The Thief's Mistress

"You needn't take her money, Robin," the younger man said earnestly. "Surely the sight of her beauty is reward enough?"

"Not quite, Will, not quite," the outlaw said smoothly. "But I know a compensation that would suffice."

Almost before she saw him move, he had grasped her arms and pulled her against him, locking her within his embrace. He kissed her full on the mouth, a slow, hard, relishing kiss. Stunned, Marian felt every sense inundated. She inhaled the scent of him, the pungent spice of male inextricably mingled with vibrant forest scents. She felt the ruthless grip of his hands and thighs, the hard tension of his chest against her breasts, and the moist, seductive movement of his lips against her own. Most shocking of all, though her gaze encompassed only the lineaments of his face, she envisioned his nakedness and her own pressed close, as if the leather, silk, and linen that covered them had vanished at his touch. . . .

Also by Gayle Feyrer

The Prince of Cups

GAYLE FEYRER

The THIEF'S MISTRESS

A Dell Book

Published by
Dell Publishing
a division of
Bantam Doubleday Dell Publishing Group, Inc.
1540 Broadway
New York, New York 10036

ISBN 0-440-21778-4

Printed in the United States of America

Published simultaneously in Canada

September 1996

10 9 8 7 6 5 4 3 2 1

OPM

To my husband, Richard,
a man of action

Prologue

Marian woke before dawn, her nerves strung with terror. The dream had vanished, but the aura of blood tainted her senses, an odor, a taste, an invisible color staining the darkness. Whispers came, a sinister rustling. "No, not whispers," she said, her own voice scarcely louder. "Leaves. Leaves stirred by the breeze." Sitting higher on the wide bough of the oak, she pressed her back against its solid trunk, drawing deep, even breaths until her racketing heart was quieted, the chaos in her mind contained. Deliberately she sharpened fear to anticipation, willed anticipation to a cold, detached calm.

At the first light she buckled on her sword and climbed down to the ground. After relieving herself, she stretched, exercising muscles cramped from sleeping wedged between branches in her chain mail. Her body limber, she climbed back to her weapons cache in the oak and placed her quiver and short bow ready to hand. She had chosen her tree carefully, looking for leafy cover that still allowed a clear line of vision across the forest pool, and for branches set wide enough for her to draw her bow and let her arrows fly true. Then she waited with enforced detachment, watching the leisurely progress of the warm sun through the bright early green of the leaves.

It was midmorning when she heard the first faint drumming of horse's hooves. Slinging the quiver over her shoulder, she straddled the bough and tested her bowstring. Simon of Vitry was coming, as Marian had known he would. The lure of the white stag was too tempting to resist—just as she had surmised when she heard the legend and plotted her trap.

Last night two separate villagers, woken from slumber by strange noises, had glimpsed a white stag moving in the darkness of the woods. At dawn they hurried with the tale to their lord, certain it was an omen, for the family chronicles said that the first Baron was granted his lands by Charlemagne in return for the skin of just such a marvelous beast. The present Vitry knew the villagers were too terrified of him to lie. If he suspected dreams or hallucinations, he did not suspect the head of a buck painted white and glimmering with pearl dust, harnessed to an enemy's back. Too superstitious to ignore the story, Vitry was far too skeptical to arrange a massive hunt without searching first for some sign of the fabulous animal. He did not want to look a fool, so he would come here, to the pool where the tales said the stag had first been sighted. And here Marian had waited.

Now three riders emerged from the forest and entered the clearing. Marian's gaze went to the man in the lead. His horse was the finest, his hunting leathers topped by a surcoat of fine scarlet wool, but she did not need any mark of distinction to recognize him, though she had seen him but once in her life, and briefly.

That once had been in the palace gardens in Paris. The stranger, a big man, turned from her mother as Marian approached and stormed toward her on the gravel path. Like a blundering bear, she had thought, until she saw his expression, the scheming malevolence in his eyes. Her mother laughed off her warning as a twelve-year-old's silliness. Beautiful and flirtatious, Eva Montrose had disappointed men far more powerful than Simon of Vitry. "You did not see his face," Marian had said, then not seeing it again, forgot—until the outlaws waylaid her family on the road.

Though no thoughts of murder transformed its lineaments now, cruelty had seamed itself into his features. Time had grizzled his black hair and thickened his body; otherwise he looked little different from ten years ago.

Reining his mount beside the pool, Vitry ordered one of his men to search for signs of the stag. The guard dismounted, and Marian turned her attention to him. Fat and balding, he circled the edge the pool, checking for tracks and droppings. His face was in profile, the features almost obliterated by scar tissue. The other guard remained mounted. He was young and impatient, eagerly scanning the surrounding woods for a glimpse of their quarry. Perhaps thinking to climb for a better view, he began to survey the trees surrounding the pond, but the foliage kept her position concealed.

The scarred man stood, shaking his head, and turned to Vitry. "Nothing, my lord. I see fox spoor and *fumes* of lesser beasts, but no recent deer sign."

Marian had braced herself to see Vitry, but now a new shock of recognition cut her, and she drew a hissing breath at the pain of it. Even without the disfigurement, she would not have known the bearded villain of ten years ago in this bald and corpulent figure, but the thin, acidic voice was the same, vinegar poured on a wound. "Vitry wants you dead," he had said to her mother, before his obscene sword thrust had taken her life.

And so she had learned her enemy's name. She had not thought to avenge herself on his hirelings, except by chance. Outlaws protected by anonymity, hidden in the forests of France, she had believed them beyond reach. But this one, at least, had been the Baron's man. Yet even now she hated him for Vitry's creature more than for himself. The other guard she did not know, nor did she doubt his history was much the same. Vitry had no use for any but the worst.

Marian had not known she had been waiting until she felt her readiness harden into implacable resolve. Drawing her bow, she took careful aim at the younger guard and shot him through the heart. Even as the first arrow found its target, she had drawn her second and let fly, taking the scarred man in the throat. Now both guards were dead, and the desperate baron was wheeling his mount to escape. With regret, she loosed a third arrow into his horse. As it went down, she leapt from the oak and ran forward. Jumping free of the falling animal, her quarry scrambled for the cover of the trees. Marian stopped and swiftly aimed.

"Vitry," she shouted. "Hold or you die."

The threat, or the sound of a woman's voice, checked him. He turned to face her and frowned, wondering if he had misheard, for she was tall as most men. But the helm she wore did not disguise the feminine cut of her lips and chin. Keeping the arrow in line with his heart, she gestured him away from the fallen bodies, away from the guard's mounts that hovered at the edge of the woods. "Move."

"Who are you?" Vitry asked, his voice tinged with contempt. His terror had faded had lessened the instant he recognized his adversary was not male. But he feared the arrow.

She backed him around the pool until they reached the site she had chosen, a clear strip close-edged by trees. Laying the bow aside, she drew her sword. "My name is Marian. I am the daughter of Eva Montrose."

He repeated her mother's name silently, then aloud, relishing the memory. Grinning, Vitry unsheathed his own heavier blade and brandished it before her. "Then you will die as she did. And this time I will have the pleasure of it."

She did not answer him. The hate, the hurt, were too deep to bandy words.

"I told her I loved her, and she put me off with smiles and pretty protests, as if my need were some trifle. It was one of the hardest things I've ever done, denying myself the joy of killing her," he told Marian, moving slowly closer as he talked. "But I could not afford any suspicion. Since I could not have her, I had to have her dead. But first I wanted her humiliated as she had humiliated me."

So he had given the order for the rape as well as the murders.

Vitry gestured toward the bodies, but she did not look. She knew they were dead. "I gave Otto those scars. I put a torch in his face when I found out you'd escaped. He said you had no way of knowing it wasn't the outlaws who killed her—and the rest of them."

The rest of them. After slaughtering their guards, Vitry's hirelings had disemboweled her father and left him writhing on the ground. Then, judging her three-year-old brother too young for sport, they slit his throat to stop his screaming. Her mother and she were to provide the amusement. They were herded into the woods, their clothing ripped from them. Her mother's body was far more voluptuous, her terror more visible. The men wanted their turn with her first, before they despoiled her gawky daughter. She watched as three of them raped her mother, until the man holding Marian grew impatient and dragged her out of sight for an uninterrupted ravaging. But he was careless in his eagerness.

"How did you get away?"

She answered that. "I killed the man who tried to rape me. With his own knife."

"And ran away. So you didn't see your mother die, Marian?"

She had seen, hidden, knowing she could do nothing against a dozen men.

"I told Otto to swive her with his sword. Will you scream as sweetly when I push mine up in you?"

He thought to make her angry and careless, frightened and careless. Instead his words iced her heart. Yet if Vitry thought he had achieved his purpose, it would serve her well, so she rushed him. The rage, however cold, was real; the carelessness was not. In a flurry of blows and parries she tested his strengths and weaknesses. Marian had no intention of underestimating him, as she hoped he would underestimate her. His power was formidable, and he had been fighting more years than she had yet lived.

Nonetheless, as she countered his attack, she saw that Vitry was past his prime and did not know it. No doubt his men-at-arms feared to confront him with his weaknesses, and his technique had grown slack. Overconfident of his strength, he relied too much on the sheer force of his blade, favoring slashing blows to the quicker driving point. His backhand was slovenly. Her greatest concern was the sword itself. Though from its ring she judged its steel inferior to her own weapon's metal, it was more massive. There was the danger it could break her blade.

Glancing about her in feigned panic, Marian began a calculated retreat. She led Vitry out of the clearing and into the woods, dodging to keep the trees between them. Here her dexterity and stamina had greater advantage than his strength. At first, certain of victory, he did not think to save his energy and followed apace wherever she led, his fury growing the longer she eluded him. When his breathing grew heavy, he had sense enough to recognize her strategy's effect and retreated back toward the clearing. She had no choice but to follow.

Suddenly he lunged at her, and though Marian leapt back, she took a glancing cut across her rib cage. The tight mesh of her chain mail deflected the edge of the blade, but its impact staggered her. Pressing his advantage, Vitry chopped at her legs, cutting through her boot to her calf, forcing her to roll. She was on her feet before he reached her, but her balance was shaky. The wound was shallow, but if she had been slower, it would have crippled her. Vitry moved in, stepping up his attack. He knew every dirty trick, but her grandfather had taught her those, as well as finer tactics. She countered and scrambled, and countered again, fighting with fierce concentration but without desperation. She did not mean to die, but she had accepted that possibility in exchange for the chance to kill him herself, by the sword, as her family had died. If she did not come home, a letter would tell her Grandfather the name of the man who had killed his kin. One way or the other, Simon of Vitry was a dead man.

His own rush was telling on him. In his eagerness for the kill Vitry had expended too much energy. As he thrust at her again, he stumbled over a root. Though he recouped before she could counterattack, Marian regained her balance and her surety. She saw that the great sword had grown too heavy for him, showing its weight in his faltering backhand. Deliberately she edged around him, letting him follow with his strongest cuts, then quickly reversed direction, playing to his weakest maneuver. The backslash came at her, aiming to open her chest. She brought her own sword under his blade and turned it, then instantly drove her point home, taking him deep in the belly. Vitry screamed, surprise and outrage rising to a shrilling agony as she pulled her weapon free. With a surge of cold triumph she saw him fall to the ground. He lay at her feet, clutching the wound and thrashing. She did not answer when he begged her for his death.

Implacable as fate, Marian sat by the edge of the pool and watched Vitry die, wondering if her father had taken as long. After an hour it was over. Rising, she went to stand over his corpse. Though all around the bright May greenery fluttered in the breeze, looking down on him, she felt encompassed by winter.

1

"Eleanor—
By the wrath of God, Queen of England . . ."

The quill scratched as Eleanor signed the letter she had just dictated to Pope Celestine III. Hovering behind her, the clerk who had framed the body of the arguments in Latin more impeccable than her own, stifled a small noise of distress. A grim smile curved Eleanor's lips. "Such will my signature be," she avowed, "until the ransom is secured, and King Richard released."

No one would contest her, certainly not the obsequious clerk. Richard had a wife, but Berengaria had not the will to be a Queen and neither the wit nor the power to save the Lion Heart from the jackals threatening to devour him.

After folding the letter, Eleanor dripped hot red wax over the edge and impressed her seal. Then she handed the missive to the chagrined clerk. "Take this to the courier who waits in the hall and tell him to saddle the chestnut gelding," she instructed. "I want him to leave London without delay. You may refresh yourself, but return here to the solar in two hours. This afternoon we will address the Bishops of Aquitaine and Anjou."

"Yes, Your Majesty."

When the clerk had departed, Eleanor told her little page to summon Marian to her chamber. Silently cursing her stiff bones, she rose from her chair and paced the length of the room, deliberating on the best approach to the Bishops. Even as she composed her phrases, a sweet scent distracted her. Roses. She had ordered new rushes laid on the floor, and now she saw the pink and white petals of the early blooms scattered among them. In less troubling times she would have noticed such a nicety at once. Crossing to the window, Eleanor gazed beyond the whitewashed walls of the castle to the vivid gardens and lush green orchards without. She allowed herself a moment to savor the warm breeze, laced with the fragrance of blossoming things. June already . . . and her son had been taken at Christmas, the year of our Lord 1192. Six months already lost.

Restlessly she resumed her pacing, shoring her turbulent emotions within a calculated framework of action. Despite the latest outrageous ransom demands from Austria, it was doubtful the Pope would excommunicate Henry Hohenstaufen, Emperor of the Holy Roman Empire, as she had asked. In this confrontation Celestine III must needs be dainty in his maneuvers. Fierce conflict waged between the Pope and Henry Hohenstaufen over certain lands in Italy, and the Holy Roman Emperor had already slit the throats of papal emissaries without remorse or fear of reprisal.

Celestine feared to undermine his authority any further. He could picture as clearly as she did the contemptuous sneer with which Henry Hohenstaufen would greet the order of excommunication. But not all the Emperor's vassals would duplicate his arrogance or his skepticism. Many of the barons surrounding him would fear both for his soul and their own, and the pressures they brought to bear would affect the Emperor in realms practical rather than spiritual. However unpredictable its influence, excommunication was a powerful sanction, and the Pope had no excuse to procrastinate employing it. Richard the Lion Heart was a crusader returning from a holy war. His person was sacred, or should be, to other Christian sovereigns, whatever personal enmity existed between them. But as always, a great gap yawned between what should be and what was.

Neither did I pay heed to such "shoulds" as were preached me, Eleanor thought sardonically. *Not as Duchess of Aquitaine, Queen of France, nor as Queen of England.* Eleanor had galloped roughshod through such gaps. She had gone on crusade for adventure, and severed her consanguineous marriage to the tediously sweet, tediously pious Louis VII in favor of one with the reckless, shrewd Henry II. Defying God had cost little; it was defying Henry that had cost her dear—sixteen years' imprisonment. The rich years of her maturity had been hostage to her husband's whim. She had grown old in that confinement, and feared she must die there.

"Well, it was you who died, Henry," she said under her breath. "And your death set me free." The instant that news came, her jailer had unlocked the door and Eleanor had ridden forth into the world. Acting as regent for her soon-to-be-crowned son, Eleanor had opened every dungeon door in England and released all the prisoners. True, the maneuver was successfully calculated to win favor for Richard and so quash the murmurs of patricide. But the satisfaction it gave her was vast. It seemed she could breathe more deeply with each new wide-flung door.

Now, scarcely four years after his coronation, Richard was prisoner. Her favorite, her fierce golden cub, was locked in Dürnstein Tower high above the Danube. Searching throughout Austria, his own troubadour had heard him singing from the tower and capped the couplet of his bawdy rhyme—

A short breath of laughter was drawn back as a sob, and Eleanor dug her nails into her fists. The prison was secure. There was no hope of rescue. She must command, argue, wheedle, bully, beg if need be, to raise Richard's ransom. She must also quell every treacherous plot to stop her before it came to fruition.

Eleanor had many spies, of diverse nature. Even when Henry had her in close confinement, her informants had fed her news of the world, though stripped of all but the flimsiest shreds of authority, she could do little then to alter it. Locked away, she had played games of power that were purely imaginary. There were moments in those chess games of the mind—a knight falls, toppled by a bishop, the bishop in turn sacrificed to seize a castle—fleeting moments when she perceived that the human game was almost as illusory. Perhaps a few more years in durance and she would have been ready to embrace the nun's habit Henry had tried to force upon her. Perhaps. But with freedom life had regained its sweetness, power its savor. And curiously those symbolic games had taught patience and honed skills in statecraft that survived her return to a more perilous arena. Now there was no time for the one, but great need for the other. In this game time and information were vital. The pieces lost might well lose their lives.

Since her release Eleanor had enlarged and fortified her network of spies. Now, all across the kingdom, those who served her were turning their skills to the crisis at hand. Although a neophyte, Marian was her most promising agent. Philip II, King of France, was once Richard's bosom friend, but envy had twisted his heart, until he became her son's bitterest enemy. Hearing that the granddaughter of an old and dear friend would soon visit relatives in France, Eleanor had summoned the young woman to Westminster for an interview and quickly assessed her potential. Impressed by her composure, Eleanor suggested to Marian that she would be grateful to hear whatever information might come her way, the glossy scraps of court gossip, rumors, judicious conjecture. It was apparent that Marian had her own purposes in going to France; still, the proposal caught her interest, and she agreed. It was the simplest role, no more complex than that of any worthwhile lady-in-waiting. But the girl proved to have a keen mind for intrigue and the ability to piece the paltry scraps into whole cloth. Sensing disaffection, she had recruited a highly placed Parisian courtier to spy for them. And it was Marian who had sent warning of King Philip's attack on Rouen.

She had performed brilliantly, and Eleanor had decided on a new assignment for her. But dabbling at the edges of Philip's court was less dangerous than insinuating herself into the heart of Nottingham Castle. However clever, Marian was inexperienced. Nonetheless, the game was played to protect the King. As Queen, as mother, Eleanor would risk anything, sacrifice anyone to save Richard.

Recognizing the tentative knock of her page, Eleanor bade him enter. He announced the Lady Marian most prettily, so the Queen smiled at him, then indicated he should wait outside.

Eleanor watched Marian approach, her stride Graceful and resolute. She knelt with the same assurance, her obeisance offered with unselfconscious pride.

"Your Majesty." It was a low voice, cool as running water. Only a faint huskiness suggested the sharp edges that lay barely hidden beneath the surface.

"Rise, Marian," Eleanor said, and, when she did, took the young woman's face between her hands and studied it for a moment.

At seventy-two the Queen had yet to overcome vanity, though nothing remained of her own handsomeness but good bones and pride of carriage. She felt the bite of envy, but its sharp tooth was muted by a pang of greater pleasure. There was no doubt that Marian was pleasing to behold. *She is the ideal made flesh*, Eleanor acknowledged silently. *A virgin maid swooning over some minstrel's romance might envision just this face for the fair Isolde*. The smooth forehead was circled by a wreath of silver leaves set with a dew of moonstones, and beneath it finely arched brows framed eyes of vair, the favored shade of soft blue-gray. The rounded modeling of cheek and chin sweetly echoed the shapely mouth, the short upper lip and soft, fuller lower one evoking rose petals in curve and tint. Heavy pale gold hair hung in two braids over small, high breasts. Marian set off her fair coloring with a subtle gray silk bliaut, the long sleeves cascading over the tight undertunic of pure white embroidered with silver, the finely pleated skirt flowing over the gentle slope of her hips.

Dazzling, Eleanor thought, yet this ravishing prettiness might soon have cloyed had another soul inhabited this body. Two things set Marian's loveliness apart, transformed it from the blandness of a pristine and vapid icon to a striking presence. One was obvious and immediate. Eleanor, tall herself, looked up to meet Marian's eyes. Her youngest son, Prince John, was of average height for a man, five feet six perhaps, and she judged Marian to be that tall.

However impressive, her height would have been incongruous if her essence had not matched it in impact. But there was nothing vapid here, nothing mild. The softness of the eyes was only in their color. They met Eleanor's frankly, with a keen, even defiant intelligence, like a gleaming sword drawn not in challenge, but in salute. Marian was an Amazon, as her grandmother had been when she rode with Eleanor on the ill-fated Second Crusade. Comrade-in-arms and trusted friend, Marie was one of the most admirable and courageous women Eleanor had ever known. Her granddaughter had the same directness, the same essential honesty—but guarded by a penetrating, even cunning mind that Eleanor recognized as kindred. In Marian fierce passion was held in check by cool intellect, and by a will the Queen suspected might be formidable as her own.

Eleanor took her place in the chair of state and indicated a pitcher and goblets of crystal set in beaten gold. "Pour us some wine; then sit beside me."

Marian first filled a goblet for Eleanor, then for herself, and drew up one of the carved stools beside the chair. "The wine is delicious, far mellower than was served at King Philip's court, Your Majesty."

"The wine masters of Aquitaine are unequaled," Eleanor answered, then moved quickly to the point. "You've chosen to leave Paris, Marian. Did you suspect you were yourself suspected?"

"No, Your Majesty, but my invitation to visit had a limit, and I felt I had reached it."

"You left the court almost a month before you returned to England." Eleanor probed.

Marian regarded her steadily. "It was understood, my lady, that I had obligations of my own to attend to in France, and once they were accomplished, I would return."

Something was different, Eleanor thought, curiosity

prickling. Some inner fire had been extinguished or contained. Marian, she did not doubt, had her own secrets. A failed love affair perhaps? Or was it the strain of subterfuge that cooled the flame she remembered?

"You have changed, Marian. Does this work for me sit ill?"

"The contrary, Your Majesty. I wonder sometimes if it is a game I play too easily, sitting within myself, watching and weighing the conversation of others."

Eleanor was not content. She probed. "When does such skill cause you to wonder?"

Marian paused fractionally. Since Eleanor had noted her ambivalence, she apparently decided honesty was politic. "The information about Rouen was the negligent slip of a friend, someone in whom I had placed trust, my lady, and who trusted me in turn, without thinking of such considerations as spies and treason. Given the import of the information, I did not hesitate to pass it on, but I cannot say that such a choice would always be easy."

"I trust you will choose wisely," Eleanor answered smoothly. Only a fool expected absolute loyalty. Part of rulership was knowing the limits of loyalty, of trust, in everyone who served you, knowing which lapses could be forgiven, which must be punished. She would probably never know if Marian should decide honor lay elsewhere; with Marian she trusted it would be a question of honor rather than one of advantage or fear. That made her more valuable, but more difficult to measure.

"Have you received news of King Richard, Your Majesty?" It was the obvious question, the necessary one, and it was also a direct evasion of further inquiry. Curiosity unsatisfied, the Queen of England bowed to necessity.

"Yes. New demands have arrived from the Emperor, couched in language exceedingly flowery and effusive, no doubt an effort to match the extravagance of his terms." Eleanor allowed herself an ironic smile. "The ransom has been raised again by half. The full sum is now one hundred and fifty thousand marks."

Marian's eyes widened slightly. After a pause she said, "That is a monumental amount."

"More than double the yearly income of the Crown. As surety for payment, the Emperor demands we increase the number of hostages as well, all to be chosen from among the first of the realm or their heirs."

"To find so many will be a difficult task, my lady, but not so difficult as collecting the ransom."

"The people love King Richard," Eleanor responded, hearing the fierceness of her own voice with bitter amusement. She knew herself enthralled by her son's glamour, even as she knew herself the wiser ruler. "His image shines in their minds with the grandeur of his coronation and the splendid courage of his deeds in the Holy Land."

"I do not doubt their affection," Marian rejoined quietly. "It is true that his handsomeness, his valour have fired their imaginations. Still, not only King Richard but King Henry before him laid a heavy tithe to finance the Crusade against Saladin. It will not be easy to procure a sum so exorbitant from already depleted coffers."

"If I have to strip the possessions of both barons and churchmen to fulfill it, I shall. If I must tax every man, woman, and child in King Richard's lands three times over, I shall raise the ransom."

"No doubt Your Majesty will have to," Marian said dryly. "I see no other way."

"Nor I," Eleanor replied, her voice level once more. Marian would be hers, as Marie had been, but through her she would serve Richard too. And Eleanor would have it no different. "It is a daunting task, and we must guard against betrayal at every turn."

"Your Majesty wishes me to return to France," Marian asked, "and hear what is to be heard of King Philip's plans? My sudden reappearance would not be impossible to explain, but it would indeed make me suspect."

There was obvious reluctance in her voice, though Eleanor would have ignored it had that been the necessity. She considered dissembling, to see what she could learn of Marian. But it was doubtful the revelations would be worth the resentment when her prying became obvious. Let Marian keep her secrets. Eleanor wanted an ally, not an antagonist. She hoped her true intention would sit better, for there she would not accept refusal.

"No, I am pleased you have left France, Marian. I have need of you here. You know that Prince John has already tried to have himself proclaimed King of England in his brother's stead. So far the knights have resisted, but fear and greed are ever active. Nottingham is the stronghold of Prince John's power. I want you to go to the castle and remain there for whatever length of time you can devise without suspicion."

"Your Majesty hopes I can determine which knights will remain loyal to King Richard and which, for fear or greed, may forsake him for Prince John?"

"I hope for more than that."

"More? That alone will be difficult to ascertain."

"No, Marian. You have a sharp eye for dissemblers. That will be the easy part."

Marian considered the problem. "Prince John intends to interfere with the ransom directly or indirectly. Your Majesty hopes that I can uncover his plan?"

"Yes, that is the crux of it," Eleanor affirmed. "A month ago we received warning from a knight in Nottinghamshire of an attempt to seize the first great tax collection from the north. The guard was increased, and the route changed. The silver arrived safely in London. Now that the Emperor has raised his ransom demand, I am certain there will be another attempt. Make a place for yourself in Nottingham Castle, and just such information may come within your grasp."

"What of the knight who gave Your Majesty warning?"

"He is dead," Eleanor said succinctly. "You are the best person to replace him."

A warning, yes. But if she read Marian aright, it was a greater challenge.

"Is he?" The most infinitesimal of smiles touched Marian's lips. Then, refusing the lure, she continued calmly. "Your Majesty may overestimate my skills. I learned of the attack on Rouen by accident. My own efforts yielded nothing so significant: A few scraps of gossip fitted together, one new informant."

"A courtier highly placed," Eleanor countered. "Yes, you are inexperienced, but you possess both audacity and caution. You have a talent for deduction, Marian, skill to discover the gold hidden in the dross. Acquaint yourself with all those who visit the castle. Befriend the Sheriff's lady if you can, and learn of the husband through her. I will provide a trustworthy woman to serve as your lady-in-waiting. She is from a rich London merchant's family. Her manners will not disgrace you, but she can also move among the servants more easily than someone higher born and gather information from sources that may elude you. On the road to Nottingham you and Agatha will rendezvous with a young gentleman who will act as messenger between the two of us. My code you know already, if you need commit your tidings to writing."

"I have no reason to visit Nottingham, Your Majesty," Marian put forward. "I can travel through on my way north, but to linger will make me seem suspicious."

Eleanor forestalled her. "Reason exists. Your grandfather has some disputed property in Nottinghamshire. He has empowered you to represent him, or rather yourself, as you can claim Fallwood Hall has been promised as part of your dowry. It is only natural that you will wish to see the property. As an unmarried woman you may represent yourself. I have no doubt you could ably present your case before the court, but with the matter of the ransom at hand, the justiciars will be too busy for such suits. It is but an excuse for you to tarry."

There was but a second's hesitation before Marian said, "I have been several months in France, my lady. I should like to visit my grandparents for a week before I undertake this mission."

Eleanor noted it was not phrased as a request and smiled.

The girl was independent and willful. If she said no, Marian
might judge, accurately, that the consequences would not be
overly severe if she returned home before venturing to Nottingham. But the Queen had no intention of being crossed
in this. "I am afraid that the King's safety must have priority. However, I have anticipated your wish to see your family and have summoned your grandmother to London. She
will be here tonight."

Marian regarded her for a long moment. Making no effort to disguise the irony in her tone, she nonetheless acqui-
esced. "Of course, Your Majesty. Whatever you wish."

■■■■■■

In her chamber Marian waited, gently stroking the chest
feathers of her sparrowhawk, Topaz. "You had best take her
to England," Raymond had said. "Her heart is yours already. I would always know she did not belong to me, no
more than you do." The light self-mockery had not disguised the pain in his voice. Remembering, Marian felt perplexed. She had chosen him so carefully. Attractive in an
amiable way, with his wide blue eyes and lazy smile, Raymond was known among the women of the French court for
his unselfish skill and for his discretion. He was charming
without the exaggerated artifice she found so absurd in
many Parisian courtiers. As he was quick-witted himself,
her intelligence neither irritated nor intimidated him. And
Raymond possessed a gentleness unsullied by weakness that
enabled her to entrust her body to him.

Memories of her mother's rape had left her fearful of
sex. Knowing she must face Vitry, Marian did not want that
lingering horror to subvert her in combat. She decided she
must overcome it. Along with fear, she felt curiosity.
Knowing she might die, she had not wanted to die a virgin,
ignorant of pleasure. She had expected Raymond to initiate
her tenderly, as indeed he had, taking her beyond the bright
new pain, the old dark fear, to fulfillment, a release sweet
yet strangely melancholy.

What she had not expected was for him to love her. It

seemed almost a betrayal—except her own, unknown, was worse. Spying had been a game to distract her while she waited for news of Vitry's return from Italy. Having cultivated useful acquaintance rather than friendship at Philip's court, she found it bitter that her one friend she must needs betray to Eleanor. No one suspected her, no harm had come to him, but still Marian felt guilty accepting his parting gift. Yet to deny his generosity would have been churlish, and it would have denied Topaz, who had chosen her.

When the knock came, she shifted the little hawk from wrist to perch, then turned to the door. "Come in."

Marian stood, facing her grandmother across the length of the chamber. This meeting was far more intimidating than her audience with the Queen, though she read no anger or distress in the other woman's expression. Instead Marie opened her arms, and Marian went gratefully into the warm solidity of that embrace, holding her tightly in return. After a moment Marie shifted her grip to her shoulders, holding her at arm's length and searching her eyes. Looking far deeper than the Queen had done.

"So . . . he is dead," her grandmother said at last.

"Yes. I would not have returned until he was."

"We feared you would not return at all," Marie said with a fine-honed edge.

"If I had not survived, a letter would have been sent you with his name."

"A sheet of parchment? I would have preferred you alive to Eva avenged."

"You have both," Marian averred.

Marie sighed. "And so . . . he is dead, by your hand and no other's. Will you tell me his name now, Marian?"

Marian lowered her eyes briefly. Though she had meant them to know eventually, the secret had become enmeshed in her being. Now it was strangely difficult to voice, even when the need for secrecy was past. Difficult or no, Marie would have it now, for honor and for love. Marian met her gaze once more and spoke the name she had held for ten years. "Simon of Vitry."

Marie shaped the words, then shook her head. "I know the family name but not the man. Was it he, rather than the thieves, who did the murder?"

"He ordered it done. The thieves and his henchman carried out his bidding. The thieves I cannot find. The henchman I killed as well."

Level and serious, Marie's gaze returned to hold her own. "And are you content now, Marian?"

"Content?" She drew a deep breath, shuddered as she released it. "No. I would do it again, but no, I am not content."

Her grandmother only waited, her patient silence more compelling than any command. Marian struggled to give shape to emotions she had kept purposefully submerged.

"I thought . . . ." She faltered, then said more fiercely, "I thought once he was gone, I would feel free. But I have been dreaming of them again. I wake wanting to kill Vitry. When I remember he is already dead, I want to weep."

"Then weep."

"Weeping is weakness." Forestalling further probing, she asked, "How is Grandfather? Still furious?"

"He trained you to fight. He let you return to France knowing why you went. When he couldn't beat the name of the man who killed his family out of you, he accepted that you would avenge us or die trying. Yes, he is furious, but he understands."

"It is why you love him, isn't it?" Marian asked. "Because he gives you full measure? Because he honors the warrior in you as well as the woman?"

"Of course," she answered, then after a pause, asked, "How did you do it? I will have to tell him myself."

"Since the Queen commands me elsewhere?" Marian remarked, humor tinged with acid.

"Did I praise her too highly, Marian? When I was young, she seemed to me all a woman should be. Have my praises embroiled you deeper than you would have chosen?"

"I find no quarrel with what you told me. For a hand that

holds the reins of power, her grip is lighter, more skillful than most. I admire her. So I will undertake this venture since the time seems crucial. But after, I shall take my leave and come home. For a time at least.''

''Well, tell me, or your grandfather will come storming down to Nottingham—and you know he cannot keep a secret.''

And so Marian told her tale, the lure of the white stag, the death of the guards, the sword fight with Vitry. And that she had watched until he was dead at last. She spoke of events, not emotions, yet when she was finished, Marie asked, ''What would you have done if there were no vengeance to be had? He might have died of some fever or beneath another's sword.''

Marian shook her head, as though it were impossible he could have died before she killed him, though she had feared it herself.

''You might have grieved then, Marian, instead of hating. You think it kept you alive, but I think it kept you dead, with them, for all these years. You have given them vengeance. Can't you at last give them grief?''

''My vengeance was my grief.''

Marie shook her head. ''I understand you better than I ever understood Eva. You are like me, like your grandfather, in your fierceness. But there is something within you that is purely your father, far more so than your pretty features. He owned a dark, secret soul for such a sweet-faced man.''

''That is when I knew he truly loved me, when he shared a secret with me. He could not give even a babe a gift without keeping it hidden first.'' Marian looked at her, facing a pain she had barely comprehended. ''You are right. I am not like my mother. I loved her, but I find no piece of her within me—no feature, no trait to nurture. She is like a flower that has bloomed and died and is gone.''

Marie sat on the bed, then reached out to take Marian's hands and draw her down beside her. ''I remember Eva's laughter. I never knew another child, another woman who took such delight in things. What do you remember best about her, Marian?''

''I remember that when I ran wild, she would sigh with exasperation and tell me that I was like you. Yet I felt she loved me more then than the moments when I managed to please her with my dancing, or my stitchery.'' She had known the truth would wound. When tears welled in her grandmother's eyes, she said, ''The best hurts most.''

''Then you will know how to recognize the best, Marian, when you find it.''

''If I find it.''

Her grandmother frowned, then sighed. ''I must tell you, Marian. When you return, your grandfather wishes you to marry soon. Have you thought of it at all?''

''With pleasure, when I think of what you have with Grandfather or the love my parents shared,'' she answered. ''But that is the best. The worst marriages I have seen lay somewhere between maiming and slow death.''

''Few are so terrible, but fewer still have found the union I share with your grandfather. Most are ordinary enough. I do not see you suited for a nunnery, though some women find freedom there. I think that cloistered life, even at its most liberal, is too constrained for you. A judicious marriage will suit you better, and your grandfather will dower you generously enough to suit any knight you select. But should he die, our sons will not be so open-handed. They would offer you their protection, certainly, but while they love you, they love the land more. I doubt your pride would bear dependence well.''

''Grandfather is not ill?'' Fear tightened her heart.

''No. But there was an incident on a boar hunt, and another man died to save him. He feels the mortal coil tighten. Most things he has settled, but knowing that you wanted to claim your vengeance and that his own lay in your hands, he never insisted you marry. Now that vengeance is done, Marian, he will want to give you your land to prevent future discord. And you must have a husband to defend it.''

Marian wanted to cry, "Then give it to me. I will defend it for myself." But even if he would agree, the price of that freedom would be bought too dearly. Her grandparents knew that Marian was fully capable of commanding her own keep—as they knew that every unlanded knight, every greedy baron who heard of an unmarried woman of property would lay siege, trying to capture her castle and force her into marriage. The cost in lives, and to the land itself, would be brutal.

"Listen to me, Marian," her grandmother said, in the tone of one who hated her own advice. "You are still beautiful, but most women your age seeking husbands are widows. I would not wish on you a husband who married you only for youth and beauty, any more than one who wanted only your land, but all these things will give you the wider choice."

"If there is no one I want, what choice is there?" Marian asked, feeling a greater hollowness within at the thought.

"The choice of the best of what can be had," Marie said quietly. "And you know as well as I that few women have as much. You must choose carefully, Marian, but you must also choose soon."

"You are right. If I cannot have love, I must be certain of respect." If any man thought to break her will to his, she would break his neck. She might be wise to marry a husband far weaker than herself, but the thought filled her with distaste. "There is still time. When I have finished my mission for the Queen, then I will think of marriage."

2 "But what of Robin Hood?" The fat Bishop questioned the innkeeper relentlessly.

"Humph." Solid in his weight as the Bishop was flabby, their bearded host sighed with exasperation, then closed his lips fast and surveyed the pestering creature in dour silence.

Marian sipped her ale and commiserated. She did not look forward to another day in the company of the Bishop of Buxton. While not stupid, the man was utterly self-absorbed, in both mind and body a monstrous yet articulate infant. Riding beside her in the caravan, he had prattled continuously. The preponderance of the monologue had been devoted first to the surpassing importance of his family and next to the obliterating ruin God was due to enact upon the Bishop's manifold enemies. Then, as the meadowlands grew scarcer and the woodlands denser, he had begun enumerating his fears of this supposedly notorious outlaw.

Now the querulous voice rose an octave. "Are you *certain* the forest is safe? I should hate to find myself robbed, with my throat cut from ear to ear."

Sitting beside her on the bench, her new maid and fellow conspirator Agatha snorted softly, obviously differing with the Bishop on the desirability of that event. The innkeeper heaved another sigh, closer to a growl, then rumbled, "Your throat's safe enough, safer than it would be in London. If you gets yourself robbed there, 'twill just be your purse that's cut . . . leastways, if you don't whine too loud."

Marian saw a shudder undulate through the Bishop's

body, so that the gold embroidery on his garments shimmered in the late-afternoon light. Seldom, she thought, had she seen such a splendidly decorated pusillanimity. All cowards should bedeck themselves so.

"But—" The Bishop began again.

"There've been no attacks on this road for nigh on a month. They say Robin Hood's moved farther north, into Sherwood."

"But I heard of an abbot who was robbed riding south, from Nottingham to London," the Bishop protested.

"Well,"—the innkeeper smiled maliciously—"they say that Robin Hood knows every tree for a hundred miles about. So maybe you should be worried after all." He turned his massive back and poured out two mugs of ale for Marian's guards, who took them to the back of the inn. Sitting on the bench under the open window, they sipped their brew in companionable silence. They were two loyal men from her grandfather's service, Baldwin voluble and burly, Ralph lean and taciturn. They did her bidding without question, and sparred with her in secret to keep her fighting skills keen.

A mass of quivering petulance, the Bishop of Buxton retreated to his table by the door, which stood open to catch the fresh breeze and gilded shimmer of the sunlight, the air dancing with motes of golden dust. Looking past him, Marian saw the day's end shadows stretched long across the empty road. There was still no sign of Eleanor's messenger.

A light strumming behind her caused Marian to turn round on the bench. Perched on the sill of the open window sat a young troubadour. His fingers caressed the strings of his lute, coaxing forth the opening phrases of a tender melody. He raised his eyes from the instrument to meet her gaze, the corners of his mouth curling in an impish smile.

Marian was amused. Since it was not a situation where she need be guarding her back, it pleased her that Eleanor's messenger had surprised her, however small the surprise. As she watched, he swung his legs through the window, stepped lightly onto the bench between the guards, and made his way toward her table. As he approached, he began to sing in a lilting tenor:

> *Her eyes as blue as summer skies, lips red as cher-*
> *ries sweet,*
> *Hair tumbling like a waterfall, all gold unto her*
> *feet,*
> *Thus will I know my mistress, sure . . . when at*
> *last we meet.*

"Your servant, lady, if you will have me," the troubadour said, bowing. "Surely no other servitude could be so sweet." He was a slender young man, with brown hair waving to his shoulders and a dainty beard and mustache. Beneath lightly sketched brows, his blue eyes gleamed with mischievous wit.

Playing out their game of chance encounter, she asked, "What song would you have sung, Sir Troubadour, had my coloring been dark?"

> *Her eyes as black as midnight sky, lips red as fire's*
> *heat,*
> *Hair massing dark as wild storm clouds, all tum-*
> *bling to her feet.*

He crooned the brunette variation in a tone more melancholy than his last rendition, then added cheerfully, "Autumn leaves for auburn hair—I am nothing if not versatile."

"Sir Versatile?" she queried, though she knew his name already.

"Alan a Dale, fair lady."

"It might be, Alan a Dale, that your services would indeed be welcome. I ride to Nottingham tomorrow, and the journey would be more pleasant for a song."

"A song for every mile, my lady," he quipped. "I go where beauty leads and would ask no other reward."

"Though you'll accept one quick enough, I expect," Agatha said, looking up from her embroidery with a calculating eye.

"Supper would not sit amiss, good woman, with some

smooth brown ale to soothe a dry throat.'' He studied Agatha's embroidery for a moment. ''Perhaps a pretty bit of thread to patch my ragged elbow?''

He displayed the torn sleeve disconsolately. His tunic was of lustrous yellow damask, but aged and threadbare.

''We've none to match.'' Agatha scowled, knotting off her design.

''Perhaps a new tunic, then,'' Marian suggested with feigned seriousness, ''to match some silken thread?''

'' 'Twould take a week to make in Nottingham.'' Agatha delineated the terms of employment.

''Blue,'' he agreed happily, meals and a new tunic being a handsome week's wage for a supposedly errant troubadour.

''Let us sit outside and watch the sunset,'' Marian suggested. ''There is a bench beneath the apple tree. After your supper you can sing me another song.''

She led the way outside, followed by Eleanor's maid and Eleanor's messenger, both hers for the duration of her Nottingham assignment. Accompanied by this unfamiliar but intriguing entourage, Marian settled herself beneath the shady apple tree. Though the inn was ordinary, its setting was pleasing. Pale dog roses and honeysuckle sweetened the surrounding air. Vivid scarlet poppies, golden trefoil, and bright-eyed daises patterned the grass about their feet, edged with plume thistle and stalks of purple belled foxglove. Giddy painted ladies and translucent blue dragonflies flitted among the blossoms.

''So, my Lady Marian, we are well met,'' Alan a Dale said. One of the particolored butterflies perched in his hair, fanning its wings.

''Indeed so,'' she answered, suppressing a smile, ''and let us hope our association will be a fruitful one.''

''Even as this tree apple has passed from blossom into leaf,'' he said, teasing the strings of his lute, ''so our labors will in time bear fruit.''

Their tone seemed conversational, but none inside would be able to discern a word they exchanged. As Alan a Dale plucked his lute, they discussed their arrangements. Depending on the circumstances in Nottingham, the week Alan a Dale was to spend in her employ might stretch to a month. Then he would to go London, ostensibly to visit his family, but in reality to convey whatever information they had gleaned to Eleanor and return with her instructions.

It was evident to Marian that the troubadour was quick-witted. Whether he was reliable was another question. The Queen had told her that he was an airy creature, but more substantial than he appeared. His fey sprightliness contrasted utterly with the maid Eleanor had provided. Agatha presented a plain and stolid exterior, her wry humor cloaked in brusqueness. She would make a good spy, a woman who could fade into the background so totally as to be invisible. If she lacked any necessary quality, it was that she did not have the gentle demeanor that would inspire easy confidence, but she embodied good sense, which would serve as well in many cases.

In France Marian had been solitary, and she still felt somewhat resentful of their presence. Nonetheless, the arrangement was sensible, and she determined to make the best of it, especially since both her cohorts possessed more experience than she did. Already she respected Agatha and was amused by the troubadour. While personal trust must needs be earned, professional confidence was immediately necessary. So they sat beneath the apple tree, sharing what information they possessed of the knights and priests in the district of Nottinghamshire, and discussing how the news of the increased ransom might affect King Richard's friends and enemies.

They talked until dusk settled into darkness, then went inside to partake of the innkeeper's plain supper of bread, cheese, and thin chicken stew, bolstered with thick brown ale. After the meal Alan sang a song of Lancelot seeking by valiant deeds to expiate his thwarted love for Guinevere. The mournful ballad had more than one guard weeping in his cups.

Marian did not doubt that Alan's seductive talent and

winsome charm would draw confidences even from the most jaded of the court ladies. While many women would find his sprightliness tempting, she found his appeal entirely aesthetic, as she might a pretty woman's. Still, she presented herself with the question of marriage with a man such as this, one whose ambitions would not conflict with her own. If he was not a warrior, neither was he a brute or a weakling. Would her grandfather sanction a match so far beneath her, a choice that would permit her to retain power over her own destiny but gain nothing for their line? To a landless knight he knew she truly loved, perhaps, but to a poor troubadour, however wellborn and clever? Marian sighed inwardly. She could not imagine her grandfather blessing such a match, nor she could not seriously imagine herself asking him to do so. Everything in her shunned the question of marriage, yet soon she must seriously consider even such wayward possibilities.

At last drowsiness beckoned her upstairs. There were but two small rooms, one for her and Agatha, the second claimed by the Bishop. The rest must make do with the floor of the inn. Agatha had laid their own sheets on the bed. Marian stripped to her shift; most slept naked, but if there was trouble, she wanted at least one garment already donned. Gratefully she slid beneath the cool linen. The mattress was lumpy, but after riding since dawn, she found it easy enough to drift asleep.

Yet ever a light sleeper, Marian woke in the night, her senses instantly searching for whatever had disturbed her. There was a faint sound from the hallway. Taking up her knife, she slipped past the gently snoring Agatha and opened the door a crack. She glimpsed the innkeeper standing at the window with a tallow candle in hand, looking into the darkness. The door hinges creaked, and he whirled round.

"Oh, you startled me, my lady," he said, then gestured toward the window with his candle. "I thought I heard something."

"Upstairs?" she questioned, regarding him narrowly, for his bedroom was below.

"On the roof, I thought," he answered easily. "There's a family of squirrels that raid the pantry. Nasty habits they has, leaving their droppings where they're least wanted. Half a dozen ways they have to sneak inside. Sorry to have wakened you, my lady. I pray you sleep well."

He took his candle and himself down the stairs, and Marian went back to her room. She did not believe him, though she could not say why.

■■■■■■

Leafy branches fluttered cool shadows on the road as they made their way toward Nottingham. Uncovering his lute as they ambled, Alan a Dale began to pluck the strings. At the sound the Bishop frowned. Marian also recognized the melody. It was a bantering ballad by Queen Eleanor's grandfather, William of Poitou, a roving Count who first set the fashion for wellborn troubadours. But when Alan began to sing, the lyrics were not William's amorous knight composing a song to his lady, but the poet's horse commenting on his rider's efforts.

> *I stomp and snort, it does no good.*
> *Alas, my rhyme's misunderstood.*
> *The poet squirms, adjusts his hood.*
>   *What shall I do?*
> *The young fool's head is made of wood*
>   *'Tis sad but true.*
>
> *He sings of love he cannot bear,*
> *Of drowning in her yellow hair,*
> *Spins words to please his lady fair,*
>   *And plots to woo.*
> *While all the time she doesn't care.*
>   *Fie such ado!*

Such wicked frivolity offended the Bishop, who gave an admonishing grunt. Relishing the Bishop's discomfort, Alan gave Marian a sly glance and continued gleefully.

> *He sings of how his heart is burning,*
> *Then of how his guts are churning.*
> *I think her thrill is in the spurning.*
> > *She's such a shrew.*
> *I know a way to douse this yearning.*
> > *I'll toss a shoe.*

Alan sang louder, steadfastly oblivious of the Bishop's disapproving glances as the caravan made its way through the thickening woodlands. The Bishop glowered at Marian, censuring her for not rebuking her wayward troubadour. Perhaps the Bishop feared that Alan might entertain them with even more salacious lyrics. If so, his fears were confirmed as Alan sang:

> *I told him we should find a mare.*
> *He's my friend, I'd gladly share.*
> *After all I'm forced to bear,*
> > *I think I'm due.*
> *You'd think he'd do it for a dare.*
> > *I like the ladies too.*

When the music faded, the singer let companionable silence replace his rakish song. After a moment the bishop's stiff-backed posture relaxed, and his pursed lips unpuckered. Happily for Marian, he did not resume his own peevish twaddle, and for a time the only sounds were the soft clopping of their horses' hooves and the trilling of birdsong. It had been a pleasant ride, clear weather and a breezy warmth to rustle the leaves of oak and larch, sycamore and beech tree, hawthorn and walnut. The woodlands here were more lush and varied than the forests of the north, though the wildness of her grandfather's lands spoke to her heart. Yet the green-shadowed depths beckoned, and Marian suddenly, fiercely wished herself alone, with no obligations, living on her own hunting skills within these woods and learning their mysteries, both fearsome and sweet.

She pushed the unavailing thought from her mind and instead permitted herself to anticipate a hot bath at Nottingham Castle and the feel of creamy, perfumed lather in her hands. Among Eleanor's gifts to her were three twig green bars of soap from Castile. Redolent of sandalwood, they were luxury indeed. With the caravan little more than an hour from its destination, they would arrive before sunset. There would be time for such an indulgence. And tonight, or tomorrow at the latest, she would be caught up in assessing the castle's inhabitants.

The road before them narrowed, and even as they entered the shadowy stretch, Marian marked it as a good place for an ambush. Trees crowded close upon the pathway, and the underbrush grew thick between. The guards became more watchful, but their caution did no good. The next moment they were surrounded by the outlaws. Concealed among the live bushes were counterfeits, shields of woven branches that fell forward to reveal twenty men with longbows ready drawn. A half dozen quickly moved forward to block the road before and behind them. Another ten were revealed in the trees overhead, aiming down on them with short bows. *The innkeeper is their informer*, Marian realized. *He showed the light to warn them of rich pickings*. In a fit of panic the Bishop cried out for their guards to attack. Most had more sense, but the youngest soldier rashly drew his sword only to have an arrow pierce his arm. He cried out, and when his sword fell, no one else lifted so much as a finger.

Marian fought against the sudden nausea of terror that spread throughout her body, the ugly memories that swarmed in her mind. She fought the rage that swiftly followed, for it would serve her little better than fear. She must keep her head. They could easily be dead already, and they were not. Only the one guard was wounded, and he not mortally. She scanned the expressions of the men she could see, assessing their intent. They were a hardened lot, but she

did not read bloodlust written there. The chances were that
these outlaws wanted no more than their money. If they
were sensible, they would escape with their lives. And if the
outlaws did not contemplate murder, she hoped that rape
was also not standard practice. She did not think it worse
than death, but the thought of it iced her with fear as death
did not.

Deliberately, on the chance she might encounter one of
the outlaws again, Marian studied their faces as best she
could, obscured as they were by their drawn weapons and
the foliage of bush and trees. Her gaze was drawn to a giant
of a man who stood at the side of the road, leaning on his
staff and surveying all of them. He was tall as her grandfather, but dark and austere, the planes of his face stark and
rough-chiseled. Although his presence was among the most
foreboding of the lot, she felt curiously reassured by the
contained, unwavering strength that emanated from him.
She presumed that this must be the infamous Robin Hood.

Then from one of the overhanging branches, a fair-
haired man descended. Swinging down to land on the road
with a taunting flourish, he laughed with a flash of white
teeth. His magnetism was palpable, and from the subtle
realignment of the outlaws' attention she knew at once that
this man, not the somber giant, was their leader. Clothed in
Lincoln green, the outlaw was above average height, two
inches or so taller than she was, Marian estimated, and in
his early thirties. Slender, but solidly built and smoothly
muscled, he walked toward them with a fluent ease of motion, and the dagged edges of his tunic added to his air of
raffish brashness. His face was a lean-jawed oval, but
though she could see he must have been a pretty, smooth-
faced youth, the strong bones had matured to a hard mascu-
line beauty emphasized by a hawkish nose and sensuous,
mocking mouth. As he approached the head of their caravan, his gaze met hers, fleetingly, before he turned his attention to the others. As he stood, hands on hips, surveying
them, the giant and a stripling youth fell in behind him.

"Dismount, gentle pilgrims, if you please," the outlaw

said with exaggerated courtesy. There was a moment's pause, and then their company dismounted as he had commanded.

"Who are you? What do you want with us?" squeaked the Bishop. It was a superfluous question, but the outlaw answered it readily enough, confirming the Bishop's worst fears.

"My name is Robin Hood, good Bishop, and I want your gold—all of it." He spoke lightly, though his voice was rough-edged, the husky low notes texturing the lightness with a delicate threat. His syllables were those of a nobleman, the underlying cadence Saxon.

"For shame, stealing from God." The Bishop tried for accusation but achieved only a whining quaver. Still, he had not fainted, more than Marian would have expected from him.

"Are you claiming divinity, Bishop?" the outlaw scoffed. "No? I assure you, my men and I will make far more Christian use of it than you."

"The Sheriff of Nottingham will hear of this outrage," the Bishop shrilled.

"Will he indeed? Nothing could please me more, save an attempt to do something about it."

Done talking to the Bishop, Robin Hood sauntered toward her, the epitome of arrogance. The particulars of his face were clearer now. Springing from a Satan's peak, his hair fell to his shoulders in disarray, a tangled skein of metallic threads, bronze streaked with pale and bright gold, light against the deeper gold of his skin. The brows were dark, a bold stroke rising to a sharp arch. Beneath them his eyes were darker still. In the leafy shadows they looked a brown hard as black, ruthless and cunning as any predator's gaze. So certain was she of their color that as he approached, she felt two successive physical shocks, one that they were not brown, as she first thought, but darkest green. Then the sun angling across his face showed them not dark at all but a green pale and warm as her own blue. The revelation was but a play of slanting light, yet it made him seem a sorcerer, transforming simple earth to precious gem.

When he reached Marian's side, the outlaw laid his hand upon her horse's neck. Stroking it with an assured caress, he smiled into her eyes, a smile so insolent it was all she could do to stay the urge to slap his face. The purely feminine response only angered her further. Hanging would be a more effective remedy.

He read it all, the impulse and the restraint, the still-seething anger, and his taunting smile broadened. Then, ignoring her, the outlaw turned to Alan a Dale, who stood beside her.

"You're smiling," he said. "Why is that, troubadour?"

"Well, Master Robin," Alan said ingenuously, "I have only a few poor coins. But if you don't cut my throat to chastise my poverty, I shall make a song of this—and consider my money well lost for the chance of it."

"You'll have your chance," the outlaw assured him. Then he turned back, as if she were no more than an afterthought. "And you, fair lady, what riches do you carry?"

Looking him straight in the eye, Marian unfastened the purse from her waist and flung it at his feet. The silver ring she wore over her glove followed it into the dirt. "No more than this," she said, her voice cold with scorn. "And you will find another purse and some jewels of small worth in my trunk." She did not tell him of the secret compartments in Agatha's humble boxes that hid the more precious stones, or of those sewn into her hem, or of the places in her saddle constructed to hide others still. However carefully he searched, she doubted he could find them all.

"You're lying through your teeth," he remarked pleasantly. Furious, Marian did not question his surety, though she prided herself on lying smoothly. As if reading her mind, he continued conversationally. "You do it very well, too well perhaps. Doesn't she, John?"

Behind him the dark giant shrugged laconically. "Aye. But then you're trying to rob her, Robin, and she's no reason to help you."

"You needn't take her money, Robin," the younger man said earnestly. He looked little more than sixteen, with thick flaxen hair wayward over his brow, generous features, and wide hazel eyes. "Surely the sight of her beauty is reward enough?"

"Not quite, Will, not quite," the outlaw said lightly. "But I know a compensation that would suffice."

Almost before she saw him move, he had grasped her arms and pulled her against him, locking her within his embrace. His eyes met hers in flaring challenge. Then he kissed her, full on the mouth, a slow, hard, relishing kiss. Stunned, Marian felt every sense inundated. She inhaled the scent of him, the pungent spice of male inextricably mingled with vibrant forest scents. She felt the ruthless grip of his hands and thighs, the hard tension of his chest against her breasts, and the moist, seductive movement of his lips against her own. Most shocking of all, though her gaze encompassed only the blurred lineaments of his face, she envisioned his nakedness and her own pressed close, as if the leather, silk, and linen that covered them had vanished at his touch. A rush of heat swept through her, terrifying in its sweetness, as though all her blood blossomed into flame, red upon red unfolding, blurring her senses. A soft gasp escaped her, but that faint parting of her lips against his was all the betrayal of her own flesh Marian would endure. Freezing that melting warmth, she willed herself to utter stillness. He might have held a statue carved of ice.

Her coldness must have penetrated his heat, for instantly he released her and stepped back. For a second he watched her intently, his eyes revealing their misted green, his expression strangely pained and hungry all in one. Then he smiled again, flashing with willful insolence, and turning strolled back toward the head of the caravan.

I could pull my knife and have it between his shoulder blades in a second, Marian thought. But the satisfaction would be brief. A moment later they all would be dead, the whole caravan no more than a heap of tumbled corpses bristling with arrows. And however insulting, it had been no more than a kiss. Yet no kiss she had shared stirred her as deeply as the outlaw's wanton mouth devouring hers. She shivered at the memory, feeling the ice that encased her senses crackle and shatter. Suddenly her lips, her breasts, everywhere his body had touched hers radiated heat. The stinging fire intensified her anger, insurgent flame warring with cold, livid rage. She shivered again, violently. *Disdain was all I gave you,* Marian thought. *Anything else you thieved.*

"Coward," she seethed, the epithet no satisfaction at all.

He heard her and turned. "And I thought it was bravely done," the outlaw said ironically, "given the fierceness of my adversary."

He gestured toward the woods, and two of his men came forward with sacks and began to search their goods.

"It seems the Bishop has lied about how much money he carries," Will Scarlett said to Robin Hood. He grinned broadly.

The outlaw clucked his tongue at such deceptiveness. "Then he shall lose it all."

The Bishop and his entourage were stripped of everything of value, but nothing of hers was touched. Marian could scarce credit such whimsy. Then she considered that most of his victims would surely lie about their goods, so the outlaw lost little by this perverse generosity. The Bishop was a rich enough catch that he could ignore one that seemed no more than middling. A tiny fish, Alan a Dale proved himself scrupulously honest about his meager purse and had half his silver returned.

"Write the song you promised me," Robin Hood said to the troubadour as he counted out the coins, "and you shall have the rest back again."

The outlaw looked to her, his gaze insinuating more than a kiss should he catch her in his net again. She glared, safe once more within a glittering mail of icy will. He shrugged, almost whimsical, though his burning eyes did not cool. Then with a swift gesture he turned, beckoning to his men, and in an instant they had melted into the green shadows of the forest. The members of the caravan stared about them, stunned at the swiftness of the outlaws' departure.

Her purse and ring still lay on the road. Alan a Dale scooped them up and, dusting them carefully, returned them.

"I wonder why he didn't take them." Perplexity muted her ire.

"I do not wonder at all, my lady," Alan said with one of his most mischievous smiles. "He stole the kiss . . . and so dared not steal more."

3 The aromas of woodsmoke, roasting venison, and fresh baked bread mingled in the air, but the tantalizing smells evoked no hunger in Robin as he wound his way through camp. He strolled from group to group, grateful that his own forced heartiness was buoyed by their exuberance. He rechecked the men at work sorting the day's plunder and found that one of the Bishop's boxes had yielded two dozen jugs of wine. They were quickly liberated from their nests of straw and passed from hand to hand. He made certain that roast meat and bread were sent to those on guard, and that the wine was not. Much, the miller's son, showed him the portion of silver that had been marked for the villagers. He nodded his approval and reminded him the innkeeper would be receiving a share. Picking up one of the jugs, Robin headed toward Little John, who stood looking down at the fair and tonsured heads of Will Scarlett and the Friar bent over a game of dice. They looked up in greeting. Tuck reached eagerly for the wine and downed a swallow that made him sputter.

"Is there any vice you don't have, Friar?" the big man asked, exasperation tingeing the affection in his voice.

"If you are speaking of gluttony, drunkenness and, when the chance presents itself, lechery, then I have them all—the better for God to forgive me," Friar Tuck said, swiftly crossing himself with the dice clutched in his plump fist. "But if you are defaming God's game, shame on you, John Little."

"You left off greed," Robin remarked just as the rotund

Friar tossed the dice, and received an injured glare for the poor showing they made. Will Scarlett picked them up and threw them, grinning all the while.

"Everything I win, I give to the poor," Tuck swore, "except what goes for wine, women, and a nice stewed capon."

"God's game?" John asked, crouching down beside the Friar as Will passed him back the dice. "Are you saying that our Lord sits about in heaven, rolling bones with the Virgin and Saint George?"

"It's well known that Providence grants all things.," Tuck answered, breathing on the bones and shaking them well. "When I throw the dice, I cast myself upon its bosom."

"You seem to have bounced off," Will said as the Friar's next throw came up. His own toss was worse, and he swore softly.

"Blasphemy!" Tuck cried happily. "I avoid blasphemy —except perhaps under extreme duress."

"Extreme duress," Robin repeated dubiously.

"When he gets a splinter in his finger," Will clarified.

John nodded sagely. "Or drops a full tankard of ale on his foot."

"I never swear when gaming," the Friar declared. Then his voice hushed, and his light brown eyes grew wide with wonder. " 'Tis said that a man who had lost all he had throwing the bones cursed God and shot an arrow into the heavens. The arrow came flying back to fix itself in the earth at his feet. When he picked it up, he found the shaft covered with blood."

"One of God's sparrows, no doubt, flying conveniently near," Robin said, his voice suddenly harsh with bitterness. Smiling defiantly, he took the wine and downed a long draft, then handed it back into Tuck's eager clutches.

He saw John and Will exchange uncomfortable glances but let the sharp comment pass. Much was oblivious, but Tuck, fond of his miracles, looked as if he'd been the one wounded. Silently gritting his teeth, Robin set himself to smoothing the Friar's ruffled feathers. Tuck seemed determined to sulk, until Providence provided a winning throw to restore his good spirits. Withdrawing while good humor reigned, Robin continued on his rounds within the camp. He lingered nowhere, successfully hiding the misery gnawing at him with nasty rat's teeth. It was easy to encourage the air of celebration. With booty in hand, other dice games were in progress. Drunkenness and gluttony were to be had with ease; even the itch of lechery could be appeased, discreetly, by those who found each other's company satisfying.

Well, if he was lecherous, he could disguise himself and pay a visit to Laurel in Nottingham. She was more than willing. Or ride up toward Lincoln—that red-headed widow had made him welcome enough. But who Robin wanted, with a sudden unassuageable hunger, was the tall beauty he had kissed in the road. He remembered her now, vividly, with her hair pale as winter sunlight and her eyes cold as winter frost. What would it take to melt her?

He picked up another jug of wine, near full from the weight of it. Skirting the edge of the camp, Robin headed into the forest. He did no more than wander among the trees for a while, wishing for their magic to take hold. But he was too caught in his own restless discontent to surrender to the quiet rhythms of the forest. A quarter mile from camp he sat down under a favorite willow, its curtain of withes sweeping over the bank and trailing in the river. Settling back against its trunk, he took a swig from the jug and coughed. The Bishop might be rich, but his wine was poor, thin and sharp as vinegar. He swallowed another mouthful and stared about him at the trees, their green filtered light more delicate and luminous than the stained glass of the finest cathedrals. Robin shifted restively, surrounded by a peace that eluded him.

There were times, when he was troubled, that he could lose himself in the subtle music of the breeze rustling the leaves, meld his being with the layered shadows and glowing patterns of sunlight. Today that escape eluded him. Still, there was comfort here. He breathed deeply, drawing in the aroma of earth and bark, the fresh green of leaf and honeyed sweetness of wildflower, their rich, warm perfumes all cooled and clarified by the scent of the river glistening in the air.

Those fragrances had come to him in the waning fever dreams when he lay on his filthy cot in Jerusalem, one more knight among the hundreds who had come seeking their fortune and found, not a land flowing with milk and honey but one pouring forth blood and horror, wretchedness and death.

The youngest of three sons, Robin had known he must make his own way in the world. With no hope of inheritance he'd lived a reckless youth, loath to leave England, to abandon the woodlands he could walk in the dark, the sweet streams that whispered in his blood. But he had craved adventure as well, and the wealth to create a future. At last he had gone on to the Holy Land, where a poor, landless knight might yet become rich. If he survived.

The first year the exotic wonders of foreign lands had dazzled and intrigued him. Byzantium was an awesome discovery, with its great domed churches gleaming with mosaics of gold and jeweled colors, its shimmering castles of translucent marble and painted tiles. His senses were ravished by cool hallways scented with fountains of perfume and by the music, eerie and seductive, that floated through the lavish castle corridors and dingiest alleyways alike, weaving its threads of sound with the ceaseless babble of foreign tongues. The marketplaces, heaped with rich fabrics, gaudy baubles, and aromatic spices, entranced him. He wandered from booth to booth, stroking the striped and spotted pelts of fabulous beasts, examining weapons as weird as they were utterly lethal. There he discovered devices so curiously contrived he could not even imagine their functions. The vast array of food was almost as puzzling. He cracked open one ruddy-skinned fruit to find a many-chambered heart glittering with tart-bright rubies. Another, orange and pulpy ripe, slid slick as woman flesh against his tongue, a texture so provocative it stirred his lust. And both the succulent fruits he sampled, the sloe-eyed houris he bedded, seemed all the sweeter for their mystery.

But there was no battle to be fought, no fortune to be won in Byzantium. So he moved on to more perilous places, Tripoli and Tyre, Acre and Jerusalem. Four more years spent fighting won him both renown and money. But never enough money. And with each passing moment he felt those bleak landscapes scouring his soul. First the slaughter, the suffering became meaningless to him, grisly rituals to be repeated over and over. Then, even as he came to respect and fear his enemy, he began truly to hate the land. As time and the desert devoured him, he began to love the blood on his sword, its red brighter than the dark, thick, sweet wines he drank that filled him with a sweeter lust for violence.

One day in the marketplace he encountered a fellow knight who had shared passage with him to the Holy Land. The man had been fervent, more pilgrim than knight, convinced his salvation awaited him in Palestine. But when he found himself utterly destitute, forsaken by the Christian lords who had hired him, only Islam had opened its arms to him. Disillusioned, he had welcomed that embrace, converted and consumed by this alien and inimical land. Though his voice was softly coaxing as he preached his new faith, fanaticism lit his eyes, bright as hellfire, and the fingers that grasped Robin's arm closed like a vise. With a surge of horror Robin pried off his hand and escaped the marketplace.

It was a common tale. He should not have been shaken. During the debacle of the Second Crusade seven thousand troops had been abandoned at Satalia. Starving and riddled by disease, they were gathered up by the enemy they had come to fight. But until that moment such stories had been no more than that, tragic tales, not a reality to reach out and seize his flesh. Robin tried to think of this time as a test of faith, but the longer he remained, the less difference he could see between those who slaughtered each other for their beliefs. The land was not holy but accursed. What was there here but an endless, sun-scorched wasteland of rock, scrub, and desolate gullies, of torturous mountains and endless barren dunes? Every tree was a blessing, a fig orchard or olive grove a miracle. Under that implacable sun, bodies baked too dry to sweat. Unless covered by a linen surcoat, chain mail blistered incautious fingers, and the most flexible armor chafed the skin raw and bleeding. Dysentery was a wasting plague, and leprosy ate the living flesh of both commoner and king. A multitude of afflictions waited, diseases that peeled the skin from the face and rotted nails from hands and feet. Flies and fleas swarmed, gluttons at a feast of misery, feeding on blood and tears.

Other things came crawling—centipedes with a bite of fire that raced along the nerves, hordes of tarantulas that raided the soldiers' camps at night. And there were snakes—dark hooded cobras long as a man was tall and humble dust-colored creatures that killed quicker still. No one knew the name of the thing he described. He did not even see it until it had bitten his hand. White as the rock on which it lay coiled, the serpent's scales gleamed with a sickly greenish tinge, and four tiny spikes, delicate as a snail's horns, crowned its head. Its eyes were green, gleaming like peridots, a green so luminous that it should have been beautiful. Instead, staring at it, he saw all the poison its body distilled and crystallized in that hypnotic gaze. It blinked at him once, in contented malice, then vanished before he could draw his sword. He walked five paces before the pain shredded every fiber of his body.

In the swarming darkness of his delirium, the knight who had converted to Islam came to him, and when the man laid his hand on Robin's arm, he could not resist. The knight led him into the abysmal wastes of the desert, guided him through an endless twisting labyrinth of mountain passages, and brought him at last to the secret fortress of the Old Man of the Mountain. Alone, Robin passed between the vast iron gates of the fortress, through the burnished bronze doors of the palace, and then through the silver gates that led to the garden. One after the other, they closed behind him, each

clang of metal resonating to the bone. But before him the
pale marble walls were draped with flowering vines of flaming pink and incandescent violet, the mazing pathways vivid
with trees laden with golden fruit. And within that luminous
and sinister sanctuary, exquisite damsels awaited, offering
all the voluptuous delights of paradise. As he entered,
Robin saw he was not alone there. He glimpsed other
knights, men he had thought dead, lying on the couches of
gauze-draped satin, drinking thick crimson wine, and drawing on pipes of hashish and opium. The hazy smoke floated
toward him, wreathing about him like ghostly arms that
beckoned him forward. He could resist none of it, though
the bodies of the women corroded his flesh like acid and the
sweet wines and sorbets, the fresh-plucked fruits lush with
juice, all burned like fire.

When he had taken his pleasure, which was purest torture, when he had eaten and drunk and smoked the poisons
he could not resist, the women dressed him in the flowing
robes of Islam and wrapped a sash of silk about his waist.
The most beautiful damsel stepped forward and showed him
a blade of steel sinuous as a snake. She stroked her breasts
with the fine-honed edge. The blood flowed serpentine from
the thin wounds, then vanished without trace. Taking the
sword from her, he felt it stir like a living creature in his
hands. He wanted to drop it, but the woman laughed, a
metallic chiming, full of mockery. The laughter went on as
he beheaded her and severed the limbs from her body. It
was her flesh, but the pain was his, and the agony drove him
to madness. Screaming, he hacked at the mutilated flesh.
The laughter went on and on until she lay in scattered bits
about the room. Then, in a slow, grotesque dance, all the
gory pieces dragged themselves together across the floor
and reassembled themselves into whole, unblemished flesh.
The woman rose again to caress the sword, smiling at him
with eyes the glittering yellow-green of peridots. The knight
returned, his face rapturous as he gave Robin a last goblet
to drink, a goblet brimming with blood. He watched avidly
as Robin raised the vessel to his lips. The first sip sickened;

the second dizzied; the third intoxicated. When he had
drained the cup, the Old Man of the Mountain came forth
and kissed him with lips dry as withered leaves. The lips
whispered at his ear, a thin, sibilant hiss. They said, "Go
forth and kill, my son. And though you die, yet shall you
return here, to paradise." So he went out through the iron
gates of the fortress, an assassin sent to murder his own
kind.

Awareness found him on a dirty pallet in care of the
Knights Hospitalers. They tended him as the fever, the delirium came and went. As the nightmare visions faded,
sweeter dreams offered solace. In them Robin wandered
through the shadowed oaks of Sherwood and the lush woodlands to the south. He breathed again the green air so moist
you could taste its scents on your tongue. And when they
gave him water, it was the fresh streams of the forest that
filled his mouth. Though he survived the bite of the viper,
and the fever passed, he was so weak they doubted he would
live. The priest had told him he was blessed to die in the
service of the Lord, in the homeland of the Savior. With a
need that burned as fiercely as the fever, Robin knew only
that he must die in England. When he was strong enough to
walk unaided, he sold all he possessed and made the slow
and wretched passage home. He was more skeleton than
man when he knelt again on English sand, the sweet, cold
rain pouring down around him, and wept with inconsolable
joy.

The day Robin returned home from Jerusalem, King
Henry declared the Third Crusade. Hearing the news
brought a chill of foreboding. Robin knew it was not for
faith that Henry took up the cross but in an attempt to unite
the factions warring about him and keep peace at home. A
futile attempt. The King rode no farther than Normandy
before that fragile unity degenerated into war and rebellion.

"Henry is a great King and shrewd judge of men—save
for his sons, and there he is a fool," his father had told
Robin as he saddled to join the King in France. " 'Tis bad
enough that he tosses them scraps of wealth and power, then

expects them to grovel in gratitude. But he thinks he can snatch back the scraps and not have his fingers bitten to the bone.

"Worst, of all his sons, dead and living, the King loves that sniveling pup John the best. He wants to give Prince John Aquitaine and Poitou, the choicest of Richard's holdings. He wants to give John the French Princess Alais, who has been betrothed to Richard from his youth. I fear he wants to disinherit Richard and make John King of England in the end. I have served him in all else, but I will not serve him in that."

And so Edward Atwood took his two eldest sons and rode to join Prince Richard's rebellion. Robin, too sick of body and mind to go, stayed to tend their lands. But even as his health mended and their estates flourished, the fortunes of the Atwoods fell. Two years later his father returned, bereft and broken, two sons dead in battle and all he owned, save Locksley, stripped away. "You have not betrayed your King, Robin," his father said, his voice thin and quavering. "It is right there should be something left for you."

Robin drank deeply from the wine, hoping to subdue the swarm of memories. Eyes closed, his back pressed against the trunk of the tree, he heard footsteps approaching. The pace told him there was no emergency, and even if he had not recognized the quiet tread, only one of his men would come looking for him when it was obvious he wanted to be alone. But the irritation was trivial. He'd found no peace and so would just as soon have the company. If John Little was the only one who'd presume to intrude, his presence was also unobtrusive, solid and reassuring as the willow at Robin's back. If it seemed best, John would sit there for hours, with no word spoken between them. But tonight, Robin predicted, John would have a thing or two to say.

He opened his eyes and smiled a lazy accusation as the big man settled down across from him. Picking up the jug of wine, he took another swig, then handed it over. "Drink it all if you want."

John took a draft, grimaced, and set the jug aside. " 'Tis

ungodly sour,'' he said. ''If you want to get drunk, Robin,
do it on ale. At least you keep your temper then. Swill more
of this stuff and you'll have us raiding Nottingham Castle at
midnight.''

Robin grinned. ''On the rare chance of catching the
Sheriff and pinning him by his ears to Nottingham gate?''

''On the rare chance you can find the gray-eyed lady and
have more than a kiss from her. Down enough of this poison and there'll be no stopping you.''

He felt himself prickle. ''Is that what your concern is
about? Not the wine but the woman?''

Little John's shrug feigned indifference, but the dark
eyes studied him. ''Christ, Rob, usually you do no more
than kiss their fingers while you slip off their rings.''

Robin shrugged in turn, an elaborated echo. ''She was
very beautiful.''

''No more than some.''

He stared in such blatant disbelief that John grinned and
said, ''I like my women warm and willing. And I've seen
some beauties you've robbed that would have been pleased
to have you swive them silly right there in the road. There's
one or two I even thought came looking for it. This one fair
hated your guts. I looked in the eyes of every man on that
caravan, and it was the woman I'd not want to turn my back
on.''

''Yes,'' he agreed, leaning back and closing his eyes
again. ''She was glorious.''

Robin knew her seething contempt had kindled him almost as much as the sheer power of her beauty. For a moment she had been all he had lost, all that had been taken
from him. He'd wanted to take it back again, needed to
break through the scorn that glittered in her eyes and touch
her, to claim her spirit through the sweetness of her flesh.
Memory gave him the sensation of her body pressed hard
against him, and he felt again the silken texture of her lips
soften and part beneath his own. It was only the barest hint
of response, but she had been moved by his kiss, he would

swear to it. *Yes*, he thought, *and hated me the more after*. . . .

"The camp's buzzing with it," John persevered.

"Setting a bad example, am I?" He refused to look at John or change his indolent posture a jot.

"Once will do wonders for you; the men'll brag you up in envy. Twice they'll mutter. Thrice and they'll be demanding the same dainties themselves, along with the silver and the wine. I killed the old Sheriff for forcing my daughter; I don't want to be numbered among such men myself."

Robin sighed, all the forced lightness suddenly heavy. He opened his eyes. "I know, John. It's a mistake I won't be repeating." When Little John said nothing, he sat up, stung with anger. "You don't believe me."

"A month ago and a month hence, but not just now. You got like this last year too, Rob. And wine makes you wolfish crazy, you know it as well as I."

Robin tensed, as if all the blood running through him had taken on a sword edge, cutting sharp through his veins. "So I do," he said finally.

It was close on two years of his father's death, and he had been drinking harder, and more often, trying to stave off the encroaching memories. Little John knew the story as well as he did. The giant had been outlawed before him, for killing the old Sheriff, though even John admitted the new one was worse. But the big man had once been Edward Atwood's yeoman. It was John who had taught Robin not only to shoot and hunt but the secret lore of the forest.

"Sometimes I believe God answered my prayers in Jerusalem. Other times I think I made a bargain with the Devil."

"That's lunacy, Robin," John rebuked him. "I doubt God dirties his fingers in our mucky little lives, and we've Devil enough in us to need no more help."

"Either way, I have the one thing I wanted most and have lost all else. When I was sick to dying, it was never Locksley Castle I dreamed of, but always Sherwood."

"It's not such a bad life, Rob," John said, quietly now.

"There's others live harder, if more honest. And those that live richer . . . well, we thieve from the thieves."

"I was wondering, before you came, if my father had remained loyal to King Henry instead of joining forces with Richard, would I be sitting in Locksley Hall now?" Robin mused. "Or would it have come to the same thing in the end?"

"The same," John affirmed. "Longchamp hated Saxons. He was the Pope's legate as well as the King's chancellor. With Lion Heart gone crusading, he thought he owned England and parceled it up to his Norman friends."

"But he only finished what King Richard began." Robin wanted the wine back, but he'd be damned if he'd reach for it with John watching. Instead he gave him a twisted smile. "The irony is thick enough to choke on. My father was a man of honor. He would have remained faithful to the end had King Henry not favored Prince John above Richard. So he gave his allegiance to Lion Heart, Henry died forsaken, and the rightful heir was crowned. But the new king rewarded those who had been faithful to the old. The knights and barons who had lately joined his ranks were treated little better than traitors. My father thought it was no more than justice when his lands were seized. We were stripped of all save Locksley. Then Longchamp took that as well."

He remembered with agonizing clarity the day the Sheriff's men rode into the courtyard, claiming Locksley Castle for Longchamp. A moat and bailey construction, it was humble pickings for the Chancellor, a sop to toss one of his minor toadies. Usually Longchamp left those he robbed with something, but they would have nothing once it was gone. The Atwoods were one of the few Saxon families not totally dispossessed in favor of some Norman lord, an oversight Longchamp meant to remedy.

Watching the Sheriff's men swagger through the hall, Robin held back the pain and anger swelling within him, knowing it was futile to fight. Anguish choked him, seeing Locksley taken from him just as he was learning to believe it would one day be his. Worse still was to see the crum-

pling despair on his father's face. When Edward Atwood
gathered his strength and protested, the Sheriff's men
laughed and told him to appeal to the King's justice. His
father's heart had given way, and as he struggled, trapped in
the agony of his seizure, they had flung him aside and
kicked him, as if he were nothing more than refuse blocking
their way. When Robin reached his father's side, it was
already too late. His fury broke then, seeing his father so
brutally destroyed.

He attacked them, blindly, killing two before he realized
what he had done, two more knowing he must flee.
Wounded, he managed to steal one of their horses and flee
into the forest.

"Well, Longchamp is gone. He was too greedy after
all," John said, drawing him back to the present. He smiled
maliciously. "I'd have liked to have been there the day that
hairy little man tried to flee England dressed as a woman
and got himself felt up by a fisherman on the shore."

Robin tried to laugh, but the pain was too close.
"Longchamp might yet be here, if Prince John hadn't lent
his support to the barons and justiciars that Longchamp
supplanted. Now Prince John's position is the strongest it's
ever been. And with Richard prisoner in Austria, the 'sniveling pup' may yet be King of England. My father risked
everything for nothing. He died for nothing!"

In a sudden fury Robin seized the wine jar and hurled it
to shatter against a further tree. The acrid smell of the wine
burned the air.

John let the silence settle around them, then said gently,
"He was a good man. Better than most. I miss him too."

It was all the epitaph his father was likely to have. His
body had been tossed in a pauper's grave, his bones mingled with a hundred others.

"It's getting dark, Rob. Let's go back to camp," Little
John suggested.

Robin still had no appetite but knew he should make
himself eat. Reluctantly he rose to his feet and followed
John back through the woods to the clearing. Once the

trencher of roast meat was set in front of him, Robin found he was hungry after all, and the King's venison, as always, tasted delicious. He drank good English ale instead of the Bishop's sour French wine and joined in telling grand tales around the campfire. Yet when he stripped and lay down inside the leafy wicket of his lean-to, he could not sleep. It was not his father and Locksley that haunted his thoughts, or the blood-soaked wastelands of Palestine, but the woman from the caravan, with her eyes bright and cool as a silver dagger reflecting the sky.

Restless, Robin rolled over onto his back. He would satisfy his curiosity at least. Tomorrow young Much would take the innkeeper his silver and pick up whatever of the caravaners' conversation he'd overheard. He'd send Tuck to Nottingham. No one knew the Friar was one of his men. Tuck could talk to Laurel and find out where that caravan was bound or if Nottingham was its destination—and discover the latest gossip from the castle as well. Maybe he should arrange to see Laurel himself, Robin thought. There was no point eating his heart out for a woman he'd never have when there were warm and willing arms to draw him down to bed.

Hungry now for the easy escape of sex, for the respite of sleep, Robin slid his hand down his torso to grasp his cock and stroke it hard. He pictured Laurel, small, dark, and voluptuous, laughing as she mounted him. Imagining the hot, tight embrace of her body sinking onto him, Robin drew a sharp breath. Perversely, as excitement grew, the image faded, and with it the promise of quick release. "Faster . . . harder," he muttered soundlessly, and his hand obeyed, searching for the rhythm that would drive him over the edge. But though he knew his body well, release eluded him. The seductive images, the swift movement built a fire that dispersed in lurid smoke. His stroking grew harsher, to no avail. Deliberately he began a subtler friction, his fingers gliding up the pulsating shaft to caress the swollen crown, a gentleness that left him straining with tension. He tried to conjure Laurel once again, the rounded curves of breast and hip, the keen bite of her teeth. But memory would not summon that familiar figure. Shadowy, amorphous, her image wavered, dissolved, and transformed. . . .

Suddenly he found himself reaching to caress a woman tall and fair. Sunlight on snow, her hair cascaded down naked shoulders and over small breasts, their rose pink nipples taut with excitement. The pale gold fleece between her legs pressed close to his own darker thatch. Pulsing inside her, his quickened flesh sent flaming arrows streaking through belly and thighs, the bright pleasure piercing them both. She gazed down at him, her cool eyes glittering, hot now with desire, urging him to ecstasy. The power of the vision swept him to the crest. He felt her body tighten about him as he came, and he heard her voice whisper, sweet, sweet and fierce, "Robin."

Even as he muffled the cry that shuddered through him, Robin felt his pleasure crack to hollow darkness, fulfillment thwarted by the sudden knowledge that he had no name to whisper in return.

4

Castle Rock rose more than a hundred feet above the meadows by the river Trent, and the stone walls and towers of the royal fortress emerged from it, seemingly one with the gray-gold stone. Visible for miles, the impregnable fortress was meant to be formidable and forbidding. Marian smiled ironically. After the attack in the woods to the south, sighting her enemy's stronghold brought only a surge of relief.

The sun was setting as the caravan crossed the bridges over the green waters of the Trent and the smaller river Leed. With a quickened pace they made their way round the base of the cliff, passing what was obviously the castle brewery. Apparently the brewmaster served Nottingham as well as its Sheriff, for close by was a small inn, the Pilgrim. Its walls of daub and wattle backed flush against the rock, opening into some natural cave, Marian presumed, the cool stone good for preserving the casks. A number of knights sat outside on rough benches drinking new-brewed ale in the waning light. Many of the caravan guards cast envious looks in their direction, but their party turned and continued up the hill, skirting the dry moat, earthen rampart, and high palisade of the outer bailey. The castle guards passed their company across the first drawbridge gatehouse. A few sheep and cows grazed the field within that wooden bulwark. Beyond it the fortifications—drawbridge, walls, and square gatetower—were all of stone. Horse's hooves clattering, the party passed over a drawbridge into the middle bailey, discovering a bustling collection of daub-and-wattle domestic buildings, a fine stable and mews. Among these mundanities was a great feasting hall meant for fine occasions, with outbuildings for temporary kitchens. Their hired men-at-arms dismounted by the stables, only their personal guards riding with them to the ultimate stone bastion of the upper bailey, standing on the high point of the rock. Set within that circular wall were the fine buildings that served the Sheriff and his household, and Marian marveled to see what appeared to be an enclosed garden, to judge by the roses of gold and crimson climbing over the top ledge. She could glance about only briefly, as their caravan was awaited. In the courtyard the marshal attended to their dismounting, ordered the unloading of the baggage, and signaled the grooms to stable the horses. The Sheriff's steward greeted them with glum formality, and the usher clucked about, full of fuss and worry.

A pretentious fanfare drew their attention to the iron-studded castle doors. They opened, pouring forth a miniature procession of flouncing pages, followed by grim, well-armored guards. There was a pause, another fanfare; then the Sheriff and his wife emerged from the castle and slowly descended the wide steps to the courtyard. Their studied pace struck Marian as both haughty and affected until something in the delicate hesitance of the young woman's movement warned her. Marian looked quickly to the lady's eyes; the unfocused gaze confirmed her blindness. But whatever practical purpose the lady's measured gait served, her husband obviously savored the chance to display his own fine vestments of rose pink brocade, the smothering weight of his jewels. A foolish, flamboyant thing he looked, Marian thought. A gaudy pink popinjay, with a crest of vivid orange.

"I am Godfrey of Crowle, Sheriff of Nottingham," he announced to them, "and this is my wife, Lady Claire. We bid you welcome to Nottingham Castle."

Studying him closely, Marian found the Sheriff's appearance bizarre as well as garish. His hair was most peculiar, its orange tint both pale and bright. Apparently proud of its glossy color and fine, thick texture, Sir Godfrey wore it elaborately coiffed. His squire must have spent a goodly time warming the master's curling tongs. Short and wide-nostriled, his nose turned up like a small snout and together with his pinkish complexion gave him a porcine appearance, an effect only aggravated by the roseate brocade. The full, almost swollen lips and plump cheeks suggested slackness, but his body showed the hardened planes of a knight's constant training, and the chill blue eyes were calculating. However foolish he looked, Marian saw he was no fool. Now that her initial surprise had passed, all her instincts were prickling with warning. *Rotten ice*, she thought . . . a strange image to conjure this midsummer's evening.

Perturbed at her fancifulness, she directed her attention to Lady Claire, the woman Eleanor had suggested she befriend as a link to the Sheriff. She was no more than twenty, and twenty years her husband's junior. Her countenance was also one of round and open features, full curvaceous lips, a snub nose—but all shapely and firm where the Sheriff's were gross and flaccid. A barbette crowned her head, the brim of the small hat embroidered with gold thread lustrous pearls, the golden netting filled with a riotous mass of chestnut brown curls. The wide, blank eyes were a variegated blue touched with flashes of other colors, like some exotic gemstone. When the Sheriff released her arm and stepped forward to greet them, Marian noted that Lady Claire's posture was not less confident but more so. She did not trust him, Marian instantly surmised. One so vulnerable would welcome an ally if Marian could win her trust.

The Sheriff greeted the Bishop first, then offered polite praises to Marian, his thin voice showing a fine tutoring in elocution. "You all had a safe journey, I trust."

The Bishop drew breath—how he had managed to restrain himself so long was a minor miracle—and regaled the Sheriff with a much-embellished version of their robbery. It did not take long before Sir Godfrey's eyes glittered with impatience at Buxton as well as anger at Robin Hood. When the Bishop paused in his sputtering, the Sheriff seized the moment and offered equally elaborate commiserations, then quickly added, ''A fine repast awaits you within, and soft beds or pallets to ease your weariness after. Tomorrow, Bishop, I have ordered a feast in your honor. Come.''

Turning, the Sheriff took his wife's hand and led her up the steps, and they followed close behind. Once within, Sir Godfrey placed them in the care of his obsequious chamberlain and swiftly departed. The Sheriff's wife did not lack for allies, Marian observed, for a soft-voiced flock of ladies-in-waiting clustered about her. Lady Margaret, in particular, stood protectively close, her face filled with an almost maternal pride and affection as her mistress introduced assorted Lady Joans and Lady Annes, before being whisked away to other duties.

The chamberlain beckoned Marian and the other guests up a flight of stairs. Sir Godfrey lived in luxury. Before his death King Henry had much expanded this royal fortress, adding several chambers to the existing edifice. Sir Godfrey had furnished these with the latest trappings. Painted tapestries were hung everywhere, and chests of fine Oriental craftsmanship were much in evidence. The Bishop received a sumptuous room, the walls covered in a checkerboard patterned with flowers. Marian was given a smaller one to share with Agatha. It was the current fashion, of course, and the Sheriff obviously liked sumptuous clothes, yet surrounding himself with an elaborate visual world in which his wife could not share seemed somehow mocking. But perhaps Lady Claire had tactile pleasures to comfort her. The cream brocade of her gown had been plain beside the Sheriff's ostentation, but the fabric was rich, with a subtle texture. And music . . . if music was a solace, what a boon Alan would be.

''Is there aught else you need for your comfort, Lady Marian? Your belongings are being carried up.''

''Then naught, for now,'' she replied. ''Save, perhaps, water for a bath?''

"There is a fine bathing room off the kitchens. The ladies usually bathe early in the morning."

"I will join them then," Marian said. She walked to the long, slitted archer's window, which afforded a view of the pastures and woodlands to the west, all suffused with the pale blue light of dusk. Gazing out beyond that density of stone defense to the drowsy peacefulness of the pastoral landscape, Marian was suddenly aware that she was indeed within the heart of the enemy's stronghold. She felt a cool frisson of fear and the sharp spur of challenge.

Her trunks were brought, and Sir Ralph appeared carrying Topaz on her block. He set her close by the bed.

"Perhaps you would like your bird to be taken to the mews?" the chamberlain suggested.

"I will keep her with me for now," Marian informed him. "She is molting and fretful, and I will wish to speak with your falconer myself about her care." Marian was curious about the mews and the Sheriff's birds. She intended to make sure the chief falconer would have the deftness to handle a temperamental sparrowhawk. But far better to go in the morning, when she could also use the trip to examine closely the fortifications of the castle and the training of the knights.

"Very well. I am at your service, my lady, should you want for anything. Supper awaits you below."

"The Sheriff said there would be a dinner for the Bishop tomorrow?"

"The most important company in Nottinghamshire." The chamberlain licked his lips and began a tally. "Sir Guy of Guisbourne, of course. Sir Ranulf of Wolverton, Sir Walter of Southwell. . . ."

Marian listened, keeping her expression politely attentive while she inwardly marked the names against the information she possessed so far. The Bishop of Buxton served some purpose after all if his presence would draw such notables for her scrutiny.

■ ■ ■ ■ ■ ■

"Ah, marvelous! Marvelous!" cried the Bishop as the roast swan appeared, resplendent on a silver platter. Dressed in its own snowy feathers, beak brightly gilded, the white bird floated gracefully on a pond of green pastry. The chef's masterpiece was carried about both tables for the admiration of the guests before being set aside to be served. "You present an impressive feast, Sir Godfrey."

"That fine slice for the Bishop," the Sheriff commanded. The server laid the juicy cut on the Bishop's trencher of dry bread. "And a portion of breast for the Lady Marian to share with Sir Ranulf."

Now that the lighter fare of the first course had been cleared away, and the swan displayed, the remaining dishes of the second course were brought in. The Sheriff's table boasted a kingly salmon, hare with honey mustard sauce, nests of woven pastry that held roasted thrush stuffed with mushrooms, a blancmanger of chicken ground to a fine paste, boiled in almond milk, then garnished with fried almonds and cinnamon, jellied eels, a creamy herring pie, fresh-caught trout, and hedgehogs in gravy. Marian noted that Ranulf of Wolverton favored this last dish above all others.

Glowering, the swart, square knight asked if she wanted one of the hedgehogs. Marian declined. Waving the dish on, he turned away from her, engaging the man closest to him in talk of boar hunting. Smiling, Marian smoothed the rustling silk of her blue kirtle, well content that Sir Ranulf was reluctant to play at courtly courtesies to a woman two inches taller than himself. The aquamanile had been passed before dinner, and they all had rinsed their hands in its rose-scented water, nonetheless, his nails were dirty. She had no desire to accept the choicest bits from his fingers.

Sir Ranulf's discourtesy also left her free to attend to any more important conversations in the great hall of the middle bailey. At the moment only their host's seemed of any significance. The knights who were not, like herself, watching the byplay at the head of the table, were debating the finer points of the boar hunt. However, the fact that these same men had steadfastly avoided politics this evening spoke of their ambivalence. Marian would have expected a balance to favor the Sheriff and Prince John, a strong presence pressuring those who still held to King Richard. Musing on this, she accepted some of the tender hare with its spicy sauce from the next servingman. There was no denying the Sheriff dined well, too well even for the power of his position. She knew Sir Godfrey came to his appointment in Nottingham as a man of only moderate wealth, but the castle furnishings, the painted hangings that draped the walls were the finest quality, and his robe was lavish, an overembroidered brocade of peach, green, and gold, festering with pearls.

"Try the eels," their host encouraged the Bishop, endeavoring to procure his influence with feast and flattery. An obvious maneuver, but Marian judged the Sheriff shrewd enough not to waste subtlety on the Bishop. She anticipated a rich dessert of bribery to follow. But perhaps that would be served in private.

Nibbling at a cheese twig from the pastry nest, Marian considered again the strong antipathy she felt for the Sheriff. Though he was superficially no worse than a hundred other sycophantic knights risen to power, there was something unnerving about the man. Perhaps it was simply his physical oddities that perturbed her. Yet there were men far more ugly whom she did not find repellent. Marian did not dismiss the uneasiness the man evoked, but for the moment her dislike was not important, that Godfrey of Crowle possessed cunning as well as power was.

"King Richard is called the foremost warrior of Christendom," the Sheriff was saying to the Bishop. His tone was dubious. "A paragon of the knightly virtues."

"None can deny his valor." The Bishop of Buxton licked the residue of jellied eels from his fingers and looked at the Sheriff expectantly. The gambit was obvious enough. He would play the game.

"Indeed not," the Sheriff agreed. "But I confess I was shocked to hear that the King tried to force his sister the

Lady Joanna to marry Saphadin, the brother of our most dread enemy Saladin.''

The Bishop provided a cluck of disapproval. ''I was told he asked the heathen to convert. Had he done so, he would have received the lady's hand in shared rulership of the kingdom of Jerusalem.''

''Saphadin was offered the True Faith only when the Lady Joanna refused, as any good daughter of Christ would, to espouse an infidel.''

''Yes.'' The Bishop nodded, his voice following the Sheriff's rhythm. ''Unrepentant, the heathen creature refused salvation.''

''And the Saracens kept entire control of Jerusalem,'' Sir Guy of Guisbourne added, his courteous tone delicately laced with cynicism. The Sheriff sent him a warning glance, a flicker of the eyelids that Sir Guy countered with a quizzical lift of his brows. Nonchalantly he turned to his dinner partner, offering her a tidbit of swan.

''Alas, it is true,'' the Bishop continued, oblivious. Sadly he shook his head. ''Finally, the King failed to reclaim our most holy of cities, and the True Cross of Our Lord remains clutched in the blasphemers' hands.''

''The Lion Heart clothed himself in glory!'' Sir Walter, the eldest knight at the table, spoke fiercely. ''Time upon time he charged into the midst of the enemy and emerged victorious and unscathed.''

Much as she admired prowess, Marian thought the King's dazzling cloth of glory cost England far too much. But she said nothing, only watched as all around the table the knights' eyes glowed with admiration that was quickly, deliberately dimmed.

''As I said, Sir Walter, the King's courage is not in question,'' the Sheriff answered smugly.

The gray-bearded knight was King Richard's sole vocal supporter. Sir Walter's outspokenness made the others uncomfortable, and Marian presumed the Sheriff had included him for just that purpose, just as he had deliberately given him the lowest place below the salt permissible for a man of his rank, almost at the foot of the table.

Now Sir Walter addressed the Bishop directly. "Though the King did not take Jerusalem, he did recapture Acre."

"The cities cannot be compared," the Bishop said testily, fighting the Sheriff's battle for him now.

"Of course not," Sir Guy of Guisbourne put forward, the silky resonance of his voice veiling a taunt. "Jerusalem is a priceless jewel, the pearl of our faith. Acre is simply a trading port . . . no matter how sumptuous, wealthy, and influential it may be. Such worldly riches can be measured only in worldly weight."

He might have cast a plush cloak upon the floor and poured onto it, gleaming, a pile of gold and gems, a bright diadem of power. Certain there was something to argue, the Bishop puffed his cheeks, yet Marian could see the gleam of that fabled wealth shining in his tiny eyes. "Acre is important," he said sulkily, "but it is not Jerusalem."

Beside the shimmering treasure horde of Acre, the single pearl now gleamed dimly. Marian was uncertain how he had managed it, but Sir Guy had disparaged both the Bishop's hypocrisy and Richard's greatest triumph of the crusade as though the King had not comprehended the prize he had won.

"Had King Richard been less concerned with his own glory, perhaps his courage would have won not only the profane, but the sacred prizes for God and the Holy Church," the Sheriff put in smoothly. "Have you considered, good Bishop, that it may well be God's will that he now languishes in Austria?"

"The ways of the Lord are mysterious," the Bishop said, but it was not agreement, merely a statement capacious enough for all situations. He pursed his lips, still vaguely annoyed.

"Have you tried the herring in pastry?" Guy of Guisbourne asked. "It is baked in a special sauce of rich cream flavored with sweet onion, garlic, and anise. The crust crumbles in the mouth."

It was the voice with which he had evoked the vast wealth of Acre. But the herring pie was within grasp. When the same greediness lit the Bishop's eyes, Marian had to repress a laugh. Presumably there was no difference twixt gluttony and avarice for the fat Bishop. A pretty serving maid laid a generous serving of the pie before him, and for the moment the Bishop was contented.

"You make it sound so delectable I must have more," Lady Alix, the lovely widow sharing Sir Guy's trencher, murmured. He broke off a golden fragment of the crust and offered it. The lady cupped his hand in hers, lips lingering on his fingertips. He smiled in answer to the lascivious teasing. The answering spark in his eyes flickered brightly but did not ignite.

Since his dinner partner seemed possessive of his attentions, Marian took care to study Guy of Guisbourne discreetly. Of the dozen men at the table, Marian judged him the most intelligent. Ever watchful, even as he played the games of courtesy with mocking skill, Guisbourne could be charming or sardonic as suited his purpose—or seemingly, as with the bishop, his whim. But if Sir Guy could soothe all the cuts he scored with such facility, he could afford to indulge a penchant for malice.

From the Queen, Marian knew but one piece of his history. Guisbourne had come to England with Longchamp and received his property here before Richard's avaricious chancellor had been driven from England. From the subtle signals of hand and eye that had passed between them, Marian discerned that Guisbourne was now working for the Sheriff. With Longchamp in disgrace, Sir Guy had no doubt found it expedient to make himself useful to Prince John's henchman. But that did not rule out his return to Richard's cause. Unscrupulous Guisbourne might be, but the King needed intelligence as well as loyalty at his command, and few knights possessed either.

Guisbourne's looks were striking. A light olive complexion was set off by hair and beard of dark, glossy brown. Under the ironic arch of his brows, his eyes compelled, their tint a deep gold of glowing clarity. Amber eyes, exquisitely feral. His powerful hands moved with a deceiving comeliness as he talked, rings flashing. Unlike the Sheriff, Sir Guy knew what suited him, and he wore it with flaunting elegance. Topping a close-fitting undertunic of scarlet silk, the damask robe was the same rich sable as his hair, its shoulders, neck, and wrists stitched with golden arabesques and semiprecious gems, topaz, garnet, agate, carnelian, and tiger's eye. She guessed Guisbourne to be perhaps thirty-six, his features of an aristocratic mode that age enhanced. The fine engraving of time delineated ruthless ambition and incisive humor, open arrogance and concealed pain, caution and ferocity. The cleverest man there, the most handsome, and it would not surprise Marian if he proved the deadliest as well. A killer of subtlety amid killers of brutality.

The Bishop finished the herring, the last crumbs of resentment swallowed with its cream sauce. His sigh was audible.

Leaning closer, the Sheriff murmured with false confidentiality, "I have heard dreadful rumors about the Bishop of Lincoln. Can it be possible they are true?"

A look of pure spite sharpened the Bishop's pulpy face. He endeavored to replace it with one of woe. "If they are dreadful, I fear they must be true."

Among the things the Bishop of Buxton had talked to Marian about on the road, besides his terror of outlaws and the immense significance of his family, was his animosity for his pious counterpart in Lincoln. The Sheriff was well informed. Bribery was not dessert but the main course, presented publicly. But could they bring about Hugh of Lincoln's downfall? She noticed that Guy of Guisbourne's countenance was deliberately blanked of expression, and she suspected the Sheriff's promise was a rash one. The Bishop of Lincoln was renowned for his good works and religious devotion, his only peculiarity his affection for a pet swan that was his constant companion. *Could a swan be considered a familiar?* she wondered.

"If he is indeed involved in such salacious and unholy

practices, his lands may well be forfeit into other, more capable hands," the Sheriff suggested.

"Fornication," the Bishop murmured. "Blasphemy. Witchcraft?"

"Prince John will hear of these abominations." The Sheriff paused delicately, then added, "He promises to come to Nottingham soon. If he gives his approval, I will initiate an investigation."

The Bishop smiled. "I believe I shall have another helping of the roast swan."

The Sheriff gestured to the server, who placed a new slice on the Bishop's trencher.

The play for the churchman was a play for the knights as well. For them the promise was one with the threat. Those who actively supported Prince John would find their estates enhanced by the property of those who did not. With Prince John's power underscoring the Sheriff's, the threat easily might become fact. If they did not battle the Sheriff's forces, the only recourse open to them would be King Richard's justiciars. And those men were preoccupied with collecting the ransom, for if they failed to do so, they would not long be his justiciars.

"When can we expect to be so honored?" An aging knight at the foot of the table spoke, and Marian heard the metallic edge of calculation in his voice. He stood to gain a great deal.

"Prince John will be here in July," the Sheriff said affably. June was well-nigh gone.

"There is much to be discussed," Sir Guy commented wryly, "now that the ransom has been raised."

"What!" the Bishop cried, and a general hubbub followed the exclamation.

"Yes," the Sheriff said. "The price is now one hundred and fifty thousand marks."

Marian drew a deep breath to quiet her quickened heartbeat. She had forgotten to pretend surprise. If the focus of attention had been on her, how easy it would have been to betray herself. Deliberately she gazed about with a dazed expression, as if the news had stunned her.

"He's already taken a quarter of what I possess," Sir Ranulf growled, and the others echoed his complaint.

"Our finest artifacts were melted down to meet the quota," the Bishop cried. "The Emperor will bankrupt us!"

"He may well do so . . . and perhaps not ever release King Richard," Guisbourne pointed out. "The Emperor has already broken his oath by raising the ransom."

The initial uproar quieted to an ominous mutter. Marian realized now why the majority of the knights here tonight were those still favoring Richard. They were the ones most likely to be swayed by the news. The Sheriff was recruiting allies tonight en masse.

"It is a terrible blow, I realize. You need wine to fortify yourselves." The Sheriff gestured for the servers to fill the goblets.

"Wine!" As if this were a cue, the Bishop raised his voice in lamentation. "Oh, if only we had not been robbed yesterday, Sheriff. I have never been so terrified. I was certain the vicious fellow was going to cut my throat from ear to ear."

He looked about him expectantly. Was he hoping for a plate of funeral meats? Marian wondered. Her exasperation with his irrelevant complaint was echoed in the ripple of annoyance that circled the table.

Sir Guy smiled, far too sweetly. "Most unfortunate," he remarked ambiguously.

"It was some of the finest wine you have ever tasted," the Bishop continued, a note of condemnation creeping into his voice. "I would have presented you with some in return for your hospitality."

"Your presence honors us, Bishop, without talk of further recompense," the Sheriff assured him hurriedly.

The Sheriff had it backward, Marian realized with a smile. For once the Bishop's whining was purely coercive. He wanted recompense for his goods, and any possibility of alliance depended on the Sheriff's paying up. No doubt everyone would have deciphered the ploy sooner had they not all been wishing the Bishop silent as the dead.

"Not to speak of the silver the ruffian wrested from me." The Bishop glowered, impatient with their obtuseness.

"We could not bear for you to suffer such a loss in our territory," the Sheriff now conceded.

Silently Marian blessed the Bishop's greedy soul. He had reminded all of the others of the Sheriff's fallibility. Promises rang far more hollow than the solid weight of gold and silver, and the power they held had more substance than either illusory gains or potential losses. The Sheriff, and Prince John, needed their help.

But her gratitude was short-lived.

"Of course, Lady Marian, you were not robbed." The Bishop made a deprecating gesture. "Though the way he dishonored you was shameful, utterly shameful."

"Your phrasing is unfortunate, Bishop," she told him coldly, furious that he now dangled the incident as tantalizing gossip. Swiftly Marian buried her own flickering disquiet at the memory. "The experience was unpleasant but trivial. Save for your overzealous guard, none of us was harmed."

"He kissed you!" the Bishop accused. "On the lips!"

"Was he a brute?" Guisbourne's dinner partner asked. Her wide blue eyes were ingenuous, but her tone was so ripe with insinuation that Sir Ranulf sniggered. Sir Guy surveyed Marian with the same guileless lift of the brows he had earlier bestowed upon the Sheriff, daring her to elaborate.

"More lout than brute," she said, and then inquired of the Lady Alix, "Does that make him more fascinating or less?"

The cold sting drew a venomous look but no answer from the brunette. Sir Guy's lucent gaze held Marian's for a second, and a corner of his mouth twitched in amusement.

Then the Sheriff giggled, making her regret her sarcasm.

More than his features, it was his voice that disturbed Marian. Cultured and smooth on the surface, his speech was tainted by a faint yet sinister breathiness, an unpleasantness that was amplified in the lewd giggle. At the sound the hairs at the back of her neck prickled. Glancing at the Sheriff's wife, silent and stiff throughout the meal, Marian felt a swell of sympathy for Lady Claire, young and blind, who had that voice to keep her company in the dark.

"We were robbed on the road through Sherwood. He kissed my hand," the youngest knight's wife said. "He was most polite." Lady Alix's innuendo had been pure malice; this woman sounded wistful.

"He stripped the rings from your fingers," her husband said sharply.

But not mine, Marian thought. For an instant she stood once more on the forest road, staring down at the silver he had refused to take, feeling the burn of his kiss on her lips, the imprint of his body on her like a brand. She doused the memory with a cold splash of anger.

Lady Claire spoke, her voice soft and musing. "The tales one hears of him make him sound quite gallant, but they are only tales, of course."

"You should not listen to such rubbish." The Sheriff frowned, and even the slight sharpening of his voice caused Lady Claire to tense. She lifted her head like a fawn scenting danger.

"He robbed me once as well," Sir Walter, the older knight who had defended King Richard, spoke up suddenly. His voice had a belligerent edge, daring the others to contradict him.

"Ah yes, Sir Walter, I had heard that. And you knew his father, did you not?" Sir Guy asked him, so blandly that Marian took note.

The gray beard seemed to bristle as the knight jutted out his chin. "Sir Edward was a fine man. And I'd no complaints of Robert, either, not until he took my money."

"This thief is some knight's son?" The Bishop interposed.

"He did not spare you, then?" Ignoring the churchman, Guisbourne pursued Sir Walter.

"Not a penny, though he fed me a fine dinner for my purse," the older man answered.

"He caught me when I rode north to Lincoln," the youngest knight said, and there were mutters of assent from others at the table.

"Sniveling Saxon whoreson robbed me once too," Sir Ranulf grunted. "Five silver marks."

"Watch your tongue, Wolverton," Sir Walter said. "He is outlawed now, but his mother was a fine and virtuous lady."

The Bishop was vexed beyond endurance. "This is nonsense. It can't be the same man, Sheriff. The brigand said his name was Robin Hood."

"He is the same," Godfrey of Crowle averred. "I outlawed him myself."

Marian had not guessed him wellborn; neither was she surprised. Despite his brashness, the outlaw's carriage and speech intimated such a lineage. "What was his crime?" she asked. An idea was beginning to shape itself in her mind, and she now wanted all the information to be had about this Robin Hood.

"He killed four of my men," the Sheriff said.

"After they'd killed Edward Atwood," Sir Walter snapped.

Sir Guy lifted an elegant brow. "I understood his heart gave way."

The old knight gave him a look of disgust.

"Although the shock of losing his property could have been the cause," Guisbourne conceded graciously.

"It seems Locksley Hall is unlucky now," Sir Walter said with asperity. "Your husband was given the hall after Robert was outlawed, Lady Alix. Now he too is dead."

From Marian's observation the Lady Alix did not seem to regard that as an unlucky circumstance.

"Did this Robin Hood kill him as well?" the Bishop quailed.

"No, it was an accident," the Sheriff said hastily. "He drowned."

"Ambrose of Blyth had an accident as well, last month," Sir Walter noted. "Of a sudden Nottingham is rife with them."

Marian recognized the name of Eleanor's former agent. She felt a finger of chill stroke her spine at this sudden multiplicity of bodies. Had both men been supporters of King Richard?

This time the Sheriff's answer was deliberate rather than quick. "Accidents are commonplace, Sir Walter. And some men more incautious than others."

There was a second of total silence. The implicit threat of death was now added to the seizure of land.

Oblivious of the undercurrents, the Bishop voiced his castigation loudly. "I am amazed, Sheriff, that you permit this Robin Hood to continue killing and plundering hapless travelers."

"Within the forests he is essentially invulnerable," the Sheriff said sharply. "I have expended too many men already, trying to track him in the depths of Sherwood. I am not fool enough to waste more."

Once again, without meaning to, the Bishop had pointed out the Sheriff was fallible.

Sir Walter glowered, still outraged at the Sheriff's threat. He pricked at him again. "Perhaps you've lost a lot of troops, Sir Godfrey, but otherwise there's less killing on the roads, not more. Robin Hood drove all the other brigands from the woods of Nottinghamshire."

"Wanted to keep all the gold for himself," the Bishop huffed.

"He is fiendishly clever," the young knight ventured. "It seems he captures any prize of worth that travels north or south from Nottingham."

Hearing that, Marian felt her simmering thoughts coalesce into a plan. She decided not to inform the Sheriff of her suspicions about the innkeeper. If the plan failed, she could easily remember the incident with the candle when and if it suited her convenience.

Thanks to the Bishop, the impetus of the conversation had floundered. Disgruntled, the Sheriff gestured for the course to be cleared, and Marian was grateful for the distraction. She saw Lady Alix signal also, and in a moment a swarthy and saturnine dwarf appeared, greeted by cries of "Bogo!" from several of the knights. Bogo proved to be a juggler and acrobat of remarkable deftness. He entertained them with his tumbling while the meats were carried off. When the desserts appeared, he somersaulted to a handstand under the fanciest platter, held high by two bearers smiling in anticipation, who placed it atop his feet. Balancing the plate on the soles of his slippers, Bogo circled the guests on his hands, displaying the confection. When he reached the head of the table, the server placed it before the Sheriff. His spirits restored, Godfrey of Crowle applauded with fervid enthusiasm and rewarded the dwarf liberally.

The Sheriff then ordered the dessert cut. There were smaller dishes as well, stewed and candied fruits, nuts and sweet wafers. But the subtlety was a centerpiece to equal the swan. The confection was a blend of almond paste, jelly, and colored sugar molded into a glistening pool fringed with elaborate bouquets of pink and red roses, violets, and green leaves. The sculptured flowers were sprinkled with flavored sugars of the same tint and perfume. This cloying triumph caused the Bishop to exclaim in delight, and the Sheriff gifted him with the largest rose. Marian had little interest in the creation but succumbed to a thrill of greed when a plate of candied ginger was passed round. Delicately she filched the largest piece.

Anticipating the delight of this luxury, she caught Guy of Guisbourne's amber gaze regarding her with lascivious humor. She smiled in return, lightly, banter rather than invitation. Then she took her first bite of the ginger, savoring the stinging sweetness on her tongue.

"I understand you are recently returned from France, Lady Marian," Lady Alix remarked, the soft-voiced courtesy undercut with a tinge of skepticism. The widow's gaze swept over Marian with delicate condescension, and she preened, subtly aching her back to display the wealth of her gown, her jewels, and the tender fullness of her bosom.

Given her height, Marian had dressed to be as inconspicuous as possible. The rustling blue sendal was the plainest cut of her silk gowns, and she covered her hair with a severe white wimple, much as she detested the things. For jewelry she wore but a single pendant, two rings of silver, and a dinner knife of silver and crystal suspended from her girdle. Though she loved the beauty of gems, she disliked the encumbrance of them. She had achieved the effect she sought with Lady Alix, at least, Marian thought with a small smile, and should not be wishing she had worn her gracefully pleated bliaut of richest crimson silk, which flowed over her skin like a cool, shimmering fire.

"Will you be with us long?" the widow inquired, honey-voiced. Her face was one of girlish freshness, all wide dark blue eyes and full, tremulous lips. Marian knew Lady Alix to be thirty, else even her keen eye would have taken near ten years from that age. What was apparent was that the sweet looks concealed a devious mind and a lickerous nature.

This last question was more pertinent, or impertinent, for the Lady Alix was the widow of the knight who had commenced the suit against her father. Although this was the smallest and most distant of her grandfather's holdings, Marian made it clear that he had no intention of relinquishing it and that she was here to safeguard his advantage and her own. Beside her, Sir Ranulf indicated new interest when he heard that her grandfather was William of Norford. She could see her worth being swiftly reassessed, not only in terms of the small holding but in her family connections. When he offered her a bite of rose-sugared subtlety from his own hand, Marian quickly made it clear that her dowry was contingent upon her grandfather's approval of her husband and was relieved when he returned to his former sullen rudeness. Few men would choose to pick a quarrel with a man as powerful as William of Norford. That her grandfather's approval of a husband rested on hers, she did not mention. She would die rather than marry such a brutish creature.

"Perhaps you would prefer another bite of ginger, Lady Marian?" Sir Guy queried.

Startled by the flush of heat that swept her, Marian hoped she was not blushing. How did he manage to make the very innocence of his tone a carnal invitation? But she met his eyes and answered coolly, "Perhaps I would."

5 The warm, honeyed glow of the midsummer sunset poured over the walls of the rose garden. Completing his move, Guy of Guisbourne sat back from the chessboard and allowed himself to savor the moment, basking in the lustrous golden light enriched by a sumptuous perfume of roses. The old garden had been a neglected tangle, and he was glad Lady Claire had begged her husband to enhance this exquisite sanctuary while the Sheriff was still of a mind to please her. Godfrey had tired of her soon enough, but the embellished garden continued to provide an idyllic retreat from the tumult within the castle.

Wondering what line of strategy Bogo was contemplating, Sir Guy returned his attention to the carved figurines on the chessboard. In the burnished light they looked more gold than ivory. For a moment Guisbourne imagined the game, themselves, the trellised bower, the garden surrounding them all encased in amber, suspended in time. He smiled at the fancy and noted that Bogo shifted infinitesimally at the smile, mistaking it for some bit of strategic speculation concerning the game. Although unintentionally roused, such doubt and suspicion were effective ploys, and he let the smile linger on his lips. But subterfuge, however effective, was no match for strategy in this game. The dwarf was a skillful player.

A minute later Bogo moved, shifting a pawn. The play was one of seeming caution, but Guy studied the alignment of the pieces, trying to foresee the traps that lay ahead. He chose an ambitious strategy, forwarding his knight—only to be instantly countered by a castle.

"A clever move," he remarked with a tinge of acidity. Despite his annoyance, Guisbourne was genuinely intrigued. This time he considered three different lines of attack before embarking on his own ambush.

The jongleur frowned and steepled his fingers, examining the resulting arrangement intently. The light was swiftly waning, and Guy summoned a guard to bring torches rather than disrupt their concentration by moving indoors. As the torch flames brightened the air, the dwarf glanced up briefly. Guy gestured to the board. "I wish we had more opportunity to play, Bogo. No one else offers me such a challenge." It was perfectly true, though he had some hope the flattery would make the other man overconfident.

"I believe we shall, my lord," Bogo remarked, his rasping voice delicately laced with innuendo.

Guy prickled with interest, though he took care not to display it with even the flicker of an eyelid. He doubted that the situation warranted any great caution, but playing this game within the game adroitly was now part of the amusement. Bogo's conversational gambit might be no more than a blind. Certainly Sir Guy had made no proposal to Lady Alix, and the dwarf was not fool enough to presume a marriage in the offing—unless Alix herself had sent her servant to test him?

"Shall we?" He invited Bogo to elucidate.

Bogo lifted his thick brows quizzically. There was no way for those black eyes to look guileless, Guisbourne thought. The man was too intelligent and had seen and suffered too much. Then, as Guy watched, something happened in the face of the dwarf. A barely perceptible tremor shivered beneath the surface of the skin, realigning the features. There was far more here than a tantalizing bit of gossip, more than an opponent's clever decoy. There was pain, and there was anger.

"As of tonight I will be serving the Sheriff," Bogo said flatly. "Lady Alix has gifted me to him."

Knowing the Sheriff's predilections, Sir Guy felt a twinge of pity for the man. Guisbourne was grateful that being handsome and of sound body, he was exempt from the Sheriff's interest and the complications of deflecting it. Still, Bogo was a fool with wit. He must have realized the inevitability of this outcome. The only surprise was that the Sheriff's lust had not been accommodated earlier, but now the delay appeared to be intentional. Guisbourne's suspicions of the Lady Alix solidified, but he forestalled any comment, choosing instead to see what had prompted the dwarf to speak to him.

"Your mistress has just informed you of her decision?"

"Once we were securely inside the castle walls, my lord," Bogo confirmed, then made his move on the board. Guy weighed the possibilities the newly shifted pawn conjured, even as he contemplated the dwarf's plight. He had no intention of interfering, but as a matter of course he considered what lines of action were possible. The jongleur was not a slave, but he had no status that would protect him from the Sheriff's desire, or the Sheriff's wrath. He doubted Bogo could escape from the castle tonight, and if he did flee and the Sheriff tracked him down, the resulting encounter would be far more unpleasant than what awaited Bogo tonight. It could possibly be fatal.

"Patience would serve you well." Sir Guy offered the obvious, the pragmatic solution. "The Sheriff is fickle in his tastes and seeks out new diversions often."

"My lord, he has also been known to cherish an affection for quite some time"—Bogo glanced at him briefly—"provided it is sufficiently unique."

Guy nodded. There was no guarantee the Sheriff would quickly tire of such a prize.

"I have heard that the longer his affection lasts, the more extreme his demonstration of it becomes." The dwarf gave him a steady look. "I am used to having my dignity disregarded. I am used to being abused one way or another. In fact, Sir Guy, even had I known what she intended, I should have come anyway."

Guisbourne waited, his curiosity increasing.

"Most people do not notice I possess intelligence. If they do, they are amused, as if a dog had learned a clever trick. They do not regard it as a human accomplishment. You are the only man who sees fit to recognize my mind as a thing of value."

"I will not stand between you and the Sheriff, Bogo," Guy warned him.

"I know that," the dwarf answered. "At least I know that you will not do it now, while you are building your power in Nottingham. But you are a clever man, more clever than the Sheriff. Too clever, I think, to serve for long a master who is so . . . deficient in certain ways."

Sir Guy studied the other man narrowly. His instincts told him that the dwarf's approach was a genuine one, but it was not impossible that Lady Alix or the Sheriff himself had set Bogo to examine him.

"I want to serve you, Sir Guy," the dwarf said with quiet vehemence. "I know I will find no better master. Use and reward my talents, and we both shall prosper. I have offered no man my loyalty. I offer it to you."

"In what capacity, exactly?" Guisbourne asked.

"As your spy now, Sir Guy, within the Sheriff's castle and closer to him in some ways than yourself."

"And what reward do you expect for such service?"

"Later . . . perhaps when you yourself are Sheriff . . . I ask that you give me a position with some dignity and permit me to serve you with honor. With your authority as my shield, no one would dare abuse me."

An interesting price. Not convoluted fantasies of wealth, revenge, or the appeasement of lust, but dignity. Dignity within his protection. And within that protection lay the promise, also, of the sweet taste of power. Guy smiled. He had learned to trust no one, but it was possible that this man's loyalty could be bought absolutely. Bogo was indeed a rare prize. Guisbourne decided to accept the dwarf's proposition. He wanted only to test his theory. "Tell me, why has Lady Alix decided to give you to the Sheriff?"

"I think you have discerned why, my lord, but I shall tell you anyway. My lady conceived a passion for you. When you displayed a minor interest in her nubile daughter, she sent the girl to a nunnery and made arrangements with the Sheriff to ensure her status as an eligible widow. Now she can both deny you the marriage that first intrigued you and present herself, and her lands, instead." Bogo sent his queen far to the side of the board, where it threatened much but was curiously vulnerable. "She has been waiting a month for you to offer marriage. Her patience is wearing thin." Bogo regarded him expectantly.

"I have been considering the possibility," Guy said, weighing the probable losses necessary to capture the enticing queen.

"Lady Alix is a handsome woman for her age, and hot," Bogo smiled unpleasantly. "She is well skilled in subterfuge and is gaining mastery in ruthlessness. All qualities I am certain you appreciate."

"Yes . . . and no." Guisbourne answered the impudence equably, settling into his new alliance with a certain relish. "I admire intelligence, but I dislike being manipulated. Nor do I want a wife who forces me to watch my back at every turn. I would prefer to dismiss the alliance entirely, though it is a more advantageous match than I would have made with her daughter."

"Lady Alix is the best mate you will find in Nottingham, but your qualms are understandable," the dwarf said. "The daughter cannot be had for the plucking, but perhaps there are roses with fewer thorns to be found in other gardens?"

"Indeed. For instance, I could marry the Lady Marian."

"For a single derelict hall, my lord?" Bogo studied him in amazement. "Swive her and have done with it."

Guy found he had to smother a flash of anger. He took the intensity of his own response as a warning not to let his cock dictate his actions. In measured tones he answered. "For an alliance with William of Norford, which could be more valuable, in time, than a rich estate here. And the Lady Marian may be given a larger dowry than she leads us to believe. Her grandfather trusts her to tend to his property, which speaks of trust." He smiled a little. "There are tales of his training his wife with sword and longbow. I wonder if he taught the granddaughter as well."

"You believe the tales?"

Guy shrugged. "It will be interesting to query the Lady Marian about it." Although Bogo's queen was alluring, he had decided it would be too dangerous to unbalance his forces. Instead he advanced his second knight, consolidating his center.

As he completed the move, a guard entered and bowed deferentially. "Excuse me, my lord, but the Sheriff wants the dwarf," he said, regarding Bogo with a combination of disgust and jeering lechery.

"In a moment," Guisbourne ordered. "Wait in the hallway."

"Very well, my lord," the guard said, and departed.

Bogo rose from the board. "Our game is ended unfinished," he said tightly. With one finger, he tipped over his king.

"On the contrary, it is just begun," Guy responded, righting the toppled piece. "I will remember our positions. I do intend to win."

"I look forward to the challenge."

"Now that we will be seeing each other more frequently, our play will be facilitated," Guy said. Then he added, "I hope the remainder of your evening is not entirely unpleasant."

"I do not expect pleasure, but if there is a shred to be had, I shall snatch it up," Bogo said with a bitter smile. "It is a small satisfaction to be desired, however perversely—"

"But?" Guy queried.

"But when the time comes to kill him, I would like the pleasure of that."

"When the time comes," Guy acknowledged, "I will try to arrange that pleasure to ensure your satisfaction."

■■■■■■

"Which gown, my lady?" Agatha asked.

"What do you think?" Marian asked in turn, forcing herself not to determine the choice. Soliciting Agatha's opinion was a small but simple way to increase their rapport.

"The pale green kirtle would be flattering, but not too lavish," the older woman suggested after surveying the selection. "Or the lavender bliaut if you want to make an impression on the ladies. It's a miracle of pleating, the sleeves as well as the skirt panels. . . ." Agatha fingered the minutely pleated silk with admiration.

Marian shook her head. "Lady Claire was eager to hear Alan sing. If I wear the lavender, her ladies will spend the morning talking of nothing but the latest fashions from France, while Claire can appreciate nothing but the texture of the fabric. Let Alan a Dale make the impression. I'll wear the green."

"And the cream-colored wimple?" Agatha asked when she had finished adjusting a thin golden girdle over the simple folds of the silk kirtle.

"No, leave my hair loose behind, and braid in front."

"It's an unfashionable style," Agatha said dubiously, but helped her with the braids. When they were done, she added, "Well, no veiling, however fine, could look as lovely as that."

"Thank you," Marian said. Though she disliked the confinement of the wimple, it was also true that she was vain of her hair.

Taking both Alan and Agatha with her, Marian made her way to the solar. The instant they arrived, the ladies laid embroidery and other gentle tasks aside to welcome them. Lady Claire held out her hands to Marian, who took them and sat beside her on a stool. Once again Marian felt a surge of pity for the young woman trapped in a world of darkness. Claire had a fresh beauty that was both vivacious and vulnerable, with none of the calculated innocence the absent Lady Alix had displayed. Like Marian, she had worn neither wimple nor barbette. Only a simple gold band

adorned her brow. The riot of brown curls suited her far
better than such severity, and the iridescent silk of her kirtle
shimmered with the same colors as her eyes. Their dense
blue was touched with fine shards of green and gold, and
they tilted delicately at the corners. Their shape and color
were so beautiful it was sad that they held no animation.
But if her gaze surveyed the world blankly, Lady Claire
radiated warmth and eagerness with the rest of her being.
Far more so now, Marian noted, when her husband was not
present to throw a pall over her natural gaiety. The other
women, russet-haired Lady Margaret in particular, treated
her with a protective affection that took care not to be cloying.

Though Lady Claire's questions about Marian's comfort
were sincere, it was obvious the Sheriff's wife was yearning
to hear the new troubadour, and Alan was soon beckoned to
the center of the room to sing. Tuning his instrument, he
began with a frolicking air about a young knight futilely
searching for valiant deeds to do, only to find all the brigands, trolls, giants, and dragons slain by other knights just
before he arrived. In the end the Queen of Faerie found him
sitting on a hillock, lamenting that nothing extraordinary
would ever happen. She whisked him away to her kingdom,
and he was never seen again by mortal eyes. Alan, Marian
noted, favored such lighthearted wickedness.

When the song ended, the Sheriff's wife laughed with
delight and called out, "I pray you, sir, play us another. No
troubadour I have yet heard sings so sweetly as you."

Alan came and knelt by her side, lifting her hand to his
lips in a tender salute. "If it please you, Lady Claire, I have
a new song that none has yet heard. Before the fair Lady
Marian took me into her service, I was wandering the south
of England. They have a sad legend there, of a lord gone
mad with grief. After I heard it, I composed this rondeau."
Rising, Alan returned to the center of the room, plucking
the wistful, eerie opening notes upon his lute. When the
room had all hushed to expectant silence, he began to sing.

"Oh, where is my lady? Is she not to be found?
She went picking flowers by the river's swift edge."
"We told you she's lost, lord, swept away to be
*   drowned."*
"Oh, where is my lady? Is she not to be found?"

"No, now deep in dark water, green weeds twine
*   her gown.*
She's lost to this world, lord. We beg you have
*   courage."*
"Oh, where is my lady? Is she not to be found?
She went picking flowers by the river's swift edge."

Alan sang exquisitely. The tune was a haunting one, and the lyrics were designed to display the full range of his voice, alternating between the deeper grieving tones of the knight and the plaintive ones of the frightened servant. The Sheriff's wife was captivated. "Oh, it is lovely," she whispered. "So sad."

"It gave me chills," one of the ladies proclaimed with delight.

"Let me sing it again," Alan said. "But this time I beg you all to join me when the servants plead with their master."

This suggestion was greeted with enthusiasm, and Alan began the song anew. With his lead to follow, the ladies-in-waiting did well enough. The Lady Claire, however, did far better than that. She had a lovely voice whose soaring tones blended in perfect harmony with the troubadour's. As they sang together, Alan looked as enchanted as Claire.

As the last strains of the song faded, Marian had a sudden sense of being watched. Turning, she saw Guy of Guisbourne waiting by the door. Marian was unsure whether to be pleased she had sensed his presence or distressed she had failed to notice his entry. He looked superb, his tunic of garnet damask inset with wide bands embroidered in gold. Now that the song was ended, he approached and greeted Lady Claire and the other ladies in the circle. She felt the shimmer of anticipation in her blood as he made his way, at last, to her side.

"Lady Marian," he said, the two words soft-napped with pleasure. "Lady Marian, I wondered if you would care to accompany me to the fair this afternoon?"

His golden eyes conjured far less innocent delights that only the two of them could share and dared her to accept them.

Marian smiled. "I would be delighted to attend the fair, my lord."

"I will return and fetch you . . . in an hour's time?"

"Yes." She smiled and agreed without hesitation. It would mean delaying her daily visit to the falconer till this afternoon, but the opportunity to learn more of Guisbourne was more important. All the more so since he was the one to seek her out.

"Until then." Sir Guy bowed and left them to their amusement.

Cautiously Marian reminded herself that it might well be the Sheriff who had asked him to question her under this flirtatious and frivolous guise. She also considered the servants' gossip, quickly gathered by Agatha, that had him soon wedded to the beautiful Lady Alix. Remembering the coolness in his eyes yesterday at dinner, Marian doubted his attraction, but attraction meant nothing when a rich widow was involved.

Already Marian was disturbed by her own sense of conflict where Guisbourne was concerned and how it would affect her ability to accomplish her purpose here. She knew well that her skills at dissembling were particular in nature. While she could keep a secret even at the expense of pain and lie with perfect sangfroid, she was not an emotional chameleon able to change the color of her character to blend with her surroundings or to match another's mood or desire. And not only was Sir Guy clever and dangerous, but she found him intensely attractive. For all the appeal of the challenge he offered, she would prefer him as an ally rather

than an opponent. If there was a way to win him back to
King Richard's side, she was determined to find it.

But for the moment he was the enemy.

■■■■■■

"She called me a lout?" Outraged, Robin dropped the
clothes he'd been about to put on and stood, hands fisted on
his hips, glowering down at Laurel.

" 'More a lout than a brute,' if you want it exact," she
answered, rather smugly, he thought. Sitting naked on the
pallet she crossed her legs, and her brown eyes regarded
him mockingly. "Were you expecting she'd swoon with
delight at the very memory of your kiss? The only one more
peeved was the Bishop—unless perhaps it's the Sheriff,
who promised to repay his losses."

"That's good news, for his losses shall be our gain twice
over," Robin said. Then, still vexed, he muttered, "I think I
would have preferred brute."

"She's cool as running water. You'd do better chasing
after the Lady Alix if it's fine lady flesh you're missing,
Robin." She lifted back the black chaos of her hair, revealing and raising her breasts with their brown puckered
nipples. The flaunting gesture caught his interest, as she
intended. And there was no need to leave just yet. Deliberately he leaned back against the wall of the hut and grinned
at her, his tilted hips offering the response he could hardly
hide.

"Lady flesh?" he questioned, with feigned innocence.
"What would I be wanting with such bland stuff as that?"

"I couldn't imagine," she bantered. Giving him her sul-
triest look, she opened her legs for him. Robin eyed the
display with the same interest she gave his nether regions,
the dark pink of her blossoming in the thatch of darkness.

"It's spice I like," he said. Kneeling in front of her, he
hooked his arms under her legs and scooped her up. She
was small and sturdily built, the full curves of her warm
against him. Smiling, he then lowered her slowly until his
upthrust cock barely brushed the wet heat of her.

"You're teasing," she whispered, her breath coming fast.

"Yes," he answered, gliding her back and forth until they meshed, the rounded head of him nudging the tender portal. She licked her lips, waiting for him to enter her. He smiled. "Yes, I am."

"That's a fine lot of teasing." Now it was his lips she licked, darting her tongue into his mouth, then whispering, "I want more. I want it all." Robin lowered her onto him, arching as she did with the wanton rush of pleasure. In a leisurely manner he set himself to discover just how much teasing she could bear.

It was an engrossing way in which to spend the morning, and he was hungry for distraction. There were too many ghosts haunting his mind and too few ways to drive them off. But the power of the charm did not last past satiation. Robin rose from the pallet and went to wash himself off at the basin, feeling the restlessness begin its rat's tooth gnawing.

Behind him Laurel said, "Dick, the blacksmith's son, asked me to marry him."

"Then you best should," he answered without pause. "He's a good man."

"He's not the one I want," she snapped. "Why shouldn't you marry me, Robin? You're no fine lord now. You're an outlaw and will be till the end of your days."

"An outlaw's hardly the best choice of husband, even one that used to be a fine lord. What good's a secret marriage? Far better to be the blacksmith's wife."

Gathering his clothes, he turned to face her. With her square face and straight brows, Laurel had a fierce prettiness that easily turned sullen. She glared at him now. "You'd best make peace with what you are, Robin Hood. You'll do no better than me."

She was right enough. He'd thought of it, briefly, because it mattered to her, not to him. Laurel was clever when she wanted to be, and she could make him laugh, but the simple truth was he didn't love her. She knew when she came to him that she wasn't the only one, any more than he was for her. He looked for pleasure freely given and tried to give it in return. It was enough at first, for they stirred a fine blaze between them. But Laurel had a possessive streak. She'd decided she wanted him, heart and soul as well as body—or wanted him to want her that much and decided marrying would prove it.

"No," he said, making it as final as he could. Little enough mattered now. He wasn't going to add to the hollowness inside him.

Laurel glowered as he tugged on his clothes. Robin wondered if she would tell him to swive himself. He groaned inwardly but said nothing. It would be a pity to lose so able a spy set right in the Sheriff's household, as well as a fiery bedmate, and her uncle, the brewmaster, was important to his plans as well. Hurt, Laurel might feel vindictive enough to try to turn her uncle against him. Robin said nothing. He'd not be dishonest with her. But Laurel held her temper, giving him a sulky shrug and the corner of a smile. After all, why douse a blaze that still burned merrily?

Hearing footsteps outside, Robin seized his sword and stepped to the door as Laurel snatched up a coverlet and a knife. But he quickly identified the soft slap of Friar Tuck's sandals hurrying up the path. The flicker of relief was brief. Tuck wouldn't come except for trouble. He opened the door to the knock, and the Friar slipped inside. "What?" Robin asked.

"I just heard," Tuck gasped. "The Sheriff's men arrested Much's father. Rickety greybeard that he is, they're saying he helped us, but you know it's just to scare folk off. They locked him in the dungeon."

"We can't attack the castle," Robin growled.

"The tunnel's not ready," Laurel said, tucking the coverlet tighter as Tuck ogled her then blushed.

"You wouldn't dare use it during the day!" Tuck was aghast. "There'd be no time, even if you did dare. They're going to take the old man to the fair and flog him there, since that's where all the townsfolk will be today."

"Just how long do have we?"

"I don't know, Robin. Maybe an hour before they begin."

"Not time enough to send to the camp and have the men come back. We'll have to do it ourselves."

"The two of us," Tuck squeaked. "Don't be crazy, Robin."

"Little John's come to see his granddaughter. Will Scarlett and Hal Potter are hereabouts. That will have to be enough."

"Enough to give them a hanging as well as a flogging," the Friar said.

"What are you going to do, Robin?" Laurel asked.

"I haven't a notion."

He gave Laurel a light kiss good-bye, which she returned with passion. As he and Tuck emerged from the hut, Robin spied a small, sturdy cart rolling down the road. As it approached, he saw it belonged to a butcher, a young fellow in a leather apron and a bright red cap. "Wait here," he said to Tuck, and ran to intercept the wagon.

"How much for your cart of meat and your horse, good butcher?" he asked.

The butcher studied him dubiously, searching out the trick. "How much?" he repeated, counting sausages one by one in his mind.

"Name a fair price and you shall have it," Robin tempted. If the fellow didn't settle soon, he'd have to rob him before he paid him.

"Four marks?" he ventured at last. "It's worth that if you sell all the meat."

"I'll give you six." Robin laughed, convincing the butcher he had a madman to hand. "But I want your clothes as well. That cap in particular takes my fancy."

"Six marks!" When he saw the silver was real, it was all Robin could do to keep the knave from dancing naked in the road. Robin traded garments and sent him on his way home a prosperous fellow.

Robin clambered into the cart and drove it back to Laurel's house. She met him at the door with a cloth filled with bread and cheese that Tuck set himself to devour. Reappraising his purchase, Robin gave Laurel the butcher's old nag then summoned his own horse with a whistle and set him in the traces. "You are entirely too handsome," he told the sorrel, shaking his head woefully. With a soft snort, the horse echoed his gesture, and Robin laughed. Gathering up dust from the pathway, he began to rub it into the glossy coat. "We must both look the part, as best we can. You can look bedraggled, can you not, my Jester?"

6 Visiting the fair made for a pleasant outing. Mingling with the high- and lowborn of Nottingham, Marian and Guy wandered the paths between the booths and decorated wagons, examining the wares. The wide meadow was crowded with local merchants, as well as those who had traveled from Lincoln and smaller towns to sell here today. The air was clotted with the potent, ever-present odors of the midden, of garbage, manure, and sweat all sharper for the warm weather. But their unpleasantness was overlaid with far more enjoyable aromas. The forest bound two sides of the meadow, adding its fresh green tang to the breeze. Closer to hand, the food sellers proclaimed their specialties. Some presented trenchers laden with stews of peas, beans, and other worts, a simple meal for those who could afford no better. Then there were the purveyors of fresh bread and ripened cheese, juicy berry tarts, ginger cakes, as well as fine Cistercian mead and new-brewed ale. Fragrant summer flowers circled almost every maiden's brow, the fancier wreaths fashioned of blossoms interwoven with glossy satin ribbons.

They paused for Sir Guy to buy her one of these, an extravagant twining of pale and dark green ribbons with white rosebuds. Marian thanked him. Such little gallantries were expected, but she thought it a pretty wreath and liked the way he solemnly fitted it to her brow, then smoothed her hair about her shoulders. They walked on investigating the sights, one of Sir Guy's guards and one of her own men following behind. The fair offered more than food and craftsmen's wares to draw the crowds. The far ends of the meadow boasted contests of wrestling and archery. At every free space among the tents and stalls, jugglers and acrobats performed their intricate feats for tossed coppers, though Marian saw not one with the skill of Lady Alix's dwarf. Minstrels sang, though none as sweetly, as sprightly as her troubadour, Alan a Dale.

After looking over the several booths offering cloth, she chose a length of brocade for Alan's promised tunic, a soft blue-violet from good woad, and ordered it sent to the castle. She had no other purchase in mind, simply the wish to acquaint herself better with the lay of Nottingham and to learn more of Guy of Guisbourne. In the latter she had been remarkably unsuccessful. Although her initial questions were not probing, each had been answered graciously and without substance, then countered with one of his own that Marian felt she could not afford to evade with the same calculation. Secrecy was obviously second nature to her escort. For the moment she quelled her impulse to challenge that polished veneer, not through a reluctance to appear impertinent but for fear of putting him on guard. Frustrated, she paused at a glovemaker's table, but even a cursory examination showed the stitching to be clumsy. She laid the gloves down and walked on through the smattering of leatherworkers.

"A paltry selection, after the markets of London and Paris," Guisbourne remarked as they passed between two cordwainers, each holding out plain slippers of soft leather for their inspection. His conversation adroitly mingled such ordinary observation with more pertinent queries concerning her life with her grandparents and her impressions of the French court.

"There is greater variety in those cities and more goods of quality. But there are fine workmen everywhere," Marian argued. "I saw handsome wool from Lincoln, both scarlet and green. The goldsmith in the second row had a deft hand, and the woodcarver's cups were distinctive. I warrant the old fletcher by the entrance to be better than any I saw in London. His arrows will fly fast and true.''

''They were well wrought,'' he agreed. ''You have a martial eye, Lady Marian.''

''I spent near ten years in the north, Sir Guy, on the borders of Scotland. My grandfather saw to it that I knew how to do more than embroider and scream prettily should one of our holds be attacked. I know good weapons when I see them.''

''And know how to wield them? I have heard that William of Norford taught the women of his family to fight.''

''You, of course, did not credit such a bizarre rumor?''

''My incredulity shames me, Lady Marian,'' he answered, ''for I suspect you are indeed sprung from a line of Amazons.''

In France, planning her revenge, Marian had carefully hidden her skill at weaponry and counted on ignorance of her grandparents to prevent just such conjecture. But she was again in England, which called for a different sort of deception. Guy of Guisbourne was asking questions to which he might already know the answers. This was a man whose nonchalant charm could instantly transform to menace if too many false notes sounded in his ears—a man who, for all that he might appreciate a foe's proficiency at deceit, would not deal lightly with betrayal. Marian had already decided to lie about nothing except what she must and then, if she had a choice, by falling short of the truth rather than invention.

''My grandmother can claim the title of Amazon. It is true that she went on crusade and there discovered she had a gift for fighting that my grandfather admired and encouraged. It is equally true my mother possessed no such penchant or skill. I am somewhere between the two. I take pride in my talent with the bow, though I am hardly the only woman who can claim some ability. I can handle a knife, which is less common. Other than that. . . .'' She gave a shrug. ''Although Grandfather attempted to show me the rudiments of the short sword, I would not want you to see me attempt to wield one. And as for the lance and the broadsword, I assure you I do not plan to be entering any tournaments, Sir Guy.''

''Should you change your mind, I will beg you to wear my favor,'' he teased.

''Your glove affixed to my helm?'' she asked.

''A crimson gauntlet, proud as a cockscomb,'' Guisbourne jested, then, guiding her to the side, added, ''Let us look down this row.'' If she were not so attuned to him, Marian would not have noticed the slight check in his step, the infinitesimal tightening of his fingers on her arm. Glancing at his face, she let her gaze skim over his shoulder and caught a brief but certain glimpse of the Lady Alix examining some lengths of iridescent silk. Marian felt a surge of satisfaction at having supplanted the sensuous widow in Sir Guy's attentions, briefly or no.

''Are you certain you have no wish to tourney, Lady Marian?'' Sir Guy asked. As if it had always been his intention, he drew her to the stall of a bladesman who displayed a small but remarkable selection. ''It might be worth perfecting your swordplay if only to possess one of these weapons.''

Since it was at his instigation, she allowed herself to stop and appreciate the excellent craftsmanship. There were two tables covered with fine crimson wool. Arrayed on the first were three swords—a tapering estoc, a curving falchion, and the short-bladed baselard. Sir Guy reached out to touch each in turn, and Marian found herself also savoring the caressing stroke of Sir Guy's hand on the swords, powerful, graceful, and knowing.

''These are very fine.'' Sir Guy hefted the falchion, testing its balance.

''They are beautiful.''

Beside the swords were several daggers, both the double-edged anelace and the thin misericorde. Marian presumed the bladesman to be a London man, for as well as his own wares, he showed several exotic versions of the weapon unlike any Marian had ever seen. She picked up a knife fashioned entirely of translucent green stone, marveling at the sculpted dragon that formed the handle. It was exquisite, but the balance was clumsy, the handle obviously carved by an artist with no sense of weapons. It was useless save for show. She laid it aside to examine another, her fingertips tracing the patterned hilt of intricately carved ivory, inlaid with gold. The same geometric designs were worked in the gilded leather of the scabbard. She slid it off to reveal a ripple-edged blade of finest steel, Saracen, she presumed, deadly as it was beautiful. Lifting it, she felt the hilt snug in her grip as if it belonged only there, a length of the shimmering blade poised in perfect balance.

Marian sheathed the dagger and laid it aside. The gold inlay priced it beyond a casual purchase, and she feared that she might have already revealed more than she intended in her hunger to possess it. Misunderstanding her gesture, the cutler offered her a little knife for cutting meat, its handle set with pretty but inexpensive agates. For politeness she admired the work.

"I can set whatever stones you wish, my lady, pearls, garnets, emeralds with the sheath fashioned the same. A worthy adornment for so beautiful a lady."

With a rueful smile Marian shook her head and walked on, Sir Guy returning to his place at her side.

"There are so many legends about your grandfather." He resumed their conversation where it would most benefit him, Marian observed, gathering information about a man who could be either a significant political opponent or a powerful ally. "One does not know how to separate fact from fancy."

"My grandfather cannot fly," Marian assured him with feigned solemnity. "Nor straddle chasms."

"I am saddened to hear it," he replied in kind.

"It is true that he tops six feet by a good three inches. I have seen but one or two men taller," she said, reminded suddenly of the dark, taciturn giant who served Robin Hood. "And he possesses strength to match his height."

"Taller even than the King. That is impressive, but I am

not surprised. William of Norford is renowned for his prowess . . . almost as much as for his loyalty.''

After the blatant machinations at dinner yesterday, she saw no reason to pretend ignorance of his intent.

''My grandfather will ever be loyal to King Richard, as he was to King Henry. He will not be swayed.'' She spoke proudly, then paused and continued with a hesitant note. ''But while he is jealous of his honor, he is a practical man. Since the King has been seized, everyone in England must needs think of what will happen if he does not return, even as they gather the ransom they hope will purchase his freedom.''

''The future is indeed uncertain,'' Sir Guy said with a small twist of a smile. ''It is always wise to consider the consequences of more than one plan of action.''

Marian waited a second before speaking. She wanted to convey a truth that could be construed as simply a granddaughter's idealism, and imply an anxiety that could suggest herself as an intermediary pawn in the game that the Sheriff and Guisbourne were concocting. ''My grandfather will serve the lawful King loyally,'' she replied at last. ''Surely such trustworthy service is a prize worth waiting for?''

''Without question. Though I would say it is his granddaughter who is in truth the prize,'' Sir Guy said smoothly. Then, as they came in view of the yeomen of Nottingham, the banal pleasantry was followed by a more surprising remark. ''You spoke of having some skill with the bow. You must show me.''

''Very well.'' She agreed smoothly, reluctance at war with pride. He led her forward, into the midst of the archers gathered from all quarters of Nottingham. To test their skill, they had arranged a line of ringed targets against straw bales, and as she watched, a gaggle of young boys raced into the field to move the targets farther back. Guisbourne's eyes narrowed as he surveyed the new placement of the bales, and Marian realized he was speculating on the range of her ability. When he glanced at her, she asked him to choose her bow. He nodded, and she was gratified he accepted the request as assurance that she would not make a fool of herself or of him.

Now that their intention was clear, the yeomen stood back, letting Guisbourne examine some of the more likely-looking short bows. He selected one for her and paid the lad for the use of it. It was lighter than Marian would have chosen but a fair selection, formed of limber wood and well strung. Sir Guy watched as she tested the bow. She could see he was amused and titillated by the rarity of the situation. But if he was certain of his own superiority, he was neither contemptuous nor hostile, as many of the men around her were. Still, not even the surliest of them would dare refuse her the chance when she was so escorted.

It was a fine test of expertise. She must not reveal her true ability or appear to hide it. Facing the target, Marian drew the bow over carefully, holding the tension a bit too taut, her elbow a fraction too high. The first flight went wide into the straw, and she hissed her displeasure. "I seldom shoot so ill," she said with perfect truth. The next arrows she put into the outer rings of the target, the last two on the far edge of the ring surrounding the bull's-eye. Flushed with the satisfaction of having placed the shots where she wanted them, Marian turned to Sir Guy. Let him think it was pride in a mediocre performance. For a woman to possess this level of skill warranted some praise.

He nodded, not dazzled but adequately impressed.

"My grandfather could put every arrow to the center circle, my lord," she said, unable to resist the temptation.

Smiling, he met the challenge, taking a heavier bow and putting three arrows into the eye of the target.

"At twice the distance," she added coolly, naming her own limit.

"My eyes are not so keen." He laughed. "At half again, yes, but at twice that distance, luck, not skill, would find the mark." He leaned closer. "However, I would wager my expertise with the sword against any challenger."

The rough-napped purr was back in his voice, ruffling

her senses. She did not doubt his skill with the carnal blade or with the metal. "Your edge is too keen," she mocked with more lightness than she felt.

"It wants sheathing."

He took her hand, curling her fingers around the hardness of his own. His kiss brushed her knuckles, too delicate to be lewd, too carefully modulated to be anything but erotic. The surprising silken quality of his beard played a subtle contrast against the softness of his lips, their inner moistness, the hint of tongue and teeth hidden within the caress.

He lifted his gaze to meet hers. There was fire in his eyes now, where there had been none for Lady Alix. But perhaps it had burned for that lady until she surrendered. For some men only conquest offered excitement. He might be pure predator.

Deliberately she met the challenge in his eyes, forcing her breathing to a slower pace. She was practiced in the erotic insinuation of the French court, well used to parrying, toying, disarming with glances and words, though she had a reputation for an acid tongue. What she was not used to was to feel the emotion, the hunger that underlay the games she had played by rote or by wit, depending on her opponent. To play her role, she wanted neither to cut Sir Guy cold nor to encourage him too much. Now an inner fire licked at her. Dismayed, Marian realized the attraction was so strong she could not separate her own desires from her judgment of the wisest course. Any banter she devised would be hopelessly clumsy. And so she let her silence, her level gaze answer him.

He released her hand, and Marian saw him glance behind her. She had not noticed when Sir Guy's guard had left, but now he reappeared carrying an object wrapped in chamois. He gave it to Guisbourne, who turned and presented it. "For you," he said simply.

As soon as he laid the gift in her hand, she knew what it was. The weight and shape were evident beneath the cloth. Strangely the first thing she felt was shame for deceiving him with her shabby show at archery. Slowly she un-wrapped the chamois and uncovered the Saracen dagger in its gilded scabbard.

"Did I choose well?" he asked.

"My lord, this is too generous," she said. The wreath was one thing. It was courtesy for gallants to offer the ladies of the court pretty trifles. But the dagger was too expensive a gift for such short acquaintance. And she doubted that he was a man lavish to no purpose.

"Be generous in turn, Lady Marian, and accept it. Not even the gems of the deft goldsmith aroused such a flame of passion in your eyes." A deprecating smile mocked the intensity of the words, but his yellow eyes burned into hers like some strange, transparent fire.

He was not fool enough to think he could buy her favors. She would fling it back at him if he tried. Though it had cost dear, the lure was not the richness of the object, such as might impress a woman like the Lady Alix. The lure, and the threat, were that he had recognized her desire—and ful-filled it.

To accept the gift was imprudent. To refuse it was tanta-mount to cowardice. "Thank you," she said finally, without embroidery. "You chose well."

Rather than carry it, she attached the sheath to her girdle. "I believe the effect is even handsomer than the jeweled meat knife," Sir Guy declared with deliberate whimsy. "Let us hope it proves less practical."

Not yet used to the weight of it against her thigh, Marian found the intimate pressure provocative, but only because the blade was his gift. Her senses tingling with unaccus-tomed desire, Marian thought she could imagine herself married to such a man as this. Except that she wondered how closely the husband's nature would match the se-ducer's. Guy of Guisbourne might well wish to dominate what he felt he owned, and his unspoken promise of heav-enly delights might prove instead a hell.

"Is there anything you wish to purchase before we re-turn?" Sir Guy asked as they walked.

So soon? They still had not seen all of the fair, and Marian wondered what drew him back to the castle. After a brief consideration she decided to prolong their stay. "The carved wooden goblets," she said easily. "The pair with the wolves racing the brim—for my grandparents."

"Of course." If he hesitated, she could not perceive it. "They were near the entrance?"

They turned and began to walk down a new row. Though the semblance was leisurely, Marian decided that his pace discouraged dawdling. They were halfway down its length when a sound captured her attention. Glancing down the cross aisle, she glimpsed a raised platform being hastily assembled at the end. The sound of hammering muffled somewhat in the noise of the crowd. At first glance she took the structure to be a small stage where musicians and tumblers might perform. Then the throng parted, and she saw the whipping post being set at its center and a half dozen guards standing about the base. Even as she watched, one of them directed a carpenter to brace the post. She felt the pressure of Sir Guy's hand on her arm tighten a fraction, subtly urging her to turn round. "We have no need to see this. I meant us to leave before they arrived."

"There is to be a flogging?" she asked, purposefully stopping where they were.

"It was decided this morning, after I asked you to accompany me." Guisbourne frowned, not bothering to hide his displeasure, though his gaze was on the platform, not on her. He took a single, steadying breath before answering in his usual casual tone. "The Bishop of Buxton felt someone should be punished for his humiliation."

"And the someone is to be?"

"The miller. His son is known to be one of the Sherwood outlaws."

"The father has aided them?"

"We set a spy on him for a time. Unless the old man has a shining gift for pretense, he is shamed by his outlaw son." He smiled coldly. "The Sheriff could do no better on such short notice."

"You think it will breed resentment," Marian stated.

"Yes, I do," he answered, looking about them at the restive crowd. "Such punishments always draw an audience, but the festive mood of the fair will be set askance by such an abrupt intrusion. It is ill timed and ill placed, effective neither as entertainment nor as warning."

Marian wondered if the Sheriff had refused Guisbourne's advice or not bothered to ask it. "The miller is old, you say. How many strokes has the Sheriff decreed?"

"Twenty."

"Then he is like to die of it."

"I believe that is the Bishop's desire."

"He values his dignity highly," Marian said. "I thought the Sheriff agreed to repay the Bishop's losses? Was that not sufficient recompense?"

"I believe the Sheriff haggled overmuch." He turned to her, an ironic glitter sparking the amber gaze. "As a result, the Bishop suffered a fit of pique and raised his price. Sir Godfrey's annoyance was likewise increased."

"And so the miller pays for two fits of ill temper," she said.

"Any association with the outlaws is to be discouraged, and flogging will be a more merciful fate than the master torturer would have shown him," Guisbourne answered grimly. "Let us go. I doubt you would find this entertaining."

"No, I would not," she answered, though she would have stayed to take the temper of the people had Sir Guy not so obviously wished them to depart. He led her back down a cross aisle, away from the workmen. Was it unsafe to stay? Obviously, not everyone knew of the flogging yet, but word was spreading quickly. She noted the crowd growing quieter around them rather than noisier. They were not anticipating watching the prisoner's suffering. Those who were strangers to the miller were no more than curious, but those who knew him were blatantly hostile.

Incongruously they heard laughter as they neared the end of the row. A small knot of people was clustered ahead of them. Two women emerged from the cluster and approached them, oblivious of the events unfolding at the other end of the fair.

"That butcher's gone sudden mad," one was exclaiming to her companion. "To give us three pennyworth of meat for one."

"I would I were a maid again and could have it for naught," the other replied. "I'd sooner trade a kiss than a penny for such fine meat—with any butcher handsome as that. I'd squeeze his sausage if I could."

"Shame on you. Your husband'll box your ears to hear you say so."

"You won't hear me saying it to him, and I'd best not hear you," she threatened. "Now, where shall we spend our twopence saved?"

Looking round, the woman saw Sir Guy and Marian just ahead of her and stepped aside deferentially. The rest of the group parted to let them through. Just ahead stood yet another wagon, with a horse tied behind. Before it was a table where a butcher had laid out his wares, with cleaver and knives beside. A very pretty maid, with wavy russet hair and fair, freckled skin, hovered before the table, while the surrounding folk dared her to take the butcher's bargain. Gathering her courage, she pointed to a cut of veal, which the butcher deftly wrapped for her and placed on the table between them. She hesitated, then leaned forward, pursing her lips for a dainty touch.

The butcher reached across the table, taking the maid's face between his hands. Mouth covering hers with lazy relish, he drew her into a prolonged and obviously lascivious kiss.

The bystanders gawked, then cheered. When at last the couple parted, the maid stood swaying a moment, quite bedazzled, the tip of her tongue tasting the lingering flavor of his lips on hers. The butcher slipped the wrapped packet of veal into her basket, and she went on her way, a blush on her cheeks, her eyes sparkling at her own daring. Grinning like a cheerful fox, the butcher turned to survey her departure.

Watching his kiss, Marian felt the shock of recognition reverberate in her body, as though he had taken her instead of the red-haired maid into his wanton embrace. Despite the loose clothes, the leather apron, and the cap that covered his hair, she knew the brazen stance of the man's body. Although the very audacity of his presence at the fair made Marian doubt her judgment, when she saw his face, certainty jolted her anew. *Robin Hood.* The bold brows with their sharply drawn arch were unique, and beneath them the deceptive darkness of his eyes met hers with mocking familiarity. With a false and goading servility he tugged his cap in salute to her. She let her own gaze go blank and skim across him disdainfully, as if he were no more than the role he played, a butcher with a too-familiar eye. She saw the fleeting puzzlement on his face, followed by an expression as blank as her own.

He should run like a fox before the hounds. Instead he assumed a brash commoner's accent and began to sing out the bizarre prices he had placed on his wares. Where a fine dame paid but one penny for threepence worth of meat, a plump priest, he declared, would be charged three for one. And fair maids, as all could see, received the finest meat for one sweet kiss.

The hardest thing was to walk on. Despite his flagrant impertinence, she was vibrant with curiosity. Her body tingled all over. Why was he here? Simply to flout the Sheriff? To stage a robbery, or perhaps to collect a share of coin from the cutpurses who frequented the fair? Or had he come to rescue the miller? The last was the most interesting possibility. If so, she wondered just how he planned to achieve it.

She felt her own body tense in readiness when another half dozen of the Sheriff's guards appeared, leading the miller between them in chains. He was a small elderly man whose once sinewy strength was fast ebbing to frailty. She had no doubt the flogging would kill him. Glancing at Guisbourne, she saw a glimmer of pity, quickly masked with cool disdain. Marian followed the progress of the procession through the crowd. It had reached the platform when she heard the cry go up behind them, a high, quavering voice exclaiming, "Robin Hood!" Then, as they spun around to see, the voice bawled louder still, "Robin Hood! There's Robin Hood!"

A plump friar stood pointing a betraying finger at the counterfeit butcher. For a second all movement and noise were suspended; then from down the row an answering cry rose from the Sheriff's guard. More than half of them leapt from the platform to give chase, even as Sir Guy whirled to his own two henchmen, ordering, "Take him prisoner." Drawing their swords, they charged toward the outlaw.

His identity revealed, Robin Hood erupted into action. He snatched up the cleaver and he sent it flying into the first of Sir Guy's men, cutting him down with deadly accuracy. Pulling a short sword from concealment beneath the table, he sprang back and overturned it with a kick, dumping the meat onto the ground. Several bystanders, as well as several eager dogs, scurried to snatch what prizes they might from the dust, blocking the second of Sir Guy's men from reaching his quarry. The fat friar rushed in from the sidelines and latched on to the cursing guard, gibbering, "He robbed me in Sherwood. Catch him!"

"Let go and I will!" the man cried. Shoving the friar aside, he forced his way through the melee in front of him.

Sir Guy unsheathed his blade but did not join the chase. Despite the skill she had shown earlier, it was clear he had no intention of leaving her unprotected. "Come," he commanded, taking hold of her arm. "I want the yeomen ready." Already the Sheriff's guards were too scattered to command, but the archers could be directed. She went with him, both of them tracking the outlaw as they ran. One or two of the townsfolk joined in the chase, but most stood back and shouted encouragement. It was unclear if their enthusiasm was meant for the quarry or his pursuers.

In the midst of the riotous noise, Marian heard a shout of

laughter she recognized as Robin Hood's and saw him leap atop a wagon. The dark leather cap flew off, and his fair hair glinted in the sunlight for a second before he jumped onto the tables waiting below. Overturning the flimsier booths, he seized impromptu weapons to impede the Sheriff's men. The guard who appeared suddenly in front of him received a face full of pepper snatched from the spice dealer's booth. The next was bombarded with pottery jars of honey that cracked upon his helm. Clambering from a wagon bed to the top of one of the sturdier stalls, Robin Hood checked the progress of the others as they scrambled through the aisles, then jumped for the clearest path. Even as she tried to calculate his plan, Marian felt a flash of pure exhilaration.

Suddenly Guisbourne stopped, and she felt his fingers dig into her arm. "The fools," he hissed, "he's acting decoy." Cursing, he grabbed one guard and ordered him to summon more men from the castle, then plunged on toward the archer's targets.

Lifting her skirts, Marian kept pace with him. She realized at once it was true. If Robin Hood were simply trying to escape the guards, he would have dashed for the cover of the surrounding woods. But he kept parallel to that tempting, leafy shelter, taunting the Sheriff's men as he ran. When she recognized him, there had been no fear in the outlaw's eyes. If anything, he had incited her to denounce him. He could not have anticipated her presence, but his outlandish behavior was designed to call attention to himself. The whole scheme was a ploy to divert attention from the captive miller.

Looking back to the platform, she could see but four men guarding the old man. Most had abandoned the prisoner to give chase. The miller seemed safely held in his chains, and Robin Hood was by far the more valuable prize. She anticipated the attack by seconds. Simultaneously two men emerged from the crowd to rush the platform, and from out of the woods Marian recognized the dark giant running to join their attack. They overpowered and swiftly dispatched the guards who remained about the miller. The big man lifted the old miller in his chains, slung him over his shoulder, and ran for the woods. Swords drawn, the other outlaws covered their retreat.

Realizing what was happening, the guards chasing Robin Hood wavered, uncertain whether to pursue the outlaw or try to retake the prisoner. A great cheer went up from the surrounding crowd, their sympathies clear at last. Following upon the cheer was a moment of relative silence, a vibrant hush of satisfaction that swept through the assembly. Sir Guy, seeing that it was impossible to retrieve the miller, seized the moment to shout orders to the Sheriff's guards, directing them to capture Robin Hood. Like an insolent echo, Robin Hood's shout of laughter answered Guisbourne's command. Then the outlaw resumed his flight, the guards their chase, the crowd its uproar. But Marian could see that where before the people had stood back and hoped, they now actively interfered.

Guisbourne reached the periphery of the field where the yeomen had been practicing. "Follow the far edges of the fair," Guisbourne ordered those who remained. "This outlaw will have to run for the forest. I'll give ten silver marks to the man whose arrow takes him down."

Despite the small fortune he had named, only a few of the men showed any eagerness to win it. Although even the most reluctant did as he commanded, Guisbourne knew as well as she did that they could not be trusted to aim true.

It took a second to locate Robin Hood again. He was amid the booths of the weavers and textile merchants, sending bolt upon bolt flying at the onrushing guards. Streams of crimson and saffron unfolded in the air as two men converged upon him, only to find themselves tangled in brilliant bonds of satin. There was a sudden barrage of color as more and more lengths of wool and linen, glistening silk sendal and damask were tossed into the aisles—so many that it could no longer be only Robin Hood who tossed them. When the profligate flurry subsided, the outlaw had vanished, and it was the Sheriff's guards who were over-turning tables and toppling booths to search for him.

The crowd would protect him now, Marian thought, for sympathy or fear of their neighbors' reprisal. Instantly she began scanning the narrow stretch of clear meadow between the fairgrounds and the forest, but he had not broken cover.

Before he vanished, Robin Hood had scanned the lay of the fair. Marian surmised that he had more than one escape route planned and would pick the least dangerous or the most accessible. The last thing she expected was for the outlaw to somersault from under a table almost at their feet. The impetus of his roll brought him into a crouch. From it he sprang up, sword in hand. Marian stood between the two men. Deliberately she wavered in their path, as if uncertain which way to move, giving Robin Hood a crucial split second to continue his flight. Instead he took the time to sketch her a mocking bow. Then Guisbourne seized her arm, and she allowed him to thrust her aside. The next instant the two men were engaged in a hail of savage blows, metal ringing sharply against metal. His face vivid with excitement, the outlaw fought with the same fiery exuberance that he had displayed in his rampant hoax of a chase. Watching their combat, she was impressed with the vigor of his strokes and his dexterous parries, but Guisbourne was no idle boaster. His technique was perfection, and he had the advantage of height and weight. Marian doubted that the outlaw's skilled audacity was a match for Guisbourne's cold-blooded ferocity. Robin Hood's ability was enough to challenge Guisbourne's, but it was unlikely he could triumph. He must have deemed himself Guisbourne's better to have risked the encounter. It was justice of a sort that the outlaw's vanity would prove his undoing.

Vain he might be, but Robin Hood was no fool. Quickly aware of the disparity, he fell back gracefully before Guisbourne's attack, using his speed and deftness to the best advantage, demanding Sir Guy expend more energy in the attack. But Guisbourne was not the only threat. Already the guards were surging down the rows toward them. Death or capture awaited Robin Hood now.

Suddenly the outlaw gave a shrill whistle. Never dropping his guard, she saw Sir Guy extend his awareness, swiftly scanning the sidelines for an attack of Robin Hood's cohorts. But it was not his comrades the outlaw had summoned; it was his horse.

Half hidden, its head hanging morosely, the dust-covered sorrel had appeared to be tied behind the wagon, but obviously the bridle's knot was set to jerk free instantly. Its quality and training now wholly apparent, the horse charged straight down the aisle. Any not fleet enough to dodge would have been trampled, but the pathway had already been cleared for Robin and Sir Guy. Now Guisbourne was forced to spring aside as the horse lunged between them. Seizing the moment's distraction, Robin Hood grasped his mount's mane and swung himself astride. With a skilled horseman's instincts, Sir Guy timed his own maneuver closely. Dodging the deadly scope of the animal's forefeet, he raced alongside, aiming a crippling blow at his adversary's exposed side. But he was anticipated in turn, as Robin Hood swung his sword down to deflect the strike. The desperate move almost unhorsed him, but he recouped his balance as his mount plunged forward, never breaking stride. Out of Guisbourne's reach, they galloped for the edge of the fair, the outlaw's golden hair a bright banner. Once there Robin Hood rode not toward the forest, where the majority of the archers were aligned, but toward the outskirts of Nottingham. It was the riskier route, with reinforcements already summoned, but the scattered daub-and-wattle cottages would cover his retreat until he could break for the woodlands.

Climbing atop the sturdiest booth, Guisbourne shouted for the archers to take aim. Marian could not see, but after a moment he cursed so viciously she easily imagined the result. He jumped down, fury hardening his features into a mask. "They missed?" she asked, if only to have him clarify.

"One for lack of skill, one deliberately. I should cut his arm off," Guisbourne grated. Marian had no doubt he was capable of it. She saw him assess his own temper against that of the crowd and decide not to indulge it. It was the Sheriff's injudicious choice of an example that had created this debacle, and Guisbourne had no intention of creating another one.

Together they walked back to where Robin Hood had set up his butcher's table, but neither it nor the wagon revealed anything of interest. The rotund friar, Marian noticed, was nowhere in sight. Even behaving rashly as he had, the outlaw could not have been certain someone would recognize him. Perhaps the friar was disguised also, a member of Robin Hood's band positioned to give the alarm at the proper moment.

"It seems fortunate I did not chase the outlaw myself," Sir Guy remarked with bitter rancor, as he stood over the body of his dead guard. "I should prefer to die by the sword than the cleaver." With a savage jerk he removed the weapon and tossed it aside. Then he closed the man's staring eyes. Hurrying forward, the Sheriff's henchmen reported to him that three of their number were dead, and as many more wounded.

Abruptly Sir Guy turned to face Marian, his gaze intent and questioning. "You saw this man two days ago, yet you did not recognize him?"

"I did," Marian confessed instantly. She lifted her chin in a gesture of shamefaced defiance. "But fool that I was, I did not trust my own eyes. I thought it was my imagination playing tricks, turning an overbold butcher into the outlaw who insulted me."

"You should have trusted your eyes," Guisbourne said, but his voice was gentled. He looked about him, a sharper suspicion cutting his features. "Where has that feckless friar gone?" he asked his remaining guard. "Find him—if you can—and bring him to the castle for questioning."

"Yes, my lord," the man said, and began the hunt both she and Guisbourne suspected would be fruitless.

"Let us go back," he said, taking Marian's arm. "I will have to give the Sheriff an account of these events."

And the Sheriff, Marian felt with certainty, would find it convenient to blame Sir Guy for his own foolhardiness. The simple fact of Guisbourne's presence during the rescue made him a perfect scapegoat. But for all the grimness in her companion's face, she had no doubt he would emerge intact from the confrontation.

As for Robin Hood . . . he had rescued the miller with a scant handful of men. A reckless escapade and a successful one. Both she and Sir Guy had underestimated the outlaw's skill and his intelligence. Guisbourne was no doubt resolved to kill him. Marian was all the more determined to recruit him.

7 For the moment the rose garden was theirs alone. The trellised bower, thickly laden with sunset-hued blossoms, provided a fragrant retreat in the center of one wall. There were other benches, of course, but the blooming bower was the one most used. The three of them looked the picture of innocence, Marian thought, Alan strumming his lute quietly as they talked, Agatha sitting decorously beside her, fingers busy with stitchery. Smiling idly, Marian traced the lowest stalks of a climbing rosebush with her fingertips. When she found another thorn she snapped it off, then searched for another. Even if they had not been alone, it was seemingly no more than an idle gesture.

They came here every day, together or separately. It was delightful in itself, ideal for a moment of solace, perfect for private conversation—so perfect that the Sheriff often chose this site for his parlays. Marian had seen the gambit at once, for the rose garden was the only place in the castle to which there was both easy access and a limited chance of discovery. Searching for a way they might be able to spy on some important meeting, Alan had pointed out that the trellis could be pulled out from the wall, and a crawl space created. Under the guise of pursuing dropped needlework and such, he had done this. Now when they came here, they each took turns breaking off the thorns on the lower stalks of the rosebushes, to minimize scratching if the opportunity to use the hiding place ever arose. Marian snapped another thorn, then stopped, needing to concentrate on their current discussion.

Agatha's needle dipped smoothly as she spoke. "It's true that no one has yet betrayed this Robin Hood. But who knows? The Sheriff may raise the reward high enough to tempt someone. If the outlaw fell, we would all fall with him."

"I concede that it is a risk," Marian said, looking to Alan and Agatha in turn, "but if I am right about Robin Hood, think of what we gain—far more extensive information of who comes and goes in Nottingham than we can acquire ourselves."

Agatha's face was somber, but she nodded her agreement. "Oh, you're right, I'm sure of it. His name is always being whispered among the servants, and I know whispers. It's not just that thin sound that's cut by fear, the worry that some overzealous guard might hear and report them; it's a whisper that's plump with secrets. And I've already heard motley tales bandied about in Nottingham: a dozen fine ladies he's said to have seduced, escapades like the fair, people he's helped, gifts he's given. A little bit of silver stretches a long way among the poor, and it's all the sweeter for being stolen from the rich. The Sheriff is despised, and Robin Hood adored. He's a Saxon, one of their own, and they feel he's been wronged. If the man doesn't reap some knowledge from that feeling, he's a fool. And he did not strike me as a fool. He'll have ears everywhere."

"And perhaps not only among the poor," Marian suggested. "I think there are knights, like old Sir Walter, who were angry enough at what happened to the father to help the son."

"We do not argue against approaching him, Lady Marian, only about the necessity of revealing yourself," Alan a Dale insisted, his blue eyes gazing at her seriously. "I can easily go alone to the forest to make contact. Robin Hood need never know you are involved. I can also speak in the Queen's name."

Marian smiled to herself. Even at his most sensible, there was something so whimsical about Alan a Dale that she wondered if Robin Hood would believe the offer of a pardon if it came from him. She was forced to ask herself if he would be any more likely to believe the offer from a woman. Why not, if the woman came from the Queen? One thing was clear. The outlaw liked audacity.

"I can be the one at risk with both Robin Hood and the Sheriff." Alan continued his argument as his deft fingers began plucking a new tune. "We arranged our first meeting to appear as chance, to prevent all of us coming under suspicion in just such a situation. I can do the same again."

"True, but I doubt now that our precaution will protect us from a man as suspicious as the Sheriff. If he captures you, he will torture you." She looked to each of them in turn. "We are at risk with one another, as well as with Robin and his men. None of us can be certain we would withstand torture without divulging the others' names."

"Eventually, but you might have a chance to escape," Alan answered, following his own line of argument. "I doubt that the Sheriff would pursue you to your grandfather's lands. To capture a spy within his domain is one thing; quite another to chase after one that's already fled."

"If you were in my service, I would accept such a sacrifice. But you are the Queen's servant, as are Agatha and I, and as such your lives are no less valuable than mine," Marian said. "Of all of us, I have the most reason to be wandering Nottingham, surveying what may one day be my home. And I am the most likely to avoid a fate of torture, since I am protected both by my sex and by my rank."

"I do not think that will protect you, my lady." Agatha frowned. "Not from what I have heard of the Sheriff and his new dungeon master."

"I do not rely on it, Agatha. And I have another quite practical counter to Alan's argument. He is to be my contact with Queen Eleanor. If she decides he is needed in London or elsewhere, I will only have to search out Robin Hood myself."

"That is no reason that the first contact should not be mine. Let me assess whether or not it is safe for you to reveal yourself to this outlaw and his men. I can be simply the troubadour, hungry for fame, and willing to risk danger for a song that will win it for me." Alan paused, then added, "Robin Hood did invite me to come back."

The wistfulness in his voice made Marian wonder if Alan's first allegiance was not to the Queen but to his art. The musician's ruse was the simple truth. He wanted to talk to Robin, alone, and gather tales of the greenwood to spin into songs.

"He will believe that, Lady Marian. Perhaps even the Sheriff would."

"Even if he did, he'd take your hands, or your tongue, if he caught you collaborating," Marian said.

"Still, it's a sensible precaution," Agatha added. "A curious troubadour might be accepted into the outlaw's fold, if only for a bit of entertainment. And Alan can see what he thinks of them."

It was indeed sensible, but Marian found she could not relinquish authority or deny herself the chance to take action. Talking things through clarified them, but sending another in her stead sat ill. "I trust your judgment, Alan, but the final appraisal must be mine. And I feel I know enough of Robin Hood already to take the risk of approaching him." She paused, knowing they were dubious. "But I will not be utterly foolhardy, I promise you. From what I've discovered of how he treats his victims, I do not fear for my life, or even my virtue. I doubt he will insult me again. I've heard nothing of ravishment. If, as rumor has it, a dozen fine ladies have bedded him, it's of their own accord. More commonly he decorates his thievery with knightly courtesy. Only my purse will be in danger, and whatever money I take will be intended for him anyway. I will not reveal the true purpose of my visit immediately, any more than Alan would have."

"You have devised a story?" Agatha asked, her plain face newly attentive.

"Yes. Once I make it clear that I believe he has a network of spies in place, I will tell him there is someone I wish to find or some bit of knowledge I wish to obtain from him.'' She pondered for a moment, then said, ''The questions will revolve around the uncertain status of my grandfather's property. Lady Alix's husband was the chief rival in the question of my grandfather's land. His fatal accident is suspicious, as is the death of Eleanor's agent Ambrose of Blyth. The latter is of more interest to us. I would like to know if the Sheriff actually had him killed or only implied his involvement after the fact, to increase fear among King Richard's other supporters. I can probe Robin Hood about both deaths, expressing worry that someone may try to dispense with me to secure my land. Perhaps I will ask what he knows of Sir Ranulf, as well. The man did no more than offer me a sweetmeat, but I can pretend his interest is serious and so perhaps dangerous.''

''That's plausible,'' Agatha said, ''but not as plausible as Alan and his songs.''

''It will have to do,'' Marian said, making it clear she intended to carry her plan through. Argument ceased, and the discussion turned at once to practicalities.

■■■■■■

''Fallwood Hall is in poor condition, Lady Marian,'' the Sheriff said when Marian informed him of her intention to spend a few days on her property.

''I wish to put that to rights, Sir Godfrey. And to make sure that it is maintained well in future.''

''Even when its future is in doubt?''

''The land is my grandfather's. I do not expect that to change.''

''Unless it becomes yours?'' the Sheriff queried.

''Unless it becomes mine.''

''Take care,'' the Sheriff said with a malicious smile. ''The Lady Alix is a woman who looks after her own interests.''

''It is a pity our interests must needs conflict,'' Marian replied, suspecting it was not only land of which the Sheriff spoke. Sir Guy was off riding with Lady Alix this morning, so for the moment the lady had that interest in hand.

"Nottingham Castle is so close," Lady Claire protested, her expression open and earnest despite her blind gaze. "Surely you can return to us in the evening?"

"It is only for a day or two. Riding to and from would consume more time than it is worth. I will organize the work I want done much faster if I am there. Once it is under way, I will return, and the amenities of Nottingham Castle will seem all the more pleasant."

Marian had no doubt that the Sheriff's wife was indeed concerned for her comfort, but she suspected Lady Claire was lamenting more the absence, however brief, of the new singer and his songs. On that point she could reassure Claire and win her gratitude. "Would you do me the favor, my lady, of tending to my troubadour while I am gone? I wish to set the hall in order, and Alan will have little to do. Better he should provide amusement for you and your ladies."

Better still, Alan a Dale could continue to observe the comings and goings within the castle. But she had also promised him that if her meeting with Robin were successful, she would later send him as a go-between. She had been wise to do so, Marian thought, smiling inwardly. The troubadour's relief had been palpable, and who knew what catastrophe might arise should she stand between a singer and his song? If Alan was hunting fame, best he did it under her aegis.

After riding to the battered old hall of daub and wattle, Marian spent one day as she had indicated, assessing the building and its surrounding property and ordering cleaning and repair work done. The steward, the brother of the man her grandfather had selected, was obviously incompetent and probably dishonest. If his work did not improve swiftly, she would replace him.

At midday she summoned her guard Ralph and reviewed his instructions. "You should reach the inn by nightfall. If you can arrange to have one of the rooms upstairs, take it, and keep a wary eye for the innkeeper. If there are other travelers, he may set the candle himself. If not, display this one. In the morning be sure he does not see you backtrack to Nottingham. We do not know what other means he has of communicating with Robin Hood. Baldwin and I will wait for you at the same narrow bend in the trail where we were robbed before. If they intercept you at some other point, you must lead them to us."

He smiled, stroking his grizzled beard. "That should perplex them greatly, my lady."

She smiled in turn. "Indeed it should. Let us hope they do not choose to rob you on your way to the inn instead of on the return."

"Normally—" Ralph sighed—"Normally, I would hope not to be robbed at all. I pray this is a profitable venture for you as well as the outlaws, my lady."

■■■■■■

Late morning of the next day Marian chose a sensible riding dress, wishing she could wear her men's leather garb instead. Her purse was filled with an amount of silver sufficient to impress Robin Hood of her seriousness and modest enough that she would not regret wasting it if all she finally accomplished today was to contrive her own robbery. She donned no jewelry, nor did she wear the exquisite knife that Sir Guy had given her. If she was to be thieved from, she meant to lose nothing she valued.

Marian bit her lips, feeling a flash of anger at the memory of Robin Hood's arms pulling her close, his mouth covering hers. The heat of the emotion surprised her, and she cooled it with measured breathing. Curiosity came to the fore, and Marian wondered again that the kiss was all he had stolen. From the tales she had garnered, Robin Hood's bawdy gallantry with women appeared entirely haphazard. Most he simply robbed, without insult, and she had no intention of tempting him with such an exquisite prize. She chose a plainer knife and wore it in full view, suspended from her girdle. Two others she concealed, one strapped beneath her sleeve, another tucked inside the top of one of her soft boots.

After giving the steward orders for the work she wanted accomplished before dark, Marian told him that she would spend the remainder of the day hunting and ordered two horses saddled. With Baldwin at her side she entered the woods near her estate and then followed the road south, heading for the rendezvous.

■■■■■■

When they reached the thickly forested bend where they had been robbed less than a week before, Marian and Baldwin sequestered under the shadows of the trees nearest the road, picking at the provisions they had brought. They could see what travelers passed, but none might wonder at them lingering there. She judged they had waited perhaps an hour when a quiet voice behind her said, "Lady Marian."

Although she had not heard the man approach, Marian did not start. She had been impressed by the silence of the outlaws' movement before. Slowly she rose and turned around, Baldwin moving close to her side. The dark-haired giant stood waiting, no weapon but his stave in his hand. "You'll remember our last meeting. My name is John Little, or Little John if you like." He smiled, amused by others' easy amusement.

"Little John," she said in greeting. "You must have received my message."

"So I did. If you will come with me, my lady. We'll join the others, and then I'll take you to meet Robin."

Without further ado he escorted them a quarter mile to where Ralph and perhaps thirty of the outlaws were awaiting them. There her guards' weapons and the knife she wore about her waist were taken, and the three of them blindfolded. With the outlaws leading their mounts, they went deeper into the woods. Although this forest was unknown territory, Marian made an effort to track their progress by sound, but she quickly determined that Little John was deliberately confusing them by circling and backtracking and accepted that the exercise was pointless. At intervals Little John hailed three sentries but Marian thought that once the same voice answered. She gauged more than an hour had passed when she heard first the sound of water, then voices in the distance. Soon a turn of the breeze brought the aroma of roasting venison to her nostrils. The foliage and brush thinned suddenly, and then she felt an uninterrupted flood of warm sunlight on her face. Voices and movement surrounded them, and someone stepped in front of her horse and grasped the bridle.

Little John removed the blindfold, and Marian found herself in a large clearing in the forest. Besides the party that had ridden with them, there were another fifty men gathered around, curious and amused by their unexpected visit. Though many were obviously hardened men, Marian felt no immediate threat from them. The wiry, cross-eyed fellow who held her mount tugged his cap and smiled at her. Reassured, she looked about the camp, tugging off her riding gauntlets with purposeful casualness. Circling the clearing were lean-tos for sleeping, and there was also a larger hut, all woven from freshly cut branches. A new encampment then. Marian wondered how often they moved. She saw the roasting pit where the deer was turning and other campfires where smaller game was spitted. There was also a rough oven that gave off the wheaty fragrance of baking bread. Including those who had gathered to greet her, Marian guessed a hundred men about, but the camp might hold double that.

"Where is he, Much?" Little John asked the fellow holding her horse.

"Down at the river, having a tilt with the staves," he answered. "No one's dumped him in yet, more's the wonder."

Little John frowned. "Fetch him, would you then. Tell him there's a lady here would talk to him."

With a grin Much set off on his errand. But someone else must have run with the news, for just as they dismounted, Robin Hood emerged from the woods directly across from them. He was bare-chested, with his stave slung over his shoulder. Catching sight of her, he stopped short in amazement. For an instant their gazes met and locked. Then he cast the stave aside and came striding across the clearing.

Immediately Marian was on guard. The tautness of his movement, the set expression on his face warned her of danger. He had the feral look of a man hungry for violence. The hardness of his mien was new, but some known quality was missing. All his vibrance was gone. She had not realized how bright the light in him was until she saw it darkened. Marian stood her ground as he approached, taking in the new details of his presence, vivid in its sensuality. His bared chest was perfectly smooth, the skin golden, the nipples tender, a deep rose. Fresh bruises from the tilting marked his arms and torso. His fair hair was darkened with sweat, and he was close enough now that she could smell the sharp tang of wine clinging to him. He paused in front of her for a second, and she saw that his eyes, even in the sunlight, were a blurred and muddy green. Then, with deliberate provocation, Robin Hood pulled her into his arms, the length of his body hot and hard against her own.

"You recognized me at the fair and chose to do nothing." His voice was harsh and grating. "You must be feeling the fire fiercely to come search me out." His mouth closed on hers, brutal and ravenous. The stubble of his beard rasped coarsely against her cheek and chin.

Even though she was braced, the voracious onslaught of his mouth, the awareness of his naked skin were an overwhelming shock. For an instant every ounce of her will was directed at holding herself tense in his arms, containing the leaping fire in her flesh within the cold, tight-linked armor of her scorn and anger. Then, as if melting within the flame he evoked, she relaxed against him, slowly lifting her arms to encircle his neck. As he pulled her even more tightly into his embrace, she reached within her sleeve to grasp the handle of her hidden knife. In a swift movement she pulled it from its sheath and pressed its edge across the back of his neck, just below the base of his skull. At the cool, pricking touch of the metal Robin Hood instantly stilled. One false move and he was dead. They stayed poised thus for a moment, locked in their inimical embrace. Then, though he dared not move back a fraction, the pressure of his body against hers ceased and his lips released hers. Tentatively he began to withdraw, and Marian let him, the keen edge of her blade incising a line to mark his retreat. When he stepped free, he lifted a hand, gingerly, to touch the narrow wound and surveyed the blood on his hand, rubbing it between his fingers with a certain perplexity.

"You're drunk," she said coldly, though the imprint of his body burned into hers like a brand. She was aware, peripherally, of her guards being released by the men who had seized hold of them, but she kept her attention fixed on Robin Hood.

The outlaw met her gaze. The dark glaze of violence had vanished, and his eyes were far less guarded than she would have expected. Within them Marian saw relief, annoyance, contrition, amusement, curiosity—a wealth of emotion welling up through the muddled wash of intoxication.

"I'd a good start on it, but you've sobered me considerably," he answered, raking his fingers through his hair. He spared a glance for John Little, who regarded him with considerable disapproval, Marian thought. Robin Hood must have thought so as well, for he looked chastened. "Give me five minutes, and I'll finish what you've begun. Then we can talk. You do have a reason for coming here, I presume?"

"I had," Marian answered sharply. She was far from sanguine about her previous plan. With a grimace of distaste she cleaned and resheathed her knife.

"She knew about the candle signal, Rob," Little John interjected. He nodded toward Ralph. "Her knight set it out at the inn last night."

Robin Hood looked at her intently and then at his friend again. "Take our guests down the trail to the oak, John. I'll join you there shortly."

He walked off in the direction of the river, and Little John escorted them down a side path that led to a smaller clearing with a vast oak. Marian settled herself beneath it and gestured her guards to sit close by. Little John sat to the side. They waited in silence a moment; then the tall outlaw spoke in a quiet voice. "Robin's been in a black mood, and the wine made it blacker. His father died two years ago today."

He said nothing else, and Marian could tell he disliked apologizing. But the words achieved their purpose. She had been ready to abandon her idea of revealing her true purpose to Robin Hood. A reckless clever man she was willing to risk, but she would have none of a reckless drunkard. She'd grant him space for a fury of grief. Then, as she remembered his wanton impudence, her fists clenched with renewed anger. No matter what answering heat his body evoked in hers, Marian thought, she would have no man touch her against her will.

But when the outlaw appeared once more, she was reassured enough to subdue her wrath. His hair was still wet from the river, but he was otherwise presentable, garbed in the Lincoln green he favored. The brutish demeanor had vanished entirely, and he greeted her with a wry, self-deprecating courtesy. "Lady Marian, how may I help you?"

His eyes, she noted, had regained their clarity. While Marian was impressed that he had managed to sober himself, she was still dubious of revealing her true plan. "I did have a purpose in seeking you out," she replied, and went on with her prepared story, explaining her distress over the recent suspicious deaths of Ambrose of Blyth and Lady Alix's husband. She expressed concern that there might be a connection, someone seeking to win a secret chess match by removing pertinent players. Sir Ranulf perhaps or the Sheriff himself? She described a fear of becoming the pawn in this hidden game. Offering to pay him for his information, she asked what he knew and what more he might discover.

All the while Robin Hood sat quite still, watching her attentively. "Tell me again," he said abruptly.

"Again?" She knew he had been listening, not drifting

back into the murky dregs of the wine. He was suspicious, but for no discernible motive. One reason she had chosen the story was that it was plausible, even accurate, as far as it went.

Marian began again, carefully, from the beginning. But she had not finished half a dozen sentences before he said, "You're lying."

She regarded him with prickling hostility. "Why do you say so?"

"Why?" His arched brows echoed her inquiry. "Well, I could have let you spin the tale out further still. But I did not think it would lead where either of us wished to go. Confronting the lie seemed more to the point."

"Everything I've told you is true."

"Then tell me what you really want, because this is not the reason you have sought me out."

"You have misjudged that already," she snapped, "with near fatal result."

But although she thought his cheeks flushed a little, the outlaw only raised his brows again, the gesture repeating his question. Marian could not think of a lie he might believe, and even if she could, to attempt it would be an obviously dangerous gamble. She must either tell him the truth or abandon the plan entirely. Finally she said, "I will tell you what I really want, if you tell me why you thought I was lying."

"Since you came to me, Lady Marian, that does not seem a fair trade," he remarked with a certain lazy insolence. "I expect you will tell me the truth anyway, rather than have wasted your time."

"Robin," Little John said quietly from the corner.

The outlaw exchanged a look with the older man, then turned back to her. "However, as has been pointed out to me, I have been lacking in courtesy where you are concerned."

It was the closest he had come to true apology. His lips twisted with a self-mocking smile, but it was not arrogance but loneliness and subdued yearning she saw in his eyes.

Without warning Marian felt again the vivid imprint of his body on hers, as though the touch of him had forever singed her flesh. Instantly Robin Hood lowered his gaze, his mobile face oddly blank, but she saw the sharp breath he drew matched the hot pulse of her memory. Against the disconcerting heat, her voice was cool and precise as she seized up the fallen thread of their conversation. "Then, for courtesy's sake, you will tell me why?"

"For courtesy's sake, I will try," he answered, with the same contained politeness. Leaning back against the hut, the outlaw closed his eyes, brows furrowed in concentration. After a moment he shrugged, then resettled himself restlessly. Marian waited, tense with frustration until finally he said, "There were no shifting eyes or betraying tic that you can guard against, if that is what you fear. And you school your face well. But when you knew I mistrusted your story, you were not angry or flustered. You spoke too carefully and repeated your words too exactly, that is all."

"Any seeking such a favor might rehearse their words beforehand," she countered, annoyed, yet pleased to turn the lingering warmth to something less disturbing.

"For me it was enough."

"Rob's good at spotting liars," Little John interposed pleasantly. He spoke rarely, but Marian noted that he was free to say what he would when he would. "I've never known him to be wrong."

"Because I say so only when I'm sure I'm right," Robin smiled.

She could not help protesting, "But—"

"Lady Marian, when first we met I told you that you lie very well. That is true. But you lie nonetheless. I have explained why I thought so as best I could. For as you say, some might rehearse their speech with no hidden intent." He shrugged again. "In all honesty, I felt it first and found a reason after. That being so, honesty is your best recourse with me. Or silence. If you have misgivings of this meeting, you will be escorted safely from the greenwood, and that will be the end of it."

She made her decision. "As I said, it is my belief that you have many sources of information throughout Nottinghamshire. It was always my purpose in seeking you out to ask you to put those sources to use, spying for me as well as yourself."

"But not, I take it, to ferret out the mystery of the body in the moat?"

"What I want is far more extensive. I will ask you to share all the knowledge you gather of who travels the road in and out of Nottingham, the why and wherefore of their journeys, as well as whatever secrets you glean from within the households where you have informants."

"You want a great deal, Lady Marian. For what purpose?"

"The news you give me will go to aid Queen Eleanor, and therefore will help bring King Richard home. Any information may prove useful, but specifically the Queen fears Prince John will attempt to seize the next ransom shipment."

He showed no surprise, only showed his teeth in his most provoking foxy grin. "I had plans for the first one myself—till it was rerouted around Sherwood. I did not find the route in time."

"You will have to refrain from stealing it once you are acting in the King's name."

"And in exchange for such superb restraint, I gather that you are offering me a pardon?"

"I have the Queen's ear, and the Queen will speak to the King."

"A full pardon, for me and all my men?" he stipulated.

"Yes."

"A pardon and restitution of Locksley?" When she hesitated, he added sharply, "It is a meager enough holding compared with what my family once possessed."

"Yes," she said again, hoping he did not intend to pile condition upon condition.

"All to be granted when, or rather if, King Richard returns?"

"Since the purpose of asking your help is to ensure that return."

"Have you thought how easy it would be for me to betray you to the Sheriff? Would that not win me an easier pardon than a futile effort to bring King Richard home again? Prince John will pay as much for the Emperor to hold his brother hostage as the Emperor would demand to free him."

"The Sheriff's honor lies only with his advantage. You've made a fool of him too often for him to spare you, much less reward you. He will take your information and kill you anyway. You have one hope of pardon. It lies with me and with the King's return."

Annoyingly the outlaw was once again all indolent arrogance, leaning back against the oak, propping his head against his hands. "But I might receive a pardon anyway, without the bother and without forgoing easy wealth. The prison gates were flung wide when Richard was anointed King, and all such sinners as I forgiven. It may happen again."

"Perhaps, but I doubt there will be a general amnesty declared on his return. Despite Prince John's pretensions, Richard has never ceased to be the King." She paused, then jabbed lightly: "Nor do you strike me as a man who prefers to sit on the sidelines and wait."

"Nor fight others' battles for them," he parried.

"What else were you doing at the fair?"

"That battle was mine. I was saving the father of one of my men."

"So you have loyalty for them but none for England?" she asked, to discover as much as to challenge.

"For Richard, you mean?"

"He is our King."

"Is he?" Robin asked, a cold glint in his eye. "I grant there's not a knight in Christendom who doesn't respect him as a warrior. Nor would I deny his courage. But I don't see that he's much of a king, except as something shiny and bright that glitters in the sun and awes the ignorant. He has

no love of England. He has not spent six months of his life
here. Our wealth is no more than fodder to feed his insatia-
ble appetite for glory. King Henry had some love for the
country at least, and wanted to make us strong. Even Queen
Eleanor has some concern for us, other than for how much
we can be milked before we run dry.''

''Has Prince John?'' she asked, since she could not deny
what he said of Richard.

Robin shook his head and gave her a bleak smile.
''That's true enough. I'd rather have Richard king than
John Lackland. And I will tell you that many of my men
love the King for his valor and will fight for him as fiercely
as you would wish, in any way you wish. But he and his
family have brought nothing but grief to mine.''

Even as Marian watched, the darkness came over Robin
again, a brooding cloud that swallowed the light he radiated,
so that she in turn felt shadowed.

''My father was a trusted adviser when King Henry first
began hunting for some land to make up for Prince John's
lack. He was seventeen then, spoiled rotten, envious, and
greedy. The King offered to make him Lord of Ireland, and
Prince John seized his chance.'' Robin's eyes met hers, and
the darkness that had taken him colored them as well, a
green-black opacity that shut her out. ''It was Easter week, I
remember, when I watched my father set sail with him,
accompanied by a grand fleet of sixty ships, three hundred
knights, and ten times that many horsemen and foot
soldiers. It was Christmas when he returned, with news of
endless disasters.

''Their arrival had been particularly calamitous. The
Irish thought the Prince had come to bring some order to
their troubled land. They sent their most honored elders,
graybeards, to greet him at the dock and offer him their kiss
of peace. Prince John stood, laughing in derision, while his
callow Norman favorites pulled the long beards of emissaries. He could hardly have planned a more malicious insult.
When the other Irish lords heard of this disgrace, they
vowed to fight rather than give homage.

"My father warned him." Anger honed his voice and cut the precision of his words sharper still. "But Prince John ignored his counsel and that of every other man of experience his father had sent with him. He listened only to the flattery of his young courtiers, men whose praises increased with each confiscated estate he bestowed upon them. He made no effort to forestall the growing rebellion. Instead he went to Dublin and squandered all his silver in drink and debauchery. His soldiers deserted because the Prince had used their wages to pay for his own pleasures. When he rode to battle against the King of Limerick, half the force he faced had but recently been his own. After that bloody and ignominious defeat he was summoned home, not Lord of Ireland, but John Lackland once more.

"My father dared to speak the truth. And so the King's heart, which had been warm, turned cold, and his sharp wits went soft as porridge." He gave her a vicious smile. "He doted on John and so blamed everyone else for his failures. My father lost favor with King Henry and King Richard in turn, all because he despised John and would not see England in his hands. It cost him his land and finally his life." A rock lay by his knee, and he picked it up and flung it across the glade with such violence that Marian had to stop herself from reaching for her knife. His skin was livid with rage, the bruises marking him like stigmata, and when his eyes met hers, they burned like green fire. "And so you see, I have no love left for any of the Plantagenets."

Abruptly Robin looked away, the flare of fury sinking within a cold and sullen disgust. Yet the rage might strike through, sudden and deadly as lightning from a storm cloud.

"I cannot change what is past," Marian said, careful in touching a pain that twisted together so many strands. She chose one that served her without belying his grief. "But if you cannot fight for King Richard, you can still fight against Prince John. I do not see that he has changed in any manner since he was seventeen, spoiled rotten, envious, and greedy."

"That's true enough," Little John said as if to himself, but the simple words threw her his support.

Marian leaned forward. Like Little John, she kept her words simple and direct and did not try to soothe the outlaw leader with sympathy. But she allowed her voice to challenge him fully. "If we prevail, Robin of Locksley, you have the chance to reclaim your lands. Or do you prefer the life of Robin Hood?"

Raising his head, he gave her a strange, enigmatic smile. "Perhaps I do," he answered. But then he looked down, rubbing his forehead as though he had a headache, and she wondered if it was rage, or grief, or simply the wine punishing him at last. "Of course I want your bargain, if it is a true one. Our freedom is worth more than the King's ransom." This time when he lifted his head, he looked simply tired. "At best, as you say, I will be Robin of Locksley once again and have earned a pardon for all my men. At worst I will end as I am now, an outlaw in Sherwood. But I want more than promises. I want you to bring me some confirmation from the Queen."

"If you can tell when I am lying, then you will know that I will honor my word. I give it to you now."

"Nevertheless, you cannot promise for the Queen, nor the Queen for the King. I want some royal token; whether it be honored later or betrayed, I will have it in my hand. Meanwhile I will expect payment for any information I acquire—in silver or in kind."

Her purse had never been taken, and now Marian untied it from her girdle and gave it to Robin. He counted it out, grinning at her in his mocking, foxy way, the darkness dissipating as quickly as it had descended. "And now, since we have no more business for the moment, will you and your men join our feast? It smells as if the venison is done at last, and I for one intend to savor it. Once I am pardoned, I will not be able to help myself so freely."

In a single easy movement Robin rose to his feet. He gave Marian a small ironic bow of acknowledgment but let Little John be the one to extend his hand and draw her to hers. Then he turned and led their way back to camp. His hair had dried, its paleness gleaming brightly in the sunlit patches of the path, and he moved with a compelling grace that drew her eye. Slender but substantial, his compact body conveyed both agility and strength, his assured carriage both ease and alertness. Marian let herself savor the rhythmic play of his leg muscles for a moment, the molded curve of his buttocks beneath his leathers, before forcing her attention elsewhere. Since he had reappeared sober, Robin had been careful not to inflict any unwanted attentions, even when her own defenses had failed her. His sexuality was ever-present, as natural, as vital as his breath. But if that vitality could not be hidden, it was carefully restrained, both to offer her respect and to regain it for himself. Now, as they entered the great clearing, Robin made certain that he treated her with discretion before his men, letting John Little lead her to a prepared place beneath one of the shadiest of the trees that edged the camp, while he walked among his men, directing them to bring her the bounty of the greenwood.

Though the food was simple, its plenitude and freshness made it indeed a feast. Aside from the venison, there was hare, partridge, and other fowl, as well as fresh fish to lay upon the trenchers. Dense loaves of fresh baked bread were passed around, with soft cheese and honeycomb. The men helped themselves, but Marian saw at least a dozen portions being sent out to the sentries and was glad to know Robin kept a careful watch on the roads. Along with the plentiful food, there were wooden goblets filled with a portion of fine ale or with the dark rich wine that Marian chose to drink.

Seated, Marian looked around curiously as she ate. She noted that Robin had selected the men with the best manners to sit by her during the meal, and she took care to speak to all within easy hearing. The presence of a lady gave the meal a celebratory air. The men were rough, and a cheerful rowdiness prevailed. Robin roved among them till all were settled, checking their boisterous spirits the instant they threatened to turn crude. That he could control them so easily, and through affection rather than fear, was a testament to his leadership.

His trencher laden with venison, Robin returned to sit beside her. He poured wine for himself but did no more than sip it, Marian noted. She continued to gaze about her as she ate, searching out how many of the faces she recognized from the robbery and from the rescue. "I do not see the false friar you had with you at the Nottingham fair," she said, turning to Robin. "Or do I not recognize him without his habit?"

He gave her a glance of such artless candor that for a moment she doubted her presumption of the man's complicity. But his puzzlement was too bland for such a sharp-witted man. "I hope you have not sent him anywhere that will place him in Sir Guy's purview," Marian warned, "for I am not the only one who thought his presence too fortuitous. The finger that he pointed at you turned back to himself."

Now Robin grinned at her. "I told him that his days of being a secret spy were at an end, but he refused to believe me."

"He may continue to play the game, so long as Guy of Guisbourne does not see him."

"Will told me he's been hiding inside the hut ever since you arrived, in fear your eye would fall upon him."

"In fear of what?" Marian chided. "I am no basilisk, to kill with a glance."

Little John gave a snort of laughter. "Fear of his own fear is quite enough for Tuck."

" 'Twas somewhat more, Lady Marian," Will Scarlett told her. "When you first arrived, Tuck was skulking in the trees just behind you. You did not see him, but he saw that demonstration of your knife work. He's been quivering in terror ever since."

"Since the Lady Marian has requested our false friar's presence, he must come forth," Robin said, and sent Will to fetch him. The others were grinning broadly as they waited, and Marian wondered what the joke would be.

The man emerged, and Marian was startled to see him dressed in the friar's habit. She had thought it only a disguise. He bobbed a greeting when Robin introduced him as Friar Tuck. Whatever terror had driven him into hiding, he was no more than nervous now and obviously curious. He settled himself among them, nibbling voraciously from a well-laden trencher.

Robin poured wine for him and refreshed Marian's goblet as well. The flavor was distinctive and familiar, and she took another sip. "This tastes like the Sheriff's wine," she commented. "Have you managed to filch some from his cellar?"

"Indirectly. . . ." Robin exchanged a glance with Will Scarlett, who burst out laughing.

"You have not heard the news at the castle then, Lady Marian?" the young man asked when he had recovered his breath.

"I was not there yesterday."

"When first we met, the Bishop of Buxton contributed some exceedingly poor wine to our holdings," Robin explained, mock-serious, a smile tugging the corners of his lips. "The Sheriff in turn contributed some very excellent wine to recompense the Bishop. Hearing of this, we thought it only proper to detain the Bishop when he set out for Lincoln and claim our proper prize."

"You robbed him again!" She found herself laughing, celebrating his audacity.

"Yes, but perhaps he can bully the Bishop of Lincoln into making good his loss," Will Scarlett said.

"I doubt that," Little John remarked. "They are adversaries."

"I can tell you that Buxton means no good to Lincoln," Marian confirmed. Whatever use they made of the news was likely to work to the detriment of the odious Bishop of Buxton and perhaps to the Sheriff. "At dinner the other day the Bishop was plotting with the Sheriff to have his rival accused of witchcraft."

"Witchcraft!" the Friar exclaimed.

"I had not heard that part of it," Robin said, making her wonder just which parts of that conversation had been reported to him.

"Bishop Hugh is a saint walking the earth," Friar Tuck avowed.

"He has been kind to many in need," Little John said. "And he's not afraid to speak his mind to the powerful."

"We cannot permit this to happen," the Friar declared, rising to his feet, his eyes aglow with zealous fervor, the half-eaten leg of some fowl still clutched in his hand.

"We can warn him certainly, Tuck," Robin assured the outraged Friar. "And since you are so eager, you can join the party that journeys to Lincoln to save him."

The Friar sat down abruptly, but though he glanced about him sheepishly, Marian could see that his anticipation of the adventure outweighed his apprehension. She began to suspect that the cowardly Friar was less a liability than he seemed. He must be well able to use his wits, or Robin would not have chosen to have him along. Perhaps Robin guessed what she was thinking, for he began spinning tales of Sherwood, amusing escapades that entertained her while praising the bravery and cleverness of his men. The timorous Friar's antics were applauded in an elaborate silliness involving a villainous baron, a beleaguered brewer, two dozen barrels of ale, six chickens, and a cow.

Her laughter kindled Robin to spin yet another tale. Now that his voice had lost the earlier harshness that wine and anger had aggravated, Marian found herself listening with a new ear. While lacking the beauty, the mellifluous menace of Sir Guy's, it had its own charm. Guisbourne's voice had the softness of the lushest sable, the glinting hardness of steel . . . an exquisite voice, all its underlying savagery cloaked with civilized elegance. Robin's voice was neither so resonant nor so refined, but the more she listened, the richer it became. Light and husky, its rough surface conjured the textures of tree bark and the glinting flow of pebbled streams. Its disarming warmth was as comforting, as caressing as the play of sunlight on wind-stirred summer leaves. A dance of elements: earth and water lightened by air and licked with a tongue of golden flame.

Marian leaned back against the tree, listening to the layered cadence rise and fall, sipping the rich wine. It was even better than she remembered; the heady draft flowed through her veins like fire and honey, burning sweetly. Senses tingling, Marian smiled. Robin smiled back at her, and that made her laugh again, for no reason. *Reason enough*, she reassured herself. Though the future was uncertain, the day was a success. She had been able to seal her bargain not only with silver but with information exchanged. Now, well fed, warmed by wine and laughter, she found herself reluctant to leave the encampment. She wanted to sit and listen to Robin's voice as he wove another tale, whether from fact or fancy she did not care. Caught in the playful camaraderie of the day, Marian felt happy, a simple, uncomplicated emotion. She could not remember when last she had felt this way. Robin offered to fill her cup with wine, but she covered the brim with her hand. It was too strong. She had become intoxicated without knowing it, flushed and giddy. Marian summoned her resolve. However pleasant the afternoon, she must leave now if she wanted to return to her hall by nightfall. Rising to her feet, she thanked them all for their hospitality with the graciousness due to fine lords.

Talking as they walked of ways and means of meeting, of signals she could send, and of avoiding suspicion, Robin escorted her back to her horse. "I'll establish a pattern of visiting my hall every few days with Sir Ralph. Once I've tended to business there, I will make it usual to spend a half day, or a full day, hunting when I do."

"In areas other than where Robin Hood does his?"

"Exactly, and I shall be sure to be seen elsewhere. I will have to remember never to return empty-handed to the hall. It will help to keep my bow arm in practice." She also planned to keep her sword arm strong training with her knights in the woods. "I won't always come myself. Alan a Dale will be go-between as well."

He nodded, then asked, ''Do you care about the deaths you inquired of before, or were they only a ruse?''

''I care—about Sir Ambrose's supposed accident in particular.''

''I do not know who killed him. But he was known to love the King. Your friend Guy of Guisbourne is a likely candidate,'' he said, giving her another of his amiable, impertinent grins. ''Or one of several other knights who look to make their fortunes under the auspices of our dear Sheriff. As for the other death, Locksley was mine. Perhaps Lady Alix has me to thank for her widowhood. Did you not consider that?''

She considered it now and answered, ''He died but recently. When it comes to vengeance, I would think you more likely to act in hot blood than in cold.'' She gave him a cool smile and added, ''I have heard it suggested that my friend Guy of Guisbourne planned it.''

He laughed. ''It seems you seek out dangerous company often, Lady Marian, though this time the gossip is wrong. Neither Guisbourne nor I is responsible. The Lady Alix made her bargain with the Sheriff. But since she did it to free her bed to accommodate your friend, you should be warned to tread lightly, lest you find yourself facedown in a puddle with a boot on your neck.''

''I will heed your warning,'' she promised as they reached the horses.

Little John appeared and returned their weapons. He drew out the blindfolds but looked the question at Robin, who shook his head no. Offering his hands to boost her, Robin helped Marian remount, then stood looking up at her. For the first time since he had sobered himself, she saw the overt flash of sexual fire in his eyes. She was glad when he dropped his gaze, giving her time to cloak her own response as he contained his. They were comrades and accomplices now. There would be no more of such insolence on his part, and she must take care to hold his respect.

He took a deep breath, combing back the tangled strands of his hair in a distracted gesture, pale gold and dark glint-

ing between strong fingers. When he lifted his gaze, the
fierce heat there was banked, the smile he gave her warm
and conspiratorial. Sunlight gilded his face and brightened
the green shimmer of self-mocking laughter in his eyes.

I like this man, Marian realized. *I was right to come here
myself.*

8 "Just how long must I play the grieving widow?" Alix asked from the bed, her voice hazy with pleasure.

Guy paused in dressing, turning to look at her. She lay in an artful sprawl amid the silk and linens, the sunlight catching the red glints in her dark hair, her blue eyes heavy-lidded. She was sated, for the moment at least, and oozed a laconic sensuality. He had taken time and care to please her, and the suspicious edge in her voice had softened. He summoned a smile, allowing his gaze to skim her body appreciatively. It was easy enough to simulate a degree of lust he no longer felt. There had always been an attraction, although her conceit overestimated its intensity.

Meanwhile he considered, then answered, "Six months, presuming tongues have stopped wagging."

"There will be something of more import between then and now. The ransom, if nothing else, will draw everyone's attention." She eyed him fretfully. "Prince John is coming to see the Sheriff this week and Nottingham will writhe in an ecstasy of speculation. After that . . ."

"The visit will prove an admirable distraction, which we could easily contravene by acting too quickly. Your husband has been dead scarce a month, Alix."

And should not be dead at all, Guisbourne thought, but did not reveal his aggravation.

Her pout was calculated, but to little effect. "It is too long."

"Let us savor our illicit relations while we may." She

smiled at that, and Guy moved to the bed. Sitting beside her, he stroked her slowly, caresses meant to soothe rather than arouse.

"Too long," she murmured again, but a purr of pleasure softened the complaint.

It was a delicate balance. Guy knew he could not play the game indefinitely. If he did not marry Alix, it would take a great toll on her pride. She would revenge herself upon him one way or another. And whomever she did wed would likely be an ally in that vengeance. Despite his growing reservations, he had not dismissed the alliance entirely. He could not afford to do so. If he made it his primary aim to consolidate his power in Nottingham, marrying Alix remained the quickest way to achieve that purpose.

He let his hands roam desultorily. Shifting sensuously under his touch, she sighed and closed her eyes. Continuing his caresses, Guy appraised her coolly. Yes, Alix was beautiful, and she possessed grace and manners sufficient to the French court. But she relied on the dewy girlishness that still clung to her to cajole and entice. He found the tactic cloying already. In another decade she would look like a fool if blind vanity could not forsake the ploy. She did not lack intelligence, but it was limited by her self-centeredness. Alix would grab what she wanted then hold fast, more likely to balk than aid him in larger plans. He would prefer someone with either less ambition or more, a wife who would tend to his castle or help him build an empire. Of course he might not need this woman at all, depending on which of his plans came to fullest fruition.

"Six months," he repeated, smoothing her flank with his palm. "Six months should be sufficient."

Dark blue eyes opened to survey him. Her hand reached up, riffling the hair on his chest. Petulantly she said, "I don't know why you're so irresolute. I've done what you wished. Your hand was not involved."

Guy did not tense or even blink. Only his hand paused, and he lifted it then deliberately, unfurling a graceful gesture before her questioning gaze. "It appears to be." He chose a chastisement that did not reveal his surprise. "So I see little difference in effect."

He recalled Alix's voice all honey-coated as she mentioned that her husband was growing feeble, that none would be surprised should he die in the near future. Old, yes, but hardly feeble. Knowing instantly what she was after, he'd told her flatly that he would have no hand in her husband's death. It seemed a clear enough disapproval to him. He had thought to warn her off, not spur her. But now it seemed she undertook the deed as a test of courage.

Guy did not entirely blame her for the act. She had been a young girl married to an aging man, then a woman in her prime married to an old one. A husband no worse than most. Guy had seen Sir Otto in his cups be casually brutal, but not with any persistent cruelty. He indulged and punished Alix as he might an unruly pet, without the wit to see the intelligence that manipulated him so expertly. Until Guy appeared, Alix had seemed content to revel in that domestic expertise and indulge her wanton appetites elsewhere. He was hardly her first paramour, but the first she loved, it seemed. Though as her pride overrated his passion, so might his overrate her infatuation. Fortuitous timing rather than obsession might have ruled these events. After so many years the burr that had rankled lightly might suddenly have cut deep—and the ponderous, boring, brutish husband become a crushing weight on her spirit—and her body, for he had remained a lecherous man.

"I did it for you." Alix murmured and, when Guisbourne lifted a mocking brow, added quickly, "For us— think what we two can build here."

"Oh, I am thinking of it," he replied with a provocative smile.

Even if Alix had conceived a passion for him, when the passion died, perhaps he would as well, to be replaced by some new lover. Done once, the deed would be easier to do again. Having tasted the power of death, could she refrain from drinking from that cup again? For whatever reason and however indirectly, she had seized power, initiating an action rather than arranging a seduction. He had thought he'd known her, but she had proved herself capable of far more than he had ever conceived.

Watching her, he concealed his wariness as she said with unanticipated sharpness, "You will find no marriage more to your advantage—not in Nottinghamshire."

He decided to provoke. "No?"

Rising, Alix wrapped her body in the silk coverlet and strolled about the room. She tarried by the chessboard, running her fingertips along the edge, toying with the pieces. Alix played well enough to let her husband win. She had some strategy, even flashes of brilliance, but no consistent patience.

"You tried to make me jealous with that gawky Amazon," she scoffed, and the scorn seemed genuine.

Jealousy or blindness? Marian was beautiful and moved with assured grace, but Alix regarded her own diminutive prettiness, her feminine wiles as her most powerful weapons. She had used them too exclusively to credit the allure of a woman whose strength of will and body was not disguised.

"The gambit worked." He smiled, as if stirring her jealousy had been his sole intent.

"With that clumsy pawn." She still loitered by the chessboard. A sly smile curved her lips, and she slid a black knight across the squares to topple a white pawn and push it from the board. "Next time choose a more worthy piece."

He froze. The gesture was too literal, the smile too smug. The "next time" dispensed of Marian entirely.

Guisbourne moved smoothly, holding his rage in check. Alix turned to him, her eyes glimmering with ill-concealed triumph. He smiled, pulling her close, then twisted her arm behind her back with one hand while the other covered her mouth. She glared at him, wild anger leaping to meet his own, and he felt a flare of lust along with his fury. Guy let the pain ease and uncovered her mouth. "Madam, tell me what you have done," he said with ominous politeness.

"Nothing!"

Guisbourne watched her melt the anger to tremulous innocence, her eyes wide, lips quivering. He preferred her fire to this poisoned honey. Ruthlessly he applied pressure to her wrist, his voice silky with menace as he said again, "Tell me, Alix."

She gasped with pain, then taunted, "I have found her a husband. Not too much worse than the one I had."

"Who?" he demanded. "Tell me who."

She cried out. He had not meant to tighten his hold, but let her think he had. "Sir Ranulf . . . he was easy enough to convince!"

Wolverton had northern lands bordering on those of Marian's grandfather. He was being squeezed out of his power base in Nottinghamshire and had not the brains to contend against his adversaries. An advantageous marriage was his best route to consolidating his power. Sir Ranulf planned to present Marian's grandfather with a fait accompli, gain a small but strategic piece of land, and a great northern alliance.

"It's done by now." Alix sneered, her girlish features abruptly coarsened.

The taste of power had indeed made her giddy. Or perhaps he had only underestimated her ruthlessness, as her husband had done. Guisbourne felt simmering rage that she should try to manipulate his life once again and anger that she now forced his hand against her. With it came a surge of disgust that she would force such a husband on another of her sex. Then he smiled, knowing he should appreciate her relish for revenge. He would choose such a fate for an enemy . . . or a pawn.

"If you think you can rule me, you are wrong." He had her by the throat. Deliberately he lowered his mouth to hers and kissed her until desire burned hotter than anger, then let her fall back on the bed. "Once you know that, and not before, then we can discuss marriage."

He left her lying there and strode out. In the courtyard he summoned his guards. He would have to bring more from his castle before approaching Sir Ranulf and say he intervened in the Sheriff's name. He did not think Godfrey had been fool enough to give consent to this abduction. Like Marian's grandfather, he was to approve afterward.

Guy wondered at his interference. Then the image of Wolverton topping Marian filled Guy's mind and fury with it. Swiftly he contained it. Whatever his attraction to Marian, however repellent the thought of Sir Ranulf bedding her, the strategies he had conceived about her were far too tenuous for the risk he was taking. With a muttered curse he dismissed his apprehension. He had committed himself when he challenged Alix. The taste of power had made her giddy. One way or the other she must lose this game.

■■■■■■

"I trust you are pleased with the work, my lady?" the steward asked, his oily eyes sliding about as he followed her toward the stables.

Slipping a light cloak over her silk court gown, Marian regarded the man contemptuously. He somehow managed to skulk while standing still. "It is much improved," she commented in a neutral voice. "Sir Ralph will remain here to oversee your efforts. I will return in a few days to consider your progress."

The steward's efforts to ingratiate himself were futile. Marian had every intention of replacing him. But she might as well let him repair more of the damage his slackness had caused first, as she had not had the chance to select another steward. She distrusted him intensely, but under Ralph's scrupulous eye the man would probably continue his efforts.

"Do you wish more guards for your return to the castle, my lady? I've ordered five men to ready themselves in case you did. They are waiting in the stables." He bobbed up and down obsequiously then cast a nervous glance over his shoulder.

Impatient, Marian started to refuse him, but reconsidered. A larger escort would be more seemly, and her private comings and goings might be less marked if she observed protocol in situations such as this. When she agreed, the steward summoned the five men. They were a mean-faced lot, though their weapons and armor were well enough tended. She wore only the knife Sir Guy had gifted her with, the gold inlay gleaming against the white silk of her gown. The men waited while she mounted, then fell in behind her and Baldwin. The steward ordered the gate opened, and they set out on the hour ride to Nottingham Castle.

The morning was cool and clear. The road wound through snatches of woodland separated by green and fallow fields. Marian relished the mild warmth of the sun, the cool fingers of breeze, the soft clop of the horses' hooves in the dirt. The others kept to her pace, and she realized their progress was more leisurely than need be. She forced her mind ahead, and the twinge of queasiness she felt at the thought of placing herself within the Sheriff's fortress only hardened her resolve to complete her mission. The wary anticipation she felt at the thought of seeing Guy of Guisbourne again was more pleasurable and more disturbing. She hoped she would find a way to overthrow the Sheriff without destroying Guisbourne as well. She did not know if she had the means to draw him, as she had Robin Hood, but Guisbourne would be an invaluable ally to the Queen. For a moment images of the two men shimmered in her mind, like a play of sunlight and shadow.

Halfway to the castle they rounded a bend to find a group of knights approaching them on the road. Twenty men, Marian estimated, recognizing one as Sir Ranulf's chief knight by a gray stallion she had admired. Perhaps it was her dislike of Sir Ranulf that prickled warning or some fixed intentness the band failed to disguise. She called Baldwin's name, sensed him moving to protect her, then heard him give a choked cry. Turning, she saw blood spewing from his mouth. One of the steward's men had drawn his sword and driven it through his back to pierce his heart. Marian shut grief and panic within as another man drove his mount forward and seized hold of her arm. The fool wore no helm. Instantly she drew the Saracen blade from her girdle and slashed his throat. Blood spurted from the gash, drenching her face, her shoulders.

Spurring her horse, she swerved from the road and raced across the field. Yelling, the traitorous guards charged after her, already far too close. There was a chance, her mount was swift, but she did not know where to run. She dared not return to the hall; the steward might have murdered Ralph as well. Galloping across the tilled earth, Marian headed her horse toward the nearest woodlands, where her maneuvering skills would give advantage. She scanned the ground for hazards, then cast a quick look over her shoulder to track her pursuers. Sir Ranulf's men could not reach her, but Marian felt a cold rush of fury, a coiling gut twist of terror, as one of the steward's guards closed on her, his powerful animal outrunning her own. Shield raised to deflect her weapon, the man passed her. Leaning forward, he seized the reins and dragged her mount to a halt. The others quickly circled to cut off her retreat.

The guard who held the reins demanded her weapon. When she gave him the knife, he backhanded her savagely. She managed to take the force of the blow and keep her seat. She did not struggle as they bound her. Any injury she received now might cripple a later chance for escape. Once her hands were tied, they blindfolded her. When she could not see them, they mauled her. She gritted her teeth and endured the heavy hands on her breasts and thighs. If she was to be Wolverton's prize, there was a limit to what they dared.

"I know whose men you are," she hissed at them, hoping they would remove the blindfold when they had done with their play. But no one untied it. When they rode again, Marian followed their progress as best she could, the concentration warding off the fear that came with helplessness. They moved swiftly along the road, then over a drawbridge. They pulled her from her horse, and dragged her through the courtyard and into a castle.

The stink of old rushes clogged her nostrils; then came the smell of sweated leather as a gloved hand touched her

face. The blindfold was jerked off. Marian glanced around
the hall quickly and saw it was as ill kept as it smelled but
well guarded. Scowling, the leader snatched off the bloodstained cloak, tossing it in a pile on a table along with her
dagger and the blindfold. For a moment she thought her
spattered gown would be ripped off as well, but these men
obviously feared Wolverton, just as they obviously did not
respect him. The knight nodded toward the stairs, and two
men seized her arms and pulled her toward them. She kept
apace, but they jerked her forward so that she stumbled;
then they dragged her up the stairs. From the landing they
led her into a large chamber and flung her onto the bed
centered on the back wall. The two men remained inside,
sliding the heavy inner bolt in place and standing guard,
eyeing her with sneering lust and rancor.

Rising from the bed, Marian went to the window and
looked out at the surrounding woodlands. She could see
nothing of the castle courtyard or the road and wondered if
that was deliberate or accidental. She gazed about the room,
trying to look distressed and confused under the guards'
scrutiny. There were few enough weapons to hand. The
chest at the foot of the bed was locked and too heavy to
move, as was the table against the wall. A pottery pitcher of
wine stood on it, and there was a small stool. A direct blow
to the face, or the back of the head, with the pitcher might
knock a man unconscious. Mentally she tested their weight
and shook her head in exasperation. Then, hearing a noise
without, she readied herself to face her adversary.

The guards unbarred the door, and Sir Ranulf entered.
She scanned him quickly and saw he'd had the sense to
wear no weapon. But even with one man dead he would
underestimate her and think luck, not skill, guided her hand.
Stopping inside, he glowered at her, as if she were to blame
for this abduction. Well, she had killed one of his men. No
doubt the venture had already cost him more than he'd
planned. He ordered the guards to stand watch outside and
bolted the door behind them.

''My grandfather will have your head on a pike.'' Marian said it coldly. Tears and entreaties would only enflame what sense of daring and lust drove him. Wolverton licked his lips nervously, but he had a look of animal obstinacy in his eyes. He had set himself to take the risk. She doubted she could reason with him.

"Better a peaceful alliance than a dishonored grand-daughter," he pronounced.

Dishonored. The word scalded, though she had not expected anything less. Wolverton would not waste time wooing her when he thought humiliation would make her tractable. He meant to rape her, presuming she would then go docilely to the marriage ceremony rather than be damaged goods. But there was something else. . . .

She regarded Wolverton unflinchingly while her mind raced, searching out the false note. He had sounded as if he were quoting, not pleased with his own phrase but mouthing another's. Could the Sheriff have urged him to this? To what effect? Then Marian thought of Lady Alix and the warnings she had received. If this was not exactly removing one's rival, Lady Alix might presume Marian would be thoroughly cowed by a forced marriage to a tedious brute. A pretty punishment for a presumptuous rival.

She could not forestall the marriage. Sir Ranulf would have found an unscrupulous priest to perform the ceremony despite her protestations. He had power enough that the Sheriff would no doubt take his side afterward, and Prince John would take the Sheriff's. Eleanor would protest, but only if Richard returned would she be assured of a petition to free herself. Months to endure, at the least.

Wolverton's glare deepened, a look of distaste mingled with growing lust. It was the idea of the rape rather than her body that appealed to him. His glance darted to the bed, then back to her again. Abruptly he stripped himself of his robe, baring a stocky body matted with hair, a limp, stumpy cock. He reached down, pulling at his flesh to harden it.

All her cool assessment was irrelevant. She would not endure being mated to this brute, not for a day. She would kill him first. If she succeeded, there were still his men to escape. But first she must rid herself of Sir Ranulf.

"Lie down," Wolverton said, jerking his head toward the bed. His hand left off tugging. It had stirred him sufficiently, and his breath came quicker. A pale pink tongue protruded between his lips.

Slowly Marian undid the ties of her bliaut. Removing the gown feigned acquiescence and gained her a few moments' time. The long skirts would only impede her movement.

"Hot for it, are you?" he asked, sounding minimally pleased. His small, brackish eyes gleamed with new anticipation.

Marian lifted the dress and slid it off, a moment of vulnerability, but he did not lunge for her. She flung it over him, the skirts covering his head. As he pawed clumsily at the cascade of silk, she seized the wine pitcher. When he tossed the gown aside, she swung the pitcher into his face, smashing his nose and cutting him about the eyes as it shattered. Wolverton bellowed with rage and pain, clutching his bleeding face. She grabbed the stool, flimsy though it was, and brought it down across his head. It broke too and brought another cry of outrage, but he did no more than stagger under the blow. His men called out. Marian felt an instant of pure panic, but Wolverton cursed them down, flushed with embarrassment as well as fury. He could not conceive that she might best him, or he might have called the guards to hold her down. He understood now that she would not submit. She saw in his eyes that he wanted to kill her, though he would dare no more than beat her senseless. Then he dropped his gaze, holding his head down to relieve the pain of his broken nose. The most useful damage the pitcher had achieved was the blood that flowed freely into his eyes. Snarling at her, he mopped it with his arm, trying to clear his vision.

There was but one more weapon within her grasp—Sir Ranulf himself. She must turn his strength against him. The room was not large, but there was enough distance from the bed to the stone wall opposite to gather some speed. Watching Sir Ranulf warily, Marian backed away as he came around the bed, finding her footing beneath the rushes. She moved slowly back until she sensed herself close against the wall. Wolverton bared his teeth in an ugly smile, certain he would corner her there. She lifted her arms protectively, as if suddenly quailing before his wrath. With a snarl Wolverton charged, rushing her like a bull, his head down, his arms outstretched. She made a last adjustment with a quick half step, planting her right foot behind her to take her weight, left foot sliding out before her. As he rushed her, Marian grabbed his hair, locking her fingers in the greasy strands. Her extended foot caught his just before it landed and knocked it aside, unbalancing him. She twisted aside as she jerked Wolverton forward, using his momentum to pull his head past her and slam it straight into the wall. Stunned, he grunted and collapsed. She was on top of him in a second, seizing the hair above his forehead and smashing his head against the floor, the first stroke dulled by the matted rushes. Wolverton glared up at her, his eyes glazed with confusion and terror. Six more strokes drove his skull to the stone, and she heard the hard shell crack. Another six and he was dead, blood and brains smearing the floor.

The guards were pounding on the door. She wondered if she should unbar it quickly, now. There were but two men outside. With luck she would secure a sword or knife, chain mail to disguise herself. The chance of snatching a mount was small, but if she failed, at least she might kill one or two before she was seized. Even with a sword, she could not destroy as many as waited below. That end would be uglier than the swift death she could give herself with a blade to her heart, but she would rather die fighting. Then she heard more footsteps, and more angry voices joined those outside. No escape. But perhaps there was a chance of rescue.

"Wolverton is dead," she announced through the door. It was a risk. She could have pretended to keep him hostage, but then the men might refuse her commands utterly, waiting for his orders. "I want the Sheriff and Sir Guy of Guisbourne brought here. Immediately. I will not charge any man who did no more than follow his master's bidding.''

There was silence, and then pandemonium broke out. The men set themselves to battering down the door. Deprived of vicarious satisfaction through Wolverton, they would seize the actual for themselves—satisfaction of lust and of bloodlust. If there was a clever head among them, they would pretend that she'd killed Sir Ranulf after he had forced her . . . and then hanged herself perhaps? The Sheriff was likely to agree. However obvious the multiple violations might be, two dead bodies would be a convenient ending to this abduction.

Marian wiped her bloody hands on Sir Ranulf's discarded robe, then tossed it over his corpse. In an equally flimsy gesture she dressed herself in her silk gown, calculating how much longer the door would hold. If it did not give soon, they would bring a battering ram.

Then in the midst of the yelling and cursing there came another burst of sound. Another surge of voices swept the hallway, and with them came the clash of weapons. Screams of agony, and of death, sounded outside the door. Marian waited, hope a singing wildness in her veins. There was a moment of stillness.

Guy of Guisbourne bade her open the door. Amazement filling her, Marian slid aside the bolt and swung the door wide. Standing on the threshold, helm in one hand, gory sword in the other, he took in the scene with a glance. He turned to face her, fierce admiration kindling in his eyes.

The sudden release from fear was a giddy potion in her blood. Marian felt a dark rushing sweetness of triumph, of survival. She smiled at him.

With that smile she saw his admiration flame to lust. Even as she saw his startlement, his attempt to subdue it, she felt the blaze of him burn through her coldness, igniting something both wild and frightening. Violence, revenge, killing had always been things she did in cold blood, not hot. This leaping heat shocked her. Her smile vanished, and she stood, her body strung with tension, nerves threaded with fire.

"Marian," he said, very softly.

She thought it first a reassurance, second a summons. Then knew it was invitation for her to acknowledge that she wanted him. She was to begin it between them. She need only speak his name in turn.

His gaze held hers for a moment, then traveled her body, laying a searing kiss each place it rested . . . on her shoulders, her breasts, her belly, her sex. She felt naked beneath his gaze. Her nipples puckered, drawing up tight and aching. Her limbs threaded with fire, and a smoking darkness consumed her. His gaze returned to her lips, and his own parted. She could feel their touch, the soft flesh of his mouth melding to hers, his tongue searching within. She could feel the hardness of his thighs pressing the length of hers and his arms closing about her back as she locked hers about his neck. It might as well have happened, it felt so vivid. But he did not move, only looked at her, his eyes burning like yellow flame.

The power of it beckoned, but it was too soon, too strange for her to reach out and seize. Yet she could not deny it either. If he kissed her. . . .

Guisbourne waited, willing her to him. "Two men have already shown you unwanted attention," he said softly, the gentleness subtly twined with seductiveness, touched with self-mockery. "I will not do that."

Two? Then she remembered Robin, who had kissed her twice unwanted. She shook her head, overwhelmed by a new rush of perplexity. "No," she whispered, drawing back.

With that answer she saw, she felt, the seething fire banked. Guy gave a small twist of a smile and said, "Let me escort you back to the castle. It is best you seem to have the Sheriff's protection as well as mine. Then no other knight will dare attempt this."

"I think few would attempt something so foolish without some sly encouragement," Marian said.

"You think rightly," Guy acknowledged.

"Then I should expect some new tactic rather than foolish repetitions."

"You would be wise to be on guard, Lady Marian. All protection has its limits."

"I will heed your warning."

"I found this outside." He held out the knife he had given her, blood-drenched still. "You have had the chance to use it, I gather."

"It deserved a better christening." Then, taking the blade from his hand, she said, "If anything is to happen between us, I would not have it begin in blood."

For an instant he looked startled; then his eyes narrowed. She thought of Lady Alix, as she realized he must. Guisbourne's gaze held hers for a moment; then he answered, "Blood can be the strongest link of all—or the weakest. You are wise to seek another one."

Reclaiming a cool demeanor, Marian accompanied him through the carnage that lay outside the door, through more in the hall below, and outside to the bailey. Strangely the warm summer sun made her shiver. There were fewer bodies here, and a man or two of Sir Ranulf's standing about. With Wolverton dead, those more cautious of their lives had opened the gates to Sir Guy and let the others bear the brunt of his attack. Guisbourne moved with absolute command, ordering the mounts and forming a party to return to stand guard here and one to return with them to Nottingham Castle.

I am in his debt, Marian thought. *I must find some way to repay it that does not compromise me.*

9 The Sheriff stood, lifting his cup high. Following his lead, Marian rose with the other supper guests to join in the toast. Sir Godfrey's voice rang out through the hall, "To he who is our Prince . . . and may yet be our King."

"Prince John!" To Marian the acclaim was loud but hollow, the lineaments of the guests those of contrived esteem and forced joviality. She wondered if Prince John could even tell the difference. As far as she knew, no one save his father had ever offered him affection unadulterated by selfish motive, nor was he likely ever to win it.

Prince John was not prepossessing, either as man or incipient monarch. The gold circlet he wore gleamed brightly, but against lackluster hair of muddy brown. His eyes were the same murky shade, close set. He was sallow skinned, with features thinly marked in a broad, flat face. Even when relaxed as he now was, his expression seemed both peevish and faintly petulant. The sumptuous bliaut of scarlet brocade and cloth of gold did not beguile Marian's eye. Beneath its artful pleating she could easily see his muscles were slack, his body thickening, though he was younger than most present. John overlooked the company with obvious condescension, but his authority sat ill, with neither the command nor the grace possessed by his mother and his brother. She did not think the Prince stupid, but he had been too long John Lackland, denied both property and power. He was testy of his honor and—despite the reek of suspicion, as heavy as the perfumed oils he wore—gullible of flattery. Nor was his avidity well enough disguised. His gaze weighed everything as if he owned it, or would soon do so. The knights and barons would fear this man without respecting him, but they knew as well as he that all that stood between Prince John and the power he craved was for the moment safely imprisoned. And if the Prince had his way, Richard would never emerge from his cell and John himself would be King.

Tonight's feast was designed for a monarch, far more elaborate and diverse than the magnificent meal the Sheriff had used to tempt the Bishop. The artful array of rich dishes brought forth was meant to impress Prince John and to stupefy the guests. Once the first toasts to the Prince were made and the guests were again seated, two servers carefully carried out a great pie and placed it in the center of the table. When the crust was sliced open, there was a sudden flurry as the little songbirds trapped beneath flew out, scattering about the great hall in a nervous frenzy of wings. Four of the Sheriff's falconers waited, one in each corner of the room. When the bewildered captives were freed, the Sheriff ordered his falcons flown. Ill fed for days, the rapacious birds rose eagerly to strike down the prey in midair. Again the cheers were flat, and the guests shifted uneasily in their seats, knowing how easily their wealth, their lives might be ripped from them so, if their feigned allegiance to the new order was too transparent. Such was the edged merriment that began the meal.

A gory feather drifted down to lie beside Marian's trencher. Looking about the table, she saw that the bloodier of the falcon's kills had left their remnants elsewhere. Lady Alix's aquamarine gown, her milky skin, were spattered with scarlet. The widow gave a little laugh, gay and brittle, her eyes glittering with annoyance. Her gaze met Marian's for a fraction of a second, instantly blanking and skimming aside as if she had not noticed her rival, before she returned her attention to Prince John. Since Marian's return to Nottingham Castle, she had moved among the women, coaxing tales about the widow. Some spoke eagerly, some reluctantly, but not one of them liked Alix. Though none seemed sure of her involvement in the abduction, they were obviously suspicious. What she heard were stories of the widow's flirtations, seductions, and small cruelties. None was as iniquitous as the kidnapping—except her husband's recent demise. It seemed Alix had but recently gained a sense of power and the will to wield it.

Marian had thought of no suitable revenge on Lady Alix as yet, only knowing that if the opportunity arose, she would seize it. The widow's ugly plan had failed, but Baldwin, who had served her family with absolute loyalty for decades, was dead. Sir Ralph had slain the traitorous steward, his coward's blood small recompense for the loss of a beloved and brave companion. Marian hungered for the same direct requital on Lady Alix, but pure physical confrontation was ludicrous against her dainty foe. Marian doubted the woman had even the most rudimentary skills with a bow, much less other weapons. Alix's sense of power would lie in what destruction she could command others to carry out, what victories she could win through manipulation. For the moment Marian must content herself with the thought of Alix's wrath at the fiasco of the failed abduction.

One idea tempted Marian sorely, if only for its fiendish irony. Presuming her mission was a significant success, she might ask favors of the Queen, perhaps even from the King. If Lady Alix were still unmarried, King Richard might command a suitable husband for the widow. Marian relished the fantasy again for a moment before dismissing it. She was willing to wish a brute on the woman, but not willing to waste the favor so foolishly. Nor was she prepared to so ensure the brute's death through her own connivance. Lady Alix had already dispensed one unwanted husband; another so forced on her was likely to have a short life span indeed. Marian glanced down the table to where Alix was flirting with Prince John and considered that the widow might well be scheming along similar lines. Alix would want revenge for her failure and must be watched carefully.

Although he now lapped up Alix's attention, Marian had
seen Prince John's gaze roving about the table, lingering too
often for Marian's comfort on the Lady Claire. Someone
would service the Prince tonight; his lascivious appetite was
well known. The only certainty was that it would not be
Marian herself. His eyes passed over her as if she did not
exist. When introduced, she had sagaciously awarded every
formal courtesy to the Prince who might be King, but she
was pleased that he had been discomfited by her height and
regarded her with ill-concealed scorn because of it. Smiling
inwardly, she had held herself more erect while she cast her
eyes down in feigned modesty. Even before the presentation
she had done what she could to forestall his interest. Elegant and rich enough to honor him, still the subtle silver
gray bliaut she had chosen did not lure with vividness as the
crimson might have done. Her hair she had enslaved with a
white wimple bound with a simple silver cord. That such
paltry precautions had proved unnecessary was a relief so
tangible it seemed a balm flowing through her. Marian did
not know how she could have endured his touch.

Sir Guy was another matter, and Marian was pleased that
the subtle elegance of the bliaut drew an appreciative
glance. He had been courteous to both her and Lady Alix
tonight, but the formality was unlike his former courtly dal-
liance. Having risked much, he was once again cautious in
how he showed his favor to either of them, and aside from
the most casual courtesies, he had little favor to spare. The
Prince was the center of his attention, and he did not stray
far from that center.

The Sheriff beckoned to Bogo and the other performers,
and they pranced to the center of the floor, performing
somersaults, building precarious towers with their bodies,
swallowing swords, and juggling lighted torches in spinning
circles of light. After a few moments of such amusement,
the Sheriff gave an imperious gesture and they rushed off.
With another the inundation of food began. Marian directed
her attention to the array of dishes being paraded past the
guests—all far more palatable than the bloody and inedible

threat that had begun the feast. Marian was much amused
by the array of toothsome monsters presented to the guests.
The most fabulous were assorted gargoyles, each uniquely
grotesque, the elaborately scaled, clawed, and fanged pastry
shell bodies enclosing tender hedgehogs. Sir Ranulf would
have gobbled them, she thought with bitter humor. There
were also a dozen cockatrices displayed on silver plates.
These creatures were constructed with the head and fore-
quarters of a piglet stitched to a capon. Other dishes were
equally fanciful, if less bizarre. There was a crusty golden
dovecote filled with birds molded of tender white-fleshed
fish and ground blanched almonds. Their tiny heads were
set with gilded beaks, and bright red currants made their
eyes. And this time, in lieu of a swan, the chef had prepared
a flamboyant peacock. The bird was skinned, roasted, then
dressed once more in its iridescent feathers, the great fan of
its glistening green-blue tail spread wide.

In Prince John's name the Sheriff had commanded roasts
of royal venison to be served, along with whole oxen,
lambs, and boars. Porpoises and seals had been brought
inland from the sea. Prince John ate greedily, favoring the
elaborate pastry-encased splendors to the roasts. The Sheriff
liked his meat well honeyed, and kept on the table a pot
heavily spiced with cinnamon and clove. Dipping into it
now, he lavished the golden syrup on his roast lamb. Marian restrained a shudder of distaste. She liked her meat less
cloyingly sweet. For flavor, she thought the best dish a rich
succulent salmon, its sauce only lightly touched with honey
and sprightly with her favorite ginger. The presentation of
the salmon was simple, the fish roasted, glazed, and laid on
a bed of pink rose petals edged with dark green leaves.

The dishes went round the table, and the wine flowed
lavishly. The meal settled into a ritual of glorification and
gluttony, with toasts, tales, and elaborate flourishes of
praise in between gorgings. Prince John demurred graciously as Sir Godfrey cited his virtues and acts of valor to
the gathering. The Sheriff played his role of praise master
well enough, given the limited material at his disposal. He

concentrated on Prince John's recent travels throughout England, where he had displayed his authority conspicuously and distributed largess with a careful hand. He had to be generous yet not so prodigal as to flaunt his wealth in the face of the heavy taxes being gathered for the ransom. When not remarking on the Prince's puissance and generosity to the room at large, Sir Godfrey leaned close to the Prince, nodding sagely as he spoke. His entire posture bespoke attentive deference to his lord.

Sir Guy she noted, carefully deferred to the Sheriff in most things. Able neither to suffer fools quite as blatantly as Sir Godfrey, nor overtly to usurp his influence, Guisbourne adopted a more reserved pose, offering considered comments at intervals, as well as occasional embellishments of flattery, praising whatever might pass for wit that passed from Prince John's lips. It was a delicate balance between a fawning that Prince John obviously desired, but might at any moment suspect, and a reserve he could equally dislike if he sensed its coldness. For Sir Guy it was sycophantic, yet she knew Guisbourne well enough to admire the discipline that kept all his sharp edges carefully sheathed. She saw no sign of the derision and contempt he had allowed to prick the Bishop of Buxton.

The Sheriff continuously flattered the Prince, but the homage was intended primarily to sway the guests. Sir Godfrey strove to perform an alchemical miracle. The knights' reluctant allegiance must somehow be transformed from dross into gold. Amid the praise the Sheriff planted sly deprecations of King Richard, attempting to tarnish the gleaming lion. Initially Prince John responded to these aspersions with the suitably melancholy reluctance of a judicious man weighing and accepting the bitter truth. But as he drank more wine, his small eyes took on a belligerent glitter, and he goaded the Sheriff with look and gesture to more elaborate sallies. The Sheriff launched into his favored tales of the King's machinations with the Saracens. When he paused, Sir Guy spoke up, his voice edged with rancor, commenting on King Richard's lack of an heir and the possibility that given his marked preference for boys, he might never beget one. Prince John savored the malice and gestured to the wine bearer to fill their cups yet again. After drinking deeply from his own the Prince glanced about him assessing the temper of the gathering.

The guests had expected such carping, and most held their tongues. Sir Walter, bristling, made an unfortunate comment about Richard's being the anointed King to the young knight beside him. It carried to the ears of the Prince, who rose, flushed with choler. "Many have said my brother's reign is cursed," he declared to the company. "I was my father's choice. He meant England to be mine. Mine."

Fool after all, Marian thought. The Prince could not hold his wine, or his tongue once the wine had loosed it.

All conversation subsided as the Prince glared about him. "King Henry denounced my brother from beyond death. When my father's body lay in the abbey of Fontrevault, Richard came to do obeisance before him. My brother was filled with cruel triumph, knowing the kingship his at last. As he knelt there, his head bowed in false reverence, blood burst from the nostrils and mouth of the King's corpse, pouring over his face in a scarlet rush and dripping onto the floor. So the great King reached out to lay his sanguinary curse upon Richard, the stripling traitor." The acid gaze swept the company once more. "Those of you who honored my father should honor me."

No one here was fool enough to challenge that spurious deduction, not even Sir Walter. Marian's opinion of the Prince sank even lower. She suspected he believed his own dupery. A clever liar she would have respected more than this seething poseur. No conjuration of his brother's misdeeds would erase Prince John's own, not when the events were so vividly emblazoned in the minds of those present.

True, it was Richard who had led the rebellion against King Henry. But King Henry had ever called John his heart, and it was his youngest son's betrayal, more than all the others, that had broken him. After Richard had vanquished his father, after the beloved city of his birth had burned, King Henry still felt the bright flow of fury in his veins and the driving hunger for vengeance. He demanded an accounting of those who had joined Richard against him. When he saw writ at the head of the list the name of Prince John, the son for whom he had entered this folly, he became in that instant an old man. Turning his face to the wall, he declared he would hear no more, for he cared for naught in the world anymore. After that there was only the low, incessant mutter, "Shame . . . shame on a conquered King."

Yet the greatest irony was that King Henry had envisioned his own ruin while John was but a child. He had even commissioned a fresco at Winchester Palace to portray it. The work depicted a great eagle with outspread wings, beset by four fledglings. Two of the eaglets rent the pinions of their father, another tore at his belly, and the last ravaged his eyes. King Henry had acknowledged himself the eagle and his sons the merciless fledglings. He had known they would harass him, beak and claw, till they destroyed him— and the one he most cherished would be, finally, the most vicious of them all.

Looking at the wrath-blotched and spiteful face of Prince John daring the assembled guests to gainsay him, Marian decided the only reason his father's corpse had not drenched him in gore was that he had not even gone to view the body before the nuns of Fontrevault entombed it. *Better vainglorious Richard than venomous John,* Marian thought once again, *and better fervent, astute Queen Eleanor than either.*

"Prince John!" The Sheriff called for a toast just as the silence threatened to fray the thin fabric of tonight's festivities irretrievably. The guests lifted their cups with a dismal cheer, then settled uneasily into their chairs. Hoping to smooth over the blunder, Sir Guy flashed his eyes at the page hurrying to refill the Prince's cup. When the boy quickly retreated, he leaned and whispered in the Sheriff's ear. Sir Godfrey quickly signaled for the dessert to be brought forward. The company seized on the diversion with a frenzied merriment.

Borne on a great tray was the most decadent and extravagant offering of the banquet. All the sugar in Nottinghamshire had gone to create the glistening marchpane hide and horn of the little unicorn lying in a bed of roses. The unicorn's sculptured head lay in the lap of a pretty young girl of perhaps fourteen. The little virgin was intended for Prince John. She was a pig-keeper's daughter, Marian had heard via Agatha, peasant stock, but golden haired and delicate, her intact maidenhead vouched for by the midwives. A bevy of young squires carried her around the room on the platter. Laughing uproariously, the knights reached out to stab the unicorn with their knives. When the dish reached Prince John, the Sheriff cut off the spiraled horn and presented it to his royal guest. Prince John eyed the girl lasciviously and offered her the horn. She reached out to clasp it with two dainty little hands and drew it to her lips. The knights cheered when she nibbled the sugary tip.

Although the Prince was obviously pleased with this pretty prize, Marian saw his gaze slide once more to the Lady Claire. Earlier in the evening he had favored Lady Alix's coy overtures, but as the night progressed, his eye had wandered more and more to Claire, flushed and radiant in a gown of coral damask, her bright, unseeing eyes like strange jewels. Before the feast Alan had sung for the guests—songs of wit and laughter that had eased the tension, songs of love that had the ladies sighing. After that, despite the anxiety among the others, Claire had remained euphoric, drinking in the night through her pores, the sound and scent of it. Her unfeigned delight drew the eye; her blindness rendered her utterly oblivious of the fate being decided for her. Marian watched as Prince John regarded her appraisingly, his eyes glittering beneath half closed lids, his lips curving in a smug, lascivious smile.

Marian felt her muscles brace for combat. She had to will herself to relax and submerge her rage in the icy waters of necessity. If Prince John wanted the Sheriff's wife, he

would have her. Sir Godfrey would not interfere. Assessing
the Sheriff's reaction, Marian saw neither jealousy nor dismay, only a fleeting expression of calculation as he weighed
how much advantage could be wheedled from the gift of his
wife's favors. His smile had the same lubricious curl as
Prince John's, and Marian realized he was taking a cruel
pleasure in both Claire's plight and her obliviousness. She
wondered if he would prefer not to forewarn her but have a
stranger appear in the night. But he would not risk surprise—if surprise there could be with Prince John's heavy
scent of musk and rose oil. Claire must be prepared. The
Prince might be less perverse in his tastes than Sir Godfrey,
but however he treated her, Claire would be expected to be
pleased or to simulate pleasure. Thinking of her vulnerability, Marian regarded the Sheriff with a surge of cold anger
and colder disgust. She pitied the little pig-keeper's daughter, but she did not know her as she knew Claire. Despite
the chilling danger of the pairing, she could almost wish
Lady Alix success in her attempt to beguile the Prince. The
noxious syrupy femininity would be just to his taste, and all
the pretty poison she spewed he would swallow, then vomit
forth on others at her bidding.

Marian knew she held no appeal for the Prince, even if
she dared try to draw his eye away from Claire. But it was
too dangerous, a game she could win only by losing. Had
she interested him, flirtation would not suffice. At best she
might anger him enough by direct refusal to be spared his
attentions but not some form of revenge. If he decided to
possess her despite her protests, no man here would prevent
him. And if faced once more with rape . . . For a brief
instant a barrage of nauseating images seized her mind,
memory converging her mother's death and Sir Ranulf's
attack. Yet this was Prince John, and the repercussion of his
death would hammer through her to destroy her family.
With so much at risk Marian realized her will could rein her
violence, if not her disgust.

But Prince John did not want her, and she was glad of it.
Whatever her unexpected protectiveness toward Claire, her

tenuous affection did not extend to a willing sacrifice of her own body. Marian looked at the pig keeper's daughter licking the sugary unicorn's horn and hoped her rapturous expression was more than the enjoyment of the sugar. Far better if the girl understood the significance of her lewd toying and saw tonight as a chance to make her fortune, even at the cost of pain. If the Prince did not take her, some knight would likely claim the prize of her maidenhead.

And it seemed certain the Prince would not. He leaned close to Sir Godfrey, whispering in his ear, then eyeing Claire with licentious certainty even before the Sheriff nodded his consent. Marian was glad that Alan's seat at one of the far tables did not afford him a good view of this exchange. As coldly as she could Marian shut down her own concern. There was no way she could protect Claire.

"Your pleasure is our command, my lord," the Sheriff said, then added, "But we have yet to talk." A slight nod of his head indicated the general direction of the rose garden. Marian felt a frisson of excitement tingle over her nerves. She had hoped, prepared for exactly this opportunity. If she timed her movements correctly, she would be able to slip into the garden unseen and hide herself behind the trellis before their meeting. The place was unguarded unless the Sheriff was within. The guests would linger by the hall. Sir Guy and Lady Alix were the only ones likely to keep any track of her whereabouts, and tonight their attention was all for the Prince. Catching Agatha's gaze Marian gave the signal they had arranged. She lifted her hand and stroked the chain of her silver necklace, a gesture she never would otherwise use. Acknowledging, Agatha adjusted the brow band of her wimple, and began looking about her casually, searching out Alan a Dale. Marian was certain her companions would do their best to ensure an easy entry and exit for her.

Between anger and impatience, Marian had lost her appetite, but she continued to nibble, listening as carefully as she could to the trio of the Sheriff, Guy, and the Prince. There were a few low-voiced comments she could not hear, but as far as she could discern, nothing of import was discussed and everything was said to the room at large. Sir Guy continued to warn off the wine bearers as well as he could, she noted, without making his efforts apparent to Prince John. The rest of the meal was a study in composure, but she did not have to wait long. Slightly more sober, Prince John had a luscious erotic goal almost within his grasp, far more delectable than the literal sweetness of the marchpane being served. He obviously wished to dispense with necessary business quickly. Soon the royal guest rose, and the others abandoned their dessert to follow him. But Prince John loitered in the entryway, politic enough to bid good night to the more important knights. Marian kept her eye on the corridor and saw Alan move ahead to check if it was clear. She waited a scant minute more and went quickly after him. There was in fact a guard, not stationed before the door but making rounds in a desultory fashion. Alan had already drawn him into conversation and had positioned the man so his back was to the door. From Alan's gestures, Marian understood he was describing the virgin and the unicorn with vivid lewdness. Batting his eyelashes, he mimicked the pig keeper's daughter nibbling and licking the phallic marchpane horn. The guard pumped the air at his crotch, laughing uproariously, totally unwitting as she slipped across the corridor and into the rose garden.

Swiftly Marian made her way to the bower. Snatching the moss green cloak Agatha had concealed behind the trellis, Marian wrapped it about her, covering the pale gown and white wimple. She lay down and inched herself into the narrow passage. The plan was simple but reasonably safe, the greatest danger now, as she squirmed into place, or later, if she was caught trying to leave unnoticed. Discovery would have no small consequence—her death most likely, and those of her comrades. She released a sharp breath of relief when she was in place without feeling any pricks or snags. Her blood was singing with the danger, the dark familiar melody coursing in her veins. She subdued her quickened breathing, knowing excitement would make her feel more impatient, perhaps even ensnared in the hampered space.

She need only lie quietly. Even in the daytime, it was almost impossible to see someone hidden here, for although the bower drew the eye, it charmed it as well. The hiding place was obscured by trellis, roses, and bench, and if an observer's gaze was not admiring the blooming bower, then it turned outward to the profusion of flowers and bushes that decorated the garden—or to whatever companion or conspirator awaited. Marian and her own two conspirators had tested the passage once, with Alan crawling behind, dressed in his brightest clothes. True, they had glimpsed the contrasting brightness of the blue doublet, but if they had not been looking carefully, she doubted they would have noticed. At night the dark cloak would render her invisible.

There was a sudden surge of noise and movement. Marian kept her breathing calm while the guards swept through the garden, aware of the movement of their torches, their voices, their footsteps as they made a cursory search. They lit the wall torches and then departed. Another moment, and she heard softer voices, lighter footsteps crunching the gravel path. Figures appeared, though she could make out their movement only barely. The men paused, and she heard the murmur of their voices, but not their words. Marian cursed silently. The garden was small, and from here she had hoped to hear them no matter where they stood. But they spoke in tones far too low to decipher, perhaps from natural caution, perhaps because a guard was within sight; she could not see. Marian recognized the soft, feline prickle of Sir Guy's tones, and then the Sheriff's breathy voice, but it was Prince John she understood first, annoyance raising his voice. "I do not see there is anything to discuss. You know my desires. You need only fulfill them."

Obviously the Prince had grown more restive in the short interval since supper. As they approached the bower, the Sheriff spoke, his voice soothing and wheedling. "I wish to serve you in all you have requested, my lord. To do so, I need to know not only your desires but your plans. And you should know and approve mine.''

''Should I? I think I need only know that they have succeeded. Then I shall approve of them,'' the Prince said. Standing beside the curving trellis, he jerked on the bushes and broke off a rose. Marian felt the quiver of the bush where she lay.

''My lord—'' The Sheriff began again.

Prince John gave an audible sniff, smelling the rose or expressing disdain, Marian did not know. ''If you feel we must talk, there is always the morning.''

''My lord, you will want to lie abed in the morning, I am sure.'' The Sheriff's voice oozed like some befouled honey, coating the very air Marian breathed.

There was a faint sound, like moist lips smacking wetly. Then Prince John queried with a spurious delicacy, ''Lady Claire's blindness . . . since she is without sight, it must mean her sense of touch is most acute?''

''I think you will find her exquisitely sensitive, my lord. But . . .'' now the Sheriff's wheedle was well laced with coercion, ''. . . I am certain she is still preparing for bed, my lord. We may as well take the opportunity to talk. Then you need not think of it again tonight . . . or tomorrow.''

''Very well,'' Prince John muttered, only partially mollified. Seating himself within the bower, he remarked, ''I trust you will make better use of this second opportunity than you did the first.''

''Last time the ransom was rerouted,'' the Sheriff said unctuously. ''I can do nothing if I do not know when the final shipment is due and where it is coming from.'' The facade slipped for a second as he added pettishly, ''I cannot perform miracles.''

''I do not expect miracles,'' Prince John snapped, in the tone of a man who expected them and found himself constantly cheated. ''I expect competence.''

There was a moment's hesitation all round. Then Guisbourne spoke. ''Information is a powerful weapon. Even weaponless we would do battle for you, my lord, for loyalty's sake. But for victory's sake, arm us well. The keener the sword we bear, the better we shall fight.''

''Yes, my lord, we must know as much as possible—what route the ransom will follow, the date, the number of guards,'' the Sheriff said. ''I can have my men ready, but I must know when to strike. Far better if we can capture the ransom before it comes through Nottingham.''

''Be assured, I will get the information for you, Sir Godfrey. I have more than one ear listening. When I know, I will send a bird.''

''They are swift, my lord, but more than one has been lost.''

''Then I will dispatch a courier to inform you—Sir Stephen, you know him by sight,'' Prince John said. Lying behind the trellis, Marian smiled. Before the Prince left, she too would know Sir Stephen's face. John's voice took on a contentious edge. ''Add that weapon to your armory, and wield it well. You must capture the ransom.''

''Yes, my lord,'' the Sheriff pledged.

''You had best . . . or you will have nothing to compensate for the taxes Nottinghamshire must supply toward the ransom. Capture it and you shall have double.''

''You are generous, as always.''

''And remember, however you arrange the robbery, no suspicion should fall on me. That is paramount.''

And ludicrous, Marian thought. Guilty or innocent, he would be suspected. Miracle indeed, if he thought that was possible.

But what the Sheriff answered was, ''Yes. I already have a plan. And no one will suspect you.''

From the small but telling pause that followed, Marian garnered her own suspicions. Much disappointed, Prince John preferred to protect himself with impossible demands. In such fashion he assured himself of someone to blame for everything. Cautiously he asked, ''What is it?''

The Sheriff's voice brimmed with smugness. ''There is an outlaw who inhabits Sherwood. He is already infamous in Nottinghamshire. His name is spreading elsewhere.''

"As far as my ears even." Prince John gloated. "His name is Robin Hood, and he has been a sharp thorn pricking your tender places."

"We have yet to dislodge him, it is true," Sir Guy intervened smoothly. "But we have found a way in which to make use of him."

"When we raid the caravan, we will disguise ourselves to make it appear that Robin Hood and his men have stolen the ransom. He is an outlaw with no allegiances. Why need anyone look further?"

Marian felt a clash of emotions, anger for Robin mingled with grudging appreciation for the plan.

Prince John paused again, but this time when he spoke a begrudging amusement leavened his voice. "I am pleased."

"My lord," the Sheriff and Sir Guy murmured as one.

Prince John went on, speaking almost to himself. "I need that money to buy the favor of the Emperor. There is no reason for him to release Richard if he can be paid as much to keep him."

"Especially if the Crown falls far short of the agreed amount. As it must if you possess the very silver that was to supply it," the Sheriff said.

"There are other pressures, of course," Sir Guy advised. "But the Emperor's greed may well prevail. If it does, my Prince, then so shall you."

Prince John went on softly, almost to himself. "My brother's health suffered in the crusade. He is confined to a cell, and the winters are colder there. Wind, hail, snow . . ." He named them as he might the most delectable dishes of a feast.

In her mind's eye Marian could hear the smile in Sir Guy's voice as he said, "Then, my lord, shall we go drink a last toast—to winter tempests and the clear skies that follow them?"

"Yes," Prince John said, rising from the bench. "And then, I think, to bed."

The Sheriff emitted one of his nastiest giggles, and the three men departed from the garden. Marian waited perhaps an hour. If she was seen returning to her room, she wanted her movements disassociated from those of the Prince. Once she was out of the garden, she was relatively safe. Seeing her darting through the hallways slightly disheveled, a guard would most likely presume she had been with a lover. But that illusion would be futile should he become suspicious and no lover could be produced. She was lucky, and no one saw her. Agatha and Alan were waiting when she slipped through the door to her room.

"Success," she whispered, alight with the triumph. She told them what she had heard, omitting the talk of Claire. She could spare Alan that knowledge, if only till the morning.

■■■■■■

The morning light was wan and misty, the sky heavy-weighted with gray clouds. Marian watched as Alan paced by the window of her room, then exchanged a quick glance of concern with Agatha, who watched him over her stitchery. The troubadour was ashen-faced, his features pinched, his eyes glittering between fury and suppressed tears. One instant his countenance seemed a decade older, the next a decade younger. Pausing to glare sightlessly out the window, he whispered, "They should be hung by their entrails, both of them."

Marian agreed, yet it disturbed her to see his pain, his anger so dangerously close to the surface. Already he cared far too much for the Lady Claire. In this condition, even if he did not do something foolish, he would bring his infatuation to the Sheriff's attention. So far it was innocent, but Claire was too responsive in return. Marian did not know Sir Godfrey well enough to guess his response; indifference was likely, but so were anger and sadistic amusement. "You must go to London."

"No," he said, lifting his head, outrage and denial glittering bright through the film of tears.

"Yes," she hissed at him. "You have given your allegiance to the same mistress as I. We serve the Queen's needs first.''

''I cannot abandon Lady Claire,'' he pleaded.

''You cannot protect her. She is the Sheriff's wife. Prince John is heir to the throne. There may be no chivalry in what these men do, but there is no help for it either. You know it as well as I.''

Alan turned on her, anger flaring. ''You killed Sir Ranulf for less.''

''He had no right to me and no family living to protest his death. I was lucky to be offered the protection of power after the deed was done. No one will try me. But that same power has offered Lady Claire up to a greater one. She is the Sheriff's property to dispense with as he wills. If she killed Sir Godfrey in retaliation for this abasement, there are many who would support her, but the law would not aid her—not Prince John's law. He would punish her defiance. There is no question that destroying Prince John himself would mean her death.''

''So you would have submitted?''

''Yes, I would have found the will to submit, as she did. If I did not, the weight of the Crown would fall not only on me but on my family.'' Marian listened with chill to her own voice. Her blood curdled at the thought of such a creature violating her—but there were many roads to vengeance. *I would still kill him, some secret way*, she thought, *even if it were as despicable as poison.*

''You'd kill him,'' Alan said, his gaze fastened to her face. ''You would find a way.''

''You will go to London,'' she ordered abruptly, angry that he had read her face so clearly. ''You must take news of Prince John's visit to the Queen. You must also tell her that I have recruited Robin Hood and report the substance of our arrangement with him.''

Alan only glared at her. If his distress were not so intense, Marian would have tried to tempt him, to tell him he could deliver Eleanor's token to Robin. But such bribery would insult him now. It would be better if the transaction made a complete circle, with Eleanor's favor passing from Marian's hands into Robin's. Marian felt a stirring eagerness for the encounter, but Alan's misery dimmed the flash of anticipation.

Agatha set her needle into the embroidery. "She is safe enough for a time, Alan. John left an hour ago."

John was gone, and too well protected for Alan to make a suicidal attack. But the Sheriff was still a target for Alan's wrath. She knew his nature did not approach the violence of her own, but he might strike out in rage. Marian considered it fortunate Sir Godfrey was bored with his wife and was not likely to approach Claire himself. Unless, she thought with a chill, the display of Prince John's favor made his neglected wife suddenly more attractive. That might influence the Sheriff, that and the pleasure of inflicting his own unwanted attentions immediately after, layering humiliation upon humiliation. Oh yes, that would appeal to Sir Godfrey.

"You will go to London, Alan," Marian repeated. "You will stay as long as the Queen needs you. You will return with whatever messages she entrusts to you and whatever token she offers for Robin Hood."

Alan ran his hands through his hair and raised such an anguished face she was filled with pity and fear. "There is no help for it, Alan, none within your grasp that will not cause dreadful damage. Remove yourself from the temptation for revenge."

"It is not only revenge. More than any pain I want to inflict on them, I want to give Claire comfort."

"Your presence will do her more harm than good. You endanger yourself, and you endanger her because you cannot hide your feelings." She did not say that those same feelings were doubtless one of Claire's few comforts. "Today. Let us trust you will have control when you return."

Alan bowed his head in defeat. He had enough wit left to accept the fact that his presence could endanger Claire further. He nodded, then raised his gaze to meet hers. "Be her friend, Lady Marian. As much as you can be."

10 Marian made note of landmarks as she rode . . . distinctive configurations of trees, a blasted stump, an unusual boulder. With perseverance she might be able to find Robin's camp herself. Not that it would be possible to arrive undetected. One sentry after another marked her passage through Sherwood, guiding her to the edge of the encampment. The men greeted her deferentially now, eager to be of service. When she asked after Robin, Friar Tuck bravely appointed himself her guide. He led her along a trail to the river, where another man pointed them to a hillside path that wound farther into the woods above the water's edge. The Friar thanked him and led her on, chattering as they walked, moving nimbly for someone so rotund.

"Just a ways more," he said after a quarter of a mile. "By the little falls. It is beautiful there. I often go there to pray."

Marian eyed the Friar dubiously. He was an odd mixture of innocence and guile, and she found it difficult to think of his garb as anything but a disguise. Yet he seemed quite serious, in his cheerful way. Was she to believe that Robin also went to the little falls to pray?

They'd just entered a small clearing when Little John emerged from the trees in front of them. He nodded a casual command to Tuck, who instantly retreated back toward the camp. Deliberately Marian started forward. Rooted and looming like some elder god of the forest, John barred her way down the path.

"Robin told me he wanted to be alone," he said to her, his tone amiable and adamant.

"I've come with important news," she responded in kind.

"It can wait a bit," he countered. "Why don't I guide you back to camp, Lady Marian, and bring some cool ale to refresh you?"

An unpleasant thought came, and she voiced it sharply. "Let me pass. If he is drunk again, I want to know it."

"He's not been drinking," Little John said quietly. "Rob's not been drunk since he made his bargain with you. And it's wine, not ale, that puts him in an ugly temper."

"Stand aside, John." It had become a matter of wills. Although she believed him already, no trust had been proved between them. He was Robin's man, not hers, and would no doubt lie to protect him—if not this time, then another. She would not have him think her easily controlled or misled. "Stand aside," she repeated.

Little John looked at her intently. "Well, perhaps you're meant to," he said ambiguously, and did as she bade.

Walking past him, Marian entered the glade and followed the path toward the river. Tree trunks lifted gracefully around her, their varied barks like rough-textured skins of brown and gray and stippled white. Overhead the foliage formed an opulent canopy, the wavering leaves tinting the grove with veiled green light, then parting to reveal the unclouded azure of the sky. Gently dispersing her impatience, a caressing breeze played over her as she sauntered along the dappled pathway. She could feel the tension bound tightly within her uncurling like a spring leaf in the mellifluous sunshine. The sensation of release was so vivid it surprised as well as soothed. All about her the soft rush of the unseen waterfall colored the air, weaving the scattered birdsong and whispering leaves into a vibrant music. The moist, cool perfume of the water enriched the other scents of earth and stone, bark and leaf, grasses and flowers. She gazed about her as she began a leisurely descent down the hillside. Sunlight and shadow shimmered in an ever-shifting mosaic, yet her awareness magnified, clarified so that she saw every leaf, every coiled vine and feathery frond limned in gold. Beneath the intricate and gilded tracery of the lush undergrowth, satin depths of shade glimmered darkly. Wildflowers shone, living jewels sparkling in their setting of brilliant green-gold. Below her the river flashed through the trees, iridescent colors rippling like a ribbon vendor's satin streamers, sapphire and slate, silver and mauve, russet and twining green.

When Marian reached the bottom of the path, she felt entranced by the beauty of the place, though she could not have said why it was more exquisite than a dozen other shaded glades abundant with oak and elm, birch and linden. Although the body of the falls was hidden by a bank of willows, she glimpsed the far edge, a shoulder of tawny sandstone with a smooth curve of water plummeting down to a foaming pool. Though louder here, the rush of the waterfall lulled like a deeper silence. Ferns sprouted in graceful arabesques about her feet, and the banks were thick with moist, plush mosses and flowering rushes. Love-in-a-mist blossomed in patches of fragile beauty. Golden trefoil and lady's slipper scattered brightness amid the luxuriant grasses, and the roseate purples of sedge, foxglove, and bittersweet tinged the greenery with their blush. A placid backwater curled, thick with white water lilies, like a wedding garland tossed carelessly among the trees. She breathed deeply, tranquillity and anticipation mingled in a subtle euphoria, like honey and wine melting into a single intoxicating draft. It was not surprising that Robin wished to be alone here, though she still meant to find him. He was not visible, but the falls were concealed behind the screen of willows. As Marian made her way through the drifting curtains of their delicate branches, the cascading water and embankment of tumbled stone came into view.

Naked, Robin lay on a bed of sun-drenched rock in the water's shallows. At first he seemed a figure carved from the amber sandstone, the contours of his body, the broad shoulders, the curves of calf and thigh, all slim yet solid in their chiseled elegance. But he was no inanimate sculpture. He was lost in sensual abandon, his head thrown back, his hands stroking his sex in a languid caress. Shock stilled her, but she did not, could not, turn away, held by the intensity of the erotic vision. Though his cock was hard, the rest of his body was relaxed, moving in a slow rhythm, offering his pleasure to the trees, the flowing water, the air itself. Marian could feel it, as though the glistening air, the warmth of the sun enveloped her in that shared communion, conjured from human need and then transformed into a singing, shimmering delight that tingled through her blood.

Sensing her presence, Robin opened his eyes, his gaze meeting hers across the water. He paused, and she felt her heart pound in the silence, marking the seconds. She questioned at first if he recognized her, then if he believed her presence, yet beyond that fierce but dazzled wonder she saw only acceptance. Marian had been holding her breath; now she drew it as one with him. She saw his chest swell, even as her own lungs filled with another sweet, reeling draft of intoxication, breathing in the warmth of the sun, the heat of desire. She felt exquisitely dizzy. Letting her watch, wanting her to, Robin resumed his caressing. The sensuous movement of his hand was like the slow evocation of a spell, each stroke spinning pleasure about them like some silken, invisible web.

Rapt, as if he had beckoned, utterly unafraid, Marian approached him, a trail of stones leading her over the swirling water to where he lay waiting. His body was dark gold and pale, burnished by sun and gleaming with sweat, the muscle swelling smooth as the river-washed rocks surrounding them. His gaze held hers as she knelt beside him, his eyes the warm green of young leaves, glimmering with light, with life.

"Marian," he said. Naming her only. Asking nothing.

Hypnotized, she reached out. Robin gasped softly as she laid a hand on his thigh, its surface hard yet yielding to her touch, the skin hot against her palm. He waited, unmoving, the clamor of her heart echoing his unspoken question, the stillness of her hand its answer. She could not move or withdraw. So his hand began again, stroking his sex with the same slow, summoning rhythm that rose and fell with her breath. She watched, enmeshed in her own fascination. A delicate wind flowed over them. The caress of the breeze seemed to pass through her body as well as over it, touching nerve and sinew with a gentle shivering pleasure she saw echoed in his flesh.

Robin closed his eyes and sighed. "Cool." The breeze entwined them, swirling and eddying in subtle harmony with the fluid music of the river, the rustling of the leaves, the soft whisper of his voice. "You are like the wind. Cool."

He shivered again, and the scorching heat of his thigh flared against her hand, as though the cool air of her fed his inner blaze. From that one point of contact, his life pulsed through her every vein and artery, elemental fire kindling an answering flame, wind and fire rising entwined. The wild beating of her heart mingled with the hidden throbbing of her sex, the visible throbbing of his. The movement of his hand quickened slightly and his body tensed beneath her touch. She drew a sharp breath. His eyes opened to meet hers, alight with the pale green incandescence of brightly tipped flame.

"Robin," she whispered, naming him in turn. The final word of the spell.

The rising torrent of his pleasure swept through her, carrying her forward. Marian reached out to touch his straining hardness. The shaft fitted her hand as if made for it, the skin like moist, clinging satin drawn taut over steel. The luxurious texture caressed her hand as she enfolded him. With a low moan, he yielded his fingers to hers, his arms outflung to grasp the edges of the rock. She felt his sex swelling in her hand, felt the jolt of his seed pulsing through to fountain in the air. A tide of flame flooded through her. She heard Robin cry out as she melted into his rapture, becoming one with him and with it. She felt them dissolving together, flesh into earth, earth into water, water into air. And the air burned coolly, sweetly, a pure transparent fire that consumed them entire.

. . . And left them shining whole, the glowing ecstasy of aftermath as exquisite as release. Their breathing slowly quieted, matched then drawn in harmony. The noises of the greenwood no longer sang in her blood but whispered around her, river and breeze, bird and fluttering leaves. Marian released a sigh of wonderment. Traces of his seed lingered on her hand, and she dipped it in the water, the swirling coolness washing over palm and fingers.

Robin raised himself up. Kneeling before her, he drew her into his embrace, his body fitting hers smoothly from knee to chest, his hands framing her face. He kissed her, his lips soft and sensuous against hers, a kiss of acknowledgment and offering. She felt the same sense of melting against him, into him, and when he tilted her back, she flowed with his movement, letting him shape their pleasure. She felt his mouth against her breast, warm through the silk, and then his hand slid down further, cupping her sex.

Reality returned with terrifying ferocity as desire flamed through her again. For all the ardor of what she had just shared with him, Marian had felt embodied not in her own flesh but in his and in the secret, eternal life of the forest. Now his tender gesture ignited a fire deep within her. No solidity of earth, no delicacy of wind or fluidity of water, but only merciless fire, burning every nerve of her body with appalling need.

Thrusting him away, Marian leapt to her feet. She discovered her body was shaking, her alarm a discordant note in the ravishing peace of the glade. She backed away, one step, still entangled in the glowing web of desire, trapped by invisible filaments that scored every limb. Another step back, and she felt the low edge of the stone like a lethal precipice.

"Marian," Robin said softly, and she stopped, as if he still bound her in his spell, possessed her through her name. He rose and laid his hands on her shoulders, a gentle, searing weight. She shivered with fever chill, fever heat. Her gown felt heavy as if drenched with water, hot and constricting. She wanted to strip it off and lie naked with him, to couple on the flat, hard bed of the sun-washed rocks.

"Marian," he repeated. And then, "Don't be afraid."

That he said the words frightened her more. Yet fear was something she was used to putting aside, an inconvenience to be dealt with when the crisis had passed. Why couldn't she master this welling panic?

"It is this place," Robin said. "There is magic here."

She had felt it, succumbed to it. But before he spoke the words, she had believed the magic no more than mood. A communion woven from a unique moment in time, a place of beauty, and the burgeoning attraction between them. Now his words stripped the encounter of any meaning, and Marian of her identity, her power. Anger cut into her fear, and anger was a weapon.

"Let me go!" she snarled.

Instantly, he released her shoulders.

"It could have been any woman," Marian accused.

Robin shook his head. "It was us, together, here."

"Not us. This place. You said so yourself."

Wrath gave her strength, but it was fear that made her turn and flee across the stones and through the willows, run up the hillside path and beyond the stand of trees to the narrow clearing between the groves. On the opposite side she stopped and sat down, leaning against the trunk of a linden, her breathing harsh and shallow. She was still too close to Robin. He might follow, but it would be worse to stumble across one of his men before she had command of herself. Intent on regaining control, Marian forced her breathing to a slower, deeper pattern.

After a moment she looked up and saw him standing at the edge of the grove across from her, his eyes dark and questioning. Her heart leapt, with desire first, then fear. The distance between them was but a few feet. She should have heard him approach; as carefully as he had trained himself to move, so she had trained herself to hear. She wanted nothing of this passion that wantonly stirred, then stripped her senses.

Watching her silently, Robin waited in the shadows, clothed now in the motley colors of the forest. A shaft of sunshine turned his hair to spun gold and, slanting across his face, transformed the seeming darkness of his eyes to misted green. A trick of light, no more, yet now that revelation seemed an act of magic. As if seeing him for the first time, Marian perceived that beyond the earthly sensuality of his beauty, Robin had the look of Faerie about him. How easy to imagine some elfen fingertip marking the points of devil's peak and angled brows, tracing the sharp-edged upper lip and pressing the sensual curve of the lower, drawing something blunt and mortal to a keener edge. This man was touched with glamour, and he could use it, Marian was sure, as skillfully as any more substantial weapon he possessed. Had he not already?

The outlaw walked across the clearing toward her, but Marian had regained her courage and did not startle. He sat down, a discreet distance away. Looking at him now, she saw a handsome man but one clearly mortal. What absurdities had she been conjuring?

"Do you feel better here?" he asked.

The question seemed strange until Marian realized that however beautiful and peaceful this grove was, the aura of enchantment had faded. She had stepped outside its circle and now felt both safe and bereft.

"Lady Marian, I don't want you to think that I will presume upon you because of this." His tone sought some meeting place between respectful formality and gentle intimacy. "I've stolen two kisses from you. I don't want you to feel this was another theft."

She shook her head. What else could it be? Did he imagine she would have chosen to respond to him so?

"It was a gift, from the forest to us. You should feel the richer for it."

"Don't tell me how I should feel!" she raged. She could not believe what she had just done—with this man she barely knew. She remembered, as if her hand still embraced his sex, the sudden wild pulsing of his climax and the joy that had engulfed her, sharing his ecstasy.

"Marian," he said, his voice demanding, pleading for a recognition she did not want to give.

"Don't touch me," she seethed at him. But he had made no move to do so. Rage fused with desperation. She felt shattered, in pieces. She wanted to cling to him, wanted the melding with his body that made everything whole. Yet if he reached out for her, she'd be as likely to stab him as embrace him. This chaos of emotion terrified her. Marian wrapped her arms about herself, rocking back and forth in a senseless mime of comfort.

Robin knelt beside her, still not touching her. "Have you had it only on your own terms then?" he asked.

She tried to tell herself the question had no meaning. In France she had taken a lover, and that lover had shown her the joys of carnal pleasure. However briefly, she had known that absolute abandon. But her pleasure had been solitary, unshared with the man who had given it to her. An exchange, not a union, shallow for all its intensity. She had wanted no more, been capable of offering no more. She sensed a power of surrender in Robin more profound than any she had allowed herself—or wished for. Only revenge was ever as powerful, and she had wielded that power, not submitted to it.

As if reading her thoughts, he asked, "Have you never felt outside yourself yet wholly yourself?"

"In fighting," she said. "In vengeance." Yet even then, immersed in the absolute necessity of the moment, she had held control not over the outcome but over herself. For ten years she had trained, and everything in her being had flowed with the stroke of her sword, reaching out toward the destruction of one man. But Simon of Vitry was dead. She had been hollow since, walking a long, empty road back from where she had left his corpse.

"You have had death for your lover then," he said. "I know how that is."

"Do you?" she asked.

"Oh yes." He met her eyes, and she saw that he did know. "But I loved life more."

It was like a judgment. She wanted to hit him. Yet there was no accusation in his eyes, only acceptance and hunger for the same. He was offering the soul-deep intimacy of true friends, true lovers. "I have been frightened too," he said unexpectedly. "The forest has many ways of claiming me. I have never denied it, or wanted to, when it enthralled me. But after it has returned me, sometimes I have been afraid that the next time I will lose myself forever. Sometimes I wish I could."

Fear chilled her, and she attacked. "It is evil then, a place of pagan witchery."

He looked at her with such reproach she felt ashamed. Shame was not something she was used to feeling, and it quelled the last of the anger and the fear.

"That its power is greater than my own does not make it evil." Robin gave her a bitter smile that softened to something sweeter. "Call the grove a lost fragment of Eden, then, if you will, where all are innocent. Friar Tuck will tell you the place is holy. He has a shrine near the falls, a little altar of rocks and flowers."

Marian remembered that Tuck said he came here to pray.

"The grove is different at different times, different with different people. Not all my men have found it, though it would seem easy enough to do." Robin touched her at last, taking her face between his hands, his gaze intent and tender. "You said it could have been any woman. I think anyone but you would have found a trail that led her half a mile downriver, not one that led her to my side."

He did not kiss her, though she could see the desire in his eyes. If only because she now had the power to fight her own hunger, she drew back from him and stood. She had wanted to talk to him alone. Now she wanted the distraction, the safety of others about them. "I have news from Nottingham. That is why I came."

"Let us go back to camp then." Accepting her decision,

he rose to his feet and led the way down the trail. Then he stopped abruptly and turned back to her, concern in his eyes. "I heard of what happened—with Wolverton."

"Nothing happened, except I smashed his skull," she said sharply.

Robin nodded, smiling faintly. Then something flared in his eyes, a small green flicker. "Guisbourne brought you back to Nottingham."

"He smashed a few skulls as well."

"Is he . . . ."

The unfinished sentence was itself an insult. What right had this outlaw to question her? She felt a fine glitter of fury and answered what he had not asked. "Sir Guy has not so much as kissed me—since more than one has been forced upon me unasked."

Robin flushed under her anger but held her gaze. Whirling, she stalked ahead of him up the trail toward the encampment. Her anger had prevailed over the confusion she felt at his recognition of her attraction to Guisbourne. She only hoped, with his fine-tuned intuition, that he did not sense her confusion now. Was what she had felt when Guy rescued her so different? Released from the death grip of her vengeance, she was awakening to fierce new passions. She must be cautious and hold control.

Although Robin quickened his pace to walk beside her, it was in awkward silence for a moment. She forced herself to walk more slowly. He asked then, tentatively, but with a genuine curiosity, "It must be true then, your grandfather has trained the women of his household to be fighters? I've wondered since you held the knife to my neck how well you might wield a sword."

Only then did Marian realize she had told him far more than she intended. "Yes," she answered, hoping the single syllable sounded easy and unthreatened. Then she added, with careful unconcern, "My grandmother and I both have some skill at arms."

She did not care that he knew—she wanted his respect— but she did not like that she had not chosen her words any more knowingly than her deeds by the falls. Marian felt a frisson of fear, and with it renewed anger. She glanced sidelong at Robin. He had contained his surprise far better than she would have expected, yet when she thought of his deft negotiations, she was well aware of his ability to conceal emotion and to manipulate others. He gave such an impression of openness, but she had not learned yet how much was his essence, how much no more than useful tool.

■■■■■■

Hiding his turmoil, Robin waited while Marian settled herself beneath the spreading branches of the oak. She had selected this position, moving ahead of him when they reached the camp. The tree stood on a rise at the edge of the glade, where they were in sight but out of hearing of his men. Robin sat across from her, choosing the most neutral distance that quiet speech would allow, and beckoned Little John to sit with them. Robin watched Marian turn to greet John. She was perfectly posed, seemingly serene as she smoothed her skirts and smiled graciously. John paused, sensing her distance, but then he sat down, nodding respectfully.

What a little scene they set, Robin thought. Marian had become a symbol to his men, of pardon, of freedom, of hope itself. She knew it and presented herself purposefully, as he and John played to it. It was a politic choice, but he knew it was not the reason she had chosen this open vantage point. She did not want to be alone with him and had shut away all but her mind. Her body she made a shield of will turned against him. The men, nodding to with her cheerful reverence, saw no particular difference. She was a lady after all. They did not expect her always to break bread with them, or always to come laughing into their midst. They admired her self-possession, her regal pride became their own, and the honor they gave her was a gift that returned to themselves.

Only Little John felt the difference, as he felt every changing breeze of the forest, every subtly shifting alliance between the men. And this shift was not subtle to such a perceiver. She had reclaimed her natural authority, but her voice, her posture were edged with tension. Robin felt John's gaze measure him in turn, but did not meet it. He had his own authority to maintain, and an alliance that must not falter because of his error of judgment. He kept his attention on Marian as she recounted the conversation she had overheard in Nottingham Castle.

Little John glared at the revelation of the Sheriff's plot, but Robin jested ironically, "I think we must needs make a truth of this lie. Else where is justice?"

Little John smiled grimly. "Aye, we'll trip them with their own rope and double knot the trick by sending the silver to the King."

"Prince John will send word of the ransom route. The Sheriff is to arrange the theft of the treasure, preferably before it passes through Nottingham." Marian smiled ironically. "He will send his own tribute as an act of good faith to London—but take double from the stolen hoard in return. The rest will go to John. The silver, the gold will swell his own coffers, but most will be used to bribe the Emperor."

"To pay him to hold King Richard prisoner longer still or to buy his death?" John's voice was a low growl.

Robin shook his head. "I do not think the Emperor dare kill him outright, or the other sovereigns will turn on him. But to play for time, yes, and perhaps to weaken his health."

"He may bleed England for yet more silver if he can prolong the King's imprisonment," Marian said.

John glowered. "It's a foul thought, that all the treasure collected to free the King may be used to hold him hostage."

Marian raised a delicate brow. "Prince John found it an amusing arrangement."

"Queen Eleanor may manage to keep the route secret, but we must plan on Prince John's discovering it. Ideally we must prevent the robbery altogether and reveal at least the Sheriff's complicity. Next best, we steal the silver from the

Sheriff's men and arrange safe conveyance to London.''
Robin frowned, considering his best sources of information.

''We will have to discover the route for ourselves or keep
close watch on the Sheriff's men when the time draws
nigh,'' Marian said.

Robin hesitated, then offered, ''I do have one spy within
the castle who may prove invaluable.''

''Only one?'' she asked coolly.

Robin held her gaze but did not answer except to continue. ''The Sheriff sometimes uses pigeons to send messages. . . .''

''So I have heard.'' Marian gave a small smile. ''And
you must know his pigeon keeper.''

''The family has reason to bear the Sheriff a grudge. The
father fears Sir Godfrey too much to retaliate. But his wife
and their son both have given us information. Prince John's
birds are specially marked, and the son often bears the messages to the Sheriff,'' Robin said then gave a small shrug.
''But he has not the learning to copy the code, so they've
been of no use to us except for their timing and what Cobb
has managed to overhear. Living within the castle, you can
make even better use of them than I, especially if you can
arrange to copy the notes and have them decoded. Prince
John will probably use the birds to send the messages.''

Marian shook her head. ''They spoke of it, but the Sheriff thought the risk of losing the bird too great.''

''Even so, Prince John is likely to send a bird to announce the messenger. I do not stop every traveler on the
road, and it would be suspicious if I started.''

''He said he would send Sir Stephen, who has a shriveled arm from an old sword cut. Otherwise he is unremark-
able, brown hair, blue eyes.''

''We will hold to this camp for a while longer then and
keep close watch for him on the roads. The news he brings
the Sheriff may be all we need. But if there are last minute
changes, they will come by pigeon, swifter than a man on
horseback. And however they come, they will be coded.''

"I can decode them. It would depend on how much time I have to study the message."

"And the intricacy of the code?" Robin smiled at her pride.

"And the intricacy of the code," she acknowledged.

"Friar Tuck can copy anything we find, and we have skill at secret searches as well as total dismantling. There's little point discovering the message if they know we've done it. And now you have the contact within the castle and the chance to learn the code beforehand." He paused, then added, "But use them with caution."

Her expression told him that was obvious, but Robin could not help his concern. "The boy's name is Cobb; the woman's Margaret. She sews for the Sheriff's wife, so it will not be difficult for you to make contact. Take her some simple present such as fruit or wildflowers, and say, 'This is a gift from the forest.' She will know then you are with us."

"What is their grudge against the Sheriff?" Marian asked.

Robin glanced at John. The tall man's brow furrowed; then he said, "Cobb took a fall, a bad one. His leg was broken. The doctor said first that it was mendable, though the boy would always limp. But the steward mentioned the fall to the Sheriff, said Cobb was lucky to keep his leg. Next thing the Sheriff had called the doctor to see him, and when he returned, the doctor looked at the leg again and said it was worse than he'd thought, that it'd go to gangrene if they didn't take it off. The father was afraid to say no. The mother argued, but the guards just took her away while they cut her son's leg off and cauterized the wound. Not even a week later, while Cobb was still suffering the agony of it, the Sheriff had the boy brought to his bed."

"That seems sufficient for a lifelong hate," Marian said when John finished.

"Margaret and Cobb have worked for us for over almost a year now, risking their lives," Robin added, offering reassurance she had not asked for.

John nodded. "They're both closemouthed, and this retribution is the honey on their bread."

"I will arrange to contact them. If this boy can bring me the messages before the Sheriff sees them, he will indeed be invaluable," Marian said, and Robin watched the cool gleam in her eyes as she sifted through the possible prizes and pitfalls. Then, remembering that he had given her this trust before he had received the Queen's affirmation of their bargain, Marian added, "Thank you."

"You're welcome," he responded wryly.

"They could be invaluable. We all know the route may be changed at the last minute, so the plans must be as flexible as possible." She was all practicality. She met his eyes as she spoke, the precise voice, the level gaze marking not their connection but its removal.

Robin ached with her nearness, her distance. The cool of her, which had been so maddening, so tantalizing, so strangely soothing, was chill now, a winter bite. He had made a drastic mistake. Yet he had done nothing but respond to the flow between them. Not coercion but offering. He doubted, held in the embrace of the forest, if he could have done aught else. Only her resistance had broken the rapturous spell. He could not imagine how one denied that power . . . yet he could, since he had chosen his enchantment and she had not.

"I must return," Marian said, rising graceful and taut.

Knowing her eager to leave, to escape, cut him. She held out her hand to John, who took it smoothly, making it all simple courtesy, as if he were the natural one to escort her. Robin bowed, letting her refuse him again. It was her right. He stood, playing the king overseeing his domain, and watched John guide her toward the horses. She did not look back.

A wave of bitterness swept him. He had lost too much and wanted now more than he would ever have. Locksley Hall, if he was lucky, but not this woman. From the instant he had seen Marian, she had personified all that had been taken from him. And he had wanted to take it back. But she was friend and ally now. It was sharing he wanted, not stolen kisses. And if it was never only kisses he had wanted, now it was Marian entire.

Even pardoned, did he dare hope for it? He was certain, not knowing why, that she had far more than the meager holding of Fallwood Hall to dower her. He could not imagine her less proud if less landed, but there was an assurance, a surety that backed her pride. Perhaps, if all his lands were returned—but he asked for no more than Locksley. Thinking that it was the most Richard would grant a traitor's get turned outlaw, he was forbidden by his own pride to ask for more.

Marian was beyond his reach.

Yet she had come within it . . . in the purest way he could imagine. Would the passion draw her back, to claim him as lover, if nothing more? That passion was more than most marriages yielded. He could not imagine how one denied that power, yet she had. It had been powerful enough to frighten her . . . and she was not one to give way to fear. He wanted her surrender, but willingly, not as an adversary. Surrender shared, not battle waged.

He must school himself to accept in advance whatever she offered. He knew already he loved her too much to refuse.

11 The morning sun lit the stone walls with a warm pale light. The last ties of her gown fastened, Marian sat on a stool while Agatha fashioned her hair. Since Marian often shunned the wimple, her companion had taken the unbound hair as a challenge to her ingenuity. Marian held herself poised as the other woman worked, in an attentive stillness she hoped masked her impatience. Whatever her own chaotic feelings, there were significant matters to attend to. "So tell me, Agatha, do you think you can trust the seamstress and her son?"

Since she had been so insistent on recruiting Robin herself, Marian had compelled herself to entrust Agatha with the first contact with the family he had told her about.

The firm fingers never ceased their weaving, laying a pattern of delicate braids over the long fall of hair. "I believe so, Lady Marian. They've both got a cold hunger for vengeance. The woman is tight and cool. The lad, Cobb, is young, but there's no child left in him. They took it off with his leg. There was risk involved in revealing ourselves, of course, but I agree the chance to read Prince John's messages is worth it."

Marian restrained a nod as Agatha began another strand of braiding. "I need only a brief time to copy the message, unless I must take special precautions to prevent the Sheriff from knowing it's been read."

"I did ask the lad what they looked like. He's not trained to judge, but there's nothing special to the naked eye, no outer markings or seal. They are tiny, so it'll be but a brief code. Couriers will bring anything of length.''

''If he's right, then I need worry only about breaking the code,'' Marian said. ''Whether or not we get to see the notes will be fortuitous. He cannot be seen going out of his way to find us, and the time between the message's arrival and its delivery must be brief.''

''He does errands for both his father and mother, so he'll have that excuse. She asked that I bring her one of the gowns you had made in Paris for her to copy for Lady Claire.''

''The lavender bliaut is cut in the newest fashion. You may as well take it now.'' She watched as Agatha knelt before the chest and lifted out the carefully folded bliaut. Then, not wanting to shirk her responsibilities, Marian asked, ''Do you want me to accompany you this time?''

Agatha shook her head. ''I want to build a stronger confidence between us. Come with me next time.''

''We must place some work of our own in her hands,'' Marian said. ''I will ask her to make a gown for me, for which she will be paid most handsomely.''

Draping the lavender bliaut over her arm, Agatha regarded her with a new intentness. ''She is quite skilled and proud of her work as well. When you come to see her, give her the Queen's cloth to fashion for you.''

''Yes,'' Marian agreed instantly. ''That will make the Queen's presence uniquely tangible.''

Agatha nodded decisively and set off to find the seamstress.

As soon as the other woman departed, Marian felt a wash of relief. She was pleased to have found a significant errand on which to send Agatha, rather than invent a flimsy one. She was glad also that Alan was still in London. Her need for solitude was fierce, but she did not want it known. She had never been gregarious, but both her companions possessed keener eyes than most for any symptoms of unease. Even a half hour alone, free of such vigilant eyes, was precious. She was almost glad of Sir Roger's abduction; that might still excuse any irritation she displayed. Her emotions were in turmoil, and she hated the sensation. She did not want such inner perplexities. Danger was everywhere in Nottingham, and such foolish distraction could prove fatal.

As dispassionately as she could, Marian examined her own conflict. For the past ten years she had been tautly aimed at one goal, and she had achieved her purpose. Simon of Vitry was dead, her family avenged. But the fulfillment of his death had left a void within her. Although she had wanted to return home, the Queen's assignment had offered diversion for her mind, a focus for her will—but her emotions had been adrift.

Suddenly she was caught in a growing fascination not for one man but two. Neither was well chosen—except in his own essence. Both had personal power, charisma, intelligence, passion. Both recognized her worth and were drawn to her strength. One was enemy, one outlaw. Even if they had been ally and equal, would this attraction to them have any meaning beyond life's reasserting itself after her obsession with one man's death? There were wellsprings not dried but dammed within her, caught behind the fixed wall of obsession and will. Was it only the passage of time, however brief, that had allowed these dammed passions to spill over, now that the deadlier one she had served was finally consummated?

If she were back in France now, would she have turned to Raymond with this same fervor? She could only judge what she had felt in his arms—and by the absence of any desire to return to them—and she could not believe it. Marian smiled ironically. She thought she had known desire, but she had experienced no more than the brush of its wing, stunning, yet how trivial compared with the piercing grip of its claws. She felt trapped by these new emotions, these wanton sensations that invaded her whether she would or no. She was used to a discipline that kept such intrusive feelings in check, and while she had kept control so far, she hated even the suspicion she might lose it.

No, that was a lie. It had been lost. Hovering on the brink, she had held control with Guy. With Robin she had been swept beyond herself, caught in the spell of his passion. Nothing she had experienced in France, not even the pinnacle of release, compared with the communion she had shared with Robin. Nothing compared with the simple touch of his hand burning through the silk of her gown. The only thing that approached it was the incendiary moment of rapport she had shared with Guy when they vanquished Wolverton and his pack of curs.

Lips curling in self-mockery, Marian remembered the rush of relief she felt when, on her last return from Sherwood, Guisbourne had come down the steps of Nottingham Castle to welcome her. He had offered her his hand to help dismount, and she had felt safe. Safe. How bizarre it had been, even at the moment, to feel so. Guisbourne was enemy still, where Robin was ally. Guy was the deadlier, the more ruthless of the men. A man filled with secrets. Yet his dark, familiar secrecy was less threatening than Robin's foreign openness. Perhaps one or two souls might be allowed to see into Guisbourne's darkness. Robin's brightness shone indiscriminately on all. And if it warmed her, his radiance dazzled, so she felt half blind, stumbling and groping in the light.

She was afraid to confront Robin again with nothing to set against an attraction that grew more powerful with every meeting. Afraid! Her own uncertainty, her trepidation disgusted, infuriated her. What she had feared in the past she had always faced. It was not her way to run. She felt she must know more, experience more than she had. She saw no other way to comprehend, to master her own passions. She would not be ruled by fear.

I will take Guisbourne to my bed, Marian thought ruthlessly. Even as she decided, she knew the danger of the choice, knew she might as easily find herself as trapped in that dark, alluring web as in the golden one that Robin had spun in his forest.

And what of the web she herself wove? She felt her

resolve checked by the specter of betrayal. Agreeing to spy
for Eleanor in France, Marian had seen herself as observer,
as manipulator, but not as seducer. Yet she had inadvertently been so with Raymond, and she found the taste of
that particular treachery loathsome. Because of that experience, she had not wanted to encourage Guisbourne beyond
certain limits. Now she found herself planning cold-
bloodedly to seduce him.

No, with calculation perhaps—but hardly in cold blood.
She would not be plotting this particular action at all if he
roused no heat in her. Knowing Guisbourne a dangerous
adversary from the start, she felt the lure of that danger
enhance his attractiveness, stirring her more deeply. But
however wayward and selfish her motives, there was no way
she could act solely for herself and simply accept the consequences, good or ill, of taking Guisbourne for her lover.
Whatever the outcome, the repercussions would affect her
mission. Rejection or a bungled liaison would distance
her from the castle intrigues; a passionate one would em-
broil her far more deeply. In Nottingham she was the
Queen's agent always, whether she would or no. As
the Queen's agent she had wished from the first to try to
win Guisbourne back to King Richard's side. If she judged
that goal achievable, she must at some point risk revealing
herself to Sir Guy. If she did not bed him, she could approach him only as an emissary, offer him wealth and position to renew his allegiance, without a qualm. But if they
became lovers, then however honest her desire for him had
been, it would instantly become suspect. However much she
relished the challenge of him as an enemy, she did not want
to destroy the possibility of his friendship or blight a passion that could endure.

True, Guisbourne might never consider relinquishing the
alliance he had established through the Sheriff to Prince
John. She might never judge the risk of revelation sufficiently safe to chance. Still, to approach him with any honesty, trust must be possible, although it might never be
attained. With desire suspect, there remained one thing she

could offer to balance the weight of deception, one thing that would say to him, "I did not act only for the Queen in this, but for myself as well." That was marriage. Marian shivered, wondering how to dance on this intricate and sticky web. To speak of an alliance at all was to admit that she could offer a dower to tempt him. She did not want their first encounter to have that lure in the forefront. Passion was the core of her motive; finding a husband, a bitter necessity.

But necessity it was. Her grandfather intended to put his estates in order, and she must fulfill her responsibilities to the family. Guisbourne knew her grandfather's loyalty to the King. Even if Sir Guy hoped to use her to draw her grandfather to Prince John's cause, he must know that she would at least hope to influence him. If that influence took hold, she could approach him by speaking for her family first and avoid compromising her position with the Queen. If Guy were willing to change his allegiance, it was possible that she could wed him.

Who else? Save for a brazen, charming outlaw, there had been no man who stirred her so, mind and body, neither in her grandfather's domains nor at the French court. She could not yet know the depth of her interest, but to acknowledge the possibility was not a lie, either to him or to herself. If the pursuit was all to Guisbourne, and he lost interest once she took him as a lover, she would dismiss him as a possible husband. Marian feared the even greater danger that although he was one of the few men drawn to her strength, as a lover he would want to control it, dominate it. But if Guisbourne would respect her strength within marriage as he did without, there would be few men who would make her a better husband.

Not Robin surely, even if he were pardoned, knight rather than outlaw. To let herself think of him that way was utter folly. Envisioning him now in her mind, Marian found it difficult to separate him from Sherwood, from earth, stone, and leafing tree, from rippling water and gleaming light. He belonged there, a wanton spirit who could not be possessed as one possessed a man.

Ruthlessly Marian thrust him from her thoughts.
She might as well fall in love with the sun.

■■■■■■

Tilting her wine goblet to her lips, Marian quickly
glanced across the torch-lit hall, keeping track of Sir Guy's
movements. Sipping the honeyed wine, she watched him
surreptitiously over the golden rim as he prowled, graceful
and vigilant, among the Sheriff's guests. She lowered her
gaze instantly when his head turned in her direction. He had
a flaunting beauty tonight, she thought, robed in deep amber
brocade with a chain of gem-studded plaques spanning his
chest. As always, his beauty, his very arrogance stirred her.

When next she glanced up, Guisbourne had paused to
talk to old Sir Walter, perhaps King Richard's last vocal
supporter among the knights and barons of Nottingham,
listening with an expression at once bemused and sardonic.
Marian directed her gaze to the musicians, while she considered the ways that part of the game might unfold. Lord
Walter possessed integrity, but little wit, speaking King
Richard's case so bluntly under the Sheriff's roof. Marian
wondered if the Sheriff would leave the old baron in place
as the token fool, encouraging derision. Or would he arrange Sir Walter's death, creating unity, however spurious,
by removing the voice of opposition? The wiser course
would be to leave him in place, she decided, if he did not
become disruptive. He was well liked by the men present,
and though most had ostensibly shifted their allegiance to
Prince John, their fealty was tenuous indeed. Sir Walter's
death would rouse anger as well as fear, rebellion rather
than obedience. Sir Guy's attitude of condescension indicated that isolation was the more likely plan. Had he discussed it with the Sheriff, she wondered, perhaps even
shaped the strategy? The Sheriff was not unsubtle, but he
would prefer fear to mockery as a weapon.

When she looked again, Sir Guy had moved on. Her eyes
sought him through the crowd and found him watching her
openly. She did not drop her gaze but raised her chin and

smiled, her lips matching the tiny curl at the edge of his.
His smile became more open, and he began to walk around
the room toward her. Watching him approach, Marian felt a
little thrill, half anticipation, half apprehension, course
along her nerves. Behind him Marian caught a glimpse of
Lady Alix, her back turned, posing before one of the
younger knights with feigned obliviousness. Another moment and Guisbourne stood before her, poised, courtly, with
the perfect edge of mockery to texture the smoothness of
his demeanor.

"You look magnificent tonight," he said, and his gaze
added fire to the compliment.

She had done her best to appear captivating. Planning for
this encounter, Marian had chosen her most vivid gown, the
flowing crimson bliaut, its soft pleats like watery flame, and
asked Agatha to redo her hair, weaving red rosebuds into a
narrow pale gold braid to form a coronet about her brow. In
her imagination she had played a deft game of verbal feint
and parry leading to a graceful surrender. Knowing her objective, she felt sure she had the skill to carry it off, despite
his greater carnal experience. But suddenly any coy stratagem coaxing Guy to become her seducer filled her with
distaste. They had come too close for her to step back into
that guileful circle where Lady Alix swayed like some lis-
some snake.

"I've had little experience of love," Marian told him
abruptly. "I should like to have more."

For a second Guisbourne was purely startled; then a delicately feral smile curved his mouth, and the golden eyes lit
with an inner lick of flame.

She had piqued his curiosity by taking the initiative. He
might have preferred controlling or believing he controlled
the seduction, but her confession of inexperience countered
the brazenness. And the very control she now wielded she
was offering to have stripped. Guisbourne would want to
dazzle her with his expertise. He would set himself to teach,
hoping no man, before or after, would match him.

"Would you?" he asked.

"Yes, "she said simply, yet knowing there was no simplicity here. "I think you are a man with many skills."

"Skill is but half the pleasure," Sir Guy answered provocatively.

Marian lowered her eyes, desire and despair surging as she remembered, vividly, the image and sensation of Robin lying beneath her on the sun-drenched rocks. Guy would have that to match. Flushed, defiant, she lifted her gaze to meet Guisbourne's. "Only half?"

"Ahhh . . ." he murmured, moving fractionally closer. "I do not think we shall lack for passion." His eyes glowed, not the color of sunlight but of torch flames in darkness. She felt again the desire to burn in that darkness with him. As her own desire flared, she could hear his breathing quicken, the subtle sound like an intimate caress. Her eyes held his, defiant still as she felt the aching pulse between her thighs, heat and moisture gathering.

"I want you now," he whispered, moving closer still, his eyes suddenly so feral she could envision him taking her here and now, both of them oblivious of all around them.

She broke from his gaze and drew a deep breath. When she raised her eyes to meet his again, the fire in them was carefully banked. To bring him to her room was possible but stupidly dangerous, to go to his castle almost as transparent. He lifted a graceful brow. "I could . . . just possibly . . . wait until tomorrow."

"Yes, tomorrow," she agreed. "Where can we meet that we will not be castle gossip an hour after?"

"I believe I know of a place." He gave another small, cryptic smile, obviously enjoying himself immensely. "Meanwhile I will savor the sweet torment of anticipation."

■ ■ ■ ■ ■ ■

With Ralph riding by her side, Marian followed the landmarks Guisbourne had described. An apple orchard burgeoning with small green fruit marked the turn off the great north road. From there a narrow, curving stream led through a lush meadow edged with birch and linden. A kingfisher skimmed past, and a flurry of magpie moths, red-tailed bumblebees, and motley winged butterflies fluttered among the flowers. The thick grass was bright with the vivid pinks and purples of Canterbury bells, foxglove, sedge, loosestrife, and bittersweet. Glossy green rushes, cloudy bursts of stinging nettles, and forget-me-nots crowded the banks of the stream. They wove through patches of light and shade as trees grew denser, meadow-land succumbing to woodland.

Discovering the blasted oak that marked the rising stretch of honeycombed hills, Marian told Ralph to wait by the tree for her return and went on alone. He might well conjecture whom she was meeting, but she hoped there were too many possible people, and reasons, for him to be certain. Nor did Marian mean to tell Agatha or Alan unless she deemed it necessary. Turning north at a tumble of boulders, she pursued the gleaming path of the stream another half mile, the banks here covered with blackberry brambles teeming with pale blossoms. She followed the serpentine windings of the water until she came upon a ridge of golden stone overgrown with creepers. Beneath it the stream suddenly disappeared into a swallet, the narrow crack in the rock face opening the way to some subterranean course. This was the final landmark. After guiding her horse around the ridge, she entered a small clearing enclosed with tall trees on one side, looming rock on the other. Guisbourne stood waiting, garbed richly but simply in lustrous bronze, his brocade tunic topped with a cape of supple leather, and fine leather trousers clinging to his legs. Behind him she glimpsed a darkness half obscured by thick foliage, the entrance to a cave.

"Lady Marian." Sir Guy came forward to greet her, offering to hand her down from her horse with an exquisite formality that made her smile. He smiled in return, with the lascivious edge of mockery that amused and aroused her. For a moment she played the game, placing her hand within his grasp and dismounting with elaborate grace. He indicated the stony mouth of the cave with an elegant flourish, then led her within, as if to his castle.

As she stepped into the darkness, cool air brushed her, flowing outward. She paused, waiting till her vision altered; then she could see a narrow passage leading sharply downward between slanting rock walls. The path curved abruptly out of sight, beyond the last glimmer of light. The obscurity edged her anticipation with apprehension, and she controlled the impulse to lay her hand to her knife.

''Go on. It's not far,'' Guy said softly behind her. His voice was reassuring and faintly amused. She knew he had deliberately chosen not to carry a torch to light their way, letting the undercurrents of danger, of fear, work their perverse erotic alchemy. Marian flashed him a look over her shoulder, ready to rebuke him, for stirring such things was like to make her cold, not hot. Yet his presence was the quintessential element of the spell, and when she met his shadowed gaze, her blood coursed through her veins with brighter heat.

She stepped resolutely into the deepening blackness, following the descending curve of the wall. Sound distorted strangely. Breathing surrounded her, and her steps echoed from some hollow place ahead—and Guy's, as if he not only followed her but also came up from the depths to meet her. Even as she rounded the turn, she saw illumination moving on the stone, not the light of day but the wavering play of flame. To her left opened a wide stone chamber, its walls marked, layer upon layer of rippling from some ancient subterranean stream now sunk far below this level. Directly ahead, at the far edge of the cave, she saw a further darkness opening beyond into those deeper, unknown regions, at once threatening and enticing.

Guy, princely in his secret domain, escorted her into the chamber. He had prepared for her—or brought others here before her. There was a thin cover of feather bedding to soften the hard floor, with another folded as a pillow. Fruit, bread, and wine waited on a ledge. All these simple pleasantries were illuminated by the extravagance of beeswax

candles, fine enough for king or cardinal, their luxury almost decadent against the primal stone. The topaz flames
flickered. Light danced on the rippled walls, catching the
metallic iridescence of the brocade tunic and sculpting the
contours of Guisbourne's face. His pupils had dilated, their
expanding blackness rimmed with gold, and the gold flames
alive within. For a moment his eyes burned, pure fire: then
the candlelight wavered, veiling them once more in shadowed darkness.

Unexpectedly tense, she turned away and began undoing
the ties of her celadon bliaut. It shocked her to be already so
roused. Her fingers worked steadily, if not as swiftly as she
would have liked. Guisbourne came up behind her and
clasped her hands. She felt his body against her back, presence more than pressure. She was suddenly, intensely aware
of his scent, the mingling of musk and sandalwood with a
smoky, burning coil of incense. Though they barely
touched, he radiated a heat that seared her skin beneath the
silk. The cool air of the cavern brushed her neck as he
moved her hair aside. He kissed the back of her neck, his
lips gliding across the bare skin, his beard surprisingly soft.
Then she felt not his lips but the hot, moist tip of his tongue
trace the high curve of her spine. He breathed in softly, the
drawn air floating, cool again over the mark. She gave a soft
gasp as shivers rippled beneath her skin. Again his tongue
laved her, a wet flame licking over the nerves.

Slowly his hands traveled down, unlacing the last fasten-
ings of her dress. He did not remove it but slid his hands
forward, cupping her breasts through the fabric, forefinger
and thumb framing each nipple. They went erect with a
small shock that made her gasp and arch back against him.
He did no more than that for a moment, holding her poised
with anticipation. Then his mouth moved up the side of her
neck. Between half-parted lips, his tongue traced a line of
fire from join of shoulder to edge of ear while his fingers
closed first gently, then harder, pinching her nipples to aching peaks. The teasing went on, precise and relentless, until

her only thought was to strip the silk away so that she could feel that tormenting grip against her skin.

He made a slight sound, as if in answer to her unvoiced craving. Taking a step back, he lifted off the gown and slipped the thin shift underneath down her shoulders. With a rustling whisper it fell to her feet, and Marian stepped free of it. Her skin tingled at the sensation of the stone-cooled air. The weight of her hair shifted against her back, a subtle, unsettling caress. Her breathing had quickened; her nerves felt bowstring taut, though he had barely touched her. The first time, in Paris, there had been carnal curiosity, but not this edged anticipation, this conflict of impulses bidding her to turn and seize Guisbourne, to stand still and trembling, waiting to see what strange magic his next touch wrought.

His tongue sought the hollow of her ear and burrowed delicately. She shivered again, violently, astonished by her own response. The single caress reverberated through her body. She felt it where he had touched her nipples and where he had not, in her moistening sex. Feeling her shudder, he began stroking her, soothing and arousing with the same smooth motion. His hands, strong and sure with their swordsman's calluses, traveled up the length of her arms, testing the archer's muscles with an appreciative touch. Moving over her shoulders, his warm palms descended her back, following the flow of waist and hips, then shaped the curve of her buttocks.

"Just watching you walk across a room stirs me. You move like a queen," he said. The slow drift of his hands, the music of his voice praised the form of her body. She heard the twist of his smile as he added, "Queen of the Amazons—regal and insolent."

Guy drew her against him once more, a tantalizing presence unseen but for his eerily flickering shadow. His brocade pressed the length of her bare back, luxurious and soft, the fabric seductive and maddening as her own fine silk had been. She knew he wanted it so and let him torment her, his touch building the lust to touch him in return. His hands cupped her breasts again, fingertips toying with her aching nipples. She pressed her breasts forward, and the soft strok-ing grew slowly harder. The almost pain of his touch did not hurt, and when he did suddenly pinch harder, even that sharper sensation sent a sweet rush to her sex. He mur-mured to her, the coaxing surety of his voice shimmering in the wake of his provocative touch. Sliding down, his hands explored the fan of her ribs, smoothed over the flat plane of her belly. His palm drifted over her loins, lightly skimming the thick floss of hair, a faint brush like wind stirring grass, so that the waiting flesh tingled. Then his hand pressed over the mound, curving to fit her, his fingertips caressing her nether lips. A single finger slipped between the tender folds, discovering her wetness. Unerringly his fingertip found the sensitive bud, stroking over and over until her knees melted with the fire his touch spun through her.

Kneeling, he laid her on the thin cover of feather bed-ding, the surface beneath hard but smooth. Resting her head on a folded corner of the bedding, he grazed his lips over hers once more and then stood back, looking down at her— a demon of this dark, deep place, with fathomless eyes. His leather cloak flared like dark wings as he stripped off his clothes. The glimmering candle flames licked his revealed body with tongues of light, scarlet and gold, and Marian reveled in this new beauty. Tall though he was, Guisbourne possessed a compact grace, the dense muscle of arms and torso showing the swordsman, the delineation of thighs and calves the horseman. The darkness of his chest hair was like streaming smoke against the pale olive gold of his skin. From the wilder thatch at his groin his cock surged up with a ruddy flush. The sight of him sent a jolt through her nerves, and she started to rise, reaching out eagerly to claim him.

"No," he murmured, stepping back. "You are already far too stirring." She suspected it was control over her he wished, as much as control over himself. But she had in-vited this and, if only for the moment, did as he bade her.

Marian lay back, watching him avidly as he knelt beside her, then closing her eyes as he leaned over to kiss her again. This time the kiss was slow and voluptuous, his tongue sliding between the tender inner flesh of her lips and hard surface of her teeth, then thrusting through to search all the intimate territories of her mouth. Still, he deliberately withheld himself, keeping the kiss their only contact, its eroticism intensified by her knowledge of his nakedness. The image of him blazed beneath her closed eyelids, and the as-yet-unknown impression of his skin burned along her own. She had only to raise her hand to touch him, but she accepted his withholding and its challenge. Lying still and taut, she let the anticipation tighten, filled with a craving for the mysterious, unbearable depths of this desire. His mouth left hers, and she felt him lean back. Opening her eyes she met his gaze, aflame with understanding.

He bent over her again, his touch singular as before, his mouth closing on each nipple in turn—lips, tongue, teeth tormenting them. He licked where his hands had traveled, the softness of her breast, the arch of ribs and curve of abdomen. His tongue dipped in to tease her navel as his hands swept down hip and flank, then up the pliant inner thigh to frame the mound of her sex.

"So fair." His whisper echoed in the hollows of stone.

Hot amid the cool cavern air, his fingers combed through the pale triangle of hair. They slid down to trace the parting of her lips. He bent forward, kissing their softness, then delved between them, tasting her moist flesh, the hotter moistness of his tongue a delicious shock threading her nerves with icy fire. The movement of his tongue was leisurely, merciless, a slow, deliberate exploration of her secret inner folds. The touch of his beard was a silken bristle against her thighs, and Marian felt the subtle pressure urging her thighs farther apart, and she opened herself to him. She thought herself utterly exposed . . . till his fingers opened the swollen lips and the faint coolness of the air licked over the wet, tender skin. His tongue licked after it, ceaseless and questing, searching out her responses, finding the bright points of sensation that lay hidden beneath the surface. His tongue tip chose the sensitive bud, flicking over it with flagrant delicacy, then with deliberate, purposeful torture.

Filled with ferocity and melting fire, she pressed herself closer, seeking the salacious caress, moaning with each hot wet stroke of his tongue. His hands caught her hips as they lifted. She felt his teeth claim the tight bud, a sweet sharpness enclosing that aching tenderness. She moaned, and his teeth tightened. The exquisite edge of pain scalded, then flared to brighter, hotter pleasure that rushed toward a piercing ecstasy. She felt as if her heart were pinned there, beating hotly beneath the flicker of his tongue. Raising her hips higher still, she pressed her sex against his devouring mouth, his ravishing tongue, then cried out when they abandoned her.

Seething in a fury of need, Marian opened her eyes expecting to see Guisbourne's provocative mockery, but his eyes scorched with flames of pure lust. His rampant cock thrust from his hips, thick yet graceful in its insolent curve, the flushed shaft wound with darker veins. "Touch me now," he whispered, and hissed when she seized the hot, hard length of him.

Gripping his shoulder, she pulled his body hard against her own, embracing the dark flames that Guisbourne stirred and burning bright in that darkness. His cock surged as her hand closed tighter around it, and her own sex throbbed in response, needing to encompass him. Her mouth found his, fusing hungrily. She drew him down on top of her, opening her legs wider as she guided him to the entrance of her body.

He lanced into her in a single swift movement, piercing her to the core. Marian gasped at the invasion, her eyes opening wide. He looked into them, savoring every nuance of her response, the eyes of a demon lover avid to possess her with pleasure, to annihilate and be annihilated by it. She wrapped herself around him, plunging into a rising tide of sensation, struggling to achieve the crest and the nadir, struggling to forget all else in the rage of need. Riptides of fire swept her, fiercer than any emotion she had known before, more savage, more fearful than combat with an enemy because she had no armor, no defense against this adversary who assailed her with the unknown darkness of her own depths. She sank her teeth into his shoulder and tasted his blood, bright and metallic on her tongue. Culmination struck her in fiery shock waves, blinding surges pulsing from the deepest center of her. Guy gave a wild cry and thrust, his tormented need one with hers. Marian felt the leashed power in him give way. He stared down at her, his eyes wide and luminous as the hot, vivid bursts of his seed spilled forth, his visage transformed, lust and amazement a single molten emotion. She cried out with him as another obliterating wave of flame swept over her, drowning her in a bright black inferno.

. . . Guisbourne lifted himself from where he lay atop her. He moaned to her as he withdrew, his incoherence tribute in itself. She answered with a low murmur of praise and satiation. Lying beside his, her body throbbed with the vibrant relaxation of fulfillment. She lay half dazed for a few moments, watching him stroke her, his strong hands moving with aimless yet evocative tenderness. The candle-light flickered over his body, gilding his skin so that he gleamed like a pagan idol.

Her mind began to clear, moving out of the warm golden haze that enveloped it. She felt the questions that had led her into Guisbourne's arms bestir themselves, demanding chill appraisal. But she did not want to answer them, not yet. Marian closed her eyes, drifting in the haze a moment more. Reality would ice this fire soon enough. Then she felt Guy's hands cease their haphazard caresses in favor of others far more purposeful. She opened her eyes to meet his challenging gaze, and a new wave of fire swept her. Pulling Guy to her, she wrapped herself around him, hungry for the oblivion of darkness that burned so brightly.

12 "What if King Richard—" Bogo began.

Guy stilled him with a quick gesture, one that might seem no more than an ambivalent hand hovering over the chess pieces. "Young lovers," he murmured. "Just entering the garden."

There was no reason for Bogo to restrain his curiosity, and he glanced over his shoulder at the young knight and lady strolling the pathways. "A bit chagrined to find us here and no doubt wishing our checkered war would yield this rose-petaled bower to love," he commented, flourishing his hands at the lavish blooms surrounding them.

"No doubt, but we shall hold fast." Deliberately Guy leaned back, eyeing the couple with an expression of bemused condescension. He trusted his regard would irk them sufficiently for a quick retreat. After a brief stroll, sniffing the rosebushes and casting covert, frustrated glances in their direction, the young lovers murmured together and departed from the garden.

"What if King Richard wins?" Bogo resumed quietly. "If you are too much to the forefront of Prince John's forces, you will never recoup his trust. Prince John is perhaps overconfident."

The tone of Bogo's voice told Guy the jongleur had no doubts that he had pondered the question.

"Perhaps," Guy echoed without the clarification Bogo obviously desired. He smiled, toying with a knight for a moment, before moving the castle instead. His play had been highly aggressive. His strategy was daring, and bold play was needed to distract from its hidden flaw. He needed to keep his attack strong and Bogo's attention fixed on the right side of the board. "Standing behind the Sheriff is therefore a good place to be until John wins."

"You are still visible. More so as time goes by."

"I have some influence with Longchamp," Guy said, from which Bogo might well surmise he had passed on enough information about Nottingham politics to retain some value. "Power bases shift endlessly. If King Richard triumphs and reinstates Longchamp, I can likely regain a foothold."

"Longchamp's taxes served Richard well, if England poorly," Bogo commented.

Guy nodded. "He is clever, and he adores the King, who may consider those sufficient reasons to reinstate Longchamp, despite how much he is detested here. But Lion Heart cares little what those here think. England gives him kingship, but it is Aquitaine and Anjou where his heart lives."

"If King Richard returns but chooses to lavish his presence elsewhere, that may itself make England a more open playing field for power."

Bogo had linked his future to Guy's. He wanted some sense of its shape, some reassurance that a place was planned for him within the various forms it might take. He wanted, fiercely, a chance to shape it for himself.

Guy continued to study the chessboard, though he had already decided on his move. How strange, he thought, to be building an alliance, perhaps what might eventually be friendship with this man. If nothing more, the dwarf could certainly become a valued steward in time. While Guy's approach was carefully calculated, he acknowledged a curious affinity with the jongleur. Bogo was reaching out, as Guy had once reached, to create a bond. It was not Guisbourne's nature to confide. He had trusted only two men in his life. One had deserved it, the other not.

To use the jongleur to best advantage, he should build upon the dwarf's need. Guy judged it best never to lie to this man if it could be avoided. Bogo was astute, and respect had been his price. A high price, in its way. Greedy the dwarf might be, but he would not accept false coin. Hungry as the man's pride was, it was prickling sensitive too. Guy knew, as surely as he knew himself, that a betrayal would be avenged.

No lies then . . . but a delicate peeling of the layers of truth would be an acceptable, an expected stratagem. There were things he was not yet ready to reveal—and best if Bogo thought each revelation earned by progressive degrees of trust. Guy smiled to himself. That true enough. Well, he could choose both the pace and the confidences. Now was the time for one. It was the wealth Bogo would most value. Although this level of the game was to do only with the Plantagenets, Guy would give the jongleur a double-sided coin, a personal revelation on one side, which would show the necessities of his strategies on the other. He met the dwarf's eyes and said candidly, "I do better to play to John's ambitions. Even with Longchamp's aid, I could never rise high in the ranks of the Lion Heart's faithful."

"No?" A shaggy eyebrow lifted. "Why not?"

"We had an altercation once, over a boy. The future King's vanity was injured."

Bogo looked at him, startled. "I did not know you had the taste."

"I don't, especially, which made the contention all the more ludicrous." Guy made a small, dismissive gesture. "It's a pleasure I've sampled occasionally but never sought. It is women who make my lance rise of its own accord. The boy would have had to coax it, but I was willing to be coaxed."

Bogo smirked, then asked, "When and where?"

"A full decade past, in Paris. I came late to a debauched banquet. The host was renowned for his food, his wine, and the entertainment he provided. Given the hour, most of the women were already busy; the ones remaining did not attract me. I waited, wondering if a more appealing one might soon be finished. Then this boy arrived, not a whore but some merchant's son whose looks had brought him noble company. He was extraordinary, with dark curls and eyes like a wounded doe's. Quite as exquisite as any woman. He had a talent for offering a woman's softness in his manner, without making a mockery of it. He presented an illusion of tender innocence that hinted at luscious corruption.''

"Quite fetching," Bogo remarked with a tinge of acid.

Guy smiled sardonically. "I did no more than note all this, a glance appreciative of the nuances of beauty, but the boy approached me. I was willing to be coaxed, as I said. What I did not know was that King Richard, still a princeling, had glimpsed this prize the previous night. He returned with hopes of claiming it. The boy and I had found a comfortable corner, though he had barely commenced his coaxing before the Prince arrived. He set himself at once to seduce the boy's attention. His power presumed the right; his vanity could not comprehend refusal. He's a handsome man, but he sees himself God's knight, radiant and irresistible. Less aware than he should have been about the monumental prize being offered, the boy decided, quite foolishly, to cling to me.''

"You are far handsomer than the King."

Guy raised an ironic brow. "It may have been no more than a taste for dark hair and eyes, rather than ruddy gold. Or that Richard was brazen drunk already. Or that the boy obviously relished the brewing conflict.

"Whatever the reason, the situation was idiotic. Richard wanted the boy. The boy wanted me. I did not want the confrontation, however much it pleased my own vanity to be chosen above Richard. But there was no graceful way to relinquish the reluctant morsel to the royal lion's slavering jaws. Already the boy would be my leavings if I departed. But a battle prize, that might salve the Prince's wounded pride somewhat. I could see a fight looming, and I could not afford a seeming cowardice in the face of his belligerence. The Lion Heart would forgive a lack of valor least of all. Yet fighting him was likely to breed a worse enmity than mere jealousy. He would hate me if I bested him, despise me if he knew I let myself lose, and he was drunk enough he might kill me if he won. By now others had gathered, half of them urging the fight, half trying to forestall it.''

Guy paused, remembering. Bogo captured a pawn and tapped his hand with it. ''You have created enough suspense.''

''Too much, perhaps, for the finale,'' Guy said deprecatingly. ''The beautiful boy . . . tittered. He was excited at being fought over, our lust, our anger toys for his amusement. Suddenly Prince Richard saw he was making a fool of himself. He turned and stalked out. Which left me with the boy, sulky now that he was deprived of his excitement. I was seething and would almost have abandoned him myself. But he set himself to turn my fire to him. I swived him rather brutally for the trouble he had caused, but he had a taste for that as well.''

Guy met Bogo's eyes. The dwarf shrugged. He had no pity to spare, especially where none was likely needed.

Guy continued. ''Richard has resented me ever since. He would accept a defeat in tournament with good grace, but not such a petty injury to his fleshy shaft. He would not be fool enough to punish me, nor has he stood in my way. He might reward my courage in battle or accept my bribes. Lion Heart took enough of those to finance his crusade. Because of that incident there is a line drawn between us that I will never pass. But few will, and that is yet another reason to favor his brother. The King keeps his counselors at a distance. Even Longchamp has limited effect upon him. Lion Heart rules, and expects others to adore and obey.'' Guy paused and went on. ''He would value my brains and valor at their true worth more than John yet be less inclined to use them.''

''You do not seem as concerned as you might with the outcome so uncertain. If the King returns, he is as like as not to strip you of your Nottingham lands.''

Guy smiled and spread his hands, a gesture accepting fate. But his eyes met and held with the dwarf's once more, their questions and evasions a provocative dance.

Then, as had happened the evening when Bogo made his offer to spy, one of Sir Godfrey's guards came to summon the dwarf to the Sheriff's bed. Bogo's face looked strained, and Guy imagined that John's visit had urged the Sheriff to new heights or depths of abasement. This guard seemed flustered. A simple man, for whom tupping the serving girls was the pinnacle of pleasure. That his master actively desired such a creature dismayed and disgusted him, and he shuffled, embarrassed, as he asked Bogo to accompany him. With a malicious smile the jongleur began to banter with the guard, tossing out a barrage of questions both explicit and oblique that served to embarrass and confuse the man further. Sir Guy hoped the guard could hide his feelings better before Godfrey of Crowle, or the man would be standing duty over the stinking garderobe.

At last gathering his will, Bogo stood. Grinning at Guy, he tipped over his knight. "It is early yet to surrender the King." With a bawdy gesture from his groin, Bogo suggested the guard lead the way out.

Guy contemplated the departing dwarf, wondering if Bogo's warped body might twist into the far reaches of his soul. Wounded deeply enough, Bogo might enjoy betraying the thing he longed for most, defiling it to free himself of hope itself. Guy was inclined to look for the worst motives, yet he knew that was a trap that could blind him as easily as undue trust. Bogo had been good to his word. Guy carefully saw the dwarf neither less nor more often than before, and only for the chess games that they had always played in the past. While they played, Bogo told him what bits and pieces the Sheriff had let slip. Sir Godfrey had not let Guy see the extent of his annoyance over Marian's rescue. The Sheriff had known of the abduction, though whether the knowledge came from Sir Ranulf or Lady Alix, Bogo had not discovered. After giving his consent to Marian's abduction, the Sheriff had been forced to support Guy's assumption of the role of her protector. Certainly his best move with Sir Ranulf dead, but it rankled nonetheless when Guy had forced his turnabout. But Marian was safe now; those who might risk her grandfather's wrath at a distance for a chance of the northern alliance would not also risk the combined wrath of Sir Godfrey and himself so near to hand. Marian was safe, unless Guy himself decided to try the same tactic—and he had far less dangerous methods he could employ. Still it would be better to wait till either John or Richard was secure on the throne before he made the choice of a wife.

Marian Montrose still seemed an unlikely choice, but seldom had a woman so intrigued him. Alix had amused his lust, but otherwise he found her almost entirely troublesome. A submissive but competent wife was acceptable, a clever partner desirable. Married to Alix, he would have to fear for his life as well. He did not want the hairs on the back of his neck prickling when he entered his own household. Challenge was one thing; threat another.

And Marian was a challenge, with her intriguing combination of directness and reserve. Her coolness held fire, bright ice burning within. Few women had so aroused him. Memory suddenly deluged him. He felt the thick spill of her hair over his hands . . . the small, tender breasts thrusting their hardened points into his palms . . . the taste of the slick salt sweetness of her flesh against his tongue. He remembered the almost shocking power of her muscles when she embraced him, the tight grip of her arms and legs about his back, the fierce heat of her sheath as he speared her.

He subdued the images and ignored the throbbing in his groin. Guy coolly considered the match with Marian Montrose again. Passion was not sufficient reason to wed a woman dowered with no more than a single hall. But if he was correct about her worth, if her grandfather could offer him sufficient land and sufficient influence, the match became not only tempting but plausible. It would be a better marriage for him if Richard remained King, since the connection would increase, indirectly, his power with the elder Plantagenet. Still, he doubted Richard would let him rise as far as his ambitions, no matter his connections. Conversely, if King Richard stripped John's followers, and Guy was counted among them, he might seem a far less attractive match himself, and his suit for Norford's granddaughter refused. Musing, he wondered if Marian would like the French court. While she did not employ the convoluted graces in style there, he thought her manners obviously refined. Yet he sensed that she preferred the relative wildness of England to France. There was an animation in her features when she spoke of her family's land. Although he had sent assorted tidbits to Longchamp, he knew he strained credulity to present himself as an ally now. Still, if it seemed Prince John was doomed to failure, a few judicious pieces of information might be enough to turn the situation back to his advantage. And a marriage into the Norford family might well assure it. Power in England under Richard. There was still the possibility for scope there. Richard cared little for England, might well leave others to develop the field. But he was likely to beggar the country with his lust for glory in the Holy Land.

Guy idly shifted the black knight forward, then back as he mulled his other options. His association with Geoffrey Plantagenet had left him a foothold with Prince John, one increased by his alliance with the Sheriff. His current position was strong, and he would continue to play the game here. But with each new encounter the plan of becoming a shaping force in the life of Henry's youngest son became not less possible but far less appealing. The Prince himself had announced he had no particular interest in intelligence for its own sake. Presented with a clever plan, he would value its worth only by its success or failure rather than weigh the value of the wit that could devise it. No liege would accept endless mistakes, but he should be able to tell the difference between bad ideas and bad luck.

Since the Prince lacked discernment, Guy wished he were even weaker—weak enough to submit his will to another. One other. That would be control worth the struggle to achieve. But John's favor went to whoever oiled him the best at the moment, and he enjoyed playing the power suitors off against one another. John might be weak, but he was wily too, wriggling from the grip of one flatterer to the next, sucking up the juicy tidbits they offered, then sliding free. Guy knew he could play the flatterer, but he wanted his own worth judged by the skill of his mind rather than the skill of his tongue. As it was, the manipulations that Guy could use to direct and control Prince John could be practiced by anyone. Guy's best-laid plans might be swept aside by someone more adept at fawning, someone whose words could lick and tickle all the sweet places that hungered for endless fondling. It would be a tedious business, pandering to Prince John's needs while balancing the necessities of power, shaping the strategies of the future for England.

But if he took only a single step back in his ambitions, the game with John as England's king became attractive once more. If Guy coddled John no more than it took to control Nottinghamshire, that might be power enough to fulfill him. To rule here was a prize within his grasp. If he and Sir Godfrey achieved success in their ploys against Richard, they would win John's favor. A timely removal of Godfrey would make Guy the most likely successor as Sheriff. Godfrey had to die. His needs were too warped, his obsession too dangerous, for Guy to continue the alliance. Sooner or later the Sheriff would feed the wrong victim to his lust. If available diversions such as Bogo began to pale, who knew what he might do to achieve satisfaction? He had already tormented, even maimed servants for his pleasure. Few left his dungeons alive. If Guy allowed the Sheriff to live, he himself would become more and more tainted in others' minds with the man's perversities. Guisbourne wanted to be feared but not despised.

But for the moment Godfrey of Crowle was a benefit. He was a stepping-stone to power, and a shield as well. Guy acknowledged that, also for the moment, he was himself more useful than threatening to the Sheriff. Still, Guisbourne knew he must take care that the Sheriff did not suddenly turn on him. He hoped that Bogo might pick up any disproportionate sense of apprehension on Godfrey's part. He did not want to wake to find himself skewered.

Guisbourne knew how murder opened new roads. He knew too how it closed them. He had always killed with discretion and vigilance. Like most men, he had tasted bloodlust in battle. But he prided himself that he'd never been drunk on the power of death, as Godfrey could be, as he feared Alix might become. Yet he had savored revenge with every atom of his being and, in doing so, closed a road before he saw its ending. The savor of revenge had come at a price—albeit the full cost was unknown and ever would be. Brooding, Guy stared at the board, no longer seeing the patterns and pieces. He could not help wondering if he had let Geoffrey Plantagenet live, would he now have the power in Brittany that he was trying to build here? Perhaps he would now be plotting with Geoffrey rather than John to keep his brother the King locked in durance.

How strange, Guy thought, spinning the black king between his fingers. *So much of my life has taken shape above such boards as these.* It was over chess that he had met Geoffrey Plantagenet, had bound himself as vassal. The Count of Brittany had seemed the perfect liege to Guy, friend rather than master. Beyond friend, for Geoffrey had told Guy that he was more a brother to him than those of his own flesh. Searching for the magic, elusive touch of Destiny, Guy had believed in that kindred spark. Geoffrey Plantagenet had been smarter, craftier than either Richard or John. He knew good counsel and did not need the truth honeyed with flattery, though he had a genius for spinning sweet lies to entrap others—a genius and a weakness. Their minds were compatible yet different enough to feed ideas and complement action. Geoffrey had a greater gift than Guy for manipulating men, Guy more skill at strategic thinking. For five years they worked together, scheming and laughing in delight at their schemes. Together they had arranged the alliances and plotted the battles that had enlarged the borders of Brittany. Guy had land and castle again, with more promised to follow.

But it seemed that Brittany was all Geoffrey would ever possess. Though Guy dreamed, and knew Geoffrey dreamed as well, other ambitions seemed farfetched. Young Henry, the King's rebellious namesake, was first in line for the throne, Richard next. Only John followed after Geoffrey. Then for a moment the world opened. Word came that the eldest brother was dead and Lion Heart the heir. Geoffrey was one life away from the throne of England. Richard might easily die. Geoffrey had valor, but not the Lion Heart's reckless surety, his headlong pride. Many things might happen, and if Richard died, Geoffrey would be King. Even now, next in line, he should gain in power. The addition of Anjou to his holdings would give him twice the power he now possessed. When King Henry summoned his sons to Angers, to redistribute the Plantagenet empire, Geoffrey and Guy rode eagerly to the parley. But the shifting power base gave Geoffrey nothing. The old eagle, ever greedy to control his rapacious fledglings, had proceeded to duplicate the mistakes with his living heir that had driven the dead one into revolt. Lavishing the trappings of power on England's new heir, he sought to strip away its substance. He told Richard he should cede the county of Poitou and the dukedom of Aquitaine not to Geoffrey but to young John Lackland. England gave Richard the title of King, but Aquitaine and Poitou were more beloved and far wealthier domains. Richard procrastinated, equivocated, then fled Angers and refused his father's command with open defiance. And so the stage was set for the next rebellion.

Guisbourne still did not understand why Geoffrey was less favored than the other sons. None of them had either King Henry's brilliance or the Queen's. But Guy had wondered if Geoffrey's parents loved him least because he was most like them, devious and cool—without the hot fires that warmed both sire and dam. But Prince John had neither cool wit nor passion's fire, and King Henry doted on him. Even if Richard died, Henry might well try to force his favorite onto the throne against the natural succession. Geoffrey had returned to Brittany steeped in bitterness.

After the fiasco of Angers Guy thought it all the more important to solidify his power in Brittany. Geoffrey had

promised him a certain castle, an important link to building
Guy's power. Like his father before him, the Count of Brittany thought to tease his courtiers with promises of riches.
He liked to toss out scraps and bones and smile as the
others snapped and snarled over them. Guy had known this,
of course, but had thought himself exempt—too important
to be trifled with. He had known Geoffrey doted on deceit
and guile and let himself be charmed, as so many others had
been, by a golden-tongued Plantagenet. Although the promise of the castle had been implicit rather than explicit, it had
been implied more than once. Landless when he entered
Geoffrey's service, Guy now possessed a small but growing
domain. Still, he needed more lands to support his position.
Guy began to woo the woman he must wed to achieve his
aims. Worse, he began to let himself care for her. Marguerite would have been a brilliant match, clever as well as
beautiful. He had informed Geoffrey when his negotiations
were well developed, casually enough, for he had never
doubted Geoffrey's word. The Count of Brittany told him,
in tones of faint surprise and reproach, that the lands must
go to another. He said that the property was too important
to be squandered.

Squandered. Wisely Guy had not lost his temper. Filled
with seething fury, he had pretended not only to concede, as
he must, but to agree. He said he could see the wisdom of
the decision, for of course he knew the reasons behind it.
Geoffrey, already vassal to King Philip, wanted to
strengthen that bond. If the French King put pressure upon
Henry, the ripe plum of Anjou might yet be squeezed from
the old King's grasp and fall to Geoffrey. To achieve that
end, the Count set himself to curry favor with King Philip
by gifting his courtiers. Geoffrey had immediately granted
Guy some conciliatory prize of smaller worth and promised
greater things to follow . . . soon. Promises or no, Geoffrey presumed Guisbourne would remain with him and take
what was to be had. After all, his vassal had no better options. So Guy had stood back and let the negotiations for his
betrothal collapse. The Count of Brittany had given the

lands, and Marguerite, to another—a puling Parisian pup who had no need or appreciation for either. With them went the last of Guy's faith in Geoffrey Plantagenet, and his belief that he himself would one day control a small empire in Brittany. Already Geoffrey's friendship with King Philip seemed more important than his own, and Philip's courtiers, men of higher birth and greater wealth, were maneuvering to cut Guy out of the inner circle, while Geoffrey smiled and made perfunctory gestures of reassurance and more empty promises. Geoffrey knew Guy was angry, of course, but not the venomous depths of his rage.

Seldom in his life had Guy given his loyalty, but he had given it to Geoffrey—and been betrayed. Geoffrey had treated him like a fool and so proved himself one as well. If only Geoffrey had not relished the betrayal, Guy would not have killed him. Sometimes, looking back, he wondered if Geoffrey might well have cared but still loved deception more than friendship. Then, enveloped in a smothering black cloud of hatred, Guy had vowed revenge and taken it. When Geoffrey ensconced himself in Paris, Guy followed, playing the faithful vassal to the last. There the young Count of Brittany followed swiftly on the heels of his eldest brother, tumbling into the grave. Shaking his head mournfully, the physic pronounced him dead of a surfeit of eels. Geoffrey had always been gluttonous when eels were served. There was no speculation of murder. All the guests who had eaten the tainted flesh were ill, including Guy himself—ill but not fatally so. Guy was willing to endure a night of twisted guts to deflect suspicion. He had tampered with the plate of eels, but it was Geoffrey's wine goblet that held the lethal poison.

That was eight years ago. After that betrayal Guy decided never to commit himself to one man as he had to Geoffrey. Spinning the white knight between his fingers, Guy frowned, cautioning himself again to be wary of Bogo. Then he shook his head slightly. Wariness was all very well; equating two such different personalities simply another mistake. Unless the dwarf's life was threatened, he had no reason to betray Guy. And if things were that desperate, his position here would be already lost. But if Guy's schemes in England did not bear the richest fruit, he did not doubt that the jongleur would be pleased with the possibility of making his home in France. Bogo knew as much as he needed to know for now. Finally he would know all. Rare as honor was, it did exist, and Guy thought the dwarf would honor his trust, so long as Guy honored his.

Trust. Honor. True rarities. Priceless in their way. There was little worth their price, though there were some cases where he might be persuaded to pay it, though he did not expect to risk being deceived. Early he had learned other values. Survival above all, and if survival could not be had, then vengeance. And if destiny, that whore, showed her favor, then perhaps both could be had. Guy stared at the chessboard as dark currents of memory spun him round, a whirlpool of hatred, revenge, and betrayal circling and pulling him down into the past.

As a child he did not understand why his father did not love him. From the first moment he could remember Guillaume of Guisbourne had loomed, dark and menacing, a violent storm ever about to break upon him. Trapped in a net of hunger, anger, and fear, he sought his father's love and approval desperately, wondering why he could not attain it. He was a better rider than any boy his age, and learned his fighting skills with ease. His mother taught him chess, and he gloried that he could beat anyone in his father's castle. He struggled to attain excellence, for anything less was met with blows or scathing derision. But when he did achieve excellence, his success was greeted with cold contempt.

When he was twelve, his father beat him, mercilessly, for some gesture of defiance, a sarcastic edge learned too well from his mother, then beat her too when she tried to intervene. The welts festered, and Guy thought he might die of the fever. But he did not die. He healed slowly, and as he lay recuperating, his mother came and played chess with him. It was then she told him the truth, in whispers, as they moved the pieces on the board. Guillaume of Guisbourne was not his father. Guy was another man's son. Guisbourne would protect his name but loathed the child of his unfaithful wife.

Guy had begged his mother to give him the name of his true father, but she would not say. "He is dead," she told him. "You need not be ashamed. He was better born than your father, a better man in all ways."

But how could Guy believe her? He did see in the fire kindled in her eyes, hear in the passion in her voice that she loved the man still. First he thought his father must be alive, for her love to shine so strongly. Then he thought the man must be dead, for the glow to be so untarnished. "What difference does it make now?" he asked. "Tell me."

"Guillaume would start a feud. His pride would not bear it. He has never been certain, but he suspects his own brother, dead in battle before you were born. It is better so. He was always jealous of his brother and accused me of taking him to my bed. I confessed a lie since the man was beyond harm. Sometimes now he beats me saying that it is a lie, because he cannot decide if it is worse believing that you are still his blood, or better. He beats me and tells me it is this man, or that other, that he has feared or envied. But he has never guessed the truth. Your true father was younger than I, and untested, young enough that Guillaume would never conceive of him as a rival, though he had both valor and tenderness. I have loved no one but your father and broke my vows only for him, for love. But Guisbourne would paint me the Whore of Babylon that he could beat me the harder."

A bastard. Guy remembered even now the vivid complex of emotions that were born with the knowledge. The discovery was humiliating, and with it came a dark wave of anger at his mother. It crashed over him . . . and swept by. In its wake came bright swells of relief, gratitude, and liberating hate. He felt released, free at last to loathe the man who had loathed him. But who was his real father? Guy begged her to tell him. His will was fierce even then, and he swore he would never reveal the name. But she refused to name him.

"You must take care. Guisbourne must not see even that you know he is not your father. He would beat you more savagely than he does now. He would beat the name from you, if he ever suspected you knew it. When you are older, stronger, then I will tell you."

But within the year she had died delivering a dead babe. He was the only child, the others all stillborn or miscarried. Guy was sole heir to Guisbourne's castle and his lands. He heeded his mother's words and never let Guillaume suspect he knew the truth. Hating Guillaume, he had taken a perverse joy in the secret.

After she was entombed, Guy asked to have one token of his mother. He knew already what he wanted, one of the rings taken from her dead hands. Sometimes when she spoke to him of his father, she had touched it. No more than a nervous gesture, perhaps, but he wanted it to believe it came from him. It was a curious ring. In poor light the stone seemed a sullen agate, dark brown, faintly mottled, set in twists of gold filigree. But held to sunlight or candlelight, it revealed itself a black opal glimmering with shifting layers of violet and deep blue, scarlet and amber. Knowing Guillaume well, Guy snatched up a handsome ruby brooch and asked if he might have it for remembrance. "Your memories are not worth so much," Guillaume said, and took it from him. Next Guy reached for a pearl, his hand hovering, then lifting, acknowledging it too fine. He did the same thing, more hesitantly, with a small emerald, starting to pick it up and withdrawing when the older man frowned. Then, tentatively, he took the opal. "This?" he asked, in discouraged tones. Guillaume took it too. Quelling panic, Guy lowered his eyes, hunting among the other jewels, fingering another ring, a faceted topaz, shifting it to catch the light. His supposed father tried the opal, but it was a woman's ring, too small for even his little finger. Guy still feared he would keep it for spite. He closed his fingers tightly about the larger topaz and let a small smile curl about the corners of his lips, the one that people said matched his mother's. "Not that," Guillaume snapped, tossing down the opal and prying the topaz from his hand. Guy tried to look sulky as he relinquished the one ring and clasped the coveted prize in the other. When old Guisbourne left, taking the jewel box with him, Guy slipped on the ring. It fitted his hand, but the filigree was too feminine. He decided he would wear it on a chain about his neck instead. When he was a man full grown, he would have another setting made and wear the ring.

He mourned his mother, but fear followed fast on the heels of grief. Not even a month passed before Guillaume of Guisbourne began to look about him for a new wife, for new lands, new heirs. One evening at supper Guy glanced up to see Guillaume staring at him. There was a hot flame of hate in his eyes, a flame that suddenly went cold. In that instant Guy saw his death born in Guillaume's eyes. What had been no more than a wish became a will to murder. It was no more than a flicker, that hot, bright flame freezing to something cold and still; then Guillaume's gaze dropped, and he smiled to himself. After that Guy watched every step, every command, planning how to run away. But he had little time to plan, for soon after Guillaume gave him as hostage to his liege.

Bertran of Anjou had once been powerful. But he had no sons or grandsons left to carry on his line. He stood alone against a powerful alliance of greedy vassals. They had forced a conflict over a single disputed bit of land, hoping to steal them all. So far Bertran had prevailed, an old lion fighting off the pack of slavering jackals. After the last battle he had demanded hostages from all who had rebelled against him, in surety for the truce while he regrouped his forces. And Guillaume of Guisbourne had handed him the prize of his firstborn son and heir.

Guy knew instantly that Guillaume meant him to die and felt a mortal fear consume his heart. Bertran would think him a precious hostage, but he was worse than worthless. Guillaume had no intention of letting his dead wife's bastard inherit his lands. Instead he would deliberately violate the truce, and Bertran of Anjou would hang his supposed son from the ramparts in retribution while Guisbourne exulted. Then Guillaume would marry again and beget sons of his own flesh.

Full of false reassurance, Guillaume escorted him to Bertran's castle. Already two corpses dangled, rotting, from the walls. But Guillaume had been careless. Guy had overheard him planning with two of Bertran's other vassals, men who planned, as he did, to sacrifice their hostages for the chance of seizing the disputed castle, already weakened and ill supported. That accomplished, they would lay siege to Bertran's own fortress. Guy knew the day, the number of men, the plan of attack. He was given a tower room. From it he could see his father ride away. Immediately Guy demanded to see Bertran. Guy would not say why, and at first the guard ignored him, telling him his lord was too busy to be importuned by a boy. But Guy was Guillaume of Guisbourne's heir, and at last the guard went to speak to Bertran and came back to fetch him.

"What I have to say is for your ears only."

The guards searched him again and bound his hands in front of him. Then, at Bertran's gesture, they left the room. The old man sat alone at his chessboard. Guy reached out with his bound hands and flicked a pawn with his fingernail. "I am less than that," he said, and told him all he knew of Guillaume's strategy.

The old man listened intently, but when Guy was done, he glowered. "You think to save your life by betraying your father into my hands?"

Guy remembered the bodies hanging from the ramparts. He felt a dark maw open and swallow him. It seemed he hung there already, rotting, the birds plucking the flesh from his face, his eyes from their sockets. His voice sounded hollow and distant as he answered. "Yes, I bargain for my life. But I think you will probably kill me anyway, for an example. You have nothing to gain by letting me live."

"And if I give you my word?"

"Then, if I live, I will know you are a man who honors it."

Bertran's voice was hard. "Perhaps you lay some other trap. You were to tell me all this, lure me into taking my men to one place, while my vassals attack at another. The alternate route is far more dangerous. If I take my men around, I will likely lose twice as many. Perhaps if I send knights to defend the lesser holding, I will be attacked here instead. Do not think that if your father attempts to break in here, your life will be saved."

Guy lifted his head and met the old man's eyes. He had no other hope now except to drag Guillaume of Guisbourne with him into the grave. "Everything I have told you is true. Guisbourne is not my father. He will have my death; then perhaps he will attack you here. I am no lamb to go meekly to the slaughter. He is my enemy, and yours." He told Bertran everything then, trusting him with his mother's honor. Bertran must believe Guy had a reason to revenge himself on Guisbourne.

When he was done with the tale, Bertran rose and held his face to the light . . . to study his honesty, Guy thought. But what the old man said was, "You have his eyes."

Guy frowned. Guillaume of Guisbourne's eyes were muddy brown, their color, their shape different from his own.

"That gold is rare," Bertran said. "My wife had eyes that color, and my youngest son's a brown touched with such brightness. Andre died in the Holy Land, years ago. He went there, against my will, not long after your mother married. I had refused to let him wed her. She was older than he by five years, and her dowry was small. I thought, after he had gone, that I should have let him wed her."

"The ring," Guy whispered, "on the chain about my neck." Bertran's fingers brushed the chain, drawing it free of his tunic. Guy felt chills run up and down his spine as

Destiny drew all the mangled threads of his life together and laid them in this man's hand.

"Yes," Bertran whispered, his face transfigured by the same awe that gripped Guy. "It was my wife's ring. Her father brought it back from the crusades and gave it to her. She gave it to Andre on her deathbed."

And Bertran of Anjou had embraced him.

So Guy had saved his own life and avenged himself on the man who would have destroyed him. Guillaume of Guisbourne died in the rebellion against his liege, and Guy inherited his lands. And if Bertran could not acknowledge him, still Guy was his heir in everything but name. For five years Guy had believed his life had form and purpose . . . until rebellion tore it asunder. His grandfather, and Guy with him, chose the wrong side in the ongoing battles between King Henry and Queen Eleanor. In the chaos that followed, his grandfather died, and all his estates were stripped from Guy. He was scarce seventeen and had nothing but his armor and his sword. His mother's ring he traded for a horse. A solitary knight, he set out to win what wealth and honor were to be had at the tourneys. He had strength and skill enough to make some future for himself. He strove, yet the sands shifted endlessly beneath his feet, and nothing he planned took shape. And then one night he had played chess with Geoffrey Plantagenet. . . .

Guy smiled bitterly, back in the present once again, yet another chessboard, another game before him. If Destiny existed, then it was a whore. He would make his own. And to do so, he must play many games at once, not stake all he had on one.

Deliberately he set the pieces in order for his continuing match with Bogo. Then, on a whim, reached out and made the dwarf's next move for him. The most obvious one, and the best, Guy thought. It would be amusing to see if Bogo took it—or chose another, determined to avoid a trap that did not exist.

13 A knock sounded at the door. Marian opened it to reveal a slender youth leaning on a crutch. Peripherally Marian was aware of his right leg, ending in a stump at the knee, but kept her gaze on the elfin face. Cobb, the pigeon master's son, had auburn hair and dark, tilting eyes. His fine features were accented by a pointed chin and slanting cheekbones. A patch of freckles spattered the bridge of his nose. Greeting her, the youth ducked his head in a gesture of humility, but when he raised it, the large brown eyes met hers. The tender-lipped boyish fragility was belied by those eyes, still and cold in their center. Deeper, in the heart of the cold, a bright dot of flame burned. She held his gaze. They understood each other wordlessly, this boy and she.

Cobb gestured with the silk he held over his arm. "I have something for you, Lady Marian," he said. As she took the gown, she felt him slip a narrow strip of vellum into her hand beneath its folds.

"Come in and I will give you money to take to your mother."

"I must be quick, lady," he warned. His voice was cool enough, and the bright cold glint in his eyes was anticipation, not trepidation.

"Oh, this will not take me long," she remarked easily, gesturing him inside.

Cobb maneuvered his way through the door. As soon as it closed, Marian handed the narrowly folded message to Agatha, then hunted in her chest for ink, quill, and vellum.

Agatha took the message to the window and examined it for any telltale signs, a hair wound about it, a bit of wax securing the folds.

"The Sheriff talks of exchanging birds with other allies, but so far it is only the Prince. Sometimes my father is instructed to seal the ends of messages we send, but not always," Cobb told them, "and we've never received one with anything visible."

"You're right," Agatha said to him, though not till she had finished her own perusal. She handed the message back as Marian laid out her things atop the flat chest and drew up a stool. "Nothing I can see. But the light's waning."

The sun was lowering, the light in the room muted and golden. "We'll look at it by candle too," Marian said to Cobb, making him as much a part of the proceedings as she could. Lighting a fine taper, she scrutinized the vellum again under its flame before unfolding it deftly, hunting for the same tiny hidden traps but finding none. She held the revealed letters over the flame, searching for hidden writing. Again nothing but what was apparent. Smoothing the note as little as possible, she briefly surveyed the code, then set herself to duplicate it on her own vellum. There was a single line with the letters run together, leaving no space between words. The shorter the message, the more difficult to untangle the code, she mused, and if too short, perhaps not possible at all. The simple text gave her something to work with. Not easy, but perhaps enough, with the advantage of knowing the coder. It read:

AGBOXVSWYUFLTZFUHBADHEDNFBGBLQBLGOFGMWGM

As Marian worked, Agatha talked softly to the youth, asking questions about his family and receiving answers in monosyllables. *He does not need to be distracted*, Marian thought. She could feel the boy's eyes on her and knew he wished that he had her skill, that he could be one step closer to his revenge. Agatha was right to gain more knowledge of his family. Who knew what might prove useful?

Marian copied the last character, refolded the note carefully, and handed it back to the youth. When Cobb had tucked it safely out of sight, she gave him a purse with enough silver to pay for this gown and another. She did it with no display. The money would be appreciated, no doubt, but it was not for the money that he did this. Marian knew from their brief greeting at the door that the boy would give his life to destroy the Sheriff. Only torture or threat to his family would cause him to betray them. But she could still enrich his revenge with silver.

As she opened the door, Marian said. "Tell your mother I am pleased with the gown, Cobb. The work is worthy of a Queen." There was no one in the hall to overhear, and the words would never be taken for anything other than praise, but the boy savored both the acknowledgment and the taste of intrigue and gave her a small conspiratorial smile, the small flame flaring in his eyes. She smiled back and said, "I do not know what I want sewn next. But come by in a day or two, and I will have chosen another length of cloth for your mother."

Cobb's eyes gleamed with triumph. "Thank you, my lady. I will," he said, bowing to her as best he could on his crutch, then moving more swiftly than she would have expected down the hall.

Closing the door behind him, Marian sat down and began to study the code by the candle flame. Agatha embroidered for a few moments in the waning daylight, then laid her embroidery aside and sat quietly watching the sunset. Marian admired her unobtrusive presence and imperturbable patience. Unexpectedly she found herself wishing for Alan and his subtle playing. She would never have imagined preferring music to silence while she worked so, but the troubadour possessed a gift, strumming tangles of thought, the very currents of the air, along with strings of his lute, and soothing tension into serenity. Then thoughts of Alan and Agatha's proximity faded from her mind as she immersed herself in solving the riddle of the code. Knowing Sir Stephen's name, she hunted its pattern among the letters. The first few decryptions she tried were unsuccessful,

and she was fairly certain it was not there. Abandoning that
search, she set herself on another path, and a third, twisting
the arrangement of the groupings, hunting for a fragment
that made sense. Then inspiration struck. She laughed softly
to herself as she watched the letters fall into place. One
word leapt out, and quickly she had deciphered the rest.
"His mother's son," Marian murmured.

Her voice was barely audible, but Agatha responded instantly. "You've found it?"

Alight with victory, Marian turned to face her companion. "It's a little twist of Eleanor's favorite code. I think
Prince John must have devised this backwards deviation
himself and thought it very clever."

Agatha's lips curled in amusement. "Show me."

Marian laid out the vellum with the intercepted cipher.
Beneath it she had written a repeating phrase and below that
stood the very message.

AGBOXVSWYUFLTZFUHBADHEDNFBGBLQBLGOFGMWGM

NHOJECNIRPNHOJECNIRPNHOJECNIRPNHOJECNIRP

MYMESSENGERDEPARTSINTWODAYSSTANDREADYNOW

"Can you read the second line?" she asked Agatha.

Agatha looked at it a moment, then exclaimed, "Why
yes, it's 'Prince John,' backwards, over and over again. The
same ten letters."

"Yes," Marian confirmed, " 'Prince John,' backwards.
That is the key." She paused and spelled it aloud,
" 'NHOJECNIRP.' The first letter of the original message
is M. The first letter of the key is N. M is the thirteenth letter
of the alphabet, and N is the fourteenth."

"I see it," Agatha interrupted. "Add them together and
you get the coded letter A. The result is greater than twenty-
six, so you go back to the start of the alphabet. It all springs
forth, but how did you guess the key?"

"Eleanor has used versions of her name as a key, so I
thought to try the same with her son. I noticed that the code
had many letters toward the end of the alphabet, so it

seemed the key should be mostly comprised of letters in the middle of the alphabet.''

''Backwards?'' Agatha inquired.

''Perhaps the Prince confuses backwards with devious,'' Marian replied. ''The instruction seems simple enough, with no hint of double meaning. Prince John is sending his messenger—presumably Sir Stephen—two days hence. That's time enough to get the message to Robin Hood. He can expect to find the knight on the road to Nottingham the day after that at the earliest.''

Agatha nodded. ''The messenger will be in no hurry. The ransom's still being collected.''

''I'll go to the hall tomorrow. Ralph can take a message to Robin to be on the watch for Sir Stephen and to hold him, if possible. Friar Tuck has the ability to copy the message.'' Then she frowned. ''But if he cannot decode it, I doubt he has the skill to detect any hidden traps.''

''This note had none,'' Agatha said, but the dubious tone judged the communication rather than Marian's concern. ''It is better to be cautious. It may be only the smaller messages they are so careless with. Perhaps you can train the Friar what to look for. You cannot be riding the south road every day till they net this fish. That's dangerous as well.''

Taking both candle and vellum to the window ledge, she held the scrap over the flame. Once it caught fire, she encouraged it to burn as quickly as possible. The code she held in her mind. ''I will teach him the tricks or tell him to wait till I can open that message myself.''

Agatha nodded agreement.

''I will go to the encampment tomorrow.'' Marian spoke decisively, but she was aware of her own rising turmoil. ''Please go tell Sir Ralph to be ready to ride early in the morning.''

Agatha nodded briskly and set off on her errand. Left alone, Marian prowled the room restlessly. The Sheriff had sent Guy on some mission he would not name, and she had not seen him since their first encounter except to bid a brief farewell. Nor had she returned to Robin Hood's encampment. She did not know if it was wisdom or cowardice that caused her reluctance to face him, but she wanted to be neither fool nor coward. She told herself there was no need to seek him out, and she had waited deliberately for Alan to come back from London with Queen Eleanor's token. Marian would have to take it to Robin Hood, but the formality of the errand would shield her—at least as long as she wished to be shielded.

Contradictory impulses clashed within her. Part of her wanted to delay the confrontation. Part of her wanted to test the strength of her attraction to Robin now that she had experienced the power, the intensity of Guisbourne's embrace. Part of her simply wanted to see him again. She was vividly aware that beneath her immediate reluctance anticipation simmered. It was impossible to ignore the thrumming of her pulse. Marian wondered what she feared most—that the intensity of Robin's effect on her would not have lessened or that it would. *Better if it has,* she thought. *Guisbourne is challenge enough for me.* They were far more suited temperamentally, and she should spend her efforts finding a way to entice him to change his allegiance.

She paused, staring out the window at the purple dusk. The outlaw had bargained his services for the pardon, and Marian was sure the Queen would vouchsafe it. There need be nothing else between the outlaw and herself than the fulfillment of that compact. But the quivering tension in her body contradicted such facile pronouncements.

■■■■■■

Sitting astride her mount, Marian watched Robin walk along the edge of the clearing toward her. From the distance he seemed at first insubstantial, moving through the shifting patterns of bright and shade beneath the trees, his hair suddenly golden in a shaft of sun. Marian felt the most curious sensation as he approached, perceiving the forest taking shape around him, within him, as though strands of light and shadow, of rustling breeze and woodland scent, of flowing stream and sap all converged here in him.

And then he was standing in front of her, vivid and entirely substantial. His strange green eyes met hers, their unwavering gaze intense and questioning. Open, as if she could step into his heart. It was too complete. His question demanded too much in answer. She had expected some wariness, some restraint, and his directness caused her every barrier to snap into place. His eyes flashed, whether in pain or anger she was not sure. In the same instant the openness vanished, and the luminosity of his presence became a bright, glittering armor, a tightly linked chain mail that deflected everything that touched it. The elemental spirit was gone, and in his place was the knight with politic skill, courteous, commanding, adamant. The facade was so polished that for a moment the woods faded and she might have been in some fine castle, with guards and courtiers standing sentry about their encounter. Then the vigilant knight smiled casually, mockingly and became Robin Hood, outlaw leader, scornful, brash, and wary as a fox.

His gaze flicked briefly over her hands; then he extended one of his own to help her dismount. Placing her gloved hand in his bare one, Marian was glad she had not yet removed her leather gauntlets, and suspected he was just as grateful to avoid the touch of skin on skin as she was.

Leading her as if in a formal dance, he guided her smoothly across the clearing to the great oak, talking of a greater one in Sherwood, displaying her presence to his men. Used to his play, his followers smiled, but the mockery in his elaborate grace set her teeth on edge, as he settled her beneath the spreading branches. With a false smile she set herself to play the forest Queen once more. His gaze called her liar, when she had every right to subdue her attraction to him. She watched him narrowly. How many women, noble or common, looked for an amorous adventure with the outlaw, that he would presume her his for the taking?

Then John Little appeared, and Robin beckoned him to

join them. When he turned to face her, Robin was formal and courteous again, with no derisive note. Little John folded his long limbs up against the oak, and Marian began to tell them about Cobb and what the note had said of the messenger's arrival. She was about to ask where Friar Tuck was, but Robin spoke first, his face intent. "We must catch this messenger. I've a good watch already, but I'll add a man or two."

"We cannot ignore the opportunity, but we must not give this exchange undue weight," Marian warned him. "By now Alan a Dale has told Eleanor of the Sheriff's strategy. This message could easily be based on false information she has deliberately let slip to Prince John's spies. Or it may have been gathered before she learned what he intends. We do not know how close Prince John's spy or spies may be to her."

"They'll likely change the route again anyway," Little John said.

"Yes, but we cannot know anything for certain, however likely it is," Robin insisted. "And even if the route is changed, if we capture other information, this message may well be used as a reference. I think it's important we have it." His eyes met hers at intervals as they spoke, the gaze holding just long enough for acknowledgment. Their green was river dark now, and his thoughts unreadable for all the candor of his speech.

"I agree we must seize it if we can," Marian said firmly.

Little John glanced up, tracking the sun. "Will should be here already, to let us know who's passed so far today."

Robin said, "We had word of a knight who stayed at the inn last night. But he had no withered arm."

"Too soon," Marian said. She was relieved to feel some of her tension lessen as they talked through their plans. "Even tomorrow would be early. You'd best not rob him or anyone else, or our quarry may take some elaborate route around."

"It would have to be very dark and twisty to escape our eyes," Little John scoffed.

"We can hope an obviously withered arm marks our messenger, but we cannot depend on its being Sir Stephen. Prince John might have found reason to send someone else," Robin said.

"True enough." Marian agreed. "Any man who travels to Nottingham the next few days should be suspect."

"If he gets as far as the inn, we can track him from there," Robin said, then glancing across the clearing, he added, "Here's Will, just come off watch."

Marian looked over to where the young Saxon was dismounting. Robin waved him over, and he came and sat beside them, nodding to Marian deferentially before turning to Robin. "Something's odd. You know the knight who stayed at the inn last night? He set out this morning, but we've not seen him since."

"Who did pass your lookout?"

"A farmer and his wife with baskets of cabbages. Another, an old man alone, with a cart full of young pigs—he was at the inn last night as well. Henry Stout and his son went by early morning. They were the only ones I knew. And there was a peddler too."

"He could be trying to take the long way round," Little John said. "But then we'd have spotted him by now. Maybe he stopped at a cottage to tend his horse . . . or is sitting drunk under a tree."

"Will?" Robin was frowning, rubbing a knuckle against his lips. "Of the ones you didn't recognize, who passed you at the time the knight should have?"

Will frowned. "Most went by this morning. The man with the pigs midafternoon, more when I'd expect. The peddler came a little while after, right before Much took my place, not an hour ago."

"You notice anything odd about any of them?"

Will furrowed his brow, which made him look younger still. "Oh . . . the pig farmer had a fine piece of horse-flesh pulling his cart."

"Good enough to be a knight's mount?"

Little John gave a raspy chuckle. "Don't tell me you think this knight's up to your sort of tricks."

Robin grinned impudently. "And why not? I never imagined I was the only man in England able to take the wit God granted him and twist it to suit."

"Most knights would not lower their dignity to such a disguise," John mocked. "Even you might balk at a pig farmer, Rob."

"I might surrender my dignity to extremity. Perhaps our farmer is carrying something more valuable than piglets." Little John and Robin nodded in concert; then Robin turned to Marian, arching an eyebrow.

Marian could see the thought plain on his face. "Not money but a message? Prince John's man was to leave today. He could not travel that fast."

Robin leaned forward, eyes gleaming, a half smile on his lips. "You said their method of communication seemed careless. Interception would not matter if the hunter went looking for his quarry days after it had passed."

"You're right," she said, angry at herself. "Prince John seems such a fool, and the message so simple, I did not consider a time switch part of the code as well."

Robin sketched a bow, the half smile broadening in a quicksilver flash. Then his smile faded. "You're frowning, Will. Where's the flaw?"

"Well, I saw the man with the pigs, Robin. He was an old man, gray-bearded and wizened. I suppose a man devious enough to think up the switch might be able to play the part, but not as well as this."

"Few would," Little John agreed, with a slow wink at Robin.

"When they closed in on King Richard in Vienna, he tried to escape capture by disguising as kitchen scullion. He lacked the proper air of humility and could not grovel convincingly," Robin said, full of scornful amusement. "His kingly pride entrapped him."

"His height might have had a bit to do with it too," Marian added wryly. "The King is hardly inconspicuous."

Will grinned at her, then turned back to Robin. "Well, this graybeard was humble enough. He was a scrawny twig of a man, Rob. No knight, now or ever. Nor cleric either, I'd wager."

"What about the peddler?"

"Oh, he was a big man. He rode slumped, but I could see him mayhap just playing the part. His horse was just an old nag, though, no knight's mount."

"He'd have been too obvious on his own mount, so he changed horses with the pig farmer. That's how I would have done it," Robin said. "Easy enough for him to trade back again once he's reached Nottingham."

To Marian it seemed fanciful but possible. "They did both spend the night at the inn."

Seeing her skepticism, Robin said, "The knight may well have gotten the idea then. We do not know that he's Prince John's man, but I'll not let this peddler pass unchallenged."

"There's a good chance you're right," Marian acknowledged. The ploy was less fanciful, after all, than the painted stag's head she had used to lure Simon of Vitry. She nodded her agreement. "I would not want the man to slip by us."

With one easy, graceful movement, Robin rose to his feet. "We can cut through the woods to the northwest and get to the last ambush site before him."

"I want to come with you," Marian said, standing as well. "I may even be able to identify him if he is one of Prince John's men."

There was no need, of course. Unless there was something that made this guess obviously wrong, Robin would bring the man back here and search his belongings. But the excitement was infectious, and she wanted suddenly to be part of the adventure.

"Not dressed like that," Robin said, but it was not refusal, only consideration. His eyes met hers again, and now they were alight with shared camaraderie. Another smile flashed. "Will, you're closest in size. Can you lend Lady Marian some hunting leathers?"

"And something to cover her hair," Little John added, not countermanding Robin's order but obviously disapproving. "And you will be keeping well back, won't you, Lady Marian?"

Robin regarded her, his expression suddenly dubious.

"I promise I will follow your orders and not put myself in the forefront," Marian told him, caught between annoyance and laughter. She'd not had time or privacy enough to train as often as she'd wish and was eager for action, however small, to warm her muscles. She looked at Little John, who was still frowning. "The risk that I'll be recognized is small."

The tall man still looked uncomfortable, and she felt a quick sharp prick of anger. She had thought herself accepted among them. Then she quieted it, for she had never proved herself, beyond some swift knife work. What she had was the reputation of an Amazon, but reputation only. "It's not as if we're off to do battle," she said tartly. "And I've the skill for that."

"I warrant you have, Lady Marian," Little John said seriously. "But it's hard not to want to protect you nonetheless, for your own sake, as well as ours."

Robin, when she glanced at him, only looked eager to share the sport. And perhaps, she considered, to see her in Will's leggings.

Will ran to fetch his extra leathers, and Little John took Marian to the hut where other clothing and supplies were stored. Will returned as John was pointing out what chest held what, and they left her alone to change. Stripping quickly, she found a soft linen shirt to wear under the tunic and leggings Will had brought. The leathers were beautifully tanned, supple and strong. She doubted Robin could steal enough to clothe his men, and this was not an amateur's work. She'd seen no leatherwork this good in Nottingham, and thought these leathers were likely from Lincoln. Further proof of Robin's connections. He had found sources for whatever he needed that the woods did not supply, or passersby yield to him. She wondered just how wide his net was stretched, to draw in both information and goods. *The wider the better*, she thought with a smile.

There was a hood and gorget to top the tunic, dagged edges fringing her shoulders. These last she slipped on after braiding her hair and binding it up with a thong. She'd worn a plain, simple shoe for riding that blended unobtrusively with the male garb. Marian quickly stretched, pleased with the ease of movement. For a moment she wished fiercely that she were home and could dress as she liked, with no one who'd lift a brow in disapproval. She girded on her own knives; her hunting bow and quiver were still fastened to her horse's saddle.

Marian rode beside Robin as they made their way northwest from the camp. The woodlands were patched with meadows thick with purple loosestrife and yellow toadflax, eyebright and devil's bit. Magpie moths spun through the air. Here and there a quiet whistle greeted them, or a man stepped forth from the trees to wave. Marian was impressed at how far to the sides and front Robin could post watchers yet keep all in constant contact. It would be impossible for an armed force to surprise him in this land.

They rode to a narrow clearing behind a thick stand of oaks. The tall trees embraced a patch of road. The horses were tethered just out of sight, and most of the men dispersed into bushes. Robin ordered the saddle stripped from the oldest of their mounts, a chestnut, and directed several men up into the trees, on either side of the road. Then he climbed, swift and agile, up into a great oak with a large branch that hung over a side of the road. Marian watched him ascend, the muscles of calves and thighs bunching and smoothing as he climbed. He turned and gestured her back toward the horses. Unable to resist, she clambered up the tree after him. Robin watched, and she could see that he stopped himself just short of admonishing her to keep farther back. He restrained himself to pointing out a more secluded branch above, where she could easily conceal herself. Marian accepted the selection with a cool smile and climbed higher, sliding a little way out onto a shaded branch. As she settled into her perch, a rope was tied high in a tree opposite and the free end was carried back beneath where Robin stood. The man holding the end of the rope flipped it, and a wave passed up through the rope, snapping it up to where Robin grasped it and secured it next to him.

Then they talked quietly among themselves until a stir went around as a young man came back from his outpost to report that the pig farmer and family were approaching. Robin pointed to Will Scarlett, designating him to deal with the pig farmer. Will waved his hat in salute. He spoke to one of the men, then bade all to draw back. Crossing his arms, he stood alone in the road, waiting.

When the farmer came around the last turn and saw Will standing there, he immediately looked all around. It was unclear to Marian if he was able to see any of the others, but she saw that he assumed they were there and drew up the wagon well short of Will, watching him intently.

"Are you a robber, then," the farmer asked Will petulantly, "standing in my way?" He could not disguise the quaver in his voice.

"Oh, not today, sir. Today I'm a horse trader, and I do most admire that charger you have pulling your wagon."

"I have no need to trade him," the farmer said, casting looks to either side as if he might try to bolt. "None at all."

Will smiled all the while, running his hand over the flank of the horse and saying, "This is a creature more suited to riding than pulling. It is too fine by far for such humble work, so I judge you must have him here on a temporary basis only. I have just the horse that would pull your cart in a happier frame of mind. You may have it in trade for this one." He motioned toward the clearing, and four men came forth leading the chestnut. A good enough beast for such service, but no match for the charger.

The farmer grew silent and did not resist as two men loosened the fine charger from the wagon and hitched up the other horse. Will and the other men climbed into the wagon and looked through it, finding nothing of note. When the horses had been switched, Will called for a piglet from the cart. He pointed to a small, plump creature, and one of the men plucked it out. He looked at the farmer and said impishly, "Just to even things a bit. You're doing very well here."

Then Will stood aside, and the farmer drove off, giving him a glare of righteous indignation as he went. It was a thin mask, Marian thought, for very evident relief that no worse had befallen him.

The farmer was long out of sight when another signal informed them of the peddler. Marian slid well back into the shade of the branches. The men also withdrew, and the glade turned quiet. Marian looked to see if Robin was delegating the peddler as well, but it was strikingly clear that he intended to handle that matter personally.

When the peddler came lurching into view on an ancient dapple gray, Marian's first thought was that the pig farmer had done exceeding well, going from that decrepit animal to what Will gave him at just the cost of a piglet. Her second thought was recognition, not Sir Stephen of the withered arm, but Sir Thomas, the most amiable of Prince John's knights. Looking down, she caught Robin staring up at her, his face alight with mischief. She mouthed the knight's name, and he grinned more broadly. Shifting his weight back and forth, the rope easy in his grip, he switched his gaze between her and the approaching peddler, sharing his eagerness with such vivid immediacy that she smiled back at him. Poised to act, he exulted the last moment before launching out. At the final second he reached up through the branches and tweaked her foot, then let out a ferocious yell and sailed out into the air swinging on the rope, still howling wild as a blue-painted Celt.

The peddler snapped alert as Robin swung down toward him, losing the slouch and sitting quite martial and erect in the saddle. Marian saw him instinctively tense and start to jolt his mount to the side, but just as quickly as that instinct came, he controlled it and reined in his weak horse.

Robin swung past the peddler and out to the further point of his arc. The peddler turned in the saddle, observing Robin's course over one shoulder, then twisted about the other way as Robin came swinging back past him on the far side, snatching the peddler's hat while coming past. The peddler went completely still and sat in the saddle without moving as Robin swung about him another full circle, brushing a foot against the horse's rear to slow his momentum. Then Robin came round a last time, caught hold of the peddler's shoulder, and plopped down behind him on the horse to a chorus of cheers from the men coming out from bushes all about.

"You're in luck, peddler," Robin said, clapping the peddler's hat on his own head. "You're to have a fine supper in Sherwood tonight. And it will not cost you much at all."

"I've not much to begin with," the peddler said firmly.

"The first payment on your price is an honest answer. How much is not much?"

Sir Thomas the peddler undid his skinny purse and tossed it over his shoulder to Robin, who caught it and began tossing it with one hand. "Such riches? Why, this is enough to buy you a meal of fine venison in the King's forest."

■■■■■■

Marian rode behind, keeping out of view as they made their way back to the encampment. When they reached the clearing, Much came forward and Robin leaned over to speak to him, then dropped back to ride beside her. "Alan a Dale arrived at the inn while we were away."

"You keep pigeons too?" she asked, wondering how he found out so quickly.

"Arrows are swift in flight," Robin answered with a smile. "We code them with paint. I was keeping watch for Alan in particular."

Marian nodded, impressed again with the intricacy of his network. She said nothing of Alan's errand in London, though surely Robin knew what it was. She hoped fervently that Alan would return with some token of commitment from Eleanor.

"I'll keep Sir Thomas till tomorrow," Robin told her. "A night tied to a tree will serve him well. Tomorrow my men will pluck Alan from the road and bring him here. Prince John's messenger will know him only as another hapless captive. We can release the two men together, peddler and troubadour. Who knows what information Alan a Dale may woo from the man if Sir Thomas sees him as a companion in adversity."

"Excellent. I was going to ask you to hold Sir Thomas, as it was," she answered. "I've got to return to my own hall tonight, preferably with some proof of my hunt, but I wanted to be back at Nottingham Castle before Sir Thomas arrived. Easy enough if I leave in the morning."

"Aye, they'll be arriving all bedraggled for dinner." Robin grinned. "And I will order a brace of hares to be tied to your saddle, to show you've been engaged in honorable pursuits this afternoon."

"Most honorable actually."

"And sufficiently dishonorable for me. I've been robbing less than I should of late, and this tale should keep my reputation lively in Nottingham." Robin smiled, teeth flashing white. "I'll continue to keep watch on the London road, but I plan to move the main force of my men back to Sherwood during the next month. I want to be prepared, and the Sheriff is most likely to try and capture the ransom as it comes down from the north, and I don't want to be adding miles of travel onto the journey when we ride to intervene." Should she need to find him, he told her the rock that marked the first of the sentry lookouts on the way north to Lincoln. "Though like as not, we'll find you if you come searching."

Robin looked into the clearing, where the men were gathered around the prisoner, obviously ready for a bit of rascality. Sir Thomas's packs were already sailing from hand to hand. Robin gestured with his head to a side path. "Go through the trees there to the hut. I'll send Tuck to help you. Except for me, he's our best at finding hidden treasures.''

As she turned her mount onto the path, he gave her a last glance, his gaze curving over the shape of her leather-clad thighs, warmly appreciative yet comradely. "You look to me as if you belong in those clothes."

She felt an unexpected flush of pleasure and answered with mild defiance, "I do."

"That's what I said." He grinned, foxlike, then went to join his men.

After following the side trail back to the hut, Marian dismounted. Once inside, she set up the trestle table to catch the best light and pulled up two benches. She drew the supplies from her own pack, readying her quill and ink on the table. In a few moments there was a timorous knock. She opened the door, and Friar Tuck came in, all shyness and bumbling until she set herself to explaining what hidden traps might be concealed within a message. Then he sat quite still, his eyes sparkling with curiosity.

They were enmeshed in their talk when Robin walked in, grinning, the messenger's tattered clothes in his arms. "He's a bit chill sitting out there in his skin. I'm tempted to let him stay that way." Robin tossed the leather packs the man had with him onto the floor. "As for these, he did not look askance at any save the largest, whether because he could not stop himself or because he wanted to mislead deliberately, I cannot say."

"Since he went to all the trouble of the disguise, I'd guess the glance was to mislead," Marian said.

"I did not want to question him too closely. If he gave way the secret by mistake, I'd not want him to guess I realized its import. I do not even want him to think I'm looking for the message. If we cannot find it on our own, then I'll question him further. He knows we'll be looking through his things." He left them again, and Marian set about searching the garments while Friar Tuck opened the large pack, which held a motley assortment of merchandise, a few soiled ribbons, copper brooches set with pretty stones, a great clump of stick figure dolls bound tightly together. Tuck set them aside and began to examine the pack. Some purses of silk and others of leather, their drawstrings knotted together. Tuck untied them and began to search each purse.

"I can't find anything in his clothes," Marian said after probing for hidden pockets and feeling inch by inch along the seams of the tattered garments. She laid them aside, resisting the urge to hand them to Tuck to double check and so give her a reason to search what he'd gone through. From what she'd seen, he had the concentration and the deftness to ferret out the hiding places. If they found nothing on the first pass, then they would examine each other's work on the second.

Just then Tuck gave a yelp of delight. He'd untied the stick dolls and found another small purse concealed in their center. Upended on his palm, it let spill a half dozen small gems of flashing crimson. "Mother Mary's veil," he murmured reverently. "Rubies."

Looking at them closely, he added with less awe, "Poor quality." He handed them to her, grinning mischievously. "Either that was too easy or he sorely underestimated us."

Marian tossed a couple in the air. "These are what we're supposed to find. Let's look for what's still hidden." Tuck began looking at the construction of the large pack while she emptied the small one. It held the peddler's supper—some wrapped cheese, bread, and a leaky berry tart. Beneath them were a soiled shirt, filthy ripped hose, and a knotted tangle of garters.

"I think he wants us to disregard this one." Marian dumped both the food and the clothing, not bothering to search them. Tuck looked at her, his sly cherubic face alight with curiosity. She explained, "This pack is smaller, but it's better made. The outer leather looks rough, but it has a fine lining."

Reaching inside, Marian began examining it by feel. The front and back panels were soft, and she could detect nothing beneath them. The side panels were one piece with the bottom, narrower and stiffer. There were no obvious lumps, but a thickness of vellum could be concealed within. The bottom felt stiffest of all.

"I've got to open the top edge," Marian said. "Can you stitch it back neatly? I'm far handier with a blade than a needle."

"There's a man here used to be the best tailor in Lincoln. He trades for our leathers and sews them. He'll set it aright."

Marian glanced at her own garb. The quality of the sewing was as good as the fine leather. Reassured, she took her sharpest blade and cut the stitches along the top edge of the seam, creating a small opening.

"Let me see your hands," Tuck said, holding up one of his own plump little ones.

Pressing her palm against his, Marian nodded. "Yours are smaller."

"And even more nimble, I'll warrant."

"The message is at the bottom, I think." She handed over the pack, and watched as the Friar frowned with concentration, set his teeth into his lower lip, and carefully wriggled his hand down inside the lining.

"Ha!" Tuck exclaimed as his hand burrowed to the bottom. "I've got them!"

"Let's see," she whispered fiercely. But it took him another minute to withdraw them. He handed her two sheets, folded together. They were sealed, but there was no other protection, and she had skill with seals. She began to unseal the documents carefully. When she had them open, she spread the documents flat. There was a map and a long coded message with several lines of characters run together as before. Handing the map to Friar Tuck, she said, "Copy this as swiftly as you can."

"I'll not be adding any curlicues," Tuck said, setting himself to copying the map, his hand swift and neat, as the quill scratched over the vellum.

Marian quickly copied the message, checked that she had made no errors, and laid it aside. With the previous solution already in her mind she scanned the lines, but to no avail. She was convinced the coding principle was the same, but the key of "NHOJECNIRP," "Prince John" backwards, did not unlock the secret, even when she started the key not at the first letter of the cipher but at later characters, trying them one by one. The puzzle eluded her, though occasionally a clarity would begin, a word or part of a word would seem to form and then degenerate again into nonsense. She considered that perhaps two keys had been applied, first one, then the second, scrambling the text in a more complex fashion. This difficulty gained Prince John a modicum of respect as she set herself once again to untangling it, but her frustration quickly grew when no meaning emerged. Under most circumstances she preferred a challenge, but she wanted to be back to her hall before nightfall. She still had not unlocked the code when Tuck made a busy buzz of noise to let her know he'd finished. When she looked up he put his quill aside with a little flourish and presented her with the original of the map and his copy. "Plain and simple," he said.

She forced herself to lay aside her own problem and quickly scan the map, searching for errors or omissions. "Perfect," she told the Friar after a minute. "More readable than the original."

"Curlicues can spin your eyeballs in their sockets," Tuck said, beaming with pleasure, then added, "I rather like curlicues."

She refolded the map and message together and carefully began to reseal the documents. The Friar had a surprising gift for silence when necessary, and he sat motionless while she did the delicate work. When she'd finished, she found her satisfaction tainted by the unsolved code that lay waiting. She gave it a baleful glare.

"It's getting late, my lady," Friar Tuck murmured. "No need to do it today. You've got the copy to work from."

He was right, of course, but it rankled.

"I'll bring in the tailor," Tuck said. "If he opens up the

other side of the pack, it will mean more sewing, but I can slide the map back in place more easily.''

Marian spared a moment to consider. Despite his comical demeanor, the Friar was quite useful, but she needed to concentrate. The documents must be replaced, but she did not want two men in here while she worked. ''If the knight is safely bound, your tailor could work out of sight in the other clearing or by the river.'' Marian saw the Friar understood. Wanting him to have something to do, she said, ''Why don't you take the jewels to Robin. We've that success at least.''

''I'll wait a bit, Lady Marian. When we've got the documents back and the pack stitched, then Robin can fling the jewels in the air and the pack at his feet and announce we've discovered his hidden treasure. Should give the knight a bit of joy amid his troubles, to see we've snapped up his bait so easy.'' He grinned at this subterfuge, tucking the map and message inside the pack and refilling the others as well. ''I'll take care he doesn't see me.''

When Tuck had gone, Marian got up and paced restlessly, fighting off irritation as the images of the letters swam in her mind. She did not want to return here tomorrow, and she did not want to chance taking the copied message back with her. Returning well after dark to her own hall after supposedly hunting overlong was no great risk; still, she preferred not to do anything out of the ordinary when something extraordinary was occurring. However, a late return would be worth it if she were sure she could break the code soon. Otherwise it was better to return in a few days' time and finish the work. That was a test of patience she would rather not endure, though she reminded herself the information might well prove worthless.

It will be worthless indeed if you cannot decipher it, she chided herself.

She stared at the copy of the map lying atop the table, looking for it to give leverage on the cipher. It laid out the area to the north of Nottinghamshire, indicating the general shape of the land, its major towns, and the movement of rivers. There were some curiously detailed marks, indicating either very small villages or places in the countryside. But it did not clarify the swarming letters, and Marian concluded that it went the other way around. She would have to clarify the message to comprehend the map.

Marian imagined a succession of new approaches, some quite abstruse, each a language of sorts, each starting to form words, then foundering into an incoherent sea of letters. She found herself growing suspicious of the independent life of these theories because they led further into abstraction and away from her starting point, her knowledge of the man who wrote the message. Perhaps in her earlier attempts, when the first part of the key was not working, she had moved on to try it on another part of the cipher rather than try all the original key to see its full effect. She returned to ''NHOJECNIRP'' and applied it again.

Marian noted just where words began to emerge, then collapsed. She marked the place, then moved on, applying the ''NHOJECNIRP'' key fruitlessly until again it started to yield something. Suddenly she noticed that the words seemed to clarify at the same interval, at fourteen letters apart, not ten as in ''NHOJECNIRP.'' Then she saw that this happened exactly at ''NHOJ.''

She forced her eyes away from the vellum. They wanted to steal glances back, so she shut them and thought it through. The first key created streaks of meaning, so this key must share the word *John*, but be fourteen characters long. She pondered what was the point of it all in the mind of Prince John. What did he imagine? What did he want? And then it was there. She knew the key, and she wanted to open her eyes and read with it, but she forced herself to keep them shut a little longer as she mentally counted off the letters again. Just fourteen. Marian kept her eyes shut a moment further, savoring the realization. Then she said, ''John will be King,'' opened her eyes and slowly read it all, word by word, thinking that by knowing the arrogance of the key she could help undo its intent.

The message gave the last major cities where the ransom

would be collected and the date of departure the guarded caravan would make for London. It laid out the route that the guards would be expected to take and the side route that they planned secretly to follow. By comparing the text with the odd details of the map, she was able to trace both routes and understand the map that the Sheriff would be examining the second day hence.

Any of that might or might not be useful, depending on later changes. But the message also named some of Prince John's new supporters in the north who could be called upon to join in the raid or help plan it. Essential information for the Queen. At the last the Sheriff was given the exact tally to date of the ransom gathered—no doubt a warning to Sir Godfrey to skim this rich cream lightly.

"Ah," Marian murmured, "but who knows what might spill and be lost in the violence of such a deed . . . and who lap up the golden flow?" She supposed Prince John would hold the Sheriff accountable for every chalice, every coin, every seed pearl that was recorded before the ransom was seized.

Laying the decoded messages aside, Marian stretched with relief and satisfaction. With a hard ride she could still be back to her hall not much later than she'd planned. She would return to Nottingham in the morning. Except now that she had achieved her objective, she felt reluctant to leave. She smiled wryly, for she could hardly join in the merriment surrounding the prisoner. A swim in the river was also out of the question, Marian thought as she stripped off the gorget and leather tunic, but she would like that as well. Tossing the top down beside her on the bench, she began to undo the breeches, then looked up, startled, as the door swung open. Equally startled, Robin stood in the portal, eyes wide and dark as his gaze swept over her body.

There was no magic in this simple hut, as there had been in the grove. No magic but what sprang to life between them now. The air shimmered with desire, not air at all but some elemental, inescapable web. Fluid, crystalline, burning, it penetrated every ligament, quivered with every breath. Robin's gaze moved over her, tangible as a caress. Even as she yearned for the exquisite explicitness of his skin beneath her palm, her fingers, she felt as if she could stroke with a look, a sigh, a thought, all the slender solid grace of him. As if his own leathers had vanished, she knew the smooth golden planes of his chest with their roseate nipples, the paler silken skin that curved over the angled hipbones, and the dark tangle that framed his arrogant manhood. His answering glance grazed the slope of her shoulders, enfolded the curves of her breasts, then slid down her hollowing belly and licked tenderly at her sex. She felt her own nipples hardening, her sex flowing, under his ardent gaze. That palpable, incorporeal touch returned to her face to brush her lips, before his eyes met hers again, their green transparent as sunlit leaves—the sweet blaze behind them hotter than mortal fires.

He was waiting, she felt it, waiting for her in the doorway, his whole body taut with the question he posed. Reality splintered around her, and for a moment she was in Sir Ranulf's castle. Guisbourne was standing at another door, the air about them thick not with the scent of warm earth and leaves, but cold granite and hot blood. Guy stood unmoving, his dark voice whispering her name. . . .

"Marian," Robin whispered, beckoned, and she returned to the moment, to that green gaze that was so tenderly merciless. Guy's glance had stripped her clothing to touch her skin. Half naked already, Marian felt Robin bare not only skin but her very nerves, flaying her with pleasure, a sensation so acute it bordered on pain. She trembled, the exposure terrifying and exquisite. Now his searching look penetrated deeper still, intimate as flesh, as if he were inside her already, as if she held him vibrant and alive within her core. Mesmerized, she gazed into his eyes, her body melting more with every heartbeat.

No! she thought. She wanted to choose, and the only choice was no. Anything else was surrender so absolute it was annihilation. Summoning her will, she forced herself to turn her back to him, if only to prove to herself that she could.

Robin moved behind her in one swift, almost silent movement. Feeling the warmth of his skin radiating against her own, Marian tensed in mounting anger and excruciating anticipation. She gasped with a fierce jolt of desire as he ran his fingertips down the length of her naked back, sweeping trails of invading fire in their wake. Involuntarily she closed her eyes, arching her back to the touch as every bone glowed molten. Warm, moist, his lips touched her neck, close to the spine. The soft touch struck like lightning, shattering the dark of her mind's eye with bright, clashing images, crazing her nerves with blistering sensation. Robin's lips became Guy's, touching her exactly there. The sun-licked branches of the hut transformed into the dense stone of the candlelit cave. She saw Guy lying naked beside her, his body patterned with flickering flames and veiled shadows. She wanted to reach out and seize him, the clandestine darkness a haven. Then Robin's tongue, hot and moist, licked over her neck, and the vision of him sprawled in abandon on the waterfall rocks captured her once more. He lay there, his body, his face, gilded with sunlight and incandescent rapture. She need only extend her hand to claim him. . . .

Robin's hands glided over her, spinning their shimmering web, enmeshing her body, her soul, in a spell of desire beyond her control. He cupped her breasts, his fingertips barely touching the nipples, and her whole body contracted in a deep pulsation of pleasure that made her moan. Her body glowed, her womb luminous with heat, with light. Another second and she would dissolve entirely—

She whirled on him in a surge of fury. "No!"

"Yes," he whispered.

"No!" she snarled, holding the edge of her control like the edge of a knife blade, denial cutting deep.

His eyes had gone black, their darkness flaring with green flame—a bright burn of rage and hunger—and his hands closed hard on her arms. Even as Marian hissed at the flash of pain, she welcomed this new ferocity, letting the pain spur her surging anger. Her body tightened for battle with a savage exhilaration. Better fight than surrender. But even as she tensed for battle, a sudden wash of shame swept Robin's face, extinguishing the hot flame. Eyes downcast, he lifted his hands, palms out, and stepped back. Visible tremors coursed through his raised arms, and he closed his hands into tight fists. He stood a moment, still trembling, then spun around and stalked from the hut.

Shocked, Marian stared after him. Gasping and panting, she fought to control the cold shivers that coursed over the hot anger. She cursed him silently for stirring her, then for leaving—two betrayals. Reason struggled with frustrated wrath, telling her any outcome wrought from that burst of violent passion would have been a disaster. Yearning blossomed, a traitorous weakness that urged her to follow him, to summon him back.

Cursing herself as well as Robin, Marian stripped off the breeches. She had let her own conflicts jeopardize the venture to which she had committed herself. Slipping into her own shift and gown, she stuffed her pack with the ink, quills, and vellum she had brought and slung it over her shoulder. Still seething, Marian closed her eyes and breathed deeply, muffling the rioting storm within her to a hollow clamor.

She knew now with utter certainty that her encounter with Robin by the waterfall had woven some strange bond of desire between them. The power of her attraction to Guy was unquestionable, but was it enough to supplant what she felt for Robin of Locksley? *It is enough to marry on*, Marian thought with utter calculation. Few felt such fervid desire as she and Guisbourne had shared, and surely Sir Guy was the better ally. More surely still, he would not steal the soul from her body. She wished with sudden urgency that she had succumbed to Guy not in the cave but on the floor of Wolverton's castle. *If only I had let him kiss me*, she thought. Perhaps that blaze of passion would have ignited a fire raging bright enough to blind her to any other. Perhaps then the magic path through the grove would have led her not to Robin but away from him.

She wished now she had never set foot upon it.

Mailing herself within a chill disdain, she went outside. Robin was waiting, standing under the shadows of an oak. He stepped forward to meet her, but her eyes forbade him.

"I would not have tried to force you," he said, his voice rough and cracked. "Only to force you to acknowledge—" He stopped abruptly, his eyes pleading with her.

It was a lie, she thought. At that moment in the hut, his hands gripping her, one would have been no different from the other. So she gave him a cold lie in answer. "There is nothing to acknowledge. Surely you can look elsewhere to satisfy your lust."

She wanted the wound she saw in his eyes. If she could hurt him enough, he would close off this openness that stripped her past any known self.

"Lust, yes. But lust does not satisfy for love," he said quietly, letting the pain cut him deeper, opening more. "I love you."

He did not ask, only admitted, yet she felt again as if he were a well of light, boundless, into which she would plummet and be lost. Marian stood, icy and scornful, until he dropped his gaze. "I've left the documents inside," she said flatly. Turning her head, she narrowed her eyes at the lowering sun. "I must leave. It will soon be night."

He lifted his head abruptly, and she made herself meet his eyes, opaque now, the clear green clouded with the secret he had revealed and then reclaimed. "Yes," he said. "You ride into darkness."

14

Lady Alix pressed her hand to her bodice and leaned across the supper table, her voice oozing sweet malice. "Tell me, Alan . . . while Robin Hood had you bound and trussed, did he ask after the Lady Marian?"

Alan's sprightly narrative faltered, and a flush appeared on his cheeks. Luckily his discomfort need have no meaning other than resentment of Lady Alix's obvious impertinence to his mistress.

Beside him Sir Thomas cocked his head, perplexed and intrigued. "And why should he?" He gave Alan a Dale a puzzled look. Obviously the troubadour had not included that tidbit in his version of their first encounter with the outlaw. Marian wondered just how he had described the meeting to the knight, alternately entertaining him and delicately prying information on their shared trek back to Nottingham. Sir Thomas had been sufficiently amused to keep Alan by his side for supper, saying, "The whelp made me laugh when I was glum."

"The outlaw was quite taken with her, and he has a reputation for gallantry," Lady Alix drawled, making the word faintly obscene, "though Lady Marian thought him quite the brute."

"Lout," Marian said lightly. "Brute was your choice, I believe, Lady Alix."

Dark amber eyes alight with candle flame, Guisbourne's gaze sought Marian's across the supper table. His expression mingled concern and wry amusement, and Marian smiled easily to let him know the concern was unnecessary. She did not want him to think any memory of Robin Hood still distressed her.

Lady Alix caught the exchange of glances and remarked, "You must find it provoking indeed, Lady Marian, to have this outlaw invading your life at every turn."

Silently Marian cursed the woman's spiteful prattling. "I can deal with such disruptions, Lady Alix," she murmured in answer, laying a cool silk of menace under the tranquil surface of her words. Then, letting it glide away, she continued, "It is Alan who needs your sympathy. I was not, after all, involved in this misadventure, and my troubadour escaped unharmed, if poorer."

"He does not appear fretted," Lady Alix remarked tartly.

"My lute is well fretted, but I am smooth and unmarred as a bowl," Alan jested. "Though to keep my purse well rounded, I must be sure to have a song ready for Robin Hood the next time I make a journey. He is certainly everywhere I turn."

"He did not waylay you on your journey to London," the Sheriff snapped.

"If he had, my Lord Sheriff, I would have made certain to compose a song by the time I had returned. Perhaps then he would have plumped my purse instead of cutting it." He mimed the action with an elaborate flourish, his eyes skimming over all the guests, resting on none for more than a second.

Marian eyed Alan consideringly. He was not fretted enough. That the troubadour might enjoy the tale of a dangerous encounter, once he'd safely escaped it, was understandable to all. That he did not feign the encounter as worse than it was did not bother her. Best he play the deception as close to the truth as he could. What did disturb Marian was his seeming nonchalance about Lady Claire. Despite Claire's obvious happiness at his return, the glow that now warmed her features, she looked pale and tense compared with when Alan had left. Tainted by fear, her vibrant energy went still and silent at the sound of her husband's voice, even the sound of his footfall. She moved awkwardly whenever the Sheriff was near, and it was an effort of will for her not to flinch under the most casual gesture of his hand reaching to cover hers.

Marian had not seen Alan's first encounter with Claire today, when the shock of her appearance might have revealed more of his true feelings. When Marian did see him, scant moments later, he had disclosed neither by word nor by gesture any of his previous apprehension concerning the Lady Claire. The only clue that he might still care at all was an artificial brightness glossing over his usual easy warmth. Such a high polish seemed no more than the best court manners to the Sheriff and his entourage, but it glittered falsely to her eyes. She should be relieved that Alan had succeeded in covering his emotions so well. Instead Marian was suspicious. Despite his frivolous demeanor, she did not think Alan's affections trivial. She disliked the idea of his hiding them from her now, however necessary he conceal them from the others. Well, perhaps the only way he could control was to hide what he felt completely. She should feel respect rather than apprehension.

Sir Thomas's hearty laughter broke into her mulling. "Oh, I think Robin Hood captured young Alan solely to give me company on the road to Nottingham."

Watching the troubadour join in the laughter with perfect naturalness, Marian felt a surge of respect. She raised her eyebrows in mock disbelief and took a sip of her wine. How bizarre that Sir Thomas would put forward the exact reason why Robin had plucked Alan from the road. She thought of the fine white silk scarf, embroidered with Eleanor's seal, that the troubadour had brought back with him, skillfully stitched into the lining of his spare doublet. Robin had searched Alan's things, she was sure. Robin could have kept the promised token and spared her the trip to present it. Was he forcing her return or refusing to usurp her authority? It did not matter. He was right either way. She should stand for Eleanor and bestow the scarf on Robin before his men, simply but with some sense of ceremony and honor.

"It was most obliging of him to ensure I had a companion." Sir Thomas went on. "I wish he'd left me the horse as well, sorry swaybacked beast that it was. At least I didn't have to walk here stark naked. The outlaw gave me clothes for my back—and boots. Though it was Alan's songs that kept my feet stepping lightly on the road, else they be far more sore this evening."

Marian saw Lady Alix flash a quick, assessing glance at her and Sir Guy. Then Alix turned toward Sir Thomas, her eyes wide and misty with admiration. She leaned forward, no hand rising to guard the low bodice of her gown, her breasts swelling forward. "You are remarkable, my lord . . . to endure such manhandling with a show not of wrath but of easy mirth. It shows a unique courage."

"Oh, I had a goodly wrath at the time, Lady Alix." Sir Thomas preened a bit at her praise, his eyes dropping to admire the deep cleavage she presented. Alix smiled at him with girlish innocence. "But I escaped in one piece, so it's easy enough to be mirthful now. And in truth Alan's songs on the road made the journey swifter. I might have appeared in a foul temper indeed, with naught but my own bile to sip as I trudged along."

"You have more reason for good spirits than I," Alan complained airily. "You were forced to swallow a supper of fine venison, washed down with the sweetest of stolen wines. I had scarce more than bread and water to fortify me for the road."

"Robin Hood lays a good table—at Prince John's expense. But eventually this outlaw will find himself spitted and roasted." Sir Thomas gave Alan a quick wink. Then, obviously taken with Lady Alix's charms, he leaned across the table and added smugly, "The thief is clever, but not near so clever as he thinks."

Marian sat, a small smile curled into the corners of her mouth, pleased to know Sir Thomas was oblivious of the fact that his documents had been discovered and copied.

She was also pleased to watch him tumbling into the dark
waters of Lady Alix's gaze. Although Alix only wanted to
make Guy jealous and feed her own vanity, the new conquest would keep her occupied for the evening—perhaps
for days. Sir Guy, she noticed, encouraged it skillfully, paying Alix a modicum of brooding attention each time she
flirted with Sir Thomas, provoking her to encourage the
knight's attentions even more. The next time Alix leaned
forward, seducing Sir Thomas in voracious earnest, Guy
sent Marian a quick conspiratorial glance.

Sir Thomas, drowning in honey, begged Alan for a love
song. Lute in hand, Alan set a stool in the midst of the
company and plucked the strings in a delicate evocation of
mood. Then he began to sing, his voice soft yet soaring with
poignant longing.

> *In dreams our winged souls entwine.*
> *There we meet and there embrace.*
> *Love, there I am yours and you are mine*
> *In dreams, if in no other place.*
>
> *Our arms encircle, vine round vine.*
> *Lips brush lips, hands interlace.*
> *In dreams our winged souls entwine.*
> *There we meet and there embrace*

Fretted indeed, Marian thought as she listened to his
chosen song. Yet it was only a courtly lament, imploring
like many others. She saw no suspicious glances, and
Claire's blind eyes were not the only ones welling with tears
as Alan's sweet voice soared with renewed ardor.

> *By day we drink of bitter brine.*
> *At night cares fade without a trace.*
> *Darkness pours down sweet as wine.*
> *At last sleep brings us face-to-face.*
> *In dreams our winged souls entwine.*
> *There we meet and there embrace.*

■ ■ ■ ■ ■ ■

After dinner Guy invited her for a stroll in the rose garden. They were circumspect, for others had the same idea. Marian was relieved that the bower was already occupied, for she might have felt she was spying upon herself sitting there. Instead they wandered along the paths until they were certain they were beyond the others' hearing. Drawing her toward one rose laden wall, Guy lifted her hand to his lips and kissed it—a seeming gentlemanly tribute, though his tongue washed silken against her skin. She shivered, remembering other touches, hotter and more intimate he had given her.

Yet his touch stirred memories of another, and a quiver of cold dismay threaded through the soft heat of pleasure. She shut them from her mind, concentrating on this man who could be ally or deadly foe.

"For the next two days I must discuss plans with the Sheriff and his guest. The day after that, if all goes well, I will be free." He spoke quietly, but his golden eyes were like caressing flames. "Will you meet me again . . . in the cave?"

Marian lowered her gaze, but her hand tightened in his, not wanting him to think it was refusal or false coyness. His fingers tightened lightly in response, as he waited for her answer. She had determined to say something, but what? She was considering this man for her husband. There must be truth offered, even in the midst of deception, to build toward that future, however tenuous it was. Still, Marian knew she would not risk admission with so devious and dangerous a man as Sir Guy unless she were well-nigh certain of his response. Meeting his eyes, she said quietly, "You know my family's allegiance. It will not change."

"Pleasure has allegiance only to itself," Sir Guy murmured, drawing closer. "That is the only allegiance we need have to each other—for now."

"And if I wanted more?" she asked, the boldness followed by a sudden tremor. She had the right to probe so, yet fear blossomed within her that she was doing something irrevocable. What if she won what she sought?

"Do you?" he asked, the amber gaze sharpened, a sudden piercing intentness she forced herself to match. Few would look so deep, and it excited and frightened her to have him move so close.

"I do not know." Honest, at least. And then, because she had determined long since to accept: "But I will meet you in the cave."

Guy nodded, his gaze holding hers. Everything, and nothing, were changed. After all, she had simply agreed to come to him for one more adventure. But the pretense that it were ever only that was gone. His voice deepened, roughened with desire and a touching hesitancy, as he said, "Perhaps then you will discover your answer."

■■■■■■

She dreamed of Guisbourne for three nights, uneasy dreams of searching a subterranean labyrinth, like but far more convoluted than the cavern he had shown her. The first night she spiraled down and down, finding him at last in the candlelit heart of the dark cave. He took her in his arms and kissed her, pressing her close, the candles tumbling around them as he drew her down on the cool stone. She burned for him, her blood bright as flame, and when she looked down and saw the flowing hem of her gown on fire, she did not care. Nor did Guisbourne, who only smiled at her, wrapping his arms around her and pulling her onto him. She mounted him, surging with him while the fire rose higher and higher, consuming them both in an obliterating ecstasy.

The second night she only remembered running through the forest, the streaking sunlight pouring off her like ribbons of water, of flame, its caress a soothing, burning torment she must escape. Afraid, she ran wildly, searching for the safety of the cave. It opened before her, and she saw Guy standing, waiting, in its shadowed mouth. She woke when he caught her in his arms, and the swift footsteps she only then realized were chasing her stopped.

The third night, the night before she was to meet Guisbourne, she dreamed again that she searched through the tunnels of rock, winding deeper and deeper, spiraling down and down until she found the cave. There were candles unlit but smoking, as if he had just been there, but the cave was empty. She felt a tumult of emotion, rage and grief and fear, for if she had arrived only a moment sooner, he would have been there waiting, and she would have been safe in his arms, safe in the dark. As she stood in the empty cave, the rock trembled and shook, then began to collapse around her. She curled in the deepest corner, covering her head with her arms, knowing the sun would pour in and consume her. . . .

Marian started awake to the sound of pounding at the door. She leapt from the bed, her movement causing the tiny light of the tallow dish to dance wildly. Her heart fluttered with the same erratic pulse. Agatha rose also, staring at her with wide, uncertain eyes in the flickering darkness. Slipping her gown on quickly, Marian went to the door and laid an unsteady hand on the bolt. She did not want to lift it, but bellowing back and forth was absurd. After undoing the bolt, she opened the door a small way to see one of the Sheriff's guards, his mailed fist raised. Glowering, he lowered it, and she asked him, coldly, "What do you want?"

"It's the Sheriff that wants you," was the growled answer.

"In the middle of the night?" She spoke with sharp outrage, though there was no question but that she would obey the summons.

"Now." The guard's eyes glittered, and his tone was laden with menace, but that did not mean he knew anything—except it was unlikely he would use such a belligerent tone unless the Sheriff himself was angry. And he had not seized her.

"In a minute," Marian answered, keeping her voice even.

"You'd best hurry," he snapped. She closed the door in his face.

She and Agatha finished dressing quickly and tamed

their disheveled hair as best they could before opening the
door to face the hostile guard again. "Take us to the Sheriff," Marian ordered instantly, seizing what modicum of
control she could. She would have stridden forward if she'd
known whether Sir Godfrey was in the hall or his own
chamber. She was relieved when the guard led the way
down to the hall. But when she walked in, her relief
withered before the Sheriff's ire. His porcine face was
flushed red, and his eyes glittered like shattered ice. Sir Guy
stood behind him, his impeccable control chilling Marian as
much as the Sheriff's searing wrath. There were a few
soldiers and fewer courtiers, but Lady Alix stood to one
side, gloating. Sir Thomas, whose bed she had been warming recently, stood beside her, observing her with unexpected aversion. She was heedless of his reproachful gaze.
Marian had no doubt, seeing her triumph and her malevolence, that it was she who had uncovered whatever crime so
enraged the Sheriff.

Marian reconsidered the possibilities swarming in her
mind. If anyone had searched their belongings, she would
have detected it. Cobb had not been about for days, and
there was no sign of him or his family here. The spyhole
behind the bower could not be linked to her. She could not
fathom Lady Alix's learning of the connection with Robin
and his men, for it was impossible that anyone could have
followed her to his camp without being discovered. That left
one obvious choice.

"Your sniveling troubadour has violated my wife." The
Sheriff seethed. "What do you know of this treachery?
How have you abetted it?"

Guilty already. Yet she was, for she had misjudged the
intensity of the infatuation and Alan's control. Marian drew
herself up and addressed Sir Godfrey with cold hauteur.
Arrogance might anger him, but fear would rouse the most
debased of his instincts. She spoke tersely. "I knew he admired Lady Claire, certainly, yet it is his bread and meat to
pay court to women of rank and flatter them. I am horrified,

as you are, at this breach of trust. I thought he had more sense!"

Marian said the last with such vehemence that she saw the Sheriff believed her. Then, clearly, she saw the will to disbelieve settle onto his features and a rapacious flame shine in his eyes. She thought of what she had heard of his dungeons, and his master torturer, and felt cold fear squeeze her guts, insidious and repellent. She remembered Cobb, taken to the Sheriff's bed, his newly amputated leg a torment, and felt both spirit and body vibrate with rage, with terror. Marian felt a cold sweat break out on her skin. She prayed that nothing showed on her face and was grateful for Agatha's sober countenance. The Sheriff's eyes held hers. An unholy fire smoldered, crackled behind their thin blue ice.

Then Guy stepped forward, murmuring in the Sheriff's ear. Sir Godfrey looked at her the whole time, and she saw the fire flicker and subside. The Sheriff glared at her sullenly. Then the fire reignited—but not for her. The Sheriff's eyes looked inward, contemplating some appalling scene as he said, "The two of them were abetted by Lady Margaret. She will be punished . . ." the Sheriff paused to smile lewdly at her, ". . . along with your troubadour."

Marian shivered, relief and nausea warring within her. Guy's intercession might just have spared her life, but at the horrific price of another woman's pain. Lady Margaret was the most faithful of the ladies-in-waiting who served Claire, and the most dependent, the remnants of her family poor and powerless. She would have no defenders . . . and Alan's behavior was indefensible.

"It is well you've had no part in this," the Sheriff said abruptly. He dismissed her with a wave of her hand.

"Where is Alan a Dale? I would like to see him," Marian dared, keeping her voice firm and reasonable. Guisbourne's eyes flashed a warning at her.

"He will see no one. I have locked him in the darkest part of the dungeon," the Sheriff snarled. Then he met her eyes and smiled. ''And there he is as blind as my lady wife.''

Marian tried not to show the horror she felt at the thought of Alan blinded, his torment already begun, but she could feel her face pale. The Sheriff's phrasing, his glacial, obscene smile, made her think that the darkness was as yet metaphorical. His next words confirmed and stripped that hope. ''Your troubadour pitied her blindness. He shall regret his pity. I will have his eyes, his hands, his voice. I will have every part of him that has insulted me. And then I will have his life.''

Fury at his cruelty flashed through her. Instantly she dropped her gaze and stood, trembling to hold control, wanting to kill him on the spot.

''Take Lady Marian back to her room, and make sure she stays within,'' the Sheriff said smugly. In command of herself once more, she raised her eyes as he gestured to the men who had brought her here. Sir Godfrey must have glimpsed something of her rage, for as they came forward, he gave a snide smile and added, ''Have a care she does not bash your skulls in.''

The guards moved to surround her, and this time Marian did stride out of the room ahead of them, Agatha moving quickly and quietly behind her. The guards hurried their pace, marching them back to the room. Marian bolted the door from within, but it did little to alleviate her sense of impotence. Pacing, she weighed the possibility of a rescue and escape and hissed with fury at the impossible odds. With surprise, with luck, she might kill her way through the men that stood guard between here and the dungeons. But she did not imagine she could then get herself and her companions, much less Lady Claire and Lady Margaret, out alive again. She was bound to serve the Queen, and the possibility of thwarting the capture of the ransom was good—but not worth Alan's life, not to her. But getting all of them killed served no purpose whatsoever. She cursed Alan again for embarking on this foolhardy love affair. Yet, loving Claire, how could he endure to see her trapped, without comfort, in such a heinous marriage? She should have insisted he remain in London, away from temptation and of some use to Eleanor.

Was she any wiser in her entanglements? Her liaison with Sir Guy was dangerous, but not the sort of idiocy that Alan had permitted to happen. Unless, of course, she was discovered as a spy. And Robin—allowing herself to be entangled in his strange snares, that was foolhardy indeed. The risk she took for Eleanor in recruiting him was justified. The risk to herself seemed madness.

Yet at the thought of him she felt a surge of hope. If she could get word to Robin, perhaps he could organize a rescue. She shook her head again. There was not enough time, and the Sheriff's eye would be upon them. They would incriminate whomever they talked to, possibly destroy Robin's network within the castle, for nothing. Rescue from the open fairgrounds was one thing; invading the Sheriff's dungeons another entirely. Robin could not help.

Agatha sat silently, watching her stalk back and forth. Her voice was hoarse as she asked, at last, ''Do you think we can bribe him . . . the torturer?''

''To free them?'' Marian was astounded.

Agatha shook her head. ''To give Alan a quick death.''

Marian glanced at her sharply, but Agatha's face showed no real hope. ''No. We've both heard how much the Sheriff's torturer enjoys his work. He would rather have blood than gold.''

''At least the torturer will not be looking for buried secrets,'' Agatha said. ''They suspect nothing but adultery.''

''We are all in danger. The Sheriff means to hold us here. Not because of suspicion but to luxuriate in the fear and suffering he creates all around him. The torturer will make Alan's agony last as long as he can. Who knows what he will say of his own accord if the pain drives him mad?'' Marian answered grimly.

''Alan can hardly betray us with no voice,'' Agatha said

harshly. "You heard the Sheriff. The torturer is going to cut out his tongue."

"He will do it, but it will be at the last, to create a final despair. I think they will blind him, even castrate him, before they take his voice or his hands."

"You may overrate the torturer's subtlety, though nothing else. They will take his manhood last."

Marian sat down abruptly. Her gaze sought Agatha's, and she asked with grim purpose, "Do you carry any poison? For preference something delayed . . . and painless. If he is to have a quick death, we are the ones to give it."

"No, I haven't," Agatha said, then nodded to the door and the guard outside. "Besides, they would not take you in to see him."

"Perhaps not, but I've heard the Sheriff sometimes exhibits his torturer's handiwork to those he feels will be most impressed. He may take us there simply to horrify us. If I could be ready to seize the chance—"

"Even if they display Alan to you, how could you give him any poison unnoticed?"

"I have only to beg to give him a dipper of water, and slip it in."

"If I were the Sheriff, I would make you drink it too, just as a precaution."

"I could saturate my handkerchief and let it dry. If I could wet it again, and wring it out across his face, whisper for him to drink—"

"Where are we to get this poison? It must look natural, as if his heart gave way. Perhaps there Cobb and his mother might help us."

"We cannot compromise them. It would threaten Robin's network."

"His network is threatened now if Alan talks."

Marian tried to think. "Poison is the best chance. If they realize I have killed him, not only will they be infuriated to be deprived of their victim, but they will look on us with new suspicion for risking so much for a simple troubadour. The Sheriff might well have me put on the rack then, or you, to see if something besides compassion prompted the deed or to punish the defiance of his authority.''

"Or for his pleasure," Agatha said tightly.

Marian nodded. They both had looked into the Sheriff's eyes. His lust could easily drive him to some madness. She was afraid to rely on her grandfather's power and the threat of reprisal to protect her. Whatever her friendship for Alan, there was no point to giving the Sheriff three victims instead of one. Even if Sir Godfrey was sane enough to stay his hand from her, he would think nothing of torturing Agatha in her stead.

She met the other woman's eyes and saw the same knowledge mirrored there, yet she also saw that despite Agatha's arguments, she was willing to take the risk. "They might think no more than that Alan was your lover as well, that you would risk the Sheriff's rage to spare him pain. Some no doubt think so already. And Lady Alix will encourage the rumor to discredit you further.''

"A lover who has deceived me, and I spare him pain?''

Agatha smiled faintly. "Yes, love might well spare him pain. It is certainly as believable as your being a spy who would silence him to spare yourself the implication.''

Marian tried to think of another solution. "You've talked with some of the guards, the servants. Is there no one we can bribe who might get close?''

"Perhaps a guard. . . ." Agatha thought and shook her head. "I know of one or two who might be trusted with some lesser risk, but not this.''

"And guards are likely to betray the asking, to win the Sheriff's favor.''

Agatha raised her head abruptly and asked, "Would Sir Guy do it?''

Marian glanced at her, wondering if her liaison was known. She thought that she had concealed it from Agatha—not the mutual attraction, of course, that was far too obvious, but the tryst itself. She decided it was secret still. Guy's intervention tonight was sufficient to prompt the question. She realized she had put Lady Margaret from her thoughts and shivered again. But Alan, and the mission, were her responsibility. One prisoner might die by chance, but not two. "Sir Guy would have the opportunity more easily than I. But if there were any chance suspicion would fall on him. . . ." Marian shook her head helplessly. "No, he would not. I would have to communicate with him somehow, and that alone would arouse suspicion. He has too much at risk here. He would not betray me for asking, of that I'm sure. But he would think me a fool to risk it." And if there was no hope of it, better he did not think her a fool. Or worse, crystallize suspicion.

Marian sat on the bed beside Agatha. They stared at each other, each hoping the other would offer some other idea. But there were no more. Not wanting to contemplate the horror to come, Marian tried to think of what might be salvaged after. When it was over, when Alan was dead, and they not betrayed, she and Agatha would at least be free to depart unharmed, but then their plotting, and Alan's suffering, would go for naught. She would have Lady Margaret's suffering on her conscience for naught. Perhaps Robin would have enough information to foil the attempt to capture the ransom. He had his own spies within the castle, and would keep close watch on the Sheriff. But he would have a far greater chance of success if she were here to observe, to decode whatever messages they intercepted. But if she stayed, would that not be suspicious in itself? If she were not a spy, would she stay to tend to her holdings after the troubadour who was not her lover had been tortured to death by the Sheriff of Nottingham?

For a moment it was all madness. Once Alan was dead, there would be the will to revenge to sustain her. Marian reached for it now, desperate for its cold steel fury to sustain her, but it eluded her. There was only this helpless sickness. As she sat, waiting, the soft light of dawn stole through the window, the day bringing only the promise of pain and horror.

■■■■■■

Guy sat at the chessboard, twiddling with a pawn, wishing Bogo would reappear. Frowning, Guy tried to concentrate on developing strategies, but the movement of the pieces was snarled in his mind. The game had been interrupted at noon, when the dwarf had been summoned to the dungeon. Guy had returned at intervals since then, ostensibly to study the pieces, and now the sun was setting. Hearing footfalls, he looked up quickly from the chessboard, but it was two of Lady Claire's ladies-in-waiting who entered. Pale, their eyes red from weeping, they stopped abruptly when they saw him, then forced themselves to continue on a brief circuit, smelling a blossom here and there, before making their way back quickly into the castle.

The household had been unusually silent while the Sheriff entertained himself in the dungeon today. They all sensed this event as a turning point. The Sheriff had given way to his worst nature, and it was not likely he would do anything but journey deeper. Even Lady Alix had looked pallid this morning, her victory subdued by the realization that the Sheriff might turn on her. For a moment Guy considered the advantages of that. He could tell Godfrey that Alix had confessed to murdering her husband, declaring it an act of obsessed passion in which he had had no part. Godfrey probably knew Alix was behind it already, so it would be no more than a request to have an obstacle removed from Guy's path. Convenient, but he did not hate Alix enough to wish hideous torture on her. Even if he did, she had enough power to make the request a risk, though not the same sort of risk he had taken last night, stepping to deflect the Sheriff's wrath from falling on Marian. Godfrey had not been beyond reason then, but if Guy had not spoken, revenge and lust might have taken the Sheriff anywhere, as the hapless Lady Margaret was learning even now. And the troubadour was a dead man, with only suffering to pass through before the fact.

Guisbourne examined the board and finally chose what seemed the safest move. The door opened again, and this time it was Bogo who entered and crossed the paths of the rose garden. Guy read nothing on the other man's countenance until he slid into the bower beside him; then he saw the muscles of the swarthy face quivering with minute tics of stress. "Lady Margaret is dead," Bogo said. Their eyes met briefly; then the dwarf lowered his head and pretended his attention was fixed on the board, a hand pressed to the nervous flesh beneath his eye. Though no one was there to observe him but Guy, he obviously hated displaying any sign of weakness. After a moment Bogo looked up and hissed, "I think the Sheriff has gone totally mad at last, and his torturer always was."

"To torment and kill Lady Margaret will turn men against him when he is seeking allies," Guy answered. "He could have done as he pleased with the troubadour."

"I shall wish that dulcet fool cut into even smaller bits if I am caught in the wake of this blood frenzy," Bogo growled.

"Alan a Dale is still alive, I take it?"

"Oh, alive, and all his bits are still in place, if somewhat bloodied. He is worth more, for the moment, as a tool to wring pangs of terror and dread from Lady Claire. They've stopped for the night, partly for shock, as they did not expect Lady Margaret to die, even with the atrocities they were committing, but also to rebuild their own lust. The Sheriff wants his wife to spend the night suffering what her lover has yet to endure."

"Tell me what happened," Guy said. Talking might help Bogo purge the horror, if only by inflicting the knowledge of it on another, and it was best Guy know what ugly twists the Sheriff's passions were following.

Bogo glanced at him briefly, then began to talk. "In the past it was the physical peculiarities that whetted the Sheriff's appetite most keenly. He was cruel, but the cruelties were but a spice to the meal. Lately his taste has been changing. Not so long ago he made the boy Cobb into what he wanted, and he would have done the same with Lady Margaret. I think it will be his new pleasure not to search out deformity and ravish it but to make it from whole flesh.

Creatures such as I will become his condiments. The normal will walk in fear of his hunger, and that fear will feed his craving and make it grow.''

"He mutilated Lady Margaret?''

"Utterly,'' Bogo said. "He wanted her his ultimate plaything, and his torturer set himself to creating it. The man is worse than the Sheriff if it comes to relishing the pain of his victims. He wants their deaths as well, though hers was an accident. The Sheriff made her watch the handiwork at first, then had her blinded, as he had promised. They amused themselves with minor agonies for a few hours, and then the torturer began to dismember her. The pain was too much. The shock of it killed her. It is far better, she would have been nothing but a maimed lump of flesh, a wailing thing, by the time he was done.''

"He wanted you to witness all this?''

"Rather more than that,'' Bogo said, and now there was black hate burning in the black eyes. "The Sheriff had me service him while he watched the torturer at work. Whether I was forced to observe depended on my position at the moment. Later he had the guards bring in Lady Claire to do the same, telling her what caused each rising scream while he swived her and promising Alan a Dale would suffer it tomorrow. They'd pause now and again, to give her troubadour a taste of what was to come and to add his cries to the music in the air. The torturer wondered if he might sing more sweetly still once they castrated him.''

"I doubt he will be as lucky as Lady Margaret and escape quickly into the dark.''

"He has no luck at all. Since Lady Margaret is beyond his reach, Sir Godfrey now says he will keep the troubadour alive instead. The torturer can take as long a time as he wants carving him. But finally he will be deaf, blind, and mute in some cell, a limbless husk awaiting the Sheriff's pleasure. Perhaps he will bring Lady Claire upon occasion when he goes there to amuse himself.''

Looking up, fear and revulsion pooled deep in his black eyes, Bogo whispered fiercely, "Why not kill Sir Godfrey now? You mean to do it sooner or later. The world would be well rid of him. The others are terrified. No one in this castle will question a fortunate accident—save the torturer, and I warrant he would follow his master fast. If we act together, we can make it appear they killed each other in some vicious frenzy."

Guy considered it, and shook his head slightly, keeping his voice low and even as he answered. "It is too soon—not for his death, I'll grant you, but for us to benefit. I will not dispense with him until I have more surety that Prince John will make me Sheriff. I am more closely linked with him than I would choose for any reason except his influence with Prince John. If I replace Sir Godfrey and am less vicious, the people will be grateful. But if I do not replace him, I am likely to be punished in his stead."

Bogo nodded, but his eyes were filled with apprehension. Guy could do nothing to belay that. Despite the escalation of the Sheriff's lust, Guy did not feel himself threatened. Not unless he ventured on some betrayal and lost. Sir Godfrey was not insane enough yet to strike totally at random. It was the helpless dependents who were truly at risk. Not wanting Bogo to resent his decision, Guy judged this a good time to draw the dwarf into the scheme for stealing the ransom. He began outlining the plan, emphasizing its imminence. He too wanted to be free of Godfrey as soon as possible. "There are shipments coming from all the cardinal points of England, but this will be the largest. The Emperor will be sending his counselors to count what has been collected. They must set out for London soon." Given something else to think about, Bogo relaxed a little, smiling at Guisbourne's suggested ruse of dressing the Sheriff's men as Robin Hood's outlaws.

"Be careful he does not steal the ransom back again," Bogo jested, managing a grim smile. He moved his knight.

"That would be ironic, would it not?" Guy smiled in return. "But I will avoid their known territory." He frowned at the knight and moved a pawn. "The sun is setting; we had best go in. We can finish the game tomorrow."

"If I am not otherwise occupied." Bogo rose, surveying the board one last time. "You are more disturbed than you admit," he remarked, moving a castle forward. "Check."

■■■■■■

Marian and Agatha had not been permitted out that day, nor anyone permitted in but the servants who brought them food. The early meal was brought by a scrawny little creature who was terrified to utter a word, almost spilled the tray, and scuttled quickly out again. But dinner was brought by a dark-haired young woman who served the Sheriff's table sometimes. She was obviously flirting with the guards when they opened the door, and she strode in with insolence. "I'm Laurel," she said casually, but her sidelong questioning glance at Marian made her look back more carefully.

Seeing Marian's attentiveness, the wench raised her chin and said, low-voiced, "We thought you might like to know your troubadour has lived out the day with legs to walk on. And that means he will be free tonight. Robin will see to it."

Marian and Agatha glanced at each other, caught between hope and fear of some elaborate betrayal. But if Alan had talked, the Sheriff would not bother with such nonsense. His guards would have already dragged them to the dungeon.

"Thank you," Marian said, surprised at the choked whisper of her voice.

"Got to be off," Laurel said, but continued to eye Marian not with the edgy fear of being caught in the conspiracy, or with pride of being involved, but with a sort of sulky defiance that made no sense. It stirred Marian's wariness once again, until she realized how closely the shape of her body, the flow of her hair, were being observed. A flagrant, arrogant sensuality informed Laurel's stance and her square face with its bold dark eyes, sulky, pouting lips, all framed with a mass of frizzled dark hair.

Marian thought, *She is Robin's lover . . . or wants to be.*

Instantly she chastised herself for such surety. Laurel lived in the castle and had observed Marian with Sir Guy. She might have been, might still be, Guisbourne's lover, and that made her dangerous indeed. But since Laurel brought Robin's message, and spoke of him in such possessive tones, Marian thought it was the outlaw she laid claim to and wondered what Robin had said or done to stir this hostile response in the woman. The idea made her prickle with antagonism, though she buried it swiftly.

Laurel gave her a satisfied smile, then turned and left them. Once she was gone, Marian turned to Agatha, the news Laurel had brought again more important than any aspect of her demeanor. Relief and gratitude rushed through her in a fierce flood caution could barely control.

Agatha took her hand and whispered, "Let's pray he succeeds."

15 The air was saturated with the scent of beer as the brewmaster led Robin and Little John through the yard. Stopping at the side door to the brewhouse and glancing unhappily from one of them to the other, the burly man drew breath to resume his plea. He gestured toward the upper bailey looming above them, Nottingham Castle commanding the town from the high cliff much as the full moon ruled the clouded midnight sky. "All this work was to be for attacking the Sheriff himself," he complained. "Why should I risk my life, my business to rescue some pretty, prattling troubadour the Sheriff's wife wanted to swive?"

"Not one word more." Robin cut him off sharply. He had thought of carrying out the plan to assassinate the Sheriff tonight as well. It was a very efficient way to prevent him from stealing the ransom. But he had no idea of its repercussions on his agreement with Marian and reluctantly dismissed the idea. "The troubadour helped us. Even if the passage can be used only once, now will be that once, and we will finish the Sheriff another time. Lead on."

The brewmaster remained still for a brief moment of protest, then acceded to Robin and opened the door for the three of them. He lit a candle and led the way into the quiet of the brewery. Faint moonlight filtered through vents by the eaves, and the tallow candle smoked and flickered as he guided them past row upon row of barrels stacked three high. Reaching the back wall, he took them through a door to the tool crib. The brewmaster pulled four coils of rope out from under a pile of burlap and held them out, announcing, "Five fathoms each, more than enough for the wall. Each looped at an end as we said."

Robin took the ropes, passed two to John, and uncoiled them on the floor of the tool crib. "Too long," Robin judged them. He smiled at the brewmaster and pulled his sword. Swinging his blade, he hacked two of the ropes in half. Then he and little John quickly looped and retied the ends. Finished, he nodded at the brewmaster. "The door."

The brewmaster wedged a post over a chest and under the end of a heavy wooden cabinet. He grunted, pulled down, and in one try levered the rack away from the back wall. He reached into the opening and pulled wooden dowels out of the joists. Then he swung a panel of the back wall out past the joist and dragged it free.

Before venturing into the darkness, Robin turned to John. "The horses?"

"Tethered in place," John answered, "which I did myself. Six here, one behind the upper bailey, two beneath the middle bailey wall, another by the outer bailey postern. There's a bow and a quiver full on each."

"Why bother with one at the postern?" Robin asked.

"You don't have to try the most outlandish thing." John answered him evenly. The dark eyes met his directly, the measuring gaze weighted with disapproval. "Chancing less could serve just as well."

Robin returned the look silently but combatively. He'd drunk neither wine nor ale, but the intoxication of adventure was lighting a giddy fire in his blood. The brewmaster was confused by the sudden tension between them and stepped back in embarrassment. Unexpectedly Little John flicked out his foot, his speed startling for such a large man, and kicked Robin in the backside. With a saturnine smile he added, "And it might save you from coming hard off a bailey wall to land on that."

Collapsing onto the pile of burlap, Robin crowed with laughter. Seeing the brewmaster's perplexity, he only laughed harder. John watched, smiling grimly all the while, till Robin finally muffled his own noise and slowly relaxed into the burlap, savoring the quiet joy he felt at John's efforts to keep him from his own wildness. John raised his dark brows, silently asking if Robin intended to see sense. Robin gave a little snort of defiance. He'd be damned before he reined himself in too tight, that was a far more likely way to stumble. But when he stood, he gave John a quick hard hug for his vigilance, his steady wisdom. Unable to make any sense of it, the brewmaster looked back and forth between them. Robin cocked his head at the man and said, ''Mother him instead, John Little, if it will soothe your mind.'' Chortling, Robin pushed the brewmaster ahead and followed him through the hole.

A long crawl space opened into a large stone chamber filled with nooks and crevices. The tunnel led to another hole in the rock above. They boosted and hauled each other to the next level, then made their way through a succession of winding passages climbing upward, stooping and moving forward by the flickering candlelight. At some places the path turned down briefly, but it always went back up again. Here and there the way forked into obscure choices, but the brewmaster found the proper course again by shining a candle against the wall to see marks that had been cut into the rock to guide them.

The air was a curious blend of acrid and bracing, not as oppressive as Robin had feared it might be. It was adequate for breathing as they climbed upward through narrow passages. Occasionally a draft coursed through the dark tunnel, hinting at other ways to the outer world. Sometimes there would have been no natural way to proceed except that small passages had been hollowed out and rocks removed to open a way to another crack of cave above. Short beams were wedged into cracks, and timbers were lashed against them, forming a crude stair up to the next level above. Robin slithered easily through such a narrow upward tunnel, then lay on the stone floor resting, watching with the brewmaster as Little John laboriously pulled his long bulk through.

Little John looked up at his watchers and said, "Caves are meant for the wee. The wee and the cruel." He pulled himself through the hole, then growled loudly, "Brewmaster, why didn't you pull more rock from here?"

"Shush," the brewmaster answered, "sound moves oddly through the rock. It mostly dies, but it can carry far. Be quieter from here." He began climbing again then said, "And you might appreciate the work that went into this."

"Aye, any work under the earth I do appreciate," Little John answered, "though you are better with rock than wood. The lashing on those little stairs behind could have been tighter with less rope and better knots. Strange, though, I thought I'd be crawling through the wet, but these rocks are near dry."

"What did you do with the rock you cleared from here?" Robin asked.

"Right under the Brewhouse it went. We built over a hole, then filled it in beneath us from the caves. No Sheriff's inspector ever saw how deep that hole was before we began, nor the rock we put into it later."

Robin followed the brewmaster upward, and John trailed last. They climbed and crawled for almost an hour until they came to a rock pile that nearly blocked the way. A pyramid of carefully laid stone went from the floor of the cave three feet up to the ceiling, partly held in place with timbers. The brewmaster turned and signaled for quiet as they approached it and kept them silent as they crawled on past the pile. They went another ten feet, turned to the side, and then crawled on into a recess, the low ceiling half a man's height. Three stout timbers were wedged between the floor and the ceiling of the recess and tied together with ropes.

The brewmaster pointed back to the pyramid and confessed, "My mistake, that first one. We couldn't make out Laurel's tapping very well and started to go up through the floor of the kitchen. She said she could sniff the candle from above, and between the smell and the scraping, she thought a cook would get on to us for sure. She crashed a tray of dishes right there to get us to stop. A fine pheasant for the Sheriff's dinner it was.''

He held the light up to Robin's face to see if he was running on too long. Not being stopped, he continued. ''Punished her for that. Stopped the work for three months, until she got reassigned to the kitchen. In the end she drove an arrow through a crack in the storeroom floor, knocked it right down through. It was the last guide stick, and we moved rock to get to it.'' He pointed to a faint gleam coming down from above and said, ''Right here.''

''You did well, all of you,'' Robin whispered, praising him, ''You and Laurel especially. Now get us up there.''

''When we cut through,'' the brewmaster said quietly, ''it took three of us to hold that stone up while the others moved the timbers.''

''Ha,'' Little John said, and moved in close to the timbers. He reached up between them, set his hands, and pushed the stone up two inches, immediately loosening the timbers. ''Not heavy,'' he grunted, ''just tunnel awkward.''

Robin and the brewmaster pulled the timbers away; then Little John put down the two-foot-square floor stone. Robin stood up through the floor, chest high into the small storage room, looked about, then sprang up. Little John followed straight after.

The brewmaster stood up through the hole in the floor and started to climb into the room. Robin motioned him to stay. Little John bent over him and said softly, ''Wait here and stay sharp. Have the rope ready. If any of the Sheriff's men come down this hole after us, you best grab one of those horses for yourself and ride for the woods. My men will find you once you're there.''

■■■■■■

They brushed each other off, found the white hauberks Laurel had filched from the laundry room and slipped them on. Worn over their hunting leathers, the cloth tunics would not pass any but the most cursory glance, but they would do better than nothing. Laurel often took food and beer to the dungeon guards, and Robin had memorized the route she described. The storage area was empty, but they moved cautiously down behind the kitchens where workers might have late-night tasks. No cooks were about, but they had to draw back when a guard appeared in the doorway and glanced about suspiciously. Robin's hand went to his sword, but the guard had not heard them. Instead the man sneaked quietly over to one of the cold ovens, opened it, and removed a hidden cache of meat. A love gift from some kitchen maid perhaps?

Robin waited two minutes, restless but cautious, before seeking out the next corridors and the stairs that branched down into the cliff once again. As Laurel had said, they encountered no one else until they peered around the next torchlit corner and saw the doorkeeper sitting in a chair right beside the dungeon door. Robin nodded to John. Together they stepped out smiling, and strode forward easily. The man looked up as they appeared, started to smile in return, then froze and reached for his sword. Robin sprinted forward and seized him, twisting his sword arm. Fast on his heels, Little John clapped a huge hand over the man's mouth and squeezed his jaw. When John pulled him, the doorkeeper came right to his feet, eyes wide with terror at the strength of the grip.

"See him," Little John said, turning the man's face toward Robin, "that's Robin Hood, and you are well pleased to help him tonight. Tell me this is true."

The man couldn't speak or move his head in assent. Little John moved his head up and down for him. "Yes, I see you are well pleased to help."

Robin took the key from him, opened the dungeon door, and led the way down several stone steps. The air was dank and old, far worse than the cave, laced with an odor of garbage, urine, and blood. They walked down to a tunnel about a dozen feet wide with a high, curiously slanted ceiling that angled down somewhat from a wall with three doors. Through the flickering candlelight they saw another guard, sitting on the floor against the wall away from the cells. He was balancing a wooden cup of beer on his knee and glanced over at them as they approached, his head weaving a little with drunkenness. His expression was puzzled, but the drawn brows relaxed when he recognized the guard. Smiling, he raised his cup and said conspiratorially, "There's enough hidden away for us all."

"You've an important prisoner hidden away too, I hear," Robin said cheerfully to the guard sprawled on the floor.

"That singer?" The guard snorted, gesturing at the door opposite, hardly looking up. "Important? Not what I'd call an important man. Couldn't hold a sword over his own head. And when he did pull his short dagger,"—the guard leered—"he stuck it to the wrong target."

"Important enough to such as us," Robin assured him, "don't you think? Else why are we here?"

The befuddled guard peered more closely at them and scrambled to his feet.

"Who are you? Why'd the doorkeeper let you in here?" he demanded, and pulled his sword.

Robin and John made no response to the sword. John jerked the other guard forward and let him go. "Ask him yourself."

The guard peered at the terrified doorkeeper, who only muttered, "Robin Hood."

Robin and John still had not drawn weapons. They just smiled. "Are you going to put that sword down," Robin asked him quietly, "or do I put you down?"

The guard looked back at the doorkeeper, then laid his sword on the floor and backed away.

"Unlock it," Robin commanded.

The doorkeeper turned the key, then stood aside, fearful under the stern watch of Little John. Robin threw back the door and stepped inside, knowing his body would be no more than a darkness outlined by the candlelight coming in from the hall behind. The wan light fell on Alan a Dale. His clothing was tattered, his face and hands were bloodstained, but naught was broken that Robin could see. Roughening his voice, he demanded in a sharp, commanding tone,

"Where's your ransom, minstrel? Pay now or to the rack with you."

Alan rose uncertainly to his feet, peering at him suspiciously. "Ransom?" he answered bitterly. "For me?"

"Or wergeld."

"Wergeld?" Alan repeated apprehensively as the dark figure approached and circled about him. "My family has little wealth, and I doubt the Sheriff would release me for any price. Take me to the rack if that is what you intend."

"No, ransom surely, for a swordless one such as you could have dropped no foe in battle and would not owe wergeld. Ransom. It must be ransom. And I'm told you have a voice as pure as gold with which to pay it." Robin then stepped behind Alan and turned back so that the light from without fell upon his suddenly smiling face.

"Robin," Alan cried in astonishment, and threw his arms about him. "How did you get here? Out of the very air above?"

Robin winked and whispered, "Nay, out of the rock below."

Robin led the troubadour out into the hallway. When Alan saw the guard, he recoiled. "He's the worst of the guards, though sweet as a babe compared with the torturer. Whatever pain I had, he sought out and worsened," he hissed, stroking his blood-streaked hands.

Robin smiled sweetly at the guard, then at Little John. "I think this man enjoys his work. A lucky fellow, seemingly."

"Lucky—till now," John growled back.

Summoning himself, Alan demanded of the doorkeeper, "Where do you have the Lady Claire? Take us there."

The doorkeeper took a tallow candle and led the way deeper into the stone tunnel. They went on another twenty paces and turned into the undercroft. The doorkeeper stopped and pointed at a door. "There's her cell." He backed away, standing close to the guard under Little John's watchful eye. Robin saw John's hand ready on the sword handle.

Alan grabbed the keys ahead and fumbled with the lock. Robin took the candle and held it steady, while Alan opened the door as swiftly as his shaking hands allowed, then rushed into the large, stark room. Robin watched from the doorway, the weak rays of candlelight casting faint glimmers in the darkness of receding shadows. The only object in the space was a pile of straw against the far wall. On it a figure in stained silk turned at the sound. Alan hurried toward it and was stopped in his dash when the figure called out, "Alan, however have you escaped?" Then he surged forward again, threw himself onto the straw, and embraced Lady Claire. Overcome with the joy of holding her, he rocked her in his arms, then smoothed back the tangled mass of her hair.

"Claire, how did you know it was me? How did you know I was free?" He covered her face with small, tender kisses.

"Why, Alan, you should hear yourself." Turned to the light, Claire's face was tear-streaked and swollen, but she laughed softly, kissing him back, lost in the same gentle delirium. "I know your step. You would not dash to me here that lightly if you were not freed. Now, tell me how."

"I really don't know, except that waiting at the door to your cell are Robin Hood and Little John, and that explains enough."

Robin knelt beside her, taking her hand and kissing it gallantly. "Lady Claire, your new home will not be so fine as you are used to, but far better than your current abode."

"I will be grateful for any shelter you offer me, Robin of Locksley," Claire said softly. "There is no room in the castle that is not a vile prison."

Robin's eyes met hers. Despite her blindness, he felt she looked straight through him. Her trust stirred his heart. "I am grateful you accept it," he answered, and gave her hand into Alan's keeping. The troubadour helped her to her feet, where she swayed unsteadily, as much from the maelstrom of emotion as weariness, Robin judged.

"I still do not know how you came here," she murmured to Alan.

"Later you'll hear all, my lady, but now we have business," John told them. Drawing his sword, he walked the guards up against the wall, then looked over at Robin. "Do we finish these?" he asked.

"Leave them to make up a song for the Sheriff," Robin suggested airily. "He'll make them sing higher than we would."

"Bright my eyes, sharp my guardian blade," Alan sang forth, suggesting a beginning, as Little John nudged the guards toward Claire's cell with his sword.

"They can yell for hours down here and not be heard," Robin said with a smile.

"We know that too well," Claire said somberly, reducing the mood to anxiety.

"Wait," John said, in a suddenly roughened voice. "I know a better place." He walked past the farthest cell and knelt to lift a metal lid from the floor. A fetid odor wafted up. "The Sheriff of Nottingham has his own hole. I had a small taste of this little hell when I was prisoner here. Lower them down and see how they like it. There's room enough for two. They can practice their singing until dawn."

"Ah . . . an oubliette," Robin cooed softly, peering into the darkness. "A taste of hell indeed. Suitable storage for two of the Devil's minions."

Alan looked suddenly pale and nauseous in the flickering gloom. His face contorted as he glared at the guard. "Yes, that's where he put me the first night. From the smell I believed him when he said I'd be left till the skin rotted from my bones."

The doorkeeper took it well enough, but the guard cringed and groveled at the thought of being locked in the putrid darkness of the deep hole. Robin had no pity for anyone serving the Sheriff's cruelty and forced them down. His face creased and hardened with bitter memory, Little John lowered the lid.

"It's a pity the torturer isn't here too," John said, "though the dark hole I'd see him in would be his grave."

Robin led them out of the dungeon, retracing the passage beneath the upper bailey redoubt and guiding them back toward the small storage room. Once he stopped and traced the outline of some admirable stone joinery with his fingers, admiring the quality of the work.

"Shouldn't we hurry?" Alan chafed at their pace.

"Hurry's for later," Robin told him languidly, filled with a delicious euphoria he knew preceded the risk yet to come. "Nobody is about, to enjoy the luxury of the place for a while. You'll not be wanting to return here again until there is a King returned to England."

"Or till we come back to slit the Sheriff's throat," Little John said under his breath.

Lady Claire's head rose high at his words. She said nothing, but her soft features bore the same quiet grimness as Little John's.

They continued along the halls, once stopping while the tones of distant voices receded. Soon they reached the storeroom and opened the door again. Robin went to the hole, leaned in, and called in a low voice, "Still there, master brewer?"

"Indeed, though not liking it overmuch," the rumbling voice whispered up.

"We're not going down there?" Alan asked, not wanting to hear the confirmation. "It looks little better than the oubliette."

"Alan, smell the air. It's of a cave, but there is a freshness behind it. It's an easy passage out," Claire told him.

The brewer passed up a coil of rope.

"You could go straight down the narrow ledge of the berm and across the outer bailey to the postern," John said, counseling a change of plan.

"Could," Robin agreed cheerfully. "But I'm taking the wall to the middle bailey."

"That's a chancy way and not needed," John argued

stubbornly. His eyes glinted as he added, ''Don't be too sure you'll impress anyone but yourself.''

It stung, but not as it would if he had no other reason. ''The more noise I make, the better. The less a gaze will come to rest later on Lady Marian.''

''Or Laurel,'' interposed the brewmaster.

''Or Laurel,'' Robin echoed. ''I intend to kick over the water barrels, annoy the citizens, and rouse the troops. You have one hour—time to crawl through the tunnel and be off.''

John hefted Alan, then Claire and handed them down the hole to the brewmaster. Then he turned and tried to curb Robin once again.

''Do you have to disturb their sleep so utterly?''

''It will save them from their nightmares,'' Robin answered, eyes glittering with defiance now. ''Get them safely away. I'll meet you in Sherwood.''

Robin waited in the storeroom, watching as Little John lifted the floor stone back into place. Once they had it shored up from below, he stepped on the stone, testing its strength. The floor was solid again, and he tapped the rock to signal them. He stood awhile in the dark listening to the kitchen about him and knew that no one was near. Then he took three small pots from the shelves and carefully walked down the hall. He went silently along the route described to him by Laurel, not at all incautiously despite his pose to John and the others.

■■■■■■

Hidden in a dark corner overlooking the wall and the berm that descended beneath it, Robin waited on the outer bailey wall. Obscured in murky clouds, the full moon yielded little light for inspecting the way ahead. He already had one long and one short rope fastened. The long rope went over the upper bailey battlement and down by where the extra horse was tethered. If he were surprised, this would be the back door out. If not, it would fuel misdirected speculation on how the prisoners had escaped in the night.

Better to help them theorize about flight over the walls than to lead them to consider too closely the rocks below. Or, worse still, search out connivance within the castle walls.

The other rope was fastened to a crevice and dangled down to the wall between the upper bailey and the middle bailey. In the faint predawn light Robin could not see exactly how he would get over the guardpost at the far wall and into the middle bailey. Both Laurel and Cobb had looked over the general route this morning earlier, but neither had been able to see the exact spot in daylight, and now it was too dark to discern. So he put it out of his mind, knowing his feet would find a way when the time came.

He imagined Marian somewhere above. If his hands could not have the luxury of caressing her, he could at least give his mind leave to rove over her form. He looked at the walls overhead, searching out a likely window to her chamber. Then he traced a climb to the window, scouring the wall inch by inch above, foothold by foothold, thinking of the exquisite pleasure that would not be his that night. It was too impossible a climb to try in the dark. And too dangerous in the Sheriff's castle. Worst of all, even if that was her very window, he had made himself unwelcome there. That put a bright arrow of pain into the pleasure of pretending. Yet another bright shaft followed after, hope, its sharp, sweet pain piercing him.

"Fool." Robin laughed, but he let the icefire vision of her burn through his mind, his blood.

When it was close enough to dawn, he returned. Walking along the narrow allure behind the battlement wall, he ducked back into the interior hall and walked to the quarters of the sergeant of the guard. He pulled back his arm and tossed a pot, shattering it with a loud crash against the sergeant's door. Then he began yelling, "Whoa, hold there. After them, man. It's Robin Hood. Get him." He threw another pot against another door and bellowed out, "Robin Hood. It's Robin Hood. After him." Instantly he heard them stirring. He threw the last pot down the hall, yelled again, then stepped back onto the walkway of the allure.

From there he was over the battlement down onto the wall in a flash, running in exultation as a pursuit formed behind him.

Laurel was right. The wall was not patrolled at night but was always guarded at set points. As he ran toward the guardpost, he was readying a short rope. A doorkeeper, blade in hand, came out to meet him. Robin stepped to the side as the man swung at him, deflected the sword, and swept the doorkeeper's feet from under him. The man went down in a heap then struggled to stand. Robin pivoted about and cracked him with an elbow to the head. The doorkeeper fell to the stones and was still.

Robin started to reach for his rope again to find a way over the guardhouse, but then he looked through the open door and saw too good a chance. He ran right in, shoved the other guard against the back wall, and tossed the short rope after him, tangling the man. Robin burst out the far door and dashed into the middle bailey, yelling his name and shouting all awake. It was glorious. He knocked over anything convenient, picked up a rock and threw it against the barracks door, and ran on, yelling all the while.

They were coming awake. Looking back, he could see men milling about, but they didn't know which way to chase or what was happening. He ran on, shouting again, trying to rouse them all. Suddenly a group of men had formed behind him, running together, coming directly at him, more joining them from the sides in a suddenly focused chase. On he dashed, past the gate, out the far side of the central square, outrunning the lot, grinning with ferocious delight. It was a splendor to know he had the speed to leave them all, even carrying his last rope.

He loped along beneath the back wall. Two guards with swords drawn were coming down the first stair aloft. He just ran past them. The second stair was clear, and the next beyond as well. He kept going past the second stair and then up. Some of the quicker ones were closing on him from behind as he looped the rope around a turret. A doorkeeper came suddenly along the allure toward him. He could have swung over, but if the man hacked the rope, it would be a hard fall down. Robin waited for him with his own blade out, though others were already on the stair up to the allure.

Robin waited, waited, waited endlessly for the man to arrive and raise his sword. Then Robin stepped inside the descending arc of hard metal and ran the man through. He pulled out his sword and kicked the body of the man down the stairs into the path of those rushing up after him. He ducked to the side, and an arrow skittered off the rock wall right where he'd been standing a second before.

Over the battlement he went, and down the rope. Kicking out from the wall, he let the rope pass through his hands as he swung back in, then kicked out and down again and again. He saw one guard, then another appear at the battlement above him. A third man showed, pulling back a bow. Robin thrust out to the side, and the arrow whizzed through the space where he had been. He went down even faster, too fast, burning his hands. As the bow was drawn again, he let go and fell the last ten feet. Landing on both feet evenly, he tucked over and rolled away from the wall, dissipating the force of the landing. Then he was under an oak, leaping to his feet—and suddenly had all the time there ever was. He ran down the shoulders of the hill that rose to meet the wall, using trees to screen himself from the arrows whistling down from above, hardly needing to rush. He felt as if he could have plucked them singing from the air.

Jester was tethered behind a small cottage and bowed a greeting when he saw Robin approach. He leapt to the saddle and reared the sorrel while yelling back at the figures gathering on the wall, then plunged into Nottingham. He knew that on that horse, one of his fastest, none of the Sheriff's men would ever catch him. Robin thundered along the just-stirring streets, windows opening, then slamming shut all about him. Deliberately he took the long way through the town to provide the greatest disruption, looking about for any threat. He loved racing alone, no other man or mount about to slow him.

At the edge of Nottingham town he reined in before the

last guardpost. The door began to open. In a blur of speed Robin shot an arrow through it. There was a cry within, and he followed two more arrows that struck the slamming door. Tossing off the white hauberk, he plunged Jester through a sleepy lane, thrilled by the escape, seeing always the image of Marian before him, and galloped off for Sherwood.

16

"You cannot suspect me of collusion. You yourself had me under guard while Alan a Dale was in the dungeon." Marian studied the Sheriff with cold defiance that iced over the sickly fear within.

She was back in the great hall, though even fewer courtiers were here. Sir Guy not among them, and Marian wondered if he would appear. Foreknowledge of the rescue had let Marian prepare herself for this confrontation with Sir Godfrey. She had dressed elaborately and richly, the intricately pleated lavender bliaut and a gauzy wimple scrolled with silver embroidery, milky seed pearls, and glittering amethysts. Her fingers were jeweled with rings: sapphire, moonstone, a coruscating diamond. Summoned, Marian presented herself in this silken armor of wealth and position. She had also bidden Agatha to remain in their room, for fear the Sheriff would deflect his anger on to her in a fit of spite.

Garbed even more richly in robes of vermilion brocade weighted with gem-encrusted chains, Sir Godfrey eyed her venomously. "Your troubadour has escaped. Therefore I can and do suspect you, Lady Marian. You have had contact with Robin Hood."

"Contact? Yes, I had contact with him. I was manhandled and insulted, all against my will. I would have killed him, given the chance. If you look to blame, blame yourself, for you have failed to capture this outlaw." She let her anger out. It was dangerous, of course, for he was unpredictable. But he preyed on the weak. Her own strength was only a small sharp dagger of courage; the sword was the strength of her family. "I will not be blamed for another. Not with impunity."

For a moment his eyes glittered with a manic flame. Her grandfather would indeed avenge her, Marian was sure, if the Sheriff dared to kill her. But the thought held small consolation. At that moment Sir Guy strode into the hall. His gaze met hers once, briefly but with flaring intensity, then fixed on the Sheriff. Marian felt a surge of relief at having an immediate protector as well as one powerful but distant. Sir Guy walked directly to his place beside Sir Godfrey and stood, impressive and vaguely ominous in a glistening bronze tunic with bat-wing sleeves, his shoulders spanned with chains of agate-studded gold. At his entrance the vindictive blaze in the Sheriff's blue eyes slowly cooled.

Marian allowed her voice to cool and smooth as well. "After the outlaw robbed us, Alan a Dale became fascinated with the lore of Robin Hood. Once he told me he thought to create songs about him and become famous throughout England. He even prattled of such things at the banquet. I told him that gallant knights made better heroes than outlaws, but he was foolish."

"There must be more to it than that," the Sheriff growled. "Why should Robin Hood rescue him?"

Marian shrugged with annoyance. "Perhaps he talked with the outlaw more than he told me and captured his fancy. This Robin Hood seems a fanciful knave, full of tricks and jests." Stealing the Sheriff's wife from under his nose was a marvelous trick, but she did not say so.

"I want you out of Nottingham," the Sheriff snarled at her.

If she pleaded, he would only take greater pleasure in the banishment. Marian saw only one option and took it, raising her gaze to meet Guy's dark amber eyes. Once again he bent and murmured in the Sheriff's ear. Sir Godfrey scowled but subsided. His brief glance at Guisbourne told him the favor would be repaid. To her, Sir Godfrey said,

"You may finish your work on the hall and lands surrounding before you go."

Marian thanked the Sheriff with as much civility as she could marshal and left when he waved a hand in supercilious dismissal. She climbed the stairs swiftly, cursing under her breath, and knocked for Agatha to admit her. Marian summarized what had happened as she stripped off the confining wimple and shook out her hair. Agatha made no move to help her, knowing she would not want to be touched while so tense. Deliberately Marian truncated the ending. "Sir Godfrey wants us to leave Nottingham but will allow me to finish the work on the hall."

Well aware of how little remained to be done, Agatha gave a small snort. "Still, it's lucky we are not banished . . . or chopped to mincemeat." Agatha took the embroidered wimple, folded it carefully and placed it in a chest. Taking a comb, she indicated Marian should sit on the bed beside her. "Your hair is tangled."

The edge off her anger, Marian sat and let Agatha smooth the comb through her hair as they talked, plotting a few simple ways to extend the work at Fallwood Hall. There was still tribute from a few vassals to arrange. She needed more grain to sustain the livestock through the winter. A scant week's work. Marian did not mention her best ploy would be spinning out her assignations with Sir Guy. She wondered what he thought. Despite the weight of the debt she owed him, she had never before solicited his help. The gratitude she already felt mingled queasily with this new connivance.

"The Sheriff may watch who we talk to," Agatha remarked.

"If we do not act much the same as we always have, that will be more curious still," Marian argued. "But you are right that we must take care."

There was a knock at the door. Marian and Agatha exchanged glances, and then the older woman rose and answered it. Guy of Guisbourne stepped through, uninvited. Looking at Marian, he said, "I want to talk to you alone."

If that was all he desired, he could talk to her alone in the bower of the rose garden. That he would presume so admitted reason for presumption. Agatha's face revealed nothing as she asked for confirmation. "Lady Marian?" Marian nodded. "I will return in an hour," Agatha said, and went quietly from the room. Guy bolted the door behind her. Marian bristled, but she had invited it, appealing to him as a lover. Already with his protection came this subtle dominance.

"I have been discreet," Guy assured. "I made sure no one observed me enter."

Agatha observed you enter, she thought. But of course Guisbourne would think her lady-in-waiting knew of her liaison. Few women could conduct an affair without an ally, and Marian had said only that she wished to avoid court gossip. "We were to meet in the cave," Marian reminded him.

"For the next few days the Sheriff will have you followed, and efforts to elude his men would make you look suspicious. For the moment we have more chance of keeping our secret if we meet here. Sir Godfrey has believed we were lovers ever since I intervened with Wolverton's scheme. He will not spread gossip, but his guards would."

"I hope he will soon tire of such absurdity," she said, storming inwardly.

Guy moved close to her, his golden eyes clouded. "Take care. I do not want you to leave, but it pleases Godfrey to think you were somehow involved in the escape."

At the moment Marian feared the Sheriff's suspicion less than Guisbourne's. To divert it, she offered a portion of the truth. "No. Though I would have rescued Alan if I could have done it at no risk to myself."

An eyebrow lifted, and his hand made a graceful concession. "I myself would have rescued him . . . if it had been at no risk."

She gave him a small bitter smile. "At little risk?"

His own smile was more sardonic. "Ah, that much I would not have chanced."

"I might have risked a little, but little more." She gave the lie with an ironic shrug. "His indiscretions put me in jeopardy, but I am happy he is free."

"The Sheriff also thinks, with rather more plausibility, that Alan a Dale will try to send you word of his whereabouts."

She wondered if he would tell the Sheriff what she said and if Sir Godfrey would believe it from his lips rather than hers. "If Alan a Dale had made me his confidante, I would not now be in this predicament. I presume Sherwood to be his whereabouts, and Lady Claire's. No doubt she is happier rooting for grubs and berries than she was in her silk-swaddled prison."

"Let us hope your pretty troubadour can protect her," Guy responded, "else she will be expected to service the whole lot of Robin's brigands, and be no better off than she was here."

"There is little choice for her now," Marian said, not arguing with his assumptions.

"True. Few places will be safe for them while the Sheriff lives."

Marian realized she would have no better opportunity than this. The questions she wished to ask all would seem prompted by the horrors the Sheriff had perpetrated, by gratitude, and by desire. The alternatives she could offer would seem less premeditated. Looking Guy in the eyes, she challenged him quietly. "How can you continue to serve such a man?"

He gave an odd smile, and she wondered if another had asked him the same question or if it was only that recent events had forced him to ask it himself. "To disassociate myself is impossible. Sir Godfrey would take my withdrawal as disloyalty. I would become his enemy, and he is not an enemy I can afford. For the moment the power I hold here is under his aegis."

"For the moment?"

He regarded her steadily, then said, "I want to be Sheriff of Nottingham."

To claim the position, Guisbourne would have to kill Sir Godfrey, one way or another. He would be too perilous an enemy to leave alive. Nothing was spoken, but they read the knowledge in each other's eyes. She could not disapprove; she only wished he had done it months ago.

"But if Prince John chooses me to replace Sir Godfrey, it will be because I have proven myself to him in some fashion."

"How?" she asked, though she knew he could only evade or lie. Pleased when he openly evaded, smiling and shaking his head slightly, she ventured, "And if King Richard returns?"

"I have chosen the side I believe will prevail," he murmured, but his eyes hooded slightly, and she thought he had plans far more complex.

She persisted. "If Richard returns, whatever you accomplish under Prince John will be in vain."

He gestured with an easy grace that belied the concern of a man so ambitious, but his voice was fractionally tighter as he said, "I would not necessarily lose my lands here. But if that happens, I do have small holdings in Brittany."

Marian faced him steadily. "It is not too late to ally yourself with the King. I could speak to my grandparents in your name. They have some influence if they choose to exercise it. I am in your debt, thrice over. Let me help you in this way." It admitted no more than he knew, that her family was loyal to the King, yet the hook of power was there.

The strange golden eyes met hers, shadowed flame. "I would not disregard your gratitude if the necessity arose. But gratitude is not what I desire from you."

She lowered her gaze, then fumed at herself. Disappointment would have been natural enough, but she knew that it was reluctance she had conveyed. To try feminine coyness to toy with him now would seem truly suspicious. Already it was too late for subterfuge. He was used to her directness, and he lifted her chin till their eyes met again, then raised a questioning brow. Curiosity came before suspicion. *Tell the truth*, she thought. *Some piece of the truth.* "This situation is of my own devising," Marian said. "I appealed to you for protection, yet now I feel trapped."

"There are any number of things that I would have you feel, Lady Marian, but trapped is not one of them—unless it is of the power of your own passion, as I am ensnared."

She was startled by the unexpected offering, by the flame in Guisbourne's eyes, alight with both desire and self-mockery. When his arms encircled her, she did not resist, snared by her own tumult of hunger and resistance. What she thought she had desired seemed to slip from her grasp even as she embraced it. Yet her heart ached, feeling its loss, and she clung to him more tightly. He murmured her name, his wanton lips working their magic, coaxing and demanding, as his strong, skilled hands undid the ties of her gown and slipped it off. She undressed him in turn, laying aside the gold chain and lifting off the tunic of rustling metallic silk.

Pulling her down onto the bed, Guy kissed her rapaciously. "You are too brave," he muttered before devouring her mouth again, and she knew he feared for her. Then he smiled at her, his eyes glittering with arousal. "Far too provocative." He moved down her body, tormenting her with stinging bites, the hot flush of them spreading in voluptuous ripples from her nipples, her sex. Clasping the pulsing bud between his teeth, he sucked and licked at her until she thrashed and snarled at him. Drawing back, he buried himself inside her with one lunge, coming as he entered her. The wild thrust of him woke new ripples deep within her, ripples that spun into a whirlpool, a dark swirling core spinning her around and down, so that she plummeted into ecstasy. As he climaxed, Guy buried his face against her throat, stifling his cry, covering her mouth with his hand to muffle hers. She held him, stroked him, the soft, hot flood of tenderness marred with currents of unease, satiation with melancholy.

When Agatha returned, they were seemly and composed, dressed once more in their silks. Sir Guy bade them both a courteous farewell and left with the same discretion with which he had arrived. When he had gone and the door was bolted behind him, Agatha frowned at her, her features stiff with condemnation. "Alan's secret affair was not enough? I did not expect such duplicity from you, Lady Marian."

"This is no risk to us."

"No risk?" Agatha raised her brows in exaggerated disbelief. "There is no chance that you might slip and reveal too much, while hoping he does the same?"

"I meant that discovery entailed no risk," Marian said sharply. "I have made no slips."

"Well, what have you learned?" Agatha prompted, her tone still tinged with disapproval.

"Nothing of significance. I would not dare probe for details."

Agatha nodded. "That is wise. He would distrust you instantly."

She felt again a bitter pride at the modicum of trust she had earned. Tangled in complexities, she picked the simplest explanation. "I thought there was a chance to win him back to King Richard's cause."

"And that the effort would be enjoyable?" Agatha looked at her closely. "Are you in love with him?"

"Perhaps. I don't know." Marian shook her head. Finally she offered a confidence. "I am expected to marry when I return home. There are few men I could endure. I thought he might be one."

Agatha nodded, gazing at her quietly. "He might suit you," she said at last. "But I think you are too like for happiness."

During the next week Marian and Agatha made an effort to conduct themselves much as usual. Marian went more often to visit Topaz, who was coming out of molt. Those visits to the mews allowed her to overlook the activities of the Sheriff's knights. They were busy with preparations and left the castle on frequent training maneuvers, but Guisbourne had kept them similarly occupied ever since Prince John's visit. Frequently Marian rode to Fallwood Hall or made small forays into Nottingham, as much to test the Sheriff's vigilance as anything. She chafed under the eyes of the Sheriff's spies. With his guards keeping watch she could not train in the woods with Sir Ralph, much less seek out Robin to thank him and discover how Alan and Claire fared. Neither Laurel nor anyone else had brought her word of them. At the end of the week Sir Godfrey seemed to tire of the game, though Marian remained cautious, trying to ascertain if he was simply being craftier in his. She took Topaz out hunting, following where the sparrowhawk led, keeping watch behind. Neither she nor Ralph could detect anyone on their trail.

Marian also sent Agatha off on a flurry of errands, none important save the one to take another length of cloth to Cobb's mother. When Agatha returned, she shook her head. "I do not know what will happen. The mother has taken fright since the death of Lady Margaret, though the boy looks grimmer than ever. I think she has forbidden him to help. Whether he will choose to disobey is now as much chance as whether he will have the opportunity."

But timing was not fortuitous. One day on her way to the mews Cobb passed her once on the stairs. He had no concealing silk over his arm, and she could see the folded vellum in his hand. He threw her a quick despairing glance, for there were guards and courtiers close by. Marian considered returning quickly to her room, but some guard called out for Cobb, and he hobbled past her, bearing the message from Prince John that she would have no chance to read. Still, that he had sent one at all should have some significance. The timing was right for the raid on the ransom.

Ironically, it was Sir Guy who provided confirmation. He came to her door again early the next morning. This time he waited for her to dismiss Agatha. The older woman departed quietly, and Guisbourne bolted the door behind her. When he turned, the brooding intentness of his expression concentrated her attention.

"What is it?" she asked him.

Guy came to stand beside her at the window, studying

her face in the cool morning light. ''I think you should attend to your hall for a few days. I will be away from Nottingham. I do not want you alone in the castle with Sir Godfrey when I am at Winterclere. His brain is full of perverse twists and turns. I do not think he would be such a fool as to hurt you, but I could not prevent it if he did.'' He reached out and stroked her cheek, his touch both tender and possessive.

At Winterclere. None of his other recent maneuvers had him away overnight or so far north, and the road south from Winterclere skirted Sherwood. But it was the ferment of energy in him, the mingling of excitement and resolve, more than his words, that disclosed his mission to her. Her own excitement at the revelation clashed with the dismay that it was Guy who had yielded the information, but excitement prevailed. She reined it close, answering him seriously. ''You are right. I will go at once.''

''Oh, not quite at once.'' He smiled. ''Tomorrow is soon enough. I do not leave till morning.''

Sensing his desire, she tried to forestall him. She was eager to convey the news to Sherwood, and to embrace Guy now did seem betrayal. ''Then it is better I leave today, before you go.''

''This afternoon then,'' he murmured.

As he reached for her, Marian felt her body tense to pull away. She could think of no lie that would not ring hollow as a death knell. Instead of resisting, she embraced him, twisting her eagerness back on itself, offering it in feverish kisses that he answered with urgency. But touch released too much. Anger flared—at him, at herself. She gripped him tighter, adding the ferocity of wrath to her embrace. *You should not have trusted me*, she thought, pierced with a sudden pain. Her teeth found the muscled curve of his shoulder and bit into the flesh, tasting blood. He gasped and pulled her closer, his knowing hands, his rapacious mouth, exploring with a new and subtle savagery. Marian tried to quell the schism within her, to blot all thought from her mind, subdue everything but the ravishing thrill of sensation as he thrust deep inside her. But sensation released emotion. She could not flee, only plunge deeper into the uncoiling twists of sorrow and rage, shame and desire. She struggled, seeking the escape of carnal oblivion, crying out in a frenzy of need. But there was no escape, only herself and Guy caught in the roiling darkness, locked about each other, black flame and scarlet shadow intertwining. Then flame and shadow merged and leapt, the burning blackness consuming them both together. . . .

Guy lay holding her for a long time, his face buried in her shoulder. Then a shudder ran through him, and he released her. He lifted his head back, his gaze holding hers, golden dark and devastated with pleasure. She was stunned by the power of what he had evoked and frightened, unable to hide either. Worse, the fathomless openness within his eyes pierced her anew, their offering an accusation. He had found some measure of protection, for he smiled ironically and murmured, "You continue to amaze me, Marian."

Then he rose and gathered his clothes and her own. They both were dressed and Guisbourne ready to depart before Agatha returned. He hovered at the door, his amber eyes gazing at Marian with their dark intensity. "I will see you soon," he said.

Abruptly Marian was aware that he might die.

"Take care," she whispered, wishing him safe return, if not success. She kissed him swiftly. Silently she cursed the twists of fate that placed them at odds. Enemy he might be, but he was also ally, friend, lover.

When he had gone, Marian went to the baths and soaked, her nerves strung with tension despite the pleasuring of her body. *Soon it will be over*, she thought. But escape from Nottingham would not free her from her own doubts, from the decisions that must be made. After the bath Marian told Agatha what to pack and ordered Sir Ralph to ready three horses. They rode out of the castle gates together, heading south. Marian was sure they were not followed. She sent Agatha on to Fallwood, with a list of things to occupy the new steward and the workers and orders to be ambiguous about her mistress' arrival. "Tell them I talked of a journey to Lincoln," she said, giving herself an excuse if necessary. Then, circling back through the outlying woods, she by-passed Nottingham and rode directly for Sherwood.

17

Marian turned into the forest at the landmark Robin had described. A moment later one of the men appeared and guided her and Sir Ralph to the next post. Sherwood was one of the finest hunting forests she had seen, alternating open stands of birch and darker-shadowed groves of oak, the woodlands scattered with bright sunlit clearings. The long grasses were a lush pale green blushed with the pink bloom of heather. In their midst unfurled ferns rose high, while goldfinch, sparrow, and thrush pecked at puffy thistle pods. As she passed from clearing to forest again, the trickling music of a lute mingled with the rustling breeze. Then Alan a Dale, sprightly in Lincoln green with a pheasant feather in his cap, swung down from an oak. Walking beside them, he recounted the tale of the rescue as he led them the last mile into camp.

"This is King Richard's hunting lodge." Marian gazed about the clearing, marveling at Robin's insolence. The wooden lodge was surrounded with the outlaw's usual array of huts and lean-tos. All about the camp the men were busy, some cleaning after the midday meal, some tending to the weapons. To one side a small, boisterous group indulged in a rough game of hot cockles, buffeting a kneeling, blindfolded man on the head till he could guess his attacker.

Alan grinned. "So it is. Rob says it's the most comfortable of the sites they have in Sherwood and that Claire would have more privacy here, a place she can familiarize herself with easily. The royal rangers have not dared complain that we use it, no more than the Sheriff's men."

"You're as impudent as Robin," Marian chided as she and Sir Ralph dismounted. "I warrant the rangers dare do little but catch a poacher or two on the edge of Sherwood."

"And not too much of that, or they'll have Robin Hood to answer to," Alan said, deft fingers plucking over the strings of his lute. His music began to weave a subtle duet with another lute, and Alan led them toward the lodge. Lady Claire sat to one side, playing beneath the shady branches of an oak, a small group of men listening as she played. Claire's dark hair was wreathed with daisies, her face alight with happiness. Both Alan's doing, Marian assumed. She waited while the lovers finished their duet, then greeted Claire, who rose and embraced her. Marian returned her tight hug, startled by the rush of affection she felt.

"I've got to speak to Robin Hood," Marian said. "But we must visit later."

"Oh, I've promised a dozen ballads at least." Claire laughed and settled back carefully under the tree. Marian scanned the faces of the men surrounding her and saw nothing unseemly. They seemed most tender with Claire.

Alan spoke softly as he took Marian into the lodge. "Robin makes sure she always has a protector he can trust absolutely. I think it best to get her out of the Sheriff's territory, to a place she can learn absolutely. But I am sure Sir Godfrey will send spies to look at my family."

"And mine," Marian said, tossing her gear onto the floor of the lodge.

"A blind woman will be noticeable anywhere. I think he would hear of her no matter where she went."

"Sir Godfrey may not search hard elsewhere if he thinks her living in Sherwood. I thought she might take refuge in a nunnery," Marian said, almost amused by his crestfallen face, "but I would not trust the Sheriff to honor sanctuary," Marian said. "I will ask my grandfather to offer his protection but I cannot guarantee his promise."

"Thank you." Alan gave her a look that mingled relief and dismay. He must have hoped she would offer yet now regretted his hope.

"If the Sheriff remains in favor with Prince John, he may not risk going against their alliance," Marian told him. "You and Claire must hope for the King's return."

"I do not know that she will leave me, even for a safer refuge," Alan said.

"If she understands the risks, then you should let her choose." Marian looked at him closely. "Unless she is a burden."

Alan looked so surprised that Marian was sure his love had not lessened with the new difficulty of tending Claire. He said again, "I only want her to feel safe. To be safe."

"I do not argue there are places where she might be safer. But I think she will feel so only with you close at hand."

Alan smiled at her uncertainly, heart and head at odds. He gave an elaborate shrug, and she judged heart likeliest to win.

He said no more as Will Scarlett came through the door, his arms filled with the hunting clothes she had worn before. "I thought you might prefer these, Lady Marian," he said.

"Thank you, Will." She accepted the offerings, which she vastly preferred to traipsing through the woods in her trailing skirts, however clear the paths.

When they left her alone, Marian slid into the smooth leathers, feeling them melt into a second skin over her own, clinging and supple. When she reappeared outside the lodge, Will beckoned to her, smiling, and pointed down a path. "Rob and John and Tuck all went off to the great oak. I think they're still there if you're needing to talk to them."

Setting off down the indicated path, Marian felt a rising wariness, not knowing the place it might lead to—though Will had said Robin was not alone. She followed the meandering trail amid the mingled oaks and silver birches of Sherwood, the dirt path bordered by wavy hair grass and tall coiled ferns and patched here and there with the mauve flush of blossoming heather. She had walked for perhaps five minutes when Friar Tuck appeared before her, padding along like a beer barrel in sandals, humming a jaunty tune she belatedly recognized as a hymn.

"Robin's gone down to the great oak, Lady Marian," Friar Tuck said when he reached her, beaming at his own helpfulness. "If you're wanting to see him, just follow the trail."

"John Little is with him?"

"Oh, no, John's gone off hunting. Robin's alone down there now. I'd show you, but this path goes right to the clearing. Rob's sent me to tend the new ale kegs." His eyes lit with cheerful greed, and with a wave of his hand he trundled up the trail to the camp and disappeared round a curve obscured by vine-draped trees.

Marian stood unmoving in the center of the path. Not even a crossroads, though she was already turned around, facing the spot where the Friar vanished from view. She need only follow him back up the trail. Or she could continue on to meet Robin. As simply as that she was given the choice. Even Tuck's blithe innocence was part of the freedom—necessary to it. For if it had been John Little she had encountered, with his taciturn mouth and omniscient gaze, Marian knew she would have turned and walked back with him, smiling with cool defiance that she might do otherwise. To do anything else would have been too intimate an admission.

But she was alone, with no one to account to but herself. Free yet pinioned by the necessity of decision, she stared back along the trail. She knew now what awaited her the other way. There would be no surprise this time, of discovering Robin, of being discovered. There would be no excuse of being swept beyond volition, nor any threat of it. If the great oak was magic, as the grove had been, still she was stepping into that realm with foreknowledge. If not. . . .

If Robin is there, it will be magic, Marian thought. The magic, and Robin, were hers to choose or to deny.

She could still refuse him. She could perhaps will herself to love another, as far as love could be willed. It should be possible. Once she had willed all her courage and discipline, all her spirit to serve hate. And Robin's voice whispered in memory. *You have had death for your lover then. I know how that is.* The words offering understanding . . . promising life.

I have chosen him already, Marian thought, *On a level deeper than my own will yet as utterly myself.* A self she had yet to discover, because that self existed only in Robin's embrace. Robin, whose openness was a portal, fathomless mystery and fathomless knowledge coiled in one luminous being. To enter that portal, she must open herself.

She walked down the path and came to the edge of a clearing, lush and idyllic, the wavy hair grass spangled with scarlet poppies, delicate harebells and purple heartsease. At first glimpse Robin was nowhere in sight, nor was the great oak. Then she stepped from the fringe of trees into the wide expanse of grass and, turning, saw it. Standing near the far end of the clearing, the colossal oak towered over the lesser trees of the surrounding forest. Immensely thick and tall, an acorn sprouted, a sapling stretching up from an age when giants walked the earth, its now massive being still one with their ancient spirit. She crossed directly to the great oak and looked up into the maze of its wide-spreading limbs pavilioned by a vast, rustling green canopy.

From high above Robin gazed down at her. Only his head and shoulders were visible as he leaned over a wooden platform set midway among the branches. He did not greet her, understanding, by her presence, her expression, by whatever link bound them, that she had come to him. Steadily Marian began to climb the oak, pulling herself up and up through the twisting stairway of its enormous branches. He drew back from the edge as she clambered the final rungs and pulled herself onto the platform, brushing the grit of crumbled bark from her hands. Lying on planking softened with furs, Robin met her gaze, his expression intent, aware, yet questioning. Then, in a single fluid movement, he rose to his feet. Standing before her, Robin looked mortal flesh and Faerie spirit, light tangling in the golden disarray of his hair and the dagged cowl of his tunic fringing his shoulders like a garland of dark leaves.

Without his asking, without his touching her, Marian slowly removed the leather skin of breeches and tunic, the supple outer skin an armor that must be stripped, a husk that must be shed, to expose the hidden vulnerability beneath. She stood before him, more naked than she had ever imagined herself to be, yet she felt filled with power, as if the sun poured its life into her veins. Her skin tingled from the mingled caresses of warm breeze, shimmering sunlight, and Robin's ardent gaze flowing over her, touching breast and belly and loins with licking warmth. Under that flush, something chill shivered along her nerves, frosting anticipation with apprehension. *Fear*, she thought. But it was only something to be shattered, surrendered. She felt it edging the heat in her blood, a strange icefire exquisite in itself.

Holding her gaze, he undressed slowly, peeling off his leathers and tossing them aside so that he stood nude, offering all the power and vulnerability of his body and spirit, as she had offered hers. Her eyes praised Robin's beauty, and his sex roused, flushing and swiftly lifting, as her gaze lingered there. Desire gathered, palpable around them. The curtained branches surrounded them, housed them in the pulsing green golden chamber of the forest's heart, sunlight stippling their skin through the dense ever-shifting layers of the whispering leaves. His eyes, the same sun-warmed shade, caught fire and burned with transparent, flame green light—the pure heat of life that could crack the coldest winter's shell, uncoiling tendril by tendril all the verdant splendor of spring. She had no desire left to escape the force that burned within him, at once so fierce, so tender.

The forest's heartbeat quickened, echoing through her own with a sweet eager pain. Her own heart leapt wildly in her breast, as if it longed to shatter and dissolve. Yet for a moment she held control, courage and fear still both hers to command. She thought again, *My choice*. Rapt, his gaze held hers as she reached out and touched him. Her fingers framed his face, delicately stroking the sharp angle of brow

and high curve of cheekbone, moving in to shape the
hawk's arch of his nose, then down to draw the outline of
his mouth, its mocking contours softened to a new innocence. His sighing breath touched her fingertips, its soft
warmth blending with the caressing breeze. Gliding her
hands down over the faint roughness of his jaw, Marian
stroked the strong column of his throat, feeling his quicken-
ing pulse flutter beneath her fingertips. They traveled along
the broad curve of his shoulder, then slowly skimmed inward again, following the long winged line of his collar-
bone to the small hollow. She pressed her palms flat against
the tawny satin of his skin, feeling its texture smooth and
pliant over the subtle curves and angles of muscle and bone.
Golden with the earthly glory of physical beauty, vibrant
with sylvan magic, he radiated a brightness so vivid that to
touch him scorched her with pleasure, blinded her with
wonder.

Robin still only watched her, first her face, then her hand
as she brushed her fingertips over his chest to caress the
bronzed coin of a nipple. He drew in his breath sharply, the
nub tightening at her touch, a tiny hardness beneath her
fingertips. The sensation quivered through her nerves, her
own nipples tightening in response. He reached out to cup
one breast, the small fullness shaping perfectly to his hand.
Palm centering on the aching peak, he rubbed in a subtle,
insistent caress that sent a fiery sap of sunlight and honey
branching through her limbs. She sighed, shivering again as
the poignant sensation permeated every vein and nerve. His
other hand skimmed the pale bush between her thighs, ruffling the hair as softly as a breeze, then molded to the
mound of her sex. One finger stroked the swollen lips,
pressing into the moist, yielding parting to touch the sensitive bud of flesh. She cried out softly as passion overwhelmed her, knees folding as she melted against him.

Robin caught her, and kneeling, he drew her down. Surrendering, she went with his movement, trusting herself to
his strength. For a moment his circling arms were a gentle
haven, as if the forest had enfolded her in all its warm,

whispering softness. Then they tightened around her, and it was not honeyed sunlight and stinging sweet tree sap that streamed through her, but a primordial fire flaring in her veins, in the marrow of her bones. She had denied him twice now, and he gripped her hungrily, arms hard about her, drawing her beneath him onto the plush furs. Marian wrapped herself around him with equal need, arms and legs clasping him tightly, seeking the same piercing, immediate union that he did. A deep tremor shook her as she felt his hard sex straining, pressing to her yielding center.

He drew back only enough to meet her gaze, his eyes green embers burning into her own, the fire of his spirit burning deep into her flesh. She cried out with him as he entered her, his first wild thrust demolishing everything within her that had ever struggled against him. His need penetrated the deepest recesses of her being as his body plunged into hers and she lifted to meet him. They strained together, sweat-drenched, striving, burrowing and flying all at once. Each thrust cleaved her, delving deeper and deeper into the molten fluid heart of her, and she opened and opened and opened to him. She moaned ceaselessly, wounded and healed with the searing, consuming, giving beauty of him within her. His need and her own burned through her until all that was cold and fierce in her met the blaze of what was hot and fierce in him. She felt the final icy inner shell within splinter into a million shards of light. Their unbearable brightness cut like pain, then melted, suffused into pleasure of unbearable sweetness.

The low, broken note of her cry was an uncanny harmony to his high, wild one as she came with him, contracting around him as tremor after tremor reverberated through her, the deepest core of her seized with the joy of him. He called her name hoarsely, his back arched, drawn like a bow, flying to her body, heart, and spirit. She felt the hard throb of him inside her, bathing her with the vital spill of his seed. Clinging, she dissolved in him, fusing into primal elements, rooted in earth, flowing in water, soaring in air, burning in fire. All the darkness in her flamed, pulsating with his light.

After, she clutched him, sobbing, a sound half tears, half untamed laughter. Dazed, she felt her limbs quaking, yet suffused with a brilliant energy that coursed through her, glowing like the vibrant flush of spring after winter freeze. Robin stroked her continuously, murmuring her name, his strong hands combing through the long fall of her hair, then cupping her face. He bent close, his mouth covering forehead, cheeks, lips with tender kisses, then drew back to gaze into her eyes, sharing joy. A long shudder rippled through him, and he sighed, a low crooning of soul-sated pleasure.

"Marian," he whispered, and again, "Marian . . . Marian. . . ."

"Robin," she answered, though she could not hear her own voice.

But he heard, and began again, ravenous still, but slow and savoring in his hunger. He kissed her deeply, and she opened to him, drinking from his kisses. He devoured her as she consumed him, supple tongue sliding into the heat of her mouth, hard cock sliding into lusher, wetter heat below. She wrapped herself around him again, hardness and softness melded into one ravishing sensation. They joined, body and spirit melding in the same exquisite irrefutable alchemy. Matter dissolved, fire became fluid light, as he thrust, then poured into her. The vivid flow of his being into hers was an intoxication of the spirit wilder than any wine could give, obliteration and revelation in one resplendent draft.

. . . And then at last, lying in his arms, adrift in a serene and trembling peace, she thought, *Love has chosen us*.

■■■■■

"I give my word, and that of every man here, to serve Queen Eleanor in King Richard's stead," Robin said gravely, though his lips curled in the faintest mocking smile at his own solemnity.

A shout rose as Marian wrapped Queen Eleanor's scarf around about Robin's arm and tied it, a knightly favor of purest white silk emblazoned with gold. Then he guided her down the gauntlet of cheering and exuberant men to the waiting feast, to seat her beneath the same tree Claire had played under earlier in the day. Together they supped on the bounty of Sherwood: roasted venison and hare, pheasant, and a pastry of starlings and mushrooms, along with hot bread, stewed fruits, and free-flowing ale. Robin drank lightly. He seemed intoxicated, not with the rich brown ale but with laughter and the glow that lingered between them, a brightness of spirit weaving them together with invisible filaments of light.

To ease the celebration into evening, Alan and Claire played and sang—rollicking songs and sad songs, songs of love and songs of battle. After the meal Robin summoned John and his other chosen leaders into the lodge to deploy them for the morrow. Marian, mitigating her own sense of betrayal, told them only that she had overheard Winterclere named as the destination for the maneuvers and that Guisbourne was in charge. Robin and John instantly nodded, having already singled it out as one of the most likely routes. They reasoned it would take a day for Guisbourne to skirt Sherwood and get in position. Robin had already sent Much and some others north to follow the ransom caravan as it traveled through the last towns en route to Nottingham and to mark where it turned. Now he gave Will orders to follow Guisbourne and his men as they moved toward it, and circle around before, sending back messengers as needed. "Even knowing the route, we will have to set troops at various points. More than one road branches off from Winterclere. But my men are swifter, more mobile. As soon as we learn what specific route they are taking, we will gather at a predetermined meeting place."

The others left, all save Robin and John. "It's too late for you to be riding back, my lady," the tall man said. "And there's rain coming as well. I can smell it on the wind."

"Agatha was to say I mentioned riding to Lincoln," Marian told them. "That will do unless the story is examined. Which the Sheriff may. He's looking for an excuse to punish me for Alan's escape."

"Marian will sleep with Claire tonight," Robin told John. "I'll send young Harry to the innkeeper of the Seven Horses. He can provide a story for her if anyone asks."

Little John leaned forward, looking between her and Robin. "Make it more than a story, Rob. Have Lady Marian finish the ride to Lincoln while we're doing our work for King Richard. When that's over and done, and while Lady Marian is still safe outside the castle, let's go back through the tunnel and take care of the Sheriff and his torturer."

Despite her own hatred of the Sheriff, Marian said, "His failure to capture the ransom may destroy him for you, with no more risk to yourselves."

"Neither of those men will be destroyed till they're dead," Robin argued. "A fall from power will only move the Sheriff elsewhere. And perhaps his torturer with him."

"Whoever is Sheriff will have a torturer," Marian said. "There is no help for that."

"Perhaps not," Robin answered, "but these two men together will urge each other to greater atrocities."

So far they spoke only of killing the Sheriff and his torturer, but would they not also try to destroy Guy if they could? She felt his specter hovering, neither friend nor enemy but some strange, disturbing mixture. "The next might be even worse," Marian said. But not even she, saying it, believed it.

John Little bowed his head. "I killed the old one, for raping my daughter, and look what was put in his place. I can't let it go on."

"Ever since the new torturer arrived, things have been getting slowly worse," Robin told her. "We can't let him continue terrorizing the people."

"For months the brewmaster and his men have burrowed into the heart of Nottingham Castle," John said. "I was happy to rescue Alan and the Lady Claire, but I would like to see that tunnel lead straight to Sir Godfrey's death.''

Yes, there is Claire, Marian thought, *Alan and Claire will never truly be free until the Sheriff is dead*. At last Marian voiced her hidden concern. ''The killing of a Sheriff is a serious crime, and I think you cannot escape blame. King Richard is touchy in such things.''

''I am well aware of that. He punished my father for joining him, instead of remaining loyal to the old King. Then he sold almost every office in England to the highest bidder, to finance his crusade.'' Robin smiled bitterly. ''But I have become cautious, with the hope of pardon. I too thought an assassination might sit ill with Richard, unless the Sheriff were in more open defiance.''

''Yes,'' Marian said at once. ''Far better to do it if the Sheriff resists King Richard's return.''

''But he may not resist. He may even have stolen enough to buy Richard's favor and continue ruling Nottinghamshire. Those questions will not be answered until King Richard returns—months from now, if ever. The Sheriff will not restrain himself meanwhile. When he commits his next atrocity, I will feel as if I have permitted it.''

Marian thought of Lady Margaret and nodded grimly. Then she lifted her head and declared, ''If you cannot escape blame, we will share it. If it sits ill with King Richard that a Sheriff of England was so executed, I will say it was at my order. I want it done, as much as either of you.''

''Very well, my lady,'' John said. ''We serve England as much in this as in our efforts with the ransom.''

''As for the ransom,'' Marian added. She glanced at John, then met Robin's eyes. ''I will not be hidden away in Lincoln. I will ride with you. I will fight with you. My place is by your side.''

18 Flanked by Marian and Little John, Robin stood in the drizzle beside the boulders at the top of Cooper's Mount. Shielding his eyes, he gazed intently at the rider pounding furiously across the valley toward them, not yet able to make him out through the dreary day. The man charged over rocky hillsides, between stands of trees, cut sharply down through blind gullies, then emerged again, coming always right at them.

"It can't be one of the Sheriff's men," Little John muttered. "Those must be still on the other side of the river. And not a scout of ours either. We sent them well west of the road, not toward the river."

Robin nodded a silent agreement and turned to greet Tuck, come to make a nervous nuisance of himself. Robin smiled at him nonetheless.

Marian turned to him, her blue-gray eyes keen and questioning. "Could our information have been wrong, Robin? Perhaps the King's Guard came another way and we are waiting too far south?"

"Much himself saw the King's force two days ago, following their planned course. His message was not wrong, but I may have been."

Robin stood among the others, staring at the rider who was yet far off. He felt an obscure discomfort nibbling at the back of his mind. The unease subsided momentarily as he allowed his eyes to follow their own will, caressing Marian. His gaze flowed down the startling course of her blond hair, down across her lovely back and flank, along the full, strong line of her legs. His mind melted into memory . . . the living cathedral of the oak, caressing them with jeweled light and sighing breath. He felt Marian's body curving to his, her being opening to his at last, body and spirit together taking flight. The glow of it returned, suffusing him. . . .

But not entirely. He could not keep away a sense of crisis.

He wrenched his eyes back to the charging rider and considered what sort of fool would push a horse so recklessly over that ground. He was fleeing nothing immediately behind him. He was fleeing nothing at all. He was coming ever at them. Then Robin knew this was no sort of fool at all.

"It's Will," he said, soft but certain.

"Will? How can you mark him from here?" Friar Tuck asked, peering anxiously through the drizzle. "He's too far off, even for your eyes. His horse is bay, but so are a thousand others."

"I can see him no better than you, but I do know that something has gone terribly wrong. That can only be Will Scarlett. The Sheriff's men must be across the river in front of us, and Will is rushing to us with the worst of news."

"Then we're not between Sir Guy and his prize?" Marian asked. "They couldn't have crossed the bridge and gotten past us. They had not enough time, and we would have seen them. And the ford is too far north."

Little John turned to Robin, seeming skeptical for a moment. Then John accepted the conviction in Robin's voice and summoned Much from among the men waiting farther down the hill. "Tell us again, lad," he said sharply. "What did you see?"

"But nothing," Much said in a fluster. "Or rather just the King's Guard. And the wagons. We waited at the last ford, and it was as you said. Only the King's men came. How could the Sheriff's knights be here?"

"Easy now, lad." John reassured him. "Could the Sheriff's knights have gotten to the ford before you?"

"No. Not at all. We had eyes everywhere. Will Scarlett's

rider came and reported they had left Nottingham on the Winter Road toward us. That had to put them to the south, in between as it were. Not north enough to reach the ford in time. Not south enough for the bridge. And there's no place in between for knights to cross the river.''

Marian looked at Robin and said, ''We could cross the river, couldn't we, anywhere?''

''Why did I think they should remain as themselves?'' Robin asked of no one. ''Why shouldn't they ultimately learn to do as we do in Sherwood?''

Robin ran down the hillside to where the horses were tethered. He sprang atop Jester and wheeled in a tight circle, crying, ''Mount up.''

Amid a great rush and swarm to the horses, Marian swung into the saddle of her mare and reined in close to Robin. Little John rode up beside them. Robin told him, ''Leave two dozen on the crest, John. And drop off scouts as we go.''

Horses milled all about them, riders adjusting their gear. Leaders were shouting their men into their assigned groups, looking for the signal. ''Ride,'' Robin called. ''Ride now for Will.'' And they bolted down the hillside, mounted ninety strong, their horses' hooves pounding.

Robin held back his horse just enough not to outrun the pace. No troop could match the speed of its fastest rider, and Jester was the fastest horse. But Robin could never ride smoothly at the pace of the troop. Never smoothly—except he was. Robin startled inwardly. Where was that demon today? That familiar demon who wanted to crash forth at all speed. How many times had John told him? There was no point to arriving before the force. It was foolish. It was an indulgence. And why today did it not cut him to hold back, even if just so slightly?

The riders were thundering at their greatest speed. He could do nothing more to increase that. He looked at Marian and knew why he felt so strangely tranquil. Until they reached Will, nothing more could be done. No rider needed any orders or encouragement. John occasionally nodded to riders to drop off in their wake. Robin admired how well John knew them all, how nicely he judged what each could do, how easily he commanded them, how much it freed him to imagine. He looked over at Marian riding beside him again, smiling at him as their steeds rushed on, wanting not to forge ahead but to ride with her at his side, one with her and the surging horse beneath him, one with the wind and the cool, licking rain.

■■■■■■

The lead riders parted and cheered Will as he rode through them and reined sharply left. Robin pulled his horse left, and they closed together into a narrowing orbit. Will thrust his fist into the air and called out, "Hail, Robin." The men cheered again, but Will's face was grim and taut. They circled their horses about each other, turning their momentum into a halt. Robin thought that if he were to die, then Little John would lead, but he would teach Will and raise him to ascendancy as he did so. The men would have a rock to rest on and a light to guide them.

"And hail the Lady Marian as well," Will said quietly now, with no smile, even for her.

"No greeting for such as me," Little John glowered in mock anger.

"Nay, none. You're too fierce for greeting, except perhaps with mug aloft," Will said. Then the roguish manner faded into stern resolve, and he continued. "But with news like mine, all we'll lift will be our swords."

"For the Sheriff's men have the ransom and the King's Guard lies dead in the road," Robin said starkly. Will's face flashed surprise that Robin should have divined his news, but he nodded that it was so. Robin looked right at him, asking without words, and he knew the expression of the others about them asked the same.

"And twelve at least of ours," Will confirmed.

"Damn them," Robin muttered as the mood darkened about them, then in a moment, repeating it, "Damn them all," with his voice rising, a surge of rage flowing out, steeling all about him. He felt the emotion of the band pulling into one shared resolve.

"Tell us," he commanded.

"We saw them before they reached the wood. The Sheriff's men, but not the Sheriff. He stayed safe in Nottingham, we hear. It was Guisbourne leading the Sheriff's men."

"To verify the ruse, such as it is?" Marian wondered, frowning. "Sir Godfrey wants a scapegoat if it fails?"

"Guisbourne will take the blame for failure," Robin said. "If he succeeds, Sir Godfrey will reap the glory of the success."

"He has succeeded," Friar Tuck said glumly.

"Not yet," Robin snapped, wanting to cuff him. Tuck let out a small peep at his glare and subsided. Robin reined his temper. "Go on, Will."

"Guisbourne led thirty mounted knights and ten times that in men at arms. I tell you I didn't like it from the first. Not the numbers. We've seen that before, but the order of them. The Sheriff's disciplined but ponderous. Guisbourne had them moving too quickly."

"Sir Guy has been away a great deal, training the soldiers," Marian said somberly.

"Week by week he's made them more dangerous," Robin assented. "Did they see you there?"

"Not then, but they for certain assumed it. They had small units posted to all their flanks as they moved, and we dared not get too close. Still, it looked enough like the usual grinding of knights, heavy-mailed. Once they'd all moved onto the Winter Road I sent off messengers, to you and to the ford."

Robin nodded, and Will saw that the messengers had arrived.

"They pressed north along the Winter Road and quickly, but they were not going to reach the ford before the guard. They slowed their pace and made camp early in the afternoon, too early, at Three Oak Hill. It felt wrong. Come morning we knew why.

"At first light Guisbourne formed them up and turned

back toward Nottingham with all the knights. Then the
guards broke for the river at the fastest pace that lot has ever
moved, with that devil Bruno leading. They were dressed
like us, as you said they'd be, most of them in Lincoln
green. That's when I saw it, that they'd act the part as well
as look it. Three Oaks Hill is at the very shortest distance
from the Winter Road to the Great Road beyond the river.
The knights were for show, to fool us. They meant to go for
the King's Guard just as we would have, fast on foot
through the wood, riders covering the sides.

"We were thirty then. We got out in front, to the sides,
and rained down arrows on them, but they moved forward
by groups, always covering each other, and we had to stay
well off. I hoped we could get across the river and slaughter
them as they swam, but Robin"—Will paused, shaking his
head in perplexity. "Rob, they had men at the river. Waiting, with boats."

"Sent down from York and Gainsborough," Marian surmised, "or across from Lincoln. The Sheriff has been weaving a few other men of power into this conspiracy. I learned
names but not their part of the plot."

"Boats?" Robin asked, both angry and intrigued.

"Yes, several small covered boats. We blundered into
their party. Robin, I never expected they could be in front of
us. It cost us three men there, and we barely got across the
river ahead of them. Still, we were ready on the far side, but
when they pushed off in the boats, they raised screens to
shield themselves. Very closely woven. We fired arrow after
arrow right into the screens, but it did nothing. They were
over and on top of us in numbers. We had to drop off
immediately and could not hinder their main party."

"The boats?" Robin repeated. "What did they do with
the boats?"

"Nothing. They left them and came at us. We fought
them from the front all the way to the Great Road. We hit
their longest shooters, but it didn't keep us safe. Another
four brave men were lost on the way."

"Did you get off someone to the King's Guard?" Little

John asked in the manner of a teacher knowing that the pupil would be able to confirm having taken the proper action.

"Yes, two, and they both were shot riding up to the guard to warn them. Shot as Saxons always are, no need to listen." Then he stumbled, glancing askance at Marian. "Forgive me, my lady. I forget myself."

"My family has Norman power, but we boast Saxon blood, and Viking," Marian said. "We respect anyone with fighting spirit."

"I can imagine how some pure-blooded Normans greet that boast," Robin said cynically, before turning back to Will. "What next?"

"There was nothing much after that, except dead knights. Bruno caught them strung out along the road. They had no way to close up with all the trees about and were swarmed over. It didn't take long. We shot from the sides because for a while they ignored us. But soon all the guards were dead, absolutely all, and then Bruno turned on us. We were scattered. I told the men to break it off and save themselves. Two of ours refused to flee. They stood and shot their arrows until the pikes cut them down." Will paused, hardly able to continue, head bowed. "After that, I pulled this horse free from its dead master and rode for Cooper's Mount, here to meet you with this dreadful news."

Painful murmurs went through the riders holding their horses closely in to hear a full measure of the dreadful news. Robin felt the rage of the men and damped down his own. They would charge blindly behind him, straight for any death he would lead them at. And he wanted them fervent, impetuous, but only at the right moment. Robin eased his horse next to Will's mount, put a hand on his shoulder, and looked gently into his face. "Will, you did bravely and you did well. There is fault here, but it is mine. I set you forth on the wrong plan, and we must now bear the terrible outcome. But, Will, there is no time now for the pain. We must act. We are few compared with their strength, and we cannot surprise them in the wood. You must lead us to the boats, Will, now.''

''Yes!'' Marian exclaimed, understanding instantly. ''It must be to the boats, for they could be vulnerable only at the bridge.''

''Will,'' Robin demanded, ''how many boats and how big?''

''Ten of them, each with room for seven or eight.''

''How many chests held the ransom?''

''Four.''

''If they can use our ways, then we must turn their tools against them,'' Robin said quietly, and turned to Little John. ''Send half our number back to Cooper's Mount. Pick any leader you wish. From there they must go down to the road in small parties. They are to hinder and harass, but they are not to engage Bruno and his guards. We need time from them. Time only, not dead men. And tell them to beware the bridge, for Guisbourne will be coming with a dozen knights.''

''And if we don't sink?'' Little John asked. ''The river winds wide of Sherwood—we'll need a new transfer point.''

''Skull Hollow,'' Robin said.

■■■■■■

''Higher. Pull that third one higher. It can still be seen,'' Marian called, and motioned them up with her hand.

''If it goes up another foot, we may as well take off my head, for I'll never fit beneath those beams.''

''Why not take it off, John?'' Robin laughed. ''And save your liege the trouble.''

''I have no princely liege.'' Little John's voice boomed up from the water. ''The only Norman I follow is the King. Now pull, lads. Pull as ever high as the lady's hand insists.''

Up it came, snugger and snugger beneath the deck of the bridge. Marian looked upstream to the river bend and called for more until the signal branch was lowered. ''There!'' she cried, cutting sharply through the air with the back of her hand. "Tie it off."

Robin stood on the bridge, calling out which men were for the boats and which would take their bows to the thicket just downstream. When Little John climbed up from below, Robin turned that task over to him and motioned to him a rider newly arrived on the bridge.

"How far off are they?" he asked.

"Not half an hour."

"And the wagons? How far behind the first of them?"

"Another ten minutes behind."

"Two wagons, four chests?"

"Yes, still."

"Will, any news from the Nottingham Road?"

"Guisbourne will be here within the hour."

Robin saw Much turn from Little John in disappointment and stand nearby, betrayed by his own youth, wanting to appeal the decision, yet not wanting to ask. Robin turned to him and said, "He's right, Much. This will be sword work. We need your bow over there instead, giving us cover. Remind them all. No one is to shoot until the wagons are directly over the boats. We'll go for the wagon guards. Do all you can to keep help away from them."

"Yes, Robin. I'll shoot as long as I have arrows."

"And Much," Little John called out, "don't think you have it easy. We have a nice way out of here by water, but you're going to have all the hounds of Nottingham chasing you through Sherwood."

Robin saw the thought cheered Much, for he walked off the bridge smiling.

They waited, crouched in the boats hanging under the deck of the bridge, woven mats covering their bodies. Several men perched in angles of the crossbeams. Robin felt a wonderful ease come over him. The others seemed mostly nervous, but he liked this time. No need to think. No need to plan. Only to slide inside the stillness and savor the coiled wait of the predator. Marian was beside him, her thigh pressed close. Not the distraction he'd thought it might be, because she'd slide inside the time too, weaving through the crosscurrents, the slow-spinning gyre of patience and anticipation. She refused to go anywhere without him. She would do nothing but risk it all. He supposed he should fear for her, but being companions-in-arms was too pure a joy. Dangerous as it was for her, for them all, rocking in small boats before a battle, he felt himself relax, even the tension in his shoulders. It all flowed out of him, and he luxuriated in having only to feel, at once easy and utterly alert.

The boat rocked slightly as she turned to him and asked quietly, "Do you think we were betrayed?"

"Not betrayed, I think, but anticipated. Guisbourne is even more wily than the Sheriff. We were well confronted. They could take the ransom only if there was to be a hope of putting it on us, and they've set themselves at the very limits of my territory, beyond my shield of Sherwood."

Marian nodded. "This way, whether we knew the ransom route or not, Guisbourne's plan would work."

"I expected none of this because they were never before capable of anything but being ponderous knights, easy to watch, easy to ambush. As we see, it has all become different. Guisbourne could predict me, and he could build a new force. We have the advantage still in Sherwood, but a large force so trained could wreak havoc not previously possible. It is not a war I want to wage. Best we go all out for Richard and win free of it entire."

"Fighting in his name doesn't seem to distress you any longer," Marian said quietly. Her chain mail glinted in the shadows under the bridge. Her helmet was ready to hand.

Robin gave her a slow, lazy smile, and she gave it back. The tight bud of hope she had given him weeks ago had unfurled, spreading bright petals and a perfume that dizzied him with its promise. *Love and freedom*, he thought. There was more he wanted, it was true, yet at this moment he had them both and was content. He rested, sun-drenched and golden in the light of Marian's smile, while the rain drizzled morosely around them. She started to speak, but he held up a hand to still her. "Hooves."

Quietly Marian slid on her helm, and laid her hand ready on the hilt of her sword. Together they waited for the coming battle. Robin's thigh still pressed close to hers, and he felt the rising heat of her blood burning through leather and muscle to fire his own.

Anticipation linked every man now as the riders crested the hill and crossed onto the bridge. Men and horses rattled by overhead. Robin was startled by how loud it all was. He looked up through the matted arrow screen, through cracks in the bridge deck, and saw feet and hooves trampling down. He knew it was impossible for them to look down and see anything through the cracks, yet it seemed they must be discovered. He pushed his green scarf farther into the neck of his tunic and felt that old glow again. No more space for thinking, for planning, only the delicious waiting fine-honed to seconds, to a heartbeat, feeling the wildness swelling his blood.

A cry rose when the flight of arrows rained from the thicket. Guisbourne's men bellowed in alarm, even as Robin signaled his men. They scrambled out of the boats, up the sides of the bridge and onto the deck, swords in hand. Stunned by the deluge of arrows, Guisbourne's men were slow to realize the danger beneath them but recovered quickly. The first two men coming over the rail were spotted by the wagon guards and killed straight off, but then Robin pushed past them and was the first onto the bridge. He cut down a guard and backed off two others. Then Will was beside him, and then Marian, and the three of them cut through guards and climbed onto the lead wagon. Little John appeared at the railing opposite and hacked off the head of the nearest guard. More men came over the rail behind him, and they slashed toward the back of the last wagon. And then there were more over the rail to engage all the guards on both wagons.

Despite the noise, the confusion, and the deadly arrows coming at them from the thicket, all the Sheriff's men fought fiercely. The withering fire of arrows from the thicket was perfectly concentrated, just before and just after the wagons. Guard after guard pushed toward the wagons and fell as they came under the fire of the arrows. Robin in the front and Little John behind each had a small group of men dispatching the guards who escaped the arrows.

Marian and Will charged the last three remaining guards atop the wagons. Robin saw her evade one thrust, only to have her sword tangled by the next. As she pulled free, she drew her long knife and stabbed the guard in the heart. Will hacked at a soldier beside her, then turned to meet yet another moving in from the side. Then Robin looked back again, and time stood still as the last guard raised his sword over her head, Robin seeing that not even Will was close enough to help. Marian jerked her long knife, but it was stuck in the dead guard's heart and didn't want to come free. The sword swung down on her. She jerked again, and at last her knife came out. She stepped inside the descending arc and thrust up, stabbing him in the throat.

To the front Guisbourne's guards broke from the road and ran toward the thicket. Robin's bowmen there had to divert many arrows to defend themselves. The withering rain of arrows keeping the other guards from the wagons faded abruptly, and on the bridge more guards broke toward the wagons.

The remaining boats pushed off, moving down the river toward the bridge. They held their shields to the side, shooting arrows freely as they came. They were not accurate from the water, but the surprise of firing from the other direction relieved the pressure. Robin and his men climbed on the wagons and began roping the chests.

On Robin's signal, the three boats under the bridge were lowered to the water and were held just below the bridge. Will and Marian got ropes around the chests on the other wagon, and six of Robin's strongest guided them down into the boats waiting below. The first two went smoothly, but the third chest got hung up against a piling and couldn't be controlled.

"Forget it," Marian cried, and hacked the rope, letting the chest fall into the river and sink from sight. "Get the last one."

Robin laughed wildly as they lowered the fourth chest, then signaled again. All his men near the wagons went down the lines into the boats. There was a final flurry of arrows from the thicket just as guards were poised to break through the pile of the dead. As the position in the thicket and on the bridge began to collapse, Sir Guy of Guisbourne surged onto the bridge at the head of a running file of knights, knocking their own men aside, crashing through toward the wagons.

All at once Robin feared for Marian and fought the black panic that would make him blind and reckless. He dared a glance at her, and she seemed strangely still, watching the onslaught of Guisbourne and his men. Then her eyes met his, briefly, and she was again a fierce windstorm of movement as she thrust to kill the next guard who attacked.

"Robin!" Little John cried out, and Robin swung his own sword, feeling as much as seeing the guard who struck at him from the side.

The man beside Robin was hacked down. "Jump," Robin yelled over his shoulder as he cut down the guard in a surge of fury.

The other men went over the side, and Little John and Robin backed rapidly toward each other, providing a last bit of cover. The guards were finding it difficult to get over the pile and were coming at them one by one, each cut down in turn. Robin parried blow after blow, but the broad side of a sword crashed into the side of his head. He was stunned for an instant and dizzied, but he knew he was not cut.

Then an arrow struck Little John in the shoulder with terrible ferocity, and blood poured from his shoulder and that sight was a greater hurt to Robin.

"Jump," Robin yelled as he darted at the two nearest Little John. He forced them back, but they rushed him again, their swords raised.

"Jump," he cried again.

Little John stood, swaying, drenched in blood. He dropped his sword, but he would not jump. Instead he grabbed Robin by the belt with his one good arm, and with his enormous strength, whirled and threw him off the bridge.

Robin splashed into the water beside the last boat. As he was pulled aboard, Robin saw Guisbourne rear his massive charger. Little John still would not jump; instead he picked up his sword and staggered toward his enemy. Guisbourne surged forward, lifting his sword. Robin saw the glittering weapon come crashing down on Little John and rise red-edged to fall again and again, until finally Little John fell beneath the hooves of the horse.

As archers crowded to the rail of the bridge, two men raised the shield, and the others began paddling furiously down the river. Marian was right there, pulling him into the boat. Robin stared at her, trying to focus. The blow to his head was still weakening him, and his vision began flickering, his mind swimming in darkness. He heard the whining rush of arrows coming down from above and the soft thud as they hit the shield. Different from the thud of horses' hooves.

"John," he whispered, the darkness of that wound was more grievous.

He heard Marian say, "I promise you the King will not forget this. Nor will I."

"He was worth ten of your kings," Robin said, feeling the pain at last.

19

Marian spent another night in Sherwood, tending the unconscious Robin in the King's hunting lodge. She stayed long enough next morning to see him awaken briefly and promised she would return quickly. She rode with Ralph back to Fallwood Hall, where Agatha assured her no one had asked her whereabouts. "As far as the castle is concerned, you were here. As far as your new steward knows, you were in Lincoln." Then Marian told Agatha of Guisbourne's initial capture of the ransom, of the battle that had cost so dearly in casualties, and of Robin's successful ploy with the boats. "The mission is a success. By now the ransom is in the innkeeper's cellar, and Friar Tuck on his way to London to inform the Queen."

"With no one the wiser, it will soon be in London."

"I have done for the Queen all that I promised I would," Marian said. "It is time for us to leave Nottingham."

"You'll not hear any argument, Lady Marian. I'll be pleased enough to see the last of the Sheriff's face," Agatha said with no wry humor to leaven the grim tone. "I will not ride north with you. I don't think we need devise an explanation. There's reason enough for me to flee your service with all that's been happening. And I'll be more useful in London."

Marian concurred. Wanting only to return as soon as possible to Sherwood, Marian worked late into the night, settling the last details with the new steward, tying such ends as she'd left purposefully dangling. He grumbled mildly at being kept from his bed but admitted satisfaction once everything was in order. After a restless sleep she rose early and rode with her companions into Nottingham. At the outskirts of the city they arranged for Agatha to join a troop of pilgrims leaving that afternoon, riding to Canterbury by way of London. "We will come back here after we've gathered our belongings," Marian said to Agatha. "I don't want you alone in Nottingham once I've left."

Riding into the middle bailey of Nottingham Castle, all three of them could feel the tension permeating the Sheriff's men. The unease was so strong that Marian felt free to comment on it to the head groom. He nodded sagely. "You're right, my lady. There was a battle. We've heard Robin Hood and his men planned to steal the King's ransom. Our men tried to recapture it, but they failed. We've a lot of wounded. The Sheriff is practically froth . . . is very upset. Sir Guy is in a fine fury too."

Marian sent Sir Ralph to get Topaz from the mews, while she and Agatha made their way to the upper bailey. Marian informed the chamberlain that they would be leaving and asked him to tell her when she could have an audience with the Sheriff. Upstairs in their chamber she and Agatha set about packing. Marian felt an edge of nervousness. It was necessary to pay her respects to the Sheriff, and she only hoped he would be glad enough to be rid of her not to interfere with her departure. She did not look forward to their final encounter, but the prospect of bidding farewell to Guy was more disturbing.

Marian remembered her hesitation at the bridge. Attuned to Robin, prepared for the cold necessity of battle, Marian had imagined she would feel detached from inner turmoil if she encountered Guisbourne. But the impact of his presence, her own wish for him to survive had stunned her. She had frozen, if only for a second, but that second had the excruciating intensity of a nightmare. Though the tide had turned when Guisbourne rode onto the bridge, she felt her own hesitation wedded to that turn and all that followed. Guy survived, but John Little was dead, and the bleakness of his loss weighed on her spirit. She wondered what she would have felt toward John if he had killed Guy. She had felt respect and affection for the giant. But if her feelings for Little John had not been so deep, neither were they so paradoxical as the intensity of emotion Guisbourne stirred within her. She had willed herself to love Guy and almost succeeded. If there had been no Robin Hood . . .

But there was Robin. Marian could not endure to play them both now that she knew which she loved. Robin was grieving, and she wanted to return to his side. She had done what Eleanor asked, and now she would leave. She was done with connivance.

She and Agatha packed and quickly assembled their trunks and had them sent to the stable yard. As the servants carried the trunks down the staircase, Guy came to the door. Agatha glanced at Marian and left when she nodded her consent.

"You can see I have decided to leave." Marian gestured to the trunks. "I would have said good-bye." That was not a lie. She would not be so cowardly as to leave without a farewell.

"Why now?"

"There is nothing more to pretend to do at Fallwood. And so I have stopped pretending to myself as well."

"And what pretense is there between us? I thought we understood each other admirably." His tone was ironic, but his eyes clouded with distress.

His words stung, but she faced him. "You said it yourself. We have had no allegiance but pleasure, and in that we served each other well. Intense as it was, I must return home and attend to my other allegiances. To pretend that you can belong to that part of my life is futile."

"Wait just a little longer." He said it lightly, but he moved closer, and she could feel him willing her to agree.

She shook her head. "No, my mind is made up. What has happened here preys on my mind, growing ever more bitter . . . and ever more fearful. I have indulged my desire at the expense of my spirit and my safety. Now I must leave. It's too long since I've seen my family."

He stepped close, his hands gripping her arms and pulling her close. He kissed her, his mouth hungry yet ever skillful, coaxing and ravishing at once. She felt the embers of their fire stir and leap to life, a dark sorcerous flame. Unique and powerful as it was, its potence had faded. Firmly she pulled away. He stared into her eyes, his own burning golden coals. "I desire you more than I ever have anyone." His voice was low and urgent, almost whispering. He looked disconcerted by the discovery, his eyes widening a little in surprise.

She felt something uncoil within her and reach out to him, even as another part of her wound the coil tight once more. The conflict twisted within her, a strange pain. What would she do if now, at the last, Guy sought her on the terms she had suggested? His attempt to capture the ransom had failed, and Prince John would not be kind to that failure. Perhaps his best chance lay now with her and with a renewed allegiance to King Richard. She had already offered to speak for him. She had in essence offered herself. But that was before he had committed himself to robbing the King.

And before she had committed herself to Robin.

Too late. But she could see he had determined to convince her. Knowing the futility, she was relieved when the chamberlain knocked at the door and summoned her into the Sheriff's presence.

"Farewell, Sir Guy," she said quietly.

He refused to answer her, deliberately leaving the conversation unfinished. She turned and went out the door, following the chamberlain down the stairs to the hall. The Sheriff waited, puffed with venom, but Marian was immune to his words. She let him fume, then thanked him for his hospitality, curtsied, and took her leave. Agatha, eager to join her pilgrims, was waiting outside in the entrance. Marian did not know if Guy still waited upstairs, but she went directly to the stables and mounted her horse. The trunks had been loaded onto mules, and Sir Ralph had Topaz on her perch, jesses and hood in place. Marian signaled them to leave, and a sense of oppression lifted as she rode out the gate.

■■■■■■

Guy waited, willing Marian to return. But she did not. At last he went out to the stables to confirm that her horses were gone. And her sparrowhawk was gone from the mews as well. Seething, Guy cursed his pride. He was cut that her departure came so soon after his failure to capture the ransom. If he had wanted her to stay, he should have waited outside the hall to convince her. Marian had made her farewell, and he knew that she was strong-willed. This talk of allegiances was folly compared with the passion they shared. If Richard did not return, she would be well pleased with a suitor allied with Prince John.

Except that Prince John would be little pleased with Guy when he heard of the fiasco with the ransom. Guy had heeded his warning about the outlaws but not well enough. Nothing had gone as he planned, but his life was not yet in shambles. Not quite. Refusing to deal with Godfrey's whining yet again, Guy prowled the battlements, trying to formulate the best course of action.

His mind kept returning to Marian, to the look of regret and resolve with which she had bidden him farewell. Their affair was ended, but she was not entirely lost to him. If she was committed to this decision, then he could have her again only if he changed his loyalties or if Prince John came to power. And she was looking for a husband, finally, not a lover. He could have her now only if he took her to wife. But he had been playing with that possibility almost from the day of her arrival. Guy decided he would not pursue her immediately. He needed to reconsider when he was calmer. Rather than follow her at once, he would be wise to give her time to miss him first, to lower the shields she raised against him. If he allowed passion to be such a guiding force in his decision, he wanted passion in return. But how long did he dare wait?

There was noise below. Looking down, he saw some

commotion in the middle bailey and ran down the steps from the allure to the yard below. Seeing him approach, the men parted to allow him to speak to the panting guard. "What is happening?"

"Sir Guy, I'm sure we've found the tunnel—the tunnel Robin Hood must've used to get into the dungeon. Harry and I found it, and we've been trying to force it open for ten minutes or more, but it's wedged too tight from below. We asked for help. . . ." The man paused, his look of triumph changing to anxiety.

"Whom did you ask?" Guy's nerves prickled, well tuned now to disaster.

"We told Laurel, Sir Guy. She was hovering behind us, watching. Amazed she was too, when we found the rock door in the storage room. It almost escaped us, for it was hidden behind some bales and set tight, but it shifted just a little under Harry's feet. We sent Laurel to tell you all and fetch some tools to help us lift it or break the brace."

"I saw Laurel walking out the gate of the middle bailey," said one of the guards gathered around. "That was ten minutes ago."

"And who is Laurel?"

The guard looked at him in amazement, his hands sketching a woman's form in the air. "She's the pretty little dark one, Sir Guy, who serves at supper a lot and helps in the kitchen. She's the brewmaster's niece."

Guy closed his eyes, picturing vividly the brewery and the Pilgrim, side by side at the base of the cliffs, their backs flush against the rock. He opened his eyes and saw the plot was still not apparent to the men around him, though they knew something was amiss. Only the misbegotten fool who had sent the brewmaster's niece for help had any inkling what was wrong. The look of dawning recognition might be enough to save him from a whipping.

"I thought the tunnel would come out on the far side of the cliffs," he whined.

"Ten lashes," Guy commanded, signaling one of the officers to take the man. "And five for his friend Harry."

All about him the men grew taut at the threat. Smiling grimly, Guisbourne began snapping orders. In two minutes he had an armed and mounted troop. The Sheriff's guards were inferior to his own, but they'd do well enough for this. He led them down the hill, but when they arrived, both the Pilgrim and the brewery were deserted. It was what he had expected, though he'd had a faint hope of greed interfering—that the brewmaster or his cohorts would believe they'd have time to carry off some of their ale. Fear prevailed over greed, a sensible priority when you ran afoul of the Sheriff of Nottingham.

Guy turned to the men. "Which of you come here often and can recognize the workers?"

All came often, it seemed and gossiped their heads off without doubt. Snarling, Guy chose the ones that seemed most observant to search with him and sent the others into the inn and the brewery. "Probe the back walls, the floors. You're looking for the entrance to a tunnel.

"The rest of you split up and search. You're to check every likely hiding place. If you recognize any of the workers from the brewery or the inn, take them prisoner."

He divided them up, sending them out to explore. Twenty minutes later one of the guards set to searching the inn came to him, cringing, to announce that the brewmaster was dead. "He was riding up on horseback, Sir Guy, coming from the river. He must have been away when the others were warned off. He spotted us before we really noticed and took off at a gallop. His horse looked fast enough to escape with the good start he had on us . . . so we drew our bows and shot him."

"Who is we?"

The man gave the name of his commander last, and Guisbourne hadn't a doubt that he'd been the one to order the bows drawn. "I ordered you to take prisoners."

The guard nodded, stiff with fear. Guy let him sweat and then dismissed him. It was the commander who'd violated the order, then sent his minion to take the punishment. It was the commander who'd pay. Dead was only slightly better than escaped. He'd rather the men had tried to capture the brewmaster and failed. But at least he'd have a corpse to toss before the Sheriff. Guy continued his own search, tracing the far edge of the pattern he'd laid out for the men. Then he saw a guard's horse, a big beast with a crooked blaze, tied to a withering tree in a narrow alley. Guy drew his sword and dismounted, commanding his own mount to stay with a gesture. Quietly he approached the house bordering the alley. This was one possible approach the brewmaster might have used, coming from the river to the castle.

As he moved toward the doorway of the hut, he heard sobbing and muffled grunts. He kicked open the door and found one of the guards swiving a small dark woman. Laurel, he presumed, though it might be no more than a chance seized. Half naked, the woman was struggling and weeping, but she had not dared cry out for help, not with a knife pressed to her throat. The man gaped at him and grinned sheepishly and lewdly, eyes flickering an invitation to join in the rape.

"Get off her," Guy ordered coldly. There were going to be a lot of whippings in the courtyard. Guy wouldn't have been surprised to be presented with another corpse instead of a valuable prisoner.

"It's Laurel," the guard said, as if this excused him.

"I surmised that. Get off her or I'll cut you off her."

The man backed away, already withered, and fastened his clothing. In a swift movement Laurel flung herself into Guy's arms. Instantly he had his sword to her throat, a scant inch below the thin cut of the knife. The blood ran down her throat to her bared breast. His other hand covered his knife. But she did not reach for it; instead she whispered in his ear, "I have something to tell you. You alone."

He regarded her narrowly. What? Another secret tunnel—what use was that to him? Had she overheard the Sheriff plotting to kill him? If it was a ploy, he'd find out quickly enough.

"Out," he said to the guard, who eyed him resentfully,

certain he was seizing the prize for himself. Sullenly he left the cottage, standing within earshot of the grunts and groans he expected to hear. "By your horse," Guy ordered, feeling like an utter fool now. The guard stomped over to his horse, and Guy pulled Laurel to the back of the cottage. Her bared breasts swayed. "Fix your clothes," he told her. She understood that he was not to be tempted and covered the temptation.

Laurel adjusted the bodice, which had been pulled down but not torn. Fear quivered under her boldness, but she faced him defiantly. She had sense enough to keep her voice low as she said, "Give me your word you'll let me go, and I'll tell you something you'll want to hear."

He regarded her coldly. "The Sheriff's torturer will find out everything you know."

"And tell the Sheriff. Maybe I know something you'd rather he didn't."

He laughed scornfully. "And why would you believe I'd keep my word?"

"I don't, not for certain. But servants know who's best and who's worst of the masters. You're no Sir Walter, who'd die before he broke his word, but you're not the same as the Sheriff either. Only you know what your word's worth to you. All I know is making you give it's the best chance I've got." She smiled a little. "I know your word's worth enough that you didn't lie to me right off."

"I won't pay for useless information," he warned her.

"Give me your word," she demanded, her voice low and fierce.

"I give you my word," he said carefully, "that if you tell me something I do not want the Sheriff to know, I will let you go."

"Lady Marian is a spy," she said.

He frowned. Marian had made no secret of her family's allegiance. The Sheriff needed to flaunt his control of Nottingham. The chance of subverting her family was worth allowing her to glean information from discussions at the dinner table. Guy knew he had never told her anything of import, and after their first talk at the fair she had made no effort to ferret information from him. He had thought they understood the rules perfectly. "There are spies and spies."

Laurel eyed him with exasperation. "Lady Marian went to Sherwood and convinced Robin Hood to serve the Queen. They were all in it together, she and her lady-in-waiting and her troubadour. Robin wants his lands back, and she promised them to him in return for his service. His lands and a pardon for all his men."

He could only stare at her. Could she be making this up from nothing but an awareness of his attraction to Marian?

She smiled, mocking him. "Lady Marian arranged for Robin Hood to steal the ransom from you."

Guy remembered then that he had told Marian something of import. He had told her where he was riding to intercept the ransom. He cursed under his breath. Then he remembered that Robin had kissed her on the road to Nottingham.

"Are they lovers?"

She looked down sulkily and he shook her, jerking her head back. "Is he her lover?"

"You mean is he her lover too?"

Guy almost struck her, but she did not cringe. He tightened his grip on her arms. She glared at him, but when she answered, her voice was sullen. "I don't know. I only know he hasn't touched me since she went to Sherwood, and he's not a man to do without."

That was the truth, he was sure.

"Let me go," she said, jerking her arm in his grasp.

He tightened it, then pushed her toward the pallet. "Lie down."

"You gave me your word," she whispered.

Guy relished her fear a minute longer, then said, "Lie down on the pallet. Pretend I've just swived you."

She lay back on the pallet, spreading her legs and lifting her skirts. She grasped a handful of fabric and pressed it down between her thighs.

He went to the doorway and leaned casually against the

jamb, watching the guard. If Laurel escaped while in his custody, the Sheriff would question him closely. Godfrey was angry enough without some new mishap. And there was no way to trust this weakling to hold his mouth, not for fear or money.

When the guard caught sight of him, Guy gave him a lecherous smile and nodded his head toward Laurel. The guard grinned at his good fortune and headed for the doorway. As the guard passed him, Guy swiftly drew his knife and slit his throat. The man toppled forward. He thrashed for a moment, the wound gurgling, then lay still. Guy cleaned his own knife and replaced it. He drew the guard's knife and tossed it into the pool of blood surrounding his face.

Guy beckoned to Laurel. She rose from the pallet, smoothing her clothing, and stared down at the dead guard with satisfaction. Guy pointed to the man's mount. "Keep the horse to a walk until you are clear of the city, then ride hard. The men have likely moved up from this section, so head east first. If the others catch you. . . ." He tilted his head at the corpse and gave her a cynical smile, ". . . then you will have this man's murder to answer for as well—because of course I never saw you."

Laurel looked up at him. "Robin won't hear of this," she said. "The only thing I'll be telling him is that she swived you too. Then I'll be leaving Nottinghamshire. There's nothing I want here anymore."

It was in her own best interests not to confess the betrayal, yet he saw she considered it a favor returned for her rapist's death. He nodded to her, accepting it. "Good luck to you then," he said, discovering he did wish her well. He liked her courage and cool head.

"I give you my word," she said seriously.

"Oh, I believe you," he said, mocking himself. "Though I have just been proven to have faulty judgment in women."

■ ■ ■ ■ ■ ■

Robin sat by John's grave, arms around his knees, drawn up tight around the echoing emptiness within. Above him the leaves were starting to turn, flames of gold and red burned among the green. Soon they would be a fire of glory. "I'll heap them all atop you," Robin whispered. "They'll be the finest funeral pyre a hero ever had."

He heard someone coming but paid no mind. He wished everyone had the sense to leave him be. *John would have come looking*, an inner voice said, and he answered under his breath, "John would have been welcome." The footsteps stopped behind him with a swish of skirts.

"I didn't know Little John was dead till I got here," Laurel's voice said, tight and strained.

Robin said nothing. It might be better to share the grief, but Laurel would want to make it more than that. He had nothing to give her.

"The men told me you were here," Laurel declared. "They also told me you might be wanting to eat."

"No," he said, refusing to look at her.

"Oh, but you should eat, for I've some special news to tell you. You're the first to know, and I want you well fortified."

So she was marrying the blacksmith after all. He could not care enough now to wish her good luck or good riddance. Turning his back still more, Robin wrapped himself in the cold gray blanket of his grief and willed her away. It did no good. She sat beside him, tossing a wineskin at his feet and dangling a cloth wrapped about some bread and meat in front of his nose, letting it slap against his cheek. The odors of hot bloody venison, yeasty bread, acidic wine all mingled and made him queasy. "Stop that," he snarled.

"She's done right well by you, hasn't she, your chilly bit of lady flesh?" she snapped in return.

It was not exasperation in her voice; it was anger. Robin looked up at her at last, incomprehension weaving with cold threads of trepidation. "What?"

"I hope it was worth it, spending the tunnel on the warbling troubadour to please that two-faced witch. I hope she swived you in payment because right now she's probably swiving Guisbourne, while you snivel here at the graveside. Perhaps I should sit and snivel with you, seeing as my uncle's dead too.''

''Swiving Guisbourne?'' he asked.

Laurel spat at him.

He wiped the spittle from his cheek. ''Your uncle's dead?'' he asked then, though his first question still spun ugly images in his brain. He looked at her closely. ''Your neck is cut.''

She lifted her chin defiantly. ''I was hiding, trying to warn my uncle. One of the Sheriff's men found me and raped me. Now he's dead. His own knife is lying in his blood.''

Compassion breaking through, Robin reached out for her, but she stepped back. ''I don't want your pity. I want money so I can start a new life in London. You owe me that.''

''Yes,'' he said, though it had never been a matter of debt before, but of shared desire and shared purpose. ''I owe you that and more. Tell me what happened, Laurel.''

''The guards found the tunnel and set about trying to pry it open. Since I knew where it led and that it would take them time to crawl through, I got out of the castle quiet as I could and ran down to the inn. I warned off the workers, but my uncle was trading ale. He was lucky, though. He took an arrow in the back—three actually, or so I heard—else he would have made fine stew meat for the Sheriff's torturer. And anyone else he knew who worked for you would have been thrown into the pot as well.''

Not all his spies knew one another. He tried to create a balance between ease of communication and safety from discovery. But the brewmaster had known all those in the castle because passing messages at the Pilgrim was easy, and doing it under the Sheriff's nose a delight to all.

''They'd have tortured him till he screamed every name he knew, then tortured him till he screamed whatever other names he could invent. So it's lucky he's dead, isn't it?

Except if you'd gone and killed the Sheriff, like you said you would, my uncle would be alive. It was why he agreed to risk his life digging the tunnel. Now he's paid full price for your folly," she said caustically.

If the brewmaster was dead, then Marian was safe from accusation, along with Cobb and the others. But Marian would be safe anyway if Guisbourne protected her. Robin ran his hands through his hair, his fingers tightening on the roots till he could feel the pain. He could see the brewmaster in his mind, arrows sticking up from his back. And then Little John, falling under the savage blows of Guisbourne's sword and disappearing under his horse's trampling hooves.

"How do you know?" he demanded.

"You knew as well as I did—" Laurel began.

Standing, he grabbed her and gave her a jolting shake. She laughed in his face. "How do you know Guisbourne was Marian's lover?"

"How do I know he was her lover too?" she taunted him. "Because I heard them. I was passing her door, and I heard them cry out. The sound was muffled, but I knew what it was right enough. Not who it was with her, though I could make a good guess after watching them eye each other at the dinner table. I hid around the corner, and I stole a look when I heard the door open. It was Guisbourne. He hovered there, and she kissed him, and then he left. He left to lead the Sheriff's men against yours. And to kill John Little."

Staring down at the ground, he saw the wineskin. The dark, sharp scent of it teased his mind with the promise of still darker oblivion. He picked it up. Little John's voice cautioned him not to. But Little John was dead. Little John, who was more a father to him than the one he'd already lost.

"Oh, yes, have some wine, Robin." Laurel sneered. "That'll solve all your problems."

"Sobriety at least," he answered, and drank deeply.

■ ■ ■ ■ ■ ■

Marian returned to Sherwood with a sense of rising joy. Agatha would be most of the way to the inn by now.

"Rob's down where we buried John, Lady Marian, by the great oak," Will said to her. "He said it was the only fitting place. He's barely left there. We sent. . . ." He hesitated, looking suddenly discomfited. "We sent Laurel, the brewmaster's niece, down with some food awhile ago. She's not come back."

So they were lovers, are lovers. Marian felt a swell of anger and jealousy, but she had never had any rights over him or let him claim any over her. She had fought her attraction—until their encounter at the great oak. That had changed everything for her. But that did not mean it had changed for him. Only how could it not? She had never felt such rapport with any other being. Yet perhaps, as she had thought before, it was a gift he could give to anyone, and did, a golden sun shining in oblivious blessing.

One could not rail at the sun.

She could tell Will did not want her to go down the path, but he did not know what was happening; he was only apprehensive. Despite his youth, he had enough command to try to hold her back if he knew. Robin was mourning, and Laurel had taken him food. It need be no more than that.

Marian had barely started down the path when she saw Laurel approaching. The dark-haired woman startled at the sight of her, anger flashing in her eyes. Then she smiled insolently, eyes narrowing, lips curving with secret, self-satisfied pleasure. She walked past Marian, swaying her hips and adjusting the bodice of her gown. Marian nodded to her coolly and kept on walking, following the winding path through the woods to the great oak.

She found Robin sitting beneath the great oak, head in his hands, an empty wineskin beside him. He looked totally disheveled, hair and clothes in disarray, but that might be no more than sleeplessness and drink. She had always despised drunkenness for weakness. Yet she knew his sorrow was great.

"Robin," she said quietly.

He raised his head, and she took an involuntary step back at the hatred in his face. His eyes burned black, and he gave off a haze of fury, a storm cloud crackling with lightning. He rose to his feet, swaying, still glaring at her. Then he stepped toward her. She tensed, wary but not quick enough to dodge the blow as he backhanded her savagely, knocking her to the ground.

"Whore."

He seized her, jerking her to her knees, then struck her again, the blow cracking the other way across her face. The physical blows, the force of the curse stunned her. For a moment there was only shock; then came the leap of pain, sharp without, sharper still within. He shoved her back to the grass and jerked at her clothes, thrusting up the tunic with one hand and wrenching open the waist of the breeches with the other.

"Guisbourne's whore."

He grasped the neck of the linen shirt and ripped it open, hand reaching to grip her breast roughly. Anger iced her, a freezing fire. She concentrated her will and energy, drawing everything tight within. Then she lashed out, her knee flying for his groin and striking home. He doubled over with a guttural cry, clutching himself. He swayed, hissing with pain, then lifted his head, glaring up at her, his eyes black with rage and loathing. When she reached for the knife in her boot, he lunged at her. Stepping aside, she planted her feet and snapped a backhanded blow to his temple. The hard clout from her fist staggered him, and he fell to the ground. Struggling to rise, he groaned and vomited, the smell sickly with wine. He struggled to rise once more but collapsed back, staring about with unfocused eyes.

Marian shivered violently. Her heart pounded, contracting and expanding in blinding surges of grief and violation, hot rage and cold. Then it shattered, and the golden light it held bled through the cracks to leave something gray and hollow. She turned and strode back up the path, forcing herself not to run as she circled the back of the lodge and slipped in almost unseen. Stripping off the leathers, she pulled on her own clothes, transferred her weapons, and picked up her gear.

Her face throbbed. The bruises were rising, and the others would know Robin had hit her. Well, there was no help for that. She had seen the violence in him before, if never so black a rage. There was a thin, pained voice inside her crying excuses. She knew the depth of his grief. John Little had been the bedrock of his life, and Guisbourne had killed him. Now Robin had discovered that Guisbourne was her lover. He had learned it from Laurel—who knew or guessed the truth. From Laurel, whom he had likely swived all along. Well, let Laurel take his blows. She could not give herself to a man who would abuse her so. Better he had tried to kill her. She could not trust Robin ever again. And she doubted he would ever trust her.

Walking out the door of the lodge, she saw Sir Ralph chatting with Alan and Claire. She summoned him with a gesture, and he came over, his expression shifting from smile to glower as he looked closely at her face. "We're leaving," she told him, and cut across the clearing to the horses. They were bridled and half saddled when Will appeared with four others beside him. Marian ignored him and finished tightening the girth before she turned to face him.

Will's look was hostile but questioning, hurt and disillusion close-layered under his anger. So Laurel had told them what she knew, or surmised. Marian considered lying but abandoned the idea, not knowing what Laurel had seen or invented. She felt again, under her ire, the crosscurrent of guilt. Will had the right to hate her. When she did not deny or question, Marian saw all the emotion in his face harden, showing the strong mold of the man within the youth.

She mounted quickly, and Sir Ralph followed. Before she could move, Will took hold of the reins of her horse, holding her in place. A dozen other men had appeared behind Will, moving in closer, a belligerent circle. Ralph moved his mount into place beside hers, his hand resting lightly on his sword, offering what protection he could, though he could give her little against so many. Even if they were not pierced with a dozen arrows each, bolting would do little good when they knew the paths of Sherwood so little. "You'll not go till Robin says you can," Will told her. She held his gaze, refusing to look away, and Will suddenly looked young again, and shamefaced. But he did not lower his eyes or release the reins.

"I can see you distrust me," she told him. "But I have not wronged you, and I will keep my word. You have all served the Queen faithfully, as have I. You will receive your reward."

With a cold pang she realized that Robin and his men still controlled the ransom. Word would not yet have reached the Queen to arrange for a new guard to transfer the gold and silver. If Robin chose, he could defy his promise and keep the prize for himself, if only for vengeance. And she had told Agatha there was no danger in her liaison with Guy.

Then the men moved back of themselves as Robin appeared through the trees. He looked haggard, his skin pale, his hair damp with sweat. His eyes sought her out as he crossed the clearing to stand in front of her. Their expression was accusing and bitter, but no longer crazed with drink. Meeting his glare with cold scorn, she let her bruises make their own accusation.

Her horse shifted restlessly. Robin realized at last that Will was holding her reins and saw the hostile faces of the men about her. Low-voiced, he said to Will, "Let her go."

Will complied, but she did not move forward. She held Robin's gaze. "I have kept my word to you. Will you keep yours to me and to the Queen?"

His eyes called her a liar. For a moment his face was transformed and he became a cunning enemy who saw a way to best her and taunted her with his power. But then he was Robin again, the man of honor she knew she could believe, and that man said, "Yes, I will keep my word."

"Farewell, Robin of Locksley," she said, offering what remained for her to give him.

"Robin Hood still," he said. "We shall see if I die so."

His men guided her and Sir Ralph back through Sherwood, lighting torches after the sun set and night swallowed them. Emerging from one vast tract of Sherwood, they pointed her to a tiny inn on the outskirts of the village of Edwinstowe, then returned to the forest. Marian rented pallets for them at the inn, and slept briefly and restlessly. She rose at dawn and headed northwest, riding hard for Lincoln. The image of her grandparents was like a beacon in the darkness of her heart as she drove them forward. And then she remembered, with a plummeting dread in her belly, that she had been told she must find a husband when she returned. She almost laughed aloud for the irony, but Robin's blows still ached on her face. Marian wondered bitterly, as she had before she took a lover, if she could ever endure a man's touch again. Well, that was folly, when she had learned full well that she could, after her virgin's fear. What she wished, vehemently, was that she would never again hunger for it so. At the moment freedom from desire seemed a most priceless gift, only freedom itself more valuable.

20 Topaz clutched Marian's glove, stretching her wings. The sparrowhawk had managed to kill a partridge and was glorying in her triumph. Wood pigeons had been the largest prey she had taken in the past. Those too had outweighed her, though not by so much. Marian set the jesses in place on her feet, then deftly slipped the hood over the sparrowhawk's head and drew the braces snug with her teeth. Topaz settled down, riding at ease on her glove as Marian turned her mount homeward, guiding the mare through the woodland that edged the barren face of the rock cliffs. Hawking was one of the few ways she had found to free her mind from regret for the past and turmoil about the future. The days she spent riding did not spare her the haunted nights, the dreams of twisted anguish in which Robin reviled her, struck her. Still, those did not pain her as much as the dreams of yearning passion, where she drowned in the molten sunlight of his embrace. She melted into that shared eternity . . . only to wake bereft.

Marian closed her mind on the blazing image. There was no escape from the dreams, but the days in the forest offered distraction and solace. Breathing deeply, she drew in the sharp crispness of the air, the pervasive scent of evergreens. Surrounding her, the dense evergreen richness of spruce and pine, hemlock and red-berried yew mingled with the naked branches of larch and sycamore. Their faded leaves blanketed the ground, but the oaks still rustled overhead with crisp metallic layers of gold and bronze. November—blood month, the Saxons called it, for the winter slaughtering. But the crimson of creeper leaf called it to mind too, a swath of sanguine color.

After emerging from the woodland, she rode back by the twin-tiered waterfall pouring down the rugged scar of the great ravine, then along the towering expanse of limestone cliffs. Following their looming curve till she came to the road leading up to Norford Castle, Marian turned her mount and climbed the switchbacked road to the top, where her grandfather's great fortress overlooked the surrounding woods and rivers, meadows and farmlands. She rode through the wooden palisade of the busy lower bailey to the gray stone fortifications of the upper, built on the highest rise of the cliff. Dismounting, she gave her reins to the groom, told him to send the partridge to the kitchen, and took Topaz with her into the castle. Her grandfather was climbing the stairs. He turned and looked down at her. With his great height and mass of white hair, he looked more like a Viking deity than a Norman lord. He gave her a small, quizzical smile and inclined his head toward the archway beside her. Curious, Marian followed his gesture and entered the hall.

Guy of Guisbourne stood waiting for her by the blaze from the fire. She stopped abruptly, astonished by his presence. He looked handsome as ever and as commanding in his elegance. Lined with sable, his cloak was cinnamon wool, richly embroidered in scarlet and clasped at the shoulder with a gem-studded brooch. Tunic and breeches of the richest leather fitted impeccably, their rich brown verging on red. A single glance surveyed the richness of his garments, but her gaze was held by the fire in his eyes, reflected flames of pure yellow burning within their dark translucent amber.

Guy assessed her in turn. Beneath a blue cape lined with vair, Marian was dressed in the same fashion, supple leather breeches and tunic. He smiled slightly, regarding her legs with appreciation but not insolence. When she laid the cape aside, his head inclined in a slight bow as he remarked, "Amazon indeed."

Despite her tension, Marian smiled a little. Moving closer to the fire, she placed Topaz on her perch, then turned to face Guisbourne. "Sir Guy?"

Her calm voice did not reveal her quickened heartbeat. If Guisbourne had discovered her betrayal, he would not have come here to kill her in so conspicuous a fashion. Had the Sheriff or Prince John sent him with some bargain, hoping she would intercede with her grandfather? Surely Guy would know that was futile—unless the Sheriff had received word of King Richard's continued durance or his death. All these thoughts leapt into her mind, yet as he looked at her, it was as if they still stood in her room at Nottingham Castle, their conversation deliberately unfinished. Now Guisbourne decreed it would continue.

"I do not know if I am welcome," Guy said to her. "There is no point in staying if I am not."

His bluntness surprised her, yet not. They had never spoken casually. Even when they had done no more than dabble in trivialities at the supper table, currents of meaning flowed underneath. Now she did not know what to say to him. She was not ready for this conversation. Yet he was here, and so she must speak.

"How welcome do you need to be?" Ambiguous, yet ambiguity was an answer too.

He held her gaze. "I have made it clear to your grandfather that I am interested in courting you, Marian. In turn he has made it clear that the choice is yours."

She sat down on the bench by the fire, and Guisbourne placed himself across from her. Marian wondered how clear it was that she had no choice except to choose, and soon. *Too soon.* She smiled ironically. "So I am told."

There was the lift of a brow in response, a slight nod of understanding. "In Nottingham you made it clear that mutual pleasure was no longer enough to bridge our opposite alliances, and that you thought of the future rather than the moment. If you demand an open change of allegiance, then

I must know if you will consider my suit. You grandfather says that others may offer but that you have favored no one so far.''

''They need not ask.''

Her grandfather had proposed several possible marriages, though without enthusiasm. She suspected he was provoking her to go to London sooner than planned and search on her own behalf. But all the candidates he presented were suitable, and the only ones possible locally. There was a youth five years younger, whom she might shape, if he did not rebel and seek a man to emulate. There was a widower of good property nearby, thirty years older than she, whose sons had not survived Lion Heart's crusade. And there were two stalwart young knights, of small but valuable holdings, eager to enrich themselves. While she could imagine a measure of respect for these men, Marian had felt no bond whatsoever—no likeness of mind, no spark of attraction. Deliberately garbed as she was now, she had met them all and had been treated with careful courtesy that ill concealed their consternation. Not one could accept her as she was, so not one was acceptable. Marian doubted she would fare much better at Queen Eleanor's court.

But seeing her so clad, Guy had smiled and called her Amazon. Her strengths had never angered or annoyed, had only intrigued him. From the first with him, she had known affinity of mind and desire. She was more herself with Guy of Guisbourne than she had been with any other man she had known. . . . Except that with Robin, in the sweetly terrifying, wildly intoxicating surrender they shared, she had become more than herself.

''I have missed you, Marian,'' Guy said.

''I thought there was no future for us,'' Marian said quietly. ''I have tried to put Nottingham in the past.''

''You say you have tried. Have you succeeded?''

Marian shook her head, trapped between truth and lies. She was in mourning still, lost in the dark soul rift that followed her leaving Robin. But Guy's presence brought back other memories, of which the flickering images of desire were only a part. Along with trepidation for an enemy, she felt a flow of relief, as if she had reclaimed a friend. But Guisbourne did not know how great an enemy she had been. "No. Not entirely. But I do not know how much I can retrieve."

Guy regarded her steadily. "Nothing has gone as I planned in Nottingham, Marian, and because of that, I may not fare as well under Prince John as I had hoped. I do not deny I may gain advantage if you accept me. But it is equally true that if I pledge myself to the King, I may lose all I have. Richard has no liking for me. I stand to gain far more power with Prince John, and he may prevail. I doubt the Sheriff would dare seize my Nottingham properties while he is still King, but if I quit Sir Godfrey now, he will wreak havoc in any way he can."

"You would benefit by allying yourself with my grandfather," she said candidly, "even if Richard gives you nothing, even if Prince John prevails."

"Perhaps. I do not know your dower, but I know William of Norford has great authority and influence. His loyalty is a prize that any King should appreciate, and it would cost a great deal to lay siege against him. But you have met Prince John. He will as likely be guided by vanity as reason. I do not deny your point. I have indeed considered it. I do not doubt that you and your family have already considered that John's rising to the throne could mean your fall."

Marian nodded. It was indeed possible.

"I do not pretend my own loyalty is so valuable. Outside my family I have given it entire only once—to Geoffrey Plantagenet, hoping to shape a king. He is dead now. . . ." Guisbourne's eyes burned darkly for a moment, showing some loss she could not fathom, a scorching ember of rage. Then he offered a small shrug, a sardonic smile. "I have tried to be more practical in my goals ever since. The Plantagenets, Prince and King, toss bones with destiny, and what we may gain from either is equally haphazard. At worst, if nothing remains for us in England, I have a small castle in Brittany. Whatever else fate lets fall, I can offer you that, and myself.''

He leaned forward, speaking intently. ''Understand that it is you, Marian, that makes this alliance desirable to me. And Sir Godfrey who makes the one I have now intolerable. You were right that serving the Sheriff sickens me. Since you left, it is not so much that he has degenerated more but that I can tolerate his malevolence less. I feel polluted by my association with him, enough that the promised gain no longer compensates for the disgust. Before you came to Nottingham, I was inured. Now everything is changed.''

She said nothing, though each moment that she did not speak bound her more tightly to this course. Her heart quickened again, beating painfully as he took her hand in his.

''I fell in love with you. I had not planned on that,'' Guy said, paring to the quick. It was as if she had left him no other recourse but to declare himself, and perhaps she had not. For it left no other recourse but to speak with equal honesty.

Marian forced herself to meet his gaze. Like the pale flames of the firelight, she saw the pain and anger flickering behind the careful control he held. She felt again the possibility of what had been between them. Was her own pain cause for hope or only regret?

''Shall I go?'' His hand tightened, then relaxed but did not release hers.

For a second Marian wished desperately that he would leave, for his own sake. She had hurt him already, betrayed him already. Now he asked for more than she could give, but perhaps it was not more than she was capable of giving, in time. The dark magnetism Guy exercised was muted but not entirely buried. Looking at him, seeing his beauty, his pride, his pain, Marian ached, hungering to reach out to one of the few souls who could understand her. Yet what she must tell him would only cause him more grief, more fury. Well, if nothing else, perhaps she could give Guy his freedom.

"Not yet." Marian drew a deep breath. The time to bid him go was long past. She had led him and herself to this moment when their past, their future fused. Fragile as a falcon's egg, it might hatch a new life—or shatter and decay.

"You know that I had hopes of drawing you to Richard's cause. I bedded you for desire, despite our differences, though I hoped that shared passion might influence you."

"As I did." He made a dismissive gesture.

"You do not know that while I was in Nottingham, I sent information to the Queen."

"You made no secret of your allegiance." His tone remained detached, but he tensed. His eyes narrowed, watching her speculatively. "You had no access to information others were not privy to. The Sheriff will not hold Nottingham if King Richard returns. It is in Sir Godfrey's interest to be blatant and intimidate with the power he now controls."

"Hear it all," she said. "Then leave if you will."

She told him that she had recruited Robin Hood to serve the Queen. She told of spying on Prince John in the arbor and of sending Alan to London with it. And she told him of the information he himself had given her inadvertently, which she gave to Robin.

Anger flared in his eyes, and he rose to his feet. "I underestimated you," he said, and his smile was feral. "But then, I was meant to."

"There is more," she said. And so at last she told him that Robin had been her lover. She did not want to. But Robin knew about Guy, as did Will and some of the others. Guisbourne would not forgive her if he heard of it elsewhere. She could not build upon another betrayal.

"An outlaw?" Guy sneered.

"A knight's son, and a knight," she answered, though what she thought was, *a spirit of the forest*.

"The Queen's whore, as well as the Queen's spy."

"No." It cut, though she had known he would think it, as Robin had. "I chose him as I chose you, for desire. It was unplanned and brief. It did not endure." In truth there had been only once when she had chosen to go to Robin with all of herself, mind, body, and heart. "That is all."

Looking into Guisbourne's eyes, she watched the anger burn hotter and hotter, a pure flaming rage. His hand dropped to his sword—then he pivoted and stalked from the hall. Marian followed him into the courtyard, where he mounted his stallion. He gazed at her, the wrath still an unquenched flame searing her. Then Guy spun his horse and rode away. She watched till he was out of sight, feeling a greater emptiness than before. There had been little chance that she could do anything but destroy any possibility of a future between them. Most likely she had just created a dangerous enemy. Grimly Marian returned to the castle and sought out her grandparents to tell them the essence of what had passed.

That night she slept ill, dreaming of golden-eyed peregrines swooping for the kill and blood-soaked forest leaves.

Guisbourne came again at dawn. Informed by her grandmother, Marian met Guy outside in the courtyard. "Ride with me," he said, a command.

He was demanding her trust when he knew well he did not have it. She nodded curtly and ordered her horse saddled. Guy waited in silence until she mounted, then turned his mount and rode outside the castle walls. She followed. "Where to?" she asked when he paused. Their breath frosted the air like smoke.

In answer he said, "Ride where you will."

So she took him to the twin falls of the great stone scar, the rift splitting the Pennine cliffs, masses of limestone tumbled on either side. The water spilled, two long, glittering cascades of silver. Guisbourne helped her dismount but did not release her. His hands tightened on her arms, and Marian felt the violence in him, barely restrained. The falcon eyes of her dream stared into her own, burning with a human lust.

She went taut in his arms. "No. If it is revenge you want,

take it with your sword. You will likely kill me, though I cannot guarantee it.''

''I do not want you dead.'' His voice cut with deliberate malice, conjuring violations to rival the Sheriff's torturer.

''I saw my mother raped, then put to death,'' she said harshly. ''I know you have cause to hate me, but I cannot tolerate brutality from any man. I will not.''

He looked at her, assessing. ''Brutality, no. But ferocity you have given and received already. Let us take revenge together, Marian, on life.''

Defiantly she pulled him to her, giving herself to the danger, not caring what she risked. Marian felt the embers smoldering between them catch and leap to life. Darkness choked it, a cold smoke of grief and bitterness obscuring the flame of desire. Yet the heat was welcome. And so she stepped into the fire.

Guy cast their fur-lined capes to cushion the stone, then lowered her onto a flat boulder. Jerking off her breeches, he took her in the open, the air ice around the joined fire of their bodies. It was savage but not swift. She met his ravaging thrusts with equal fury, as if they both fought to stoke the fire hotter and brighter, conjuring a blaze fierce enough to melt the iron shackles of the past.

Afterward he lay beside her on the stone, tense despite his release. ''Yesterday I did not appreciate what you gave me—the truth.'' He smiled grimly. ''I like it little better today.''

''You do not know yet if you can forgive me.'' Then she clarified. ''Forgive me enough to wed me.''

''I wish I hated you more. Or loved you less.'' Despite his control, Guisbourne's eyes were cold unwavering flames burning into hers.

For a moment Marian wondered if he might have calculated it all, plotting a betrayal to equal what he felt, made vulnerable by desire. A rape not of the body but of the spirit. She did not doubt he was capable of the cruelty. If he walked away, she would not revenge herself for this. Then a chilling fear gripped her as she thought, *His vengeance would be equal to or greater than what he suffered. He can wound me so deeply only if I love him. Would he wait for that?*

If she was to have his trust, then she must give her own. There was no better match for her now, in mind or body. "Stay with us until Richard returns. When that is accomplished, we can decide if there is a future for us as well. If Richard prevails, we will see to it that you at least hold what you have now. The Queen will swear it."

It was as close as she could come to the finality of *yes*. It gave them time, which she believed he needed as well as she did. It gave at least a chance for freedom without total enmity.

She looked at the massive cliffs rising above them, a battlement of stone more formidable than man could shape. Swords of bright water, cold molten silver, cascaded over rough stone. With painful vividness she remembered Robin by the waterfall in the grove, and all the blooming lushness that embraced them. Well, Robin and summer were gone. Winter was still to pass through. After winter she and Guy could find a spring.

"I have made my choice," Guisbourne said. "And I do not come empty-handed. I have information of value to the Queen, which you can give to her."

"You can give it yourself," Marian said. "I have been summoned to court. Queen Eleanor bids me accompany her to Austria. The time has come to bring home the King."

■■■■■■

"Rise, Sir Guy." Eleanor watched as Guisbourne rose gracefully from where he knelt before her. Marian had set two stools beside Eleanor's chair, but she decided to keep Guisbourne standing. "Marian has said you bring me news. From her tone I could only presume it unfortunate."

"Unfortunate indeed." Guisbourne looked directly into her eyes. "Prince John and King Philip have contrived a plan to prevent King Richard's release."

"And what is this plan?" Eleanor asked. The particulars were far more important than her own distress.

"They will offer the Emperor silver equal to the ransom if he will keep Lion Heart imprisoned until Michaelmas," Guisbourne said. "Or they will pay one thousand marks a month for as long as the Emperor will hold him in durance. Ostensibly the monthly payment will be until King Philip has claimed the redress he says he is due—"

"But they want the imprisonment to be permanent or lethal." Eleanor finished for him.

"Yes," Guisbourne said. "Preferably the latter."

Eleanor smiled bitterly. "The Holy Roman Emperor's last treaty with Richard was sworn on his soul. But Henry Hohenstaufen's soul is a dull and paltry thing compared with the gleaming weight of silver. Even the Devil would think himself richer for the trade."

"No doubt the Emperor wants both the ransom and the bribe," Marian interposed.

"No doubt," Eleanor agreed. "But if he is forced to choose, King Richard's ransom is collected. If he keeps his word, the Emperor can keep both silver and soul, such as it is."

"True," Guisbourne said. "But the Emperor would not be bound by King Philip's negotiation to give any part of the silver to the Duke of Austria, who captured Richard and delivered him into the Emperor's hands. This new offer will therefore bring him more wealth. He will be tempted."

"But you cannot believe he will succumb," Eleanor said derisively. *Else why are you here?* remained unspoken.

As if in answer, Guisbourne's gaze flashed briefly to Marian. He continued. "Your Majesty, I believe the outcome is uncertain. At the worst King Philip and Prince John will succeed and the Lion Heart will never leave Austria alive. At the best the Emperor will drive a harder bargain for King Richard's freedom."

"Then what is your advice, Sir Guy?" Eleanor tinged her voice with acid, challenging him still.

Guisbourne's demeanor remained unchanged, serious

and direct, as he answered her question. "The Emperor's greed is monumental, but it will not make him utterly stupid. He will be wary of the risk of holding King Richard longer. However, after King Philip's offer the Emperor will feel he must receive even more than he has been promised, or he will keep the Lion Heart in thrall. You must anticipate what demands the Emperor will use as bargaining ploys. Weigh the possibilities well, for you will have to accept one of them."

Yes, this was the advantage that he brought her and on which he made his bid for her favor.

Eleanor surveyed Guisbourne, making no secret that she was weighing him. Despite her suspicion, she was favorably impressed. He had been succinct and offered no apology. He had made no effort to charm her other than by affording her the dignity she was due. What he offered were intelligence and information, both of high value. She had not thought her younger son could raise so much silver in secret. Although the news Guy provided now did not compensate for his earlier connivance in stealing the ransom, that attempt had failed. This would do for a new beginning. When her golden cub returned, no doubt she would have to accept others of John's repentant followers who offered less.

There were those who would be loyal to the death and those who would be loyal to the rule of order. Most would make what allegiances seemed likely to prevail. Guy had tilted this way and that, but his course was directed by circumstance, not weakness. His English lands had been granted through Longchamp, but they lay in the heart of Prince John's strongest holdings. Marian had said Guisbourne had sickened of his association with the Sheriff. Eleanor placed that to his credit.

And Guisbourne had served her son Geoffrey faithfully until his death. That was in his favor.

If Sir Guy had loyalty to offer now, it would be to Marian. But Marian was loyal to her. It was enough. In truth Eleanor had made her decision that morning. She had not told Marian, but word had arrived early that the Sheriff of Nottingham had seized Guisbourne's lands. It perturbed Eleanor that John's allies were so certain of victory. But the Sheriff had chosen to flaunt his power from the first. If John lost, Sir Godfrey lost as well. Flagrancy cost him nothing and gained much. Even Lion Heart's justiciars would not intervene until they were certain of who would rule England. However ambivalent his motives, Guisbourne had put himself at risk in Richard's name. Eleanor would not see him suffer for it—not if she could prevent it.

"I am grateful, Sir Guy. You have given me time to begin another campaign. If Richard prevails, you will be rewarded."

He smiled at her now, a restrained smile that acknowledged his gratitude even as his eyes acknowledged the difficulties. He understood perfectly what he brought to this new allegiance and what he did not. "Thank you, Your Majesty."

"When the Emperor reveals this ploy, we must react with surprise and consternation." Eleanor played out the latest move of Henry Hohenstaufen in the chessboard of her mind. "The Emperor has no honor, but he is not so foolish as to believe that his power is limitless or that others have none. His barons are bound by the same oath he made, and they are not all so ignoble. Pressure can be brought to bear among them." She knew that she must work swiftly. November's end was at hand.

"Yes," Guy said. "Their pride in their own honor and their fear of the Emperor's machinations can both be used to advantage."

"Some even fear for their souls," Eleanor jested, and received a brilliant smile. It was a smile to make the Queen remember the woman and the sap of passion flowing hot in the veins. Looking from Marian to Guisbourne, she decided to be generous. "Sir Guy, you will accompany us to the Emperor's Court in Austria. We leave early in December. I want to spend Christmas with my son."

■■■■■■

The chains rattled as King Richard knelt before the Holy Roman Emperor. With a graceful gesture the King doffed his royal bonnet and laid it in his enemy's hands.

Lion Heart performs like a master, Guy thought, watching the game be played out. Richard was always aware of his audience. Beside him, Marian sent him a quick glance, irony mingled with excitement, sharing appreciation of the climactic moment. Standing close by Eleanor, it was Marian who looked the Queen. The Queen of Faerie, Guy thought, regal in her gown of white brocade banded with silver embroidery, her flood of pale hair crowned with leaves of silver dewed with pearls.

They had waited long enough for this moment. Henry Hohenstaufen had kept the English company dangling for more than a fortnight. Christmas had come and gone, as had Twelfth Night. Hope rose when the Emperor promised to release Richard on January 17, but he had put them off till February without explanation. Queen Eleanor, wasting under the strain, had kept up her secret communications, plying her influence wherever she thought it would do the most good.

Two days ago, on Candlemas, the court had reconvened at Mainz. There, finally, the Emperor had revealed King Philip's bribe. Henry Hohenstaufen presented the violation of his sworn word most innocently. If he did not release Richard, the English would be aggrieved, but if he flouted Philip, he would lose his French alliance. To compensate him for this, he asked that Richard acknowledge vassalage to the Holy Roman Emperor instead of France. The English barons were duly outraged, for the single payment of the ransom would become instead a yearly tribute. But Eleanor and King Richard had already discussed the possibility and made their decision. The Lion Heart's freedom was the greatest priority. All else could be maneuvered later.

Now, kneeling in chains before the Emperor, King Richard spoke in a ringing voice, renouncing his allegiance to the treacherous Capetian dynasty and transferring it to the Hohenstaufen. The English barons wisely held their tongues. The Emperor's barons wisely wept with joy at King Richard's gesture of homage. With a gesture betokening his generosity of spirit, the Emperor commanded the King's chains be unloosed. Lion Heart rose and walked to his mother, who fell weeping into his arms. Watching, Guisbourne thought her tears unfeigned, though equally politic as the others that flowed so freely down the face around him. *A most glorious moment*, he thought, and tried to curve his lips into a less cynical smile.

As the ritual of release was enacted, Guisbourne also saw the ransom being transferred to Hohenstaufen's coffers and the English hostages being passed into Austrian hands. Who knew how long they would have to wait to return home? Longer than Lion Heart, Guy imagined. The Emperor presented the letters of safe-conduct to King Richard. Guy wondered how long it would be before Henry started counting in his mind the sweet shining weight of the French silver he had missed. Guy knew that King Philip's emissaries would be waiting close by, with proposals that the Emperor violate the safe-conduct and recapture the dangerous lion he had just unfettered.

The Bishop of Cologne approached the royal party. Guy moved close enough to overhear as the Bishop invited the Plantagenets, mother and son, to stay at his castle on their way down the Rhine toward the sea. He was gladly accepted. Listening to their arrangements, Guy began his own reckoning. There was not time to pass that information on to Prince John, but when they reached Cologne, he would know the rest of the itinerary and be able to encode and send it to England. With Prince John and King Philip moving from the front, and the Emperor from behind, Lion Heart should not see England again.

But Fortune was playing whore to Richard now. Guy would not be surprised to see her sit in his lap awhile longer. No doubt the Lion Heart gave a sweeter ride than John or Philip could supply. At the moment Guy favored

Richard's escape. He frowned, wondering what he could do that would not be an obvious betrayal of his pact with Prince John and King Philip but abet King Richard's return.

My semblance has become my desire, Guy mused.

If Prince John triumphed, Guisbourne wondered how he would handle his reinstatement without alerting Marian's suspicion. He would tell her he had spoken to Prince John about the instability of the Sheriff, his disgust at Sir Godfrey's excesses. He could tell her he had convinced John that the failure to capture the ransom was the Sheriff's fault because Sir Godfrey had ignored Prince John's warning about Robin Hood. Marian knew John to be susceptible to such blatant flattery, true or false. That and his new affiliation with William of Norford would make a convincing enough explanation.

Guy smiled. He could even ask Queen Eleanor to plead his case for him. Prince John would enjoy that duplicitous game greatly. He hated his mother as much as, or more than, he loved her. It was the best idea so far since he would not even appear to approach Prince John directly. Only now, watching the Queen regain her composure after her display of emotion, Guy felt an annoying twinge of conscience. He admired Eleanor and found he disliked the thought of making her play the puppet. But that was folly. The Queen jerked on his strings already. As Guy had hoped, the ploy of having Sir Godfrey seize his lands had sufficed both to make his defection more believable and to create a sense of debt in both Eleanor and Marian. In Nottingham Marian had been Eleanor's servant, and the Queen would take her share of his revenge.

Brooding on Marian's betrayal, he had gone over their every encounter. Examining their dialogue carefully, he decided that Marian had not contrived to trap him but had only used the information he foolishly let escape. It made only a little difference, yet that little was enough to let her live. That, and her unfeigned passion.

He wanted revenge but had been uncertain of its shape until word came from one of Prince's John's spies that Eleanor planned to include Marian in her Austrian retinue. As soon as the Sheriff heard she was to be so favored, his suspicions revived, and he besieged Guy with questions. While admitting Marian had tried to lure him back to King Richard's camp, he had assured Sir Godfrey that her efforts had only increased his own caution in talking to her. He also argued the implausibility of a lady of her quality having any involvement with Robin Hood. When the Sheriff flung the outlaw's amorous reputation in his face, Guy had frowned and admitted she might have contrived some scheme with her troubadour. Revealing a new animosity, he had proposed to approach Marian, feigning disillusion with Prince John. "I will discover if her interest in me was anything but subterfuge. If I can revive our affair, I may well be privy to information that could be of use to us."

Guy did not know until he saw Marian again how much he was driven by desire as well as vengeance. He was in love with her still, yet the same vulnerability that enraged him worked to his advantage. She believed the truth of his passion and so believed the rest as well. He had not expected her to be so candid in return, his rage flaming first at the substance of her confession and then at her very honesty. He wanted revenge still, if only the revenge of knowing he had deceived her when she had given trust, as she had done to him. Nothing else would cauterize the pain of her deceit. Loving her made it all the more necessary to have that hidden power, yet that need played night to the day of his need for the trust she offered him, and he felt a curious bitterness to know he could never give her the full truth in return. One thing was certain—he no longer planned to throw his own betrayal in her face and abandon her. He would marry her and keep his secrets in the dark.

■■■■■■

The sun shone, a roseate gold in the bright blue of the March sky. A fresh wind whipped the King's banners as his ship sailed into the harbor of Sandwich. Resplendent as some gilded idol come to life, Lion Heart stood on the deck.

All about Guisbourne the men whispered of good omens. They gazed at Lion Heart with reverence, for Richard had been in high spirits on his way back to England, setting himself to woo the most reluctant with his bonhomie and exuberance, then basking in their adoration. Guy was one of the few on whom he had made no effort to expend his charm. He had been perfectly civil, but it boded ill for the future. The cool reserve had made Guy wary. Now seeing the King's gaze skim over him without acknowledgment, he began to wish Lion Heart's enemies had captured him en route back to England.

Their escape had not been luck entirely. King Richard had the fastest ship and the best captain, who had hidden them well from the eyes of enemy spies. Nothing could be done now. Once returned to English soil, Lion Heart would rally the knights and barons to his cause, and they would follow the heroic crusader to the death. The most committed of Prince John's allies might fight, but barring the Lion Heart's own death in battle, his victory was assured.

Guy doubted he would be faulted. The information he had sent to John and Philip in France had been completely accurate, though less complete than his actual knowledge. And he had sent one significant fabrication to the Sheriff. Fearing for the King's life, Longchamp had suggested sending a decoy to England, in case assassins lay in wait. Richard, ever hungry for glory, had disparaged this sensible idea as craven. After that confrontation Guisbourne had coded a message to the Sheriff, implying that it was not the true King who would be returning to England. If Sir Godfrey believed it and refused to surrender Nottingham Castle to King Richard, so much the better.

When Guy first proposed his plan to beguile Marian, Sir Godfrey had accused him of changing camps. Guy had readily admitted he was opening another road should Prince John's attempt to seize the throne fail, but reiterated that he stood to gain far more if John took the throne. Guy also pointed out that if King Richard reclaimed England, he himself would be able to help Sir Godfrey regain the power he was certain to lose. Guisbourne intended no such thing, but Sir Godfrey's death must wait until Guy was once again in position to replace him as Sheriff of Nottingham. He and Godfrey had worked well enough together, and the Sheriff did not question him further. Godfrey was reassured, or so it seemed. True, Guy had always disdained to besport himself with the Sheriff, but he had taken care never to disclose his revulsion and had attended any interrogations that were relevant to the security of Nottingham. He had never directly crossed the Sheriff—except where Marian was concerned. Perhaps that had been sufficient to provoke Sir Godfrey. Nonetheless the Sheriff had acknowledged that Guy's scheme would benefit him no matter what the outcome. He communicated their intentions to Prince John, who had come once again to Nottingham.

They had discussed what plums might fall their way, the Queen's inviting him to Austria being the juiciest windfall they could imagine. Then, in Prince John's presence, the Sheriff had suggested that Guy assassinate King Richard if the chance befell him. Guy did not know if Prince John had told the Sheriff to contrive the conversation, but alarm prickled all his senses. He had been instant and adamant in his refusal, addressing Prince John directly. "If it was in defense of your life, sire, I would do it without hesitation. But I am not a man to commit regicide."

Was Sir Godfrey so mad that he could not foresee the outcome, or was he endeavoring a triumph of malice? Guy wondered what sort of idiot they conceived him to be. He would never be trusted once he was known to have killed a king. He would be executed swiftly by John or by Philip. It was understood that the information Guy promised to pass might well lead to Richard's death, but Guy would not have royal blood wet and vivid on his hands. Prince John scowled at the refusal, but Guy hoped he had been moved a notch closer in trust.

Planning an independent assassination was another matter. Although he would reap no gratitude, neither would he face retribution. But he saw no reason to take so drastic a step. There were too many possibilities open to him. If Prince John lost, if Richard did not reward his present service because of old enmity, there would still be Marian's dower, which Guy was now utterly convinced would be a rich one. And he wanted Marian. Even if she did not yet love him, there had been no woman he had considered before who offered all that she did: intelligence, beauty, passion, honor even, for all her skillful duplicity. If he put all that in service to his own future, what would it not be possible to achieve?

Strange. Arriving in England, he had thought the country barbarous, and his intention had been to return to France as soon as possible. Now that scheme lay buried the deepest of all. Still, if all else failed, if the layers of his schemes were somehow revealed and he lost both England and Marian, France awaited. As soon as either Richard or John was secure on the throne, King Philip had assured Guy that he could return and claim the lands promised him for spying on the Plantagenets. Or continue in England, if he chose, secretly in service to a French king.

21

Marian was coming to see him. Word spread quickly from the lookouts to the camp. Gesturing his men to stay behind, Robin forced himself to wait in the woods just outside the clearing, imagining her guided through the still bare-branched trees of Sherwood, gauging her approach. Knowing her near, he stood taut and shivering, renewed turmoil seething within the frozen shell of anger and bitterness that had held him all winter. The instant he saw Marian riding toward him, he felt the hot burst of desire, a raging flame at his core he had hoped long quenched. It beset him fiercely, fire and ice warring, opposite elements that struggled to consume each other. The cold encasing his body tightened and tightened till he thought he would shatter.

And then he did. The icy fury and bitterness that gripped him crackled and splintered, the shell falling away. The rush of flame dissipated in the air. Robin gasped, the first new breath sharp and painful. Losing the frozen shell left him exposed and vulnerable, for without it there was only passion. And pain. Defenseless, he searched for all the sources of his rage—John's death, her betrayal with Guisbourne—but they melted in his hands. So he rebuilt his shattered walls from will alone, a thin frost of control he prayed would serve him through their meeting. When she had gone, perhaps he could reclaim his wrath.

Nothing had changed. He did not want to love her. He should not love her. But he did.

As she rode toward him, he kept thinking he saw something on her face, some response to him, kept feeling his heart try to leap, and each time he forced it down more harshly. Finally she was right before him, her mood a cipher, and he forced himself to mirror the ice-smooth exterior Marian presented as she slid off her horse and stood before him.

"I bring you a message from the King," Marian said seriously, without preamble. "All that Eleanor promised is yours if you and your men help in the siege of Nottingham Castle. Come to the great meadow south of the city tomorrow, and from the King's own hands you will have your pardon, your land, and freedom for all you bring with you."

We have done enough, Robin thought, *but King Richard will always want more*. Yet he had expected the summons, if not from Marian. Richard had a battle to fight near to hand, and it was natural enough that he would wish to see his subjects demonstrate their loyalty.

Looking into Marian's cool, clear gaze, Robin thought that he'd give all that for something else he'd once thought she promised, but he nodded acceptance and motioned her toward the assembled men across the glade. He could not trade their pardon for her love. That wealth was not his to give.

As they walked in silence, he was aware of her tension, the tightly controlled movement of her body giving more away than the impassive expression on her face. When they emerged into the clearing, the men stood waiting. Robin heard an angry rumbling. The knowledge of Marian's affair with Guisbourne had come too close on the heels of Little John's death. Looking out at the assembled men, Robin could see some still hated her and perhaps always would. But others, like him, had never stopped loving her. Soft over the muttering anger came a murmuring swell from those for whom Marian was still a beacon of light. Most waited, still hostile, but ready to pardon her if she fulfilled the promise she had made them.

In a ringing voice she announced, "Yes, it is true. I come from King Richard. Lion Heart summons you. Any man here who fights for England shall have his pardon." Cheers rose all around, and when they faded, she added, "More than that. Queen Eleanor told me to inform you the game laws of Sherwood will be eased. The laws will not disappear, but their penalties will not be so severe."

Another great cheer went up, the men's voices sounding in unison, for poaching had led many a man to come fleeing to Sherwood—where he could dine on the King's deer to his heart's content.

"We hear Richard has besieged all John's castles," a man called out to her.

"Indeed." She paused, keeping her audience keen for her news before she continued. "Though he did not have to order it done. Nobles in every corner volunteered for the work."

"Naturally, most expect to pay the King's price and become the new masters," Robin said, his voice lightly edged. He wanted to stem the fervent tide of feeling she was raising so quickly. Richard possessed the power to embody men's dreams. His did not want these men to have too harsh an awakening.

"Perhaps that is why we hear they're looting their new dominions." Will laughed. "They hope to steal enough from themselves to pay back the cost of the purchase."

"As you could expect." Marian smiled, not resentful of their cynical banter.

"And what of Saint Michael's Mount?" Much asked eagerly. "Is it true the warden died of fright even before the King's men got there?"

"It's true he's dead," she answered. "Who can say if it was fear or guilt?"

Friar Tuck laughed. "What of these bishops descending upon the court, carrying crosses through the land? Will they be paying also?"

"In truth, Tuck, I think they only pick up the cross when they come within sight of the King. But yes, they too will pay."

It is all King Richard has ever had us do, pay and pay

and pay, Robin thought. Yet what was the point in complaining when he too would prefer Richard to John? At least it appeared that fighting would buy his men their freedom, and better with stolen gold than with their lives. He hoped the Sheriff would not put up too fierce a fight.

"What of this talk," Much asked her, "that this is not the King but some impostor taking the land? Some say King Richard will not risk his life, others that he is already dead."

"Deceit and nothing more," Marian answered. "I traveled with the King from Austria."

Robin saw that Marian, playing fine lady or comrade to their need, was weaving herself into their hearts once again.

"Lion Heart has never lacked for bravery. In that his reputation scarce honors him," Robin said, aiding her at last. If his men must fight for the King, let them do it with high hearts.

"Don't such tales come only from Nottingham?" she returned. "Aren't they convenient for the Sheriff? He's cowered in his castle for two weeks already, under siege, daring no counterattack. Now the King himself is near, and this will be settled."

"What will the Sheriff pay?" Robin asked, and the mood turned immediately somber and still, awaiting a judgment from Marian.

"The King is wroth. Only Nottingham stands against him, and so the Sheriff will pay all."

Robin considered that since Richard himself was coming to Nottingham Castle, perhaps he was rather pleased to find some defiance in need of complete and final crushing.

Friar Tuck spoke saying, "And what of the crusades?"

"I do not know what the King's plans are for the future." She answered carefully. "Only that he brings peace to England now."

Marian looked over the men assembled around them. "What say you all?" she called out to them. "Are you for the King that makes you free men again?"

"Yes," they cried as one, and Robin marveled at her

sway over them—the past forgotten in the sweep of the future. Hope became a shining light in every face.

It was a light that would soon be doused in drink if they did not take care. Robin wanted them fresh tomorrow. Yet they must celebrate, as some would not live to see their freedom. He set about ordering a generous, finite portion of ale or wine served all around. Food was brought out from their stores: bread, cheese, salted meats, freshly roasted game, and tart apples. Robin led Marian to sit beneath the oak near the hunting lodge.

"You had best find some other camp," she murmured. She smiled at him slightly then, ironically, though his heart twisted to receive any smile at all from her lips.

"Yes," he said. "I promise the King will find his property empty and in fine repair." Then, regarding her curiously, Robin asked, "Will you fight for Richard?"

This time her smile was bitter. "I still represent my grandfather in Nottingham. Planning to lead his troops into battle, I wore my chain mail. The King thought it unfitting. He admires my valor but would like it clothed in flowing silks. He thinks I will be most useful as a symbol, a woman who can represent his Queens, mother and wife, to the men-at-arms. He has ordered me to dress so. . . ." Her hand gestured, indicating the pure white cloak lined with the plush softness of vair, clasped with silver glimmering with the pale light of opals, moonstones, and pearls. The pale gray gown beneath was a fine wool, soft as cobwebs. Her voice hardened. "He has ordered me to give over my grandfather's troops to other hands. I have obeyed. Sir Ralph will command them at Nottingham Castle."

A man came with goblets for them both. As Marian sipped her wine, Robin noticed her looking intently at his cup. He quaffed down a large swallow, then laid it aside. "Ale only, these days," he said, looking at her directly. "I have found the cost of wine too high to bear."

Marian tensed slightly at his words. Robin did not know if he should say more or not. Just then Alan and Claire emerged from the lodge and crossed over to the oak to join them, Claire moving with sure feet on the known path. Marian embraced them both with affection. Warm as her greeting was, when she did not relax fully with the young lovers, Robin was again aware of the tight control she still held.

Alan sat beneath the oak and smiled at Marian. ''I would have been out to greet you, but I was finishing a new song,'' he said.

''And from the smugness of your smile, I know it particularly fine, even before I hear it,'' she replied with a light laugh.

Settling himself comfortably beneath the oak, Alan plucked delicate vibrations from the strings of his lute, luminous joy birthed from sweet melancholy. He began to sing.

> With your return cold winter flowers.
> Snowflakes blossom, shining bright.
> Lily, phlox, and rose, each dowers
> The crystal air with petalled flight.
>
> Pale laden trees form blooming bowers.
> The sky lets fall new buds of white.
> With your return cold winter flowers.
> Snowflakes blossom, shining bright.
>
> Closed tight for all these blighted hours,
> My heart melts free of frozen night.
> Warm tears flow like sweet spring showers.
> The bloom unfolds to seek your light.
>
> With your return cold winter flowers.
> Snowflakes blossom, shining bright.

Robin's heart pained him, pierced by the truth of the lyrics, the yearning joy of the music. The pain pierced more deeply, for as Alan sang, Marian draw back, cooler and more aloof than before, a frost settling over the warmth of her smile. Still, when the troubadour finished, she praised his song in glowing words and said he must play it soon for the Queen.

Marian shared the wine, the meal, the talk, telling them of King Richard's release. Then she rose, saying she must return and take Robin's promise with her. He accompanied her back to her horse.

She was mounted when he forced himself to ask at last, "What of Guisbourne? We heard he sailed with you to Austria and returned with the King."

"Yes," Marian answered in a steady voice. She met his gaze, her face smooth and secret, though a myriad of emotions flickered in her eyes, pale blue fire, gray ice. Robin tried to read their shifting expression, but they stilled to match the mask of her face. She had sought the best men to serve her Queen, Guisbourne and himself. Despite her attraction, Marian had fought against him, not tried to seduce him. Because of that, Robin did not believe she would have given herself only as a lure to Guisbourne. She desired him. Or she loved him. And it was Guisbourne who would have her.

Robin's eyes caught sight of a cluster of white wood violets nestled by the trunk of a birch. Impulsively he bent and picked them. Cool and fragile in his hands, the flower's delicacy, the rising sweetness of their fragrance were both solace and torment. He almost crushed them as the pain inundated his heart again. Instead Robin laid the pale blossoms into her hands, surrendering them into her keeping.

"Good-bye, Marian," he whispered.

■■■■■■

The day was cold and clear, the sun bright as a polished coin. In the open meadow, the golden stars of celandine and glowing clusters of newly blossomed daffodils struggled to survive under trampling feet and hooves, while motley groups awaited the King's arrival. Waiting with them, Robin sat quietly in the saddle while the long lines of men at arms filed past along the road toward Nottingham. Once Will Scarlett hailed a fellow from his village, and they exchanged salutes in honor of the King. For the most part Robin's men stood at ease or sat relaxed on their horses,

filled with the spirit of camaraderie, fervently yet quietly
exulting that they would no longer have to live as outlaws.
Robin could not help questioning if King Richard would
really live up to the promises made in his name. Lion Heart
cuffed whom he would with his great paw, and he made his
own rules when loyalty was in question. The King might
use a band of outlaws to fight his battle, then refuse to grant
them pardon. Robin did not wish to disturb the mood of his
men, but he sorely wished John were beside him to compare
impressions and weigh the dangers. Robin wondered if his
last chance of flight to the wood was on him.

An array of armored knights rode past him. He snapped
his head as a sudden pale flash caught his eye, then stilled
his heart again when he saw that it was a bright flag, not
Marian's shimmering hair. She had said the King had forbidden her to fight. She was likely not to be among the
soldiers at all. Robin had not wanted to admit how much he
hoped Marian would come to him. He feared the King's
betrayal less than the destruction of the frail hope that he
could not root out of his heart. He should not want her, but
he did. Worse still, he wanted but could not have.

Knights continued to ride past, superbly mounted. He
forced his attention there, comparing their horses with his
own. He would not trade Jester for any of the powerful
animals he saw. ''Not only are you fleet of hoof, but wit is
most rare among your kind,'' he murmured to the roan, and
received a soft snort in answer. Images from his own military training came to Robin, and then scenes he had wit-
nessed on crusade, tests of skill and tests of courage. He
saw some knights of all sorts of prowess riding past. His eye
sought out the best and measured their look in the saddle
against the knight he had been. In Sherwood Robin had kept
his old skills honed as best he could and developed new
ones to compensate to fit a new mode of fighting. Looking
around, he saw few who could sit a horse as well as he, and
he would match his bow arm against any in England.

Then Robin saw a knight riding stronger than the rest, a
champion among them, and he felt a surge of anger. It was

Guy of Guisbourne, moving somewhat ahead of a larger party. Robin acknowledged that sword to sword he could not match Guisbourne, not without the hand of luck. Outlawry had taught him new skills, and they were achievements of pride, not shame. But they would give him but small advantage, if any, against a strong knight so perfectly honed, and Guisbourne was the best he had ever encountered. If he fought Guisbourne in a small space where swift movement was not an option, he would survive only by performing some utterly novel move beyond Guisbourne's expectation. Robin smiled, remembering with a rush of delight Much's father and the chaos of the rescue at the fair. He had foiled Guisbourne then, though the same trick taught Sir Guy not to underestimate him.

Then Robin saw King Richard riding in an oncoming party, cantering smoothly ahead of bodyguards who sought to protect him, moving from group to group of those awaiting his favor. The great Lion Heart loomed over the others, riding with compelling grace and power. A figure of ruddy gold, he wore a pure white surcoat over his hauberk of finest chain mail and displayed such utterly complete and radiant sovereignty that he far outshone Guisbourne or any other knight at hand. King Richard's image had tarnished and shriveled in Robin's mind. Seeing the man in the flesh was to be struck by a blaze of glory, his courage, his prowess evident as his command. Robin drew a deep breath, the memory of his father's castigated misery clouding the golden resplendence of the King. Knowing Richard's flaws, he could never be enspelled, but Robin saw why others worshipped, kneeling at Richard's throne as at an altar. *Would you were half the King you look*, he thought, *and I might kneel there gladly too*. Gladly or not, he would kneel to Richard if it meant his pardon and that of his men.

Then he felt Marian's presence, vivid as a touch. His eyes found her riding sidesaddle on a gray mare. Mantled in white wool, a gown of pale green spilling around the hem, she presented exactly the vision Richard wanted. Robin had himself used her regal presence to impress his men. Marian looked directly at him, her expression intent yet unreadable. She did not turn immediately but held his gaze and nodded formally. The flamboyant brightness of the King suddenly faded to nothing. There was only her pale, glittering perfection, like the sun shining on the first deep winter snowfall, with all the glory of spring and summer bedded beneath, waiting to awake. Like spring, an exquisite rush of hope flowed through his veins, and time itself seemed to disappear. Then she turned away, breaking the spell.

Hope quelled, Robin turned his mount and saw Guisbourne, displeased with his open admiration, staring hard at him. Anger uncoiled again, dark and bitter, that his enemy had claimed his lover. *And I thrust her to his arms*, Robin thought, wishing he could once again hate them both. *Too late*.

Now the King saw him waiting with his men. Lion Heart turned his great war horse toward them and trotted forward. As he neared, Robin's men dismounted and knelt. Robin waited a proud moment longer than the rest, with Richard's eyes full upon him. Then, defiant, he made a brief bow while still in the saddle, a bow of nobility to the lord, then slipped off his horse and went down to one knee. The King looked silently upon him, and the entire assemblage fell still.

"I hear you have become a terror of Sherwood, Robin, ruler of the wood," King Richard said.

Still kneeling, Robin looked up,

"Only in your absence, Lord, and always for England."

"I do not take the violation of my forests lightly. Or the invasion of my castles, for I hear you have accomplished that too in Nottingham." The King's blue eyes glittered dangerously, then cleared. "Nevertheless I know you have served me well, and your presence proves your pledge to assist me in taking back my own. There are eloquent voices speaking for you at court, including Queen Eleanor, and another multitude among our people praising you."

"Thank you for the kind words, Sire. I only wish to serve as a free man."

"You proved yourself loyal to England while less than free. Will you now prove yourself loyal while in my service?"

"Yes, my lord. I pledge the full strength of us all, now and always, to serve you as King."

"Then rise, Robin. Know you are once again Robin of Locksley."

He rose as the King bade him. Lion Heart looked out over the motley band of outlaws who had already saved his ransom. "All who have served Robin Hood are pardoned. Come join my service as free men."

A swell of joy passed through them, but as one they looked to Robin while still kneeling. Robin smiled and bade them rise to their feet.

The King looked less than pleased; the hard glitter was back in his eyes. "I see that all these serve you, Robin. I value discipline highly but prize loyalty above all."

"You have full loyalty, my lord. From each and every one." Robin stood aside as Richard raised his arm in summons, gesturing for the former outlaws to join his own men, and they ran forward.

A cry went up from the yeomen around the King, welcoming Robin's men, and surged with a fire through the King's force as the men of Sherwood were joined with them. The King observed the display of affection, at once pleased and uneasy with it. He lightly flicked the reins, and his charger turned back upon the road to move among other groups of nobles, knights, churchmen, and commoners who had appeared, clamoring and bickering for his attention.

While the King played strategic games of flattery and reproof, favor and penalty, the yeomen, archers, and other men-at-arms continued marching toward the castle. There was much paraphernalia of battle going forth on wagons. Two catapults were being pulled forward, their solid construction a great improvement on the unwieldy machines Robin had seen in the Holy Land. Other wagons bearing the stones for the catapults to hurl forth came along after. Robin motioned his own men into the saddle and led them off into the fields, sweeping past the entire caravan. There was nothing here but politics. He wanted to see what awaited them in Nottingham.

■■■■■■

Robin found a large force already surrounded the castle, though mainly focused on the outer bailey gate, where they were making a great commotion and raising consternation among those defenders. Robin motioned his men to follow, and they rode a wide circuit entirely around the castle. The King's men were at work everywhere, even battering through the entrance to the tunnel that the Sheriff had ordered sealed. Robin saw little point in that. Without the element of surprise, it would be a deathtrap. The Sheriff's men-at-arms were stationed along all the high stone walls towering above. Archers occasionally let fly flurries of arrows through the firing slits. At places they came forth openly upon the upper ramparts, fired, then stepped back out of sight, only to reappear at some other point, shooting again. Will caught his eye and made a disdainful gesture. Robin confirmed with dismissive expression that most of the archers were an indifferent lot.

The rest of them had also declined in military coherence, he reflected, since Guisbourne had not been training them for months. So much the worse for them, he thought. The defenders were few compared with the vast throng being brought by Richard to challenge them, but in a purely defensive role they were more than ample. They had the strength of those high walls and a massive store of provisions that Robin had seen with his own eyes. They had all they needed for month upon month of resistance—save for resolve. The Sheriff had been spreading rumors throughout Nottingham that it was not the Lion Heart who had returned to England. Those outside the castle knew the lie. Robin wondered just how long the knights and the men-at-arms within the walls would be able to persuade themselves that the Lion Heart was not before them, in all his splendor and wrath.

The main strength of Nottingham Castle was in the high stone walls of the middle bailey. The upper bailey might rise even higher, and it might contain exalted living quarters, but if it came to a final defense on a dark day, the middle bailey was the place for a stand. A wooden palisade extended out from the upper bailey at one end, swept around the outer bailey, and returned back to the middle bailey at the other end. The palisade overlooked a ditch and was anchored with posterns at either end. Right in the middle was a strong gate, and outside that gate the main force of the siege was concentrated.

The outer bailey presented an awkward initial hurdle to besiegers. Its wooden walls would not long withstand the full power of a determined army and certainly not the shattering stones thrown by catapults. But the outer bailey was an excellent barricade for bowmen who could rake the besiegers and inflict dreadful casualties throughout their ranks. The large field behind was also an excellent staging area for sallies by mounted knights who could suddenly emerge to ride down the foremost troops, blunt the sharp edge of the siege force, and then return to safety. The King was sure to lose many men at the outer bailey gate even though a determined effort by the entire force was certain to take it.

The bulk of the troops was still hours away, with the catapults even farther off. Nevertheless an immediate assault had begun. A large number of men were gathered before the gate, setting fires and trying to cover themselves with shields against a vicious deluge of arrows raining down from the palisade. More men rushed to join the besieged soldiers, but they were taking such terrible casualties that the living only briefly replaced the dead. Worse, the Sheriff's men kept pouring water from barrels on the top of the gate, putting out fires as fast as they could be started. A party of archers clustered in a tight group, shooting erratically at the Sheriff's forces before ducking under their shields, their efforts to retaliate almost worthless.

Robin was immediately concerned. If something impetuous occurred, he wanted to choose his men's place. From a distance they could use their arrows. Up close they could merely offer their flesh. Surveying the rise of the terrain, he dismounted his men on a small hillock that offered a clear though somewhat distant view of the gate. He selected his ten best archers and told Will to be ready to shoot any of the Sheriff's men who appeared on the high rampart, but to wait for his signal.

Leaving Will in command, Robin wove his horse through the confusion milling about the castle. He saw more knights had arrived. Guisbourne and several others were conferring with Sir Edwin, who had charge of organizing the gate assault. Robin knew he had to assure his chosen place in the battle at once or Guisbourne would choose it for him, lethally most likely. He trotted Jester over to the men, swinging just a bit wide as he pulled up, forcing Guisbourne's mount back. Robin turned to face Sir Edwin and declared, "The King has sent me directly to you with the best bowmen on the field. They are yours to command." Guisbourne began to speak, but Robin made a sweeping gesture, leading all their eyes to the hillock. "Shooting from there," he said, slowly turning and tracing the arc of an arrow, "my men will let no one show himself above the gate and live."

"Indeed?" Guisbourne's disdain called him a liar. "I could better use them at the wall."

Sir Edwin eyed Robin silently, then looked from his men to the gate, clearly skeptical of their accuracy at that distance. Robin knew that he was in the presence of a man both too confident and too ambitious. Sir Edwin would not be satisfied with any sort of caretaker role in arraying the force. He obviously wanted blood, action, and distinction, in any order he could get them. Robin said, "If you can't stop them putting out the fire, they will make you wait until the catapults are brought here by some earl."

They waited in silence as Sir Edwin considered. Then he challenged Robin, saying, "Perhaps I'll give them to Guisbourne, for how could any shoot as well as you claim?"

Robin turned toward Will, then thrust his finger at three

of the Sheriff's men on the ramparts, dumping barrels of water to douse the flames beneath them. Will directed the men to fire, and they loosed a long flight of arrows. All three men were hit and fell backward out of sight. Sir Edwin turned back to Robin, acknowledged the shots with a curt nod. "Keep your archers there, and deploy the rest as you think best," he said; then he rode away, his attention already turned to other matters. Guisbourne's gaze met Robin's, their bright gold burning with cold anger. Then Guisbourne smiled, a twist of mockery that conceded the victory and admired the bowmanship. Wheeling his mount, he rode off as well.

For a time other men appeared to pour water down onto the flames. Robin's men shot them as fast as they appeared. Then they stopped appearing but knelt below the level of the ramparts and poured water blindly, but to no great effect. They threw rocks aimlessly over the top, in a futile effort to keep fire starters from approaching. Soon the fire was burning at many places and could no longer be stanched.

For half an hour the fire grew in strength. Sir Edwin sent more men-at-arms to gather by the gate, an array of mounted knights forming behind them. The Sheriff's bowmen stood behind the palisade and rained arrows down on the King's soldiers. Shields rose aloft but could not stop the deadly arrows coming in from both sides. Robin's men and many others fired back, but the palisade protected the Sheriff's bowmen. A frightful toll was taken on the King's men as they stood beneath the arrows, as they struggled to stoke the flames.

Then the King's men brought forth a massive battering ram, provoking an even greater barrage of arrows. The raised wall of shields could not cover all the men, and many moving the ram forward were shot. Yeomen leading the charge jerked away the corpses, and Sir Edwin commanded more men to replace the fallen. Some attackers stumbled as they carried their burden over the treacherous footing of the stone-filled ditch, but the rush carried them forward. The massive ram crashed into the burning gate. The sound boomed in the air as the impact shuddered the timbers. But the resisting gate held. It bounced the ram backward, crushing two men who were pushing it at the very end. And then the ram surged forward again and again and again, bludgeoning the gate and weakening it.

"Couldn't they wait for the fire to do its work?" Will asked Robin.

"Sir Edwin cannot wait," Robin answered, "lest the King or another come to take his glory."

"Such glory," Will replied quietly, then fired another arrow.

Burning timbers pitched to the ground. The men guiding the tip of the ram went right into the flames and stood there a moment, their clothing igniting as they readied the ram, and then propelled it in a final smash that cracked open the wall. Sir Edwin sent fifty men with gloves and grappling tools swarming into the hellish chaos of flame and arrows. Hooking their tools into the burning wood, they jerked and pulled the timbers aside, widening the yawning gap created by the ram that was still being pounded into the wall next to them. One man rushed from the searing heat, his hair a wreath of flames, then fell and disappeared into the smoke.

Heedless of the fire tenders trampled under their hooves, Sir Edwin sent in a mounted charge. The King's knights, Guisbourne foremost among them, galloped through the flames and swept across the outer bailey accompanied by a rush of swordsmen. Unbalanced and unready, the defenders flailed clumsily at the attackers. The knights sliced through their ranks, hewing the disordered opposition. The Sheriff's forces foundered, progressively cut off from one another, isolated into small groups all trying to fight in retreat back toward the middle bailey.

The outer bailey gate collapsed completely into flames. Panic swept through the Sheriff's men, and as one they turned and fled. The King's troops gave a savage cry of triumph, plunging through the gap in a wild rush. Sir Edwin lost control in an instant as all the remaining troops ran through the flames into the outer bailey, madly pursuing the Sheriff's troops, hacking them to death as they fled across the field. Caught in the crazed excitement, Robin's men looked to him, wanting to join the dash. He could see no purpose in adding to a mindless charge against a fully engulfed, retreating enemy, and he bade them hold back.

The King's knights scattered their foes and slaughtered them with the avid help of a throng of foot soldiers. But even as Sir Edwin's men cut through the battered enemy, their own order dissipated into mindless slaughter. Then the middle bailey gate suddenly opened, and a fierce troop of mounted knights stormed out. Their ordered strength cut through the suddenly vulnerable King's men near the gate. The Sheriff's knights attacked savagely while their pinioned cohorts fought free and dashed into the middle bailey.

A trumpet sounded. The Sheriff's knights wheeled and raced back toward the middle bailey. Terrified, the remaining men-at-arms ran at their heels, all the King's men surging after them. When the last of the Sheriff's knights had passed through, the gate slammed shut, locking out twoscore men-at-arms.

Those of the Sheriff's men betrayed by their own turned in shock and horror to face the throng charging at them. Most dropped their weapons and tried to surrender, but a wave of Sir Edwin's men engulfed them and began hacking them to pieces. Then Guisbourne came riding up. His voice rose over the melee, commanding them to stop. "Take them as prisoners. We need prisoners."

It was a moment before the troops' bloodlust could be quenched, but they succumbed to Guisbourne's compelling power and did as he ordered. They shoved the prisoners forward, trudging sullenly, cheated of their easy prey.

Half an hour later Robin sat on the hillock with Will Scarlett, sharing bread, cheese, and ale. Their long shadows stretched down the hill as the sun lowered in the sky. From his vantage point Robin searched here and there for some sight of Marian, but without reward. Then King Richard, only recently arrived, emerged from a hastily assembled tent and mounted. He moved through the outlying turmoil of the camp to the forefront of the siege, then galloped through the embers of the outer bailey gate with his guard. He stopped short at the middle bailey drawbridge. "Still barred against me?" Richard thundered. "Assaulted, yet not taken? I was told the castle was mine. Where is the Commander of this farce?"

"We routed them, Sire, and lost not a knight—" Sir Edwin began, then lapsed into silence as Richard's piercing gaze cut away his momentum.

"Be off," Richard ordered him. "Guard the baggage and keep from my sight. Guisbourne, take these men in hand."

Sir Edwin skulked away, and Sir Guy set about reordering the troops. King Richard beckoned to his guards and rode closer to the middle bailey, glaring up at the ramparts.

Robin decided he wanted a closer vantage point and moved down the hill. Despite Lion Heart's ire, Robin suspected the King might be pleased that his person would be required to consummate the affair. Then, as Lion Heart studied the fortifications, a group of bowmen appeared on the wall above and fired a salvo of arrows directly at the King. Four men-at-arms fell around him, two mortally wounded. Enraged beyond measure, Richard grabbed a crossbow from an attendant, aimed, and shot one of the archers in the chest. The man clutched his heart and tumbled over the ramparts.

"Do you not know me?" he bellowed in an enormous voice. Richard's entire assemblage went silent at the force of it, and Robin marveled that even those on the walls above were plunged into silent awe. "How can you shoot at the King himself?" he roared. Then he spun in his saddle and called for his chief carpenter. "A gibbet, I will have a gibbet on this spot within an hour. I'll hang all the traitors."

The chief carpenter hurried to the King and waited nervously.

"Guisbourne," the King demanded, "how many prisoners do we have?"

"Eighteen still alive, my lord."

"A gibbet for them all, carpenter. By sundown."

"But, Sire," the man complained tentatively, "there would be so much to build. It must be for less or take longer. Six, Sire, six. We could make it for six within an hour."

Richard regarded him impatiently yet said nothing.

The other man dared not repeat himself. "Eight, Sire, eight. Within one hour."

Richard nodded assent. "Do not lose all the daylight."

The chief carpenter watched the King ride off, then turned to Guisbourne. "Please, Sir Guy, may we have the shortest ones?"

Guisbourne smiled grimly and nodded. The chief carpenter scurried off.

An hour of hurried construction ensued, with many of the Sheriff's men looking down from the walls as the crude gibbet was erected. While the Sheriff's men watched from the heights of the middle bailey, eight prisoners were dragged forward, and nooses were slipped around their necks. A blast of trumpets rang out, and the King emerged from his tent. He looked up at those observing him on the ramparts and raised a hand above his head. He called out in his powerful voice, "Observe the fate of traitors," then struck the air with his fist. Groups of hangmen pulled at the ropes, and the eight men were jerked aloft. They twisted in the air, faces enpurpled and tongues protruding, strangling slowly while the King's troops cheered. At last the twitching stopped, and the corpses were left dangling before the walls of Nottingham Castle.

The Sheriff's men disappeared from the ramparts, but the gate did not open. Robin returned to the hill, watching as the King's men clashed shields against swords and occasionally fired arrows over the wall. They shouted, raised their swords, and paraded about, but only silence was returned to them. The sun lowered behind the hills, colors mottling the sky—blood red and flame red, cold steel gray and smoldering smoke, as if war waged in heaven. Then night fell, fires were lit, and eventually an uneasy quiet reigned.

■ ■ ■ ■ ■ ■

Morning came with no sign of surrender, and so throughout the day many spectacles were enacted for the benefit of the watchers on the walls. Two different bishops arrived with their personal armies. The Archbishop of Canterbury solemnly excommunicated all those who continued resistance. The rest of the prisoners were hanged. A constant marshaling of troops paraded their force about the outer bailey and around the walls generally. Above all, the King appeared many times and stared for long periods at the gate.

Robin thought that if the King might not be able to open the gate through the sheer force of will, the terror he inspired might well do so. Catapults were brought up and were positioned with elaborate care, but Robin thought they were mostly unlikely to be used since Richard would not wish to damage further the stronghold his father had so recently improved.

The King's second day at Nottingham Castle ended with him still outside the walls, living in a tent, seething. After sundown the gate opened briefly and a delegation of unarmed constables emerged. They walked to an open space, and their leader called out, "We come to parley with your leader."

They were searched for weapons, then taken to the tent of the King. Richard made them wait for an hour with his guard close about them. Wanting to overhear what he could, Robin moved close to the King's campfire. In its flickering light, Robin saw their fear, their sweat, and their terrible uncertainty. At last the King emerged, and they all knelt before him.

"Why have you come?" he asked them

"To see with our own eyes if you be the King," the foremost constable answered.

"And what think you?" he asked them.

"You are surely the King, my lord," was the answer. The others nodded their assent.

"Then why do you defy me and bar the castle gate? Why do you call excommunication and more upon yourselves?"

"We do not mean to, Sire. There is great fear in Nottingham Castle. All who wished to open the gate have been slaughtered. And the Sheriff told us you were not truly the King." His voice quavered with apprehension.

Several of the guards moved suddenly in on the lead constable, but Richard stopped them with a gesture. "And now?" he asked, in a level voice.

"Now we only wish to stay and serve you."

Richard regarded them in silence. As he looked from each to the next, they lowered their faces to avoid his gaze.

"No. You shall not stay," Richard said, watching them wilt before him. "And you shall not serve me either, not unless you return to the castle and deliver it to me by noon tomorrow."

"But, my lord, the Sheriff—" their leader began.

Richard cut him off and shouted, "The gibbet is for traitors. Prove yourselves to me or it waits for you all."

The King stalked back into his tent, leaving them weak with fear. The guard herded them back to the gate, then backed off. The constables waited, hardly daring to breathe, willing the gate to open again. When it did, the constables vanished within.

■■■■■■

Dawn came again, and no one appeared on the walls above, either to surrender or to fight. The scene was deadly quiet. Finally, at midmorning, the head constable appeared on the ramparts.

"In the name of the King, we throw open Nottingham Castle."

The gate opened. Robin could see a pile of weaponry and unarmed troops standing behind it. Guisbourne formed up a powerful vanguard immediately, marshaling mounted knights at the very front and men at arms as a screen to either side. They rode in through the gate and met no resistance at all. In fifteen minutes they had secured the entire middle bailey and then Guisbourne rode back to the gate. "The Sheriff has disappeared," he announced. "The constables do not know if he has escaped or hidden himself, but men are searching for him everywhere."

Down the tunnel, Robin wagered silently.

There was another rush of activity in the outer bailey. Robin and his men mounted their horses and watched Richard swing up into the saddle and pull off his helmet to show himself, aglow with triumphal energy he imparted to all. At last Marian appeared from the seclusion of a tent well to the back of the assembled forces. Robin rode down to join the King as she rode up the hill to the ruined gate. Marian was gowned for the role the King had decreed she play, pristine yet sumptuous amid the charred wreckage. Beautiful as she looked, Robin's heart ached for the warrior restrained in soft silk. But despite her garb, she did not lose all her fierceness. In her bearing she would always be an Amazon, proud of her strength and skill. The vivid crimson of the gown she wore spoke of the blood spilled in the King's name, and the embroidered crown of her barbette and veil evoked a golden helmet. When Marian reached his side, the King started his horse forward. Unable to resist the temptation, Robin maneuvered Jester through the jostling knights until he rode close behind.

The King's Guard led the way, a clip-clop of hooves sounding loudly as they rode across the drawbridge of the middle bailey. They passed from the bright morning to the shadowed underpass of the stone watchtower. As Robin's eyes adjusted to the darker light, he felt a sudden coldness. For a heartbeat he thought the chill came from the slightly cooler air, but then he fixed on a small sound from above, almost too faint to hear over the pounding of the horses. Just as the King was riding through the very center of the passage, Robin looked up and saw the tip of an arrow emerge from a hole in the ceiling. Robin dived onto the King's back, knocking him from the saddle as the arrow came whizzing down from above. Robin felt the arrow strike his back, pain flaring like a torch as he fell with the King. He held fast, and they landed side by side. The impact jarred him, blazing agony along his nerves. Still, he kept the King's body covered.

Marian was somehow out of her saddle. He felt her arms encircle him and knew she shielded both the King and him with her back. She smelled of sweet herbs amid the noisome odors and blood of the siege. The King's Guard surrounded them, shouting, and Guisbourne's voice lifted above the rest. "The murder hole. It came from the murder hole!" The guards pulled the King from under him, farther away from the deadly trap. Robin gasped as he was thrust away, the bright red flame of pain burning to the edge of obliterating blackness, then fading to searing scarlet. Marian held him still, and Robin accepted the comfort of her as he had accepted the shores of home after the hell of unholy lands, with a pure joy that overflowed in tears.

Despite the pain from the arrow, Robin lifted his head at the sudden sound of scuffling overhead, followed by a scream. All about him the King's Guard raised their spears toward the darkness of the murder hole in the stone archway above. More sounds of struggle were eclipsed by a shrill scream like a slaughtered pig. Robin saw a two-headed creature fall through the murder hole onto the passage beside him. And then he saw that it was two men, or one and a half. The Sheriff was already dead in the dirt, the bow still gripped in his hands. Bogo, the dwarf, was clenched to his back, stabbing him over and over and over. Faint with pain, Robin could only watch as the knights pulled Bogo off the Sheriff.

The dwarf stared about him wildly for a second, still caught in the fervor of his bloodlust. Then his eyes focused, though it did not seem he looked at the King. As Robin tracked the line of that intent gaze, it seemed to his pain-blurred senses that Bogo looked at Guisbourne astride his mount at the end of the gateway. But perhaps not, for Guisbourne did not look at Bogo. Sir Guy stared instead at Marian, clinging to him. Turning, Robin looked at her for the first time, already knowing himself home in her arms, and saw the affirmation in her tear-streaked gaze.

"You love me," he said.

"Yes, I love you," she whispered, hawk fierce, woman tender.

Then, as if drawn by a magnet Robin turned back to face his rival. The black shock of hatred in Guisbourne's eyes struck him like another blow. With Marian's arms about him, he plunged into darkness.

22

"Only the shoulder," the doctor muttered, "though I wager it would have taken King Richard through the heart."

Marian watched, tense, as the man cleaned Robin's wound and stitched it. She wanted to tend him herself, but Lion Heart had sent his own physician. That would not have stopped her if the man had been all manner and little skill, but he was deft and expert as he sewed the ragged edges of flesh, and she had no argument with his choice of herbs for the poultice. Unconscious, Robin moaned but did not waken till he was done and the physician and his assistant turned him on the bed. His gaze was aimless at first but swiftly focused, first on the doctor tending him and then on her.

"Leave us," he said to the others. Robin's voice was hoarse, and his eyes left hers long enough to command them when they hesitated. There was an uneasy shifting, but the doctor and his assistant departed.

Marian stood looking at him, afraid for a moment that he would deny her, despite what she had seen in his eyes, despite the love they had sworn in fear of death. But the brush of death's wing had swept away the last of the enmity. Finally it was this simple. Robin had forgiven her. Robin loved her. Whatever else might once have been possible, there was no other choice for her now.

"Will he free you?" Robin asked.

She was not the only one with fears. "I am free. There was an understanding but no oath."

"Then you will marry me." His voice burned with urgency.

Whatever she did now would betray Guisbourne, but to wed him would betray Robin and herself as well. Guy must suspect or know already, for she was here with Robin, not with him.

Marian sat beside him on the bed, stroking his sweat-soaked hair back from his brow. "Yes," she answered. "Yes, Robin, I will marry you."

She kissed him, the tender touch of their lips sealing the oath she gave him.

When she drew back, Marian saw the fear and urgency in him replaced with a serene peace. "I love you," he whispered. "I swear I will never raise my hand to you again."

"I believe you," she said, trusting his word as he did hers. The same glow of peace she saw in his eyes blossomed within her.

With a sigh Robin closed his eyes. In a second he was fast asleep. She sat for a while beside him, watching him, touching him, then rose from the bed and slipped quietly out into the hallway.

Marian made her way to the staircase, meaning to seek out Guy of Guisbourne. Still, she was not prepared to meet him ascending the steps. His face was already marked with the restraint of a contained anger. She did not know what else was wrong, but she had no comfort or reassurance to offer, only the cruel stroke she must herself deliver. There were no words. As clearly as Robin, Guisbourne understood her in a glance. Everything they had struggled to attain these last months was severed. She saw the pain of it cut him, felt its echo. Then rage flared in his eyes, a black fire seething within gold, and he stalked past her up the stairs.

She stood a moment, tensed as if for battle, willing herself to calm. Then, seized with fear, she turned and ran back along the hall. Guisbourne was nowhere to be seen in the hall, but when she opened the door to Robin's room, she found him as she had left him, sleeping peacefully. Leaning back against the door, Marian exhaled sharply, relief surging in the wake of fear. She crossed to the window and sat down on the bench. Guards should be summoned to watch over Robin. Although now that she had reclaimed control, Marian could not imagine Guisbourne taking revenge on a helpless man, she had no doubt that he was now a dangerous enemy.

■ ■ ■ ■ ■ ■

Guy opened the door quickly at the knock. Bogo slipped into his room. It was one of the most paltry of the guest chambers in Nottingham, but Guisbourne was grateful now for its privacy, however minimal. He bolted the door behind Bogo. "Did anyone see you?"

"No, I took care," Bogo answered.

Fingers toying with the heavy medallion round his neck, Guy gestured the dwarf to sit on the bench. Taking a place at the other end of the narrow seat, Guisbourne regarded Bogo long and intently, and the dwarf's black eyes surveyed him solemnly in return. At last Bogo ventured, "Lion Heart makes a pretty king, and he is less stupid than John. But I hear he does not favor you."

"No, I am not favored," Guy answered, feeling a surge of cold rage. "Yesterday after the battle King Richard praised my endeavors at the siege. He smiled and said they made up for my earlier intrigues against him. He returned to me exactly the lands I held before. And though I offered to pay as much, he told me he has sold the office of Sheriff to the fool Lady Alix has just entrapped for her husband. With that power close to hand, she will find a way to ruin me."

"Nor will you wed the Lady Marian and have her lands to compensate," Bogo said in his quiet, rasping voice.

Guy did not flinch. He met the too-knowing eyes and said, "No, I will not have her now."

Marian had all but given her word to marry him, but he would not try to hold her. The King would not force her. Only her own sense of honor would be bond enough, and he had seen how she looked at Robin Hood—Robin of Locksley again, with not just his crumbling hall restored, but all his lands, since he took the arrow meant for the King. Though part of Guisbourne lusted to possess Marian at any cost, pride was stronger. She did not love him. She would never love him now. Desperately as he wanted her, Guy would not enslave himself to futile hope. Nor would he have her as Robin's leavings. Passion was ended.

Revenge was another matter.

Guisbourne had determined to challenge the upstart Saxon to a duel. He had tested steel with him and knew himself the better swordsman. If Guy did not let his fury fault his hand, he would kill Locksley. He fumed that he must wait till the man had healed, that Robin might have time to wed Marian before he died. But die he would, and Marian would be widowed or unwed. But first he would shatter the cornerstone of all their schemes and watch their world tumble as his had just done.

Once that was accomplished, he would not care if he saw England ever again. He would return to the other world that awaited him across the Channel. But for that he needed Bogo's help.

"King Richard favored you, I noted." He tinted his words with a delicate sarcasm. "Though the prize seems small reward for the deed. The Sheriff might yet have killed Lion Heart had you not struck."

"I thought he had killed him," Bogo replied in the same cynical tone. "But yes, I am indeed much favored." He displayed a fine gold ring set with a carnelian. "A pretty trinket indeed. He patted my head like a dog when he gave it me and spoke to me the same. *Good Bogo, brave fellow!*"

Guy had seen the interchange and guessed the rich ring to have a high cost to Bogo's pride. Though the gift was paltry for the service, Lion Heart had preened at his own generosity.

"So you find the outcome unsatisfactory. Do you plan to change it?" Bogo asked. The black eyes met his again. Guy willed his own gaze deeper and deeper, his questions asked and answered in silent exchange, until at last death looked into death. Murder lay between them, and Bogo did not shrink away.

"We will change it," Guy answered, and watched the dark eyes widen, not in surprise but in acknowledgment. But though the other man's gaze held his, it was wary. Guy leaned forward, summoning forth all Bogo had promised him. "I admit it is to satisfy my vengeance. I want to see them all scrabbling on the floor for power. Yet the deed will benefit us both. Do not do it if you cannot bear the burden. I will reward your service in any case."

Bogo did not want only reward. He wanted fellowship. This act would bind them, closer than lovers. And refusal created danger. Having been asked, the request could not be withdrawn. Nor could knowledge of it be forgotten. The dwarf's black eyes regarded Guy solemnly, measuring the conflicting weights of guilt and gratitude, fear and communion. "You would replace King Richard with Prince John, and so become Sheriff after all?"

"Perhaps." At Bogo's questioning look Guy at last revealed the deepest layer of his schemes. "Or if you prefer, we might return to France. I have expectations there as well, from King Philip. England is barbarous by comparison, and I long for civilized pursuits."

A slow smile spread across the other man's face, and Guisbourne knew he had won. "I would much prefer France to England," Bogo said. "And if I am in France, why should I care who rules here?"

"Then all that remains is how it is to be accomplished," Guy said. His fingers trailed down the gold chain he wore to caress the gold scrollwork of the medallion, the cool polished surface of the onyx.

"I do not doubt you have a plan. I will tell you if I think my part can be accomplished."

"Fear will be an enemy. Fortune whores for whom she will. You have the skill to do this—the swiftness, the sleight of hand, the will. I do not ask you to risk the impossible. Do not attempt it if you know you are too closely watched."

Guy's lips curled in a cynical smile, and his hands gestured gracefully, "If they catch you, we are both dead."

Bogo smiled in answer. "That would be a pity indeed, my lord. I will do my utmost to prevent it. But just what am I to do?"

Guy removed the chain from his neck and set it on the bench between them. Rimmed by crimson garnets, the onyx at the center of the medallion gleamed black as the dwarf's eyes. "See if you can open it."

Bogo set to work, his clever fingers searching out pressure points and catches to no avail. After a few minutes Guy, smiling, signaled him to stop. "It is well designed," Bogo said. "If I cannot discover the lock, I do not think others would."

Guy showed him the mechanism—four pieces of golden scrollwork shifted simultaneously with one hand, two garnets then pressed with the other to unlock the base of the medallion and open the hollowed onyx. Within it was a soft globule. "In this form the poison is most easily concealed, but it will still dissolve quickly in wine. The King commands a banquet tomorrow. You will be performing. Do your balancing trick and carry Richard's cup on a tray or contrive some other amusement." Guy deliberately did not title their victim. It was easier to kill a man than a King.

"Still . . . if he dies, they will suspect poison," Bogo said, "and question those with any contact with his cup or the food."

Smiling slightly, Guy drew a small phial of green glass from his purse. It was a small thing, easily concealed. "You have one other task—to add this to a dish that will be shared by all. Whoever eats it will be sick, but should not die. Richard still suffers from an illness he acquired in the Holy Land. If others are sick with similar symptoms, his death should be accepted as natural. A sauce would be best if you can manage it. Eat but a little from that dish if it is offered you, but eat some. With Richard dead it will be in your best interests to endure a bit of vomiting rather than feign illness and risk drawing suspicion to yourself."

Guy gave him a blue silk handkerchief of Lady Alix's to wrap the poisons in. "Fitting," Bogo said, with a bitter smile.

Guy shrugged. "I could think of no way of implicating her that did not put us at risk."

"And if Prince John becomes King, she will likely swive her way into favor." With a few deft movements Bogo folded the square of silk and tucked it into the hem of a sleeve.

"If you want recompense for her abuse, we will try to devise something. The more we do, the more cautious we must be." Guy frowned slightly, but he would not deny Bogo revenge if he needed it.

Bogo made a dismissive gesture "I had the Sheriff to satisfy me. But what of Locksley?"

"I do not need subterfuge to deal with Robin Hood. If I face him, it will be an honorable challenge."

"And Lady Marian?"

Guy tensed, then shook his head. Bogo lifted his heavy brows. "If she is to die, I will kill her," he murmured. If Bogo killed her, he would not forgive the dwarf her death. Part of him craved that absolute vengeance, yet he admitted he could do it only in a rage. "She has been honest with me, as best she could."

"Then I know I am safe with you too," Bogo said.

Guy met his gaze. "Yes. You do not need to fear me, whether you succeed or fail. I give you my word I will reward you not with death but wealth and command within my power to bestow. My respect you have already."

"And my allegiance is to you, and you alone." Bogo bowed and left the room.

Guy stared after him. If they succeeded, Bogo would have what Guy had promised, if only stewardship of the castle he now possessed in Brittany. His own fortune was more uncertain. He did not doubt King Philip would give him some reward for his service. But its richness would depend on the French King's mood, and that mood would be greatly improved if Richard was dead, even if Guy must appear to have no direct connection with the event. King Philip had cared for Geoffrey Plantagenet and thought Guisbourne a faithful follower. After Geoffrey's death King Philip entrenched himself amid existing followers of high birth and great power, his attitude toward Guy benign but indifferent. Guisbourne found no mental spark to fan between them, and unless he could move into the inner circle, he had little chance of discovering one.

Searching for a new path to power, Guy had discovered Longchamp. The little man was already close to Richard. Guy discovered that his remarkable ugliness made him an easy man to flatter for his mind. Longchamp was intelligent but unimaginative. Mentally greedy, he was inclined to usurp other's ideas for his own, adding some minor twist that made him think he had transformed the whole. Guy let him, as he let him win at chess. It amused him greatly that what little counsel Richard took was often his, bedecked with some pretty ribbon of Longchamp's. Their association was close enough that Longchamp offered Guy the chance to buy a piece of England when Richard was selling it off to finance his crusade. Guisbourne considered it. He did not think he had sufficient funds to risk, but his life in France seemed stagnant.

Then the two branches of his life interwove. King Philip summoned him, and after obscuring pleasantries murmured that he would be glad to hear of any news, of Richard or John, from a knight friendly to France. Philip had also murmured, even more softly, that neither he nor Sir Guy had any reason to be fond of Richard. Guy had nodded discreetly, wondering what version of the quarrel over that sulky boy Lion Heart had told the King. Philip, he knew, had once been overfond of Richard. Then hatred had taken the place of love. So it was King Philip who gave Guy enough money to make the purchase of the Nottingham territory. Guisbourne's conversation with King Philip was brief, but in discussing strategy the French King had at last glimpsed Guy's possibilities. Whether Philip would recall them when Guisbourne returned to France depended on his success here.

And now that success lay in Bogo's hands.

23

Marian smiled, savoring Robin's laughter as the tumblers spun about the King's table in a blur of arms and legs, entertaining the guests before the feasting began. She deduced the laughter hurt, for he drew a sharp breath, shifted in his seat, and contented himself with a smile at the cavorting. Robin looked like a forest god still, but one richly clad in shimmering brocade the color of leaves sun-splashed and shadowed. Eyes flashing with the same green light, he carefully raised his cup, toasting the performers with his uninjured arm. Marian saw he only sipped at the wine; the flush lighting his face was born of delight, not drink. The joyousness she shared with him had a more intimate source than the gaiety of those surrounding them, but they both were caught in the mood of the moment as well.

The great hall was filled with unbridled merriment, part pure exuberance, part relief that the battle was ended and the shape of the future known. In the two days since the battle there had not been time for the sort of preparation that went into the banquets for the Bishop and Prince John, but supplies had been rushed from all over Nottinghamshire and beyond to make a feast worthy of the King. Nobles and peasants alike had made special offerings to celebrate the return of their sovereign.

Marian glanced over to where Guisbourne sat watching the jongleurs. Her own elation was subdued by her awareness of Sir Guy's losses and his hidden wrath. She had, in fact, promised Sir Guy no more than he had received from

King Richard: the restoration of the lands that the Sheriff
had seized from him. Truthfully Marian did not feel he
deserved more property now since he had earlier worked so
actively against the King. She had only hoped that a knight
no more opportunistic than most would be valued for the
qualities he did bring to the King and would profit more
after faithful service. Even knowing him to be her enemy
now, she wished him well, though she feared for what
havoc he might yet wreak in her life.

She watched him surreptitiously, doing her best to weigh
the strain of events upon him. As always he was fashionably
garbed, tonight in vermillion brocade, a heavy onyx medallion draped round his neck. His manner was supremely
courteous, but Marian knew him well enough now that she
could read the signs of stress in the formality of his composure. Guy seldom laughed, but his smiles tonight were calculated responses rather than the ironic twists that were his
natural expression. Closer to the King, Lady Alix laughed,
the sound ringing with giddy triumph. Marian did not know
if the Lion Heart was aware of the antagonism that existed
between Sir Guy and Lady Alix, but he had all but ruined
the worth of his gift to Guisbourne by giving the office of
Sheriff to Lady Alix's swain.

She knew now that this was why he had been so angry
when she met him on the stairs, and the King's betrayal
magnified her own. Marian had never promised to wed
Guisbourne, but it had been implicit in her urging him to
stay. If she had not learned to love him, their journey to
Austria had bound them close. She knew that only a force
as powerful as her passion for Robin could have sundered
their alliance. Guisbourne had every right to believe her
faithless. But it was beyond mending. Regret shadowed but
did not eclipse her own fierce happiness.

She turned away, watching the celebration. All about the
room the antic tumblers whirled and juggled, each striving
to outdo the other's capering, all striving to outdo Bogo. At
the moment the dwarf was spinning a myriad of objects: a
pale green apple, both his shoes, a knight's gauntlet, and a

gemmed knife some lady had tossed into the fray. Catching them one by one, he polished the apple on his sleeve and returned it to the bowl, presented the borrowed glove and knife to their owners, slipped on his shoes, bowed, and began a flurry of handsprings.

Caught up in the reckless gaiety of the dinner, Bogo somersaulted through the air and onto their table. His handsprings carried him deftly as a cat amid the cups of silver, wood, and metal that lined the table and all the way to the King. No one else would have dared such outrageousness, but Richard only laughed uproariously as the dwarf finished with an exaggerated bow. The splendid landing threatened to become catastrophe as Bogo's sweeping hand jarred the edge of the King's wine goblet and nearly toppled it. Catching the golden goblet quickly, Bogo lifted it up and balanced it atop his forehead, a new trick to counter his clumsiness. With another flourish of his hands, the dwarf replaced the goblet in front of the King. Amid the flurry of laughter and applause, Lion Heart took hold of the goblet and lifted it in a toast.

"Sire, do not drink from that cup!" Robin exclaimed, rising to his feet. He went pale with the sudden movement, but the command in his voice stilled everyone there. Startled, Marian sat unmoving with the rest, suspended in a frozen tableau. Then Robin inclined his head toward Bogo and added evenly, "I saw this man slip something into the wine."

King Richard set down the goblet, and the guests drew back in apprehension. The dwarf made no move yet, but when Lion Heart gestured to his guards, he seized the heavy vessel in his hands. Again everyone stilled, as if the dwarf might transform wine to acid. Clutching the goblet, Bogo turned, his gaze flickering over the guests. His eyes were pools of blackness. She saw death in their depths, and judgment—of herself, of them all. Then a flicker of something else, a plea, a hunger. In a swift gesture Bogo lifted the goblet to his lips and drank it to the dregs.

Marian did not know why she looked at Guy as Bogo

drank. It did not seem that Bogo had sought his gaze, yet when the dwarf's expression changed, it seemed he had been looking toward Guy. Marian's eyes turned to him and saw an answer in Guisbourne's expression, a crack that opened to a world of puzzlement and pain. It showed for a second only, and then the crack sealed, and Guisbourne's face reflected a cooler version of the surprise and consternation that surrounded them. Bogo dropped the empty goblet to the table. For an instant Marian expected him to topple in agony, but he only stood there, his face set and grim.

"Take him to the dungeon," King Richard ordered. "I want him questioned."

The King's Guard surged forward and seized the unresisting Bogo, spilling cups of wine over the guests as they hauled him from the table. Some of the women screamed as if they had indeed been doused by acid. Others, knight and lady both, scrambled from the bench, their faces pale and sweating from fear of poison. A few hurried from the room, planning to vomit up their wine, she presumed, for one weak-stomached knight only made it to the corner. They swarmed past the guards, who held Bogo on the floor. He tried to stand up, but they jerked him off his feet and hauled him away.

"No one, soldier or commander, lady or lord, is permitted to leave the castle until the dwarf has been questioned," the King declared.

"I think the guests' fears are distorted," Robin said quietly to the King. "Still, you do not know that the wine is all that has been tampered with today."

King Richard eyed the retching knight with disdain, then ordered, "All the food prepared for this banquet is to be destroyed." Another gesture sent more guards from the hall to tighten control from the upper bailey to the far outer bailey gate. "You are in command of those men," he said, turning to Robin. "And for the service you have just done me, I will make you an Earl."

■ ■ ■ ■ ■ ■

Marian was in shock. Guisbourne left the hall, and she did not stop him. She knew because she had seen, but she did not know how to believe. It seemed so . . . base, so craven. For all his skill and pleasure in the multilayered ruses of intrigue, she thought of Guy as a man of courage, a man who strove for excellence. To outwit a foe's treacherous machinations was only an aspect of that excellence. She did not understand this ignoble act, or how the dwarf could descend from hero to assassin so swiftly. And then to drink the goblet down . . . .

Guisbourne had not expected the gesture of self-sacrifice. More than anything else, it was the surprise of that pain that revealed him to be the guiding hand behind the plot. But the look in his eyes was proof to no one save her, and even if she had proof, Marian did not know if she could bring herself to expose him. The thought of his death twisted within her, a visceral pain.

And Bogo—he had not died instantaneously. But he would hardly poison the King so blatantly if he had hoped to escape. Slow then, but not as slow as it would be for the dwarf, who had little more than half the King's height and far less than half his weight. He would be dead soon enough, though he would still have a double agony to endure. Would he have his wish and keep his master's name silent—or would the torturer pry it from him before the poison killed him?

What if Bogo died in silence? She alone would know. What must she do? Cold-blooded as the act had been, if Guisbourne would give his word . . . But how could she trust his word now?

Marian looked around. The hall was fast emptying, and panic tinged the air. This banquet had been to celebrate a triumph. Perversely, after the Sheriff's failed attempt, King Richard had seemed invincible. The courtiers acted as if arrows could not touch the King—as if it were not Robin's quick eye and courage that had saved him, or Bogo's assault on the Sheriff, but divine intervention. But the threat of poison was a poison in itself. The thought of the King's mortality, as well as their own, corroded the security of all.

Marian made her way from the hall and up the stairs toward Guisbourne's room. Her mind swarmed with questions, a plague of stinging hornets. Had Guy decided to do this only after the King's ruinous division of Nottingham? He would gain nothing—nothing except the satisfaction of vengeance. Marian knew that need as she knew hunger and thirst. Had Guisbourne deceived her all along with some secret alliance? If he had always planned to kill the King, there had been better opportunities before. Did he expect reward elsewhere? Prince John would give gold with one hand and issue Guisbourne's death warrant with the other. Surely Guy was wise enough to know that? Yet the attempt need not be on John's request. Richard's death would still have benefited Guisbourne, now that his other plans were destroyed. She knew his losses devastating, but were they great enough to drive him to so heinous a crime? If he had remained beside the Sheriff, he would have lost his lands, and likely his life as well. If the new Sheriff's being Lady Alix's husband was a threat, he still had the opportunity to marry into greater power.

Yet he had not lost only power and wealth. He had said he loved her, and her love was lost as well. Could he have feigned the intensity of his passion? She did not think so. He was not a man to show any vulnerability willingly. But she had not feigned her desire either.

She paused outside his room, her mind a whirl of confusion, hurt, and incomplete intentions. What would confrontation serve except to warn him? He would never confess. If he believed her a threat to his survival, he would kill her. She had only the knife of silver and crystal that she had worn to dinner. The blade was small but well honed. Marian owned no knife that was not a weapon. Drawing a breath, she knocked. There was no answer and so she pushed open the door. At once she saw his embroidered brown mantle draped across the bed. Her vision seemed to blur, and the intricately entwined vines became coils of writhing golden snakes.

Marian froze as she heard footsteps without, but they passed on by. She shivered. Swiftly she searched Guy's belongings. There were two small chests brought over from his own estate. She found one secret compartment, and behind it another. But there was nothing within the first and a few bits of jewelry in the second. She suspected the second compartment was another blind, She pried at every pressure point she could imagine, to no avail. If there were other secret compartments, they were cleverly wrought. Marian knew she might chop the chests up before she found them. If there was poison, he had had the opportunity to bring it from his own estate before the banquet and to destroy all traces. She did not believe Guy had planned this until she had returned to Robin and King Richard had refused to advance him—a double blow that had thwarted too many plans. Yet he must have had the poison already—and the willingness to commit regicide.

Memory swept her, sickening in its implications. Geoffrey Plantagenet had died after just such a banquet as this. And Sir Guy had been the Count of Brittany's close friend. Had the death been coincidence only? She had heard no hint of enmity. Perhaps Guy had had no hand in his death, only seized upon the idea of the banquet. She could not know, but she did not like the implications. It now seemed strange, sinister that Sir Guy spoken Geoffrey's name but once. "He is dead now. . . ." She remembered the dark depths of Guisbourne's eyes that showed her something irrevocable, a bitterness harsher than grief.

Marian had thought she understood Guy, that they were alike. Yet the secret labyrinths of his soul were far darker and more twisted than she had imagined.

I would have killed Prince John, she acknowledged, *if he had taken me against my will. And I would have done it by poison, to have my vengeance and my life. I would have thought he deserved no better, and his death worth the cost to my honor.*

Would her motive have been so much more virtuous, to submit to ravishment to spare her family, then to revenge herself secretly? She and Guy were alike after all. He had only entered more deeply into his own darkness than she had journeyed into hers.

Yet Marian knew now she could not spare Guisbourne. At the moment he would place survival foremost. But stripped of all possibility of power, he might decide vengeance sweeter than life. King Richard would not be safe while he lived, nor she, nor Robin. She must find him, before he struck again.

She went back into the hallway and made her way toward the hall. Two knights were walking past, absorbed in discussion, but she heard one of them say, "I don't know who. I only heard that the dwarf gave them a name."

If I hear such talk, then he must as well. Guy's best course had been to wait and hope Bogo died without revealing his name. If Bogo had talked, Guy must escape—unless he had been seized already. Marian walked out through a side hall, past the sergeant of the guard's chambers and made her way onto the allure. From there she looked out over the battlements, harshly carved with light and shadow by the setting sun. Scores of men-at-arms patrolled the walls and secured the portals. Moving across the outer bailey, they stopped and questioned everyone, commoner and noble alike. Guisbourne was nowhere to be seen. If he were still free, he would not brave such an obvious departure, not even by pretending to oversee security. No matter how one might reach an outer gate, absolutely none was allowed to pass through. Where would he go?

Then she knew. Dashing inside, Marian ran along the empty corridor and down the stairs. She kept going past the living quarters, past the main floor with the grand banquet hall, down toward the kitchen. Guards were questioning the panicked servants in the corridors. The kitchen itself was almost empty, the food cleared away to be destroyed. Two women were scrubbing the tables and utensils, talking as they worked. One was just finishing a sentence; "Lady Alix? Are you sure?"

"Yes. I heard from the doorkeep that the dwarf said it was the Lady Alix. He had her handkerchief tucked up his sleeve. Then the ugly thing keeled over and rolled all about the room, frothing." They looked up as she entered. They curtsied automatically, then looked at each other.

Marian looked for men at arms, but none was about. "Where are the guards?" she asked.

"No one here now but us, my lady," one of them said. "The guards are questioning the others. We didn't help prepare the dinner."

She went through the kitchen into a hallway lined with storerooms and stopped outside the first one. One servant began talking brazenly behind her back. "Torturer will have a fine time questioning her." The cold tone told Marian she had little liking for the arrogance of the nobility. Better a fine lady than one of the kitchen maids. "Was Lady Alix said the torturer was skilled and should stay at Nottingham Castle. Wonder how highly she'll sing his praises as he plays her."

It was a worse fate than she would have wished for Alix. But Marian could not think of that now. The first door was open a crack. She pulled her small sharp knife from its embroidered sheath, then shoved the door open with her foot. At the doorjamb she glanced quickly around the door, took in a small room beyond, and pulled her head back. She entered cautiously, confirming her glimpse of a stone pried up, a gaping hole in the floor—and no guard. The King had ordered both ends of the tunnel reopened for his inspection, but he would not have allowed it to be left unprotected. Moving closer, Marian saw scuff marks in the dust. She looked down into a low tunnel. The glimmering torchlight outside the storeroom cast little light below, but she could see the shape of a foot, the body it belonged to pulled almost out of sight. She took the torch from the hall and shone it down into the tunnel. The guard was dead, his throat slit. And a second lay farther back, his face blackened from a torch burn, a flood of bright red heart's blood on his white hauberk.

Enough, she thought, *I must speak, or these deaths become mine too.*

Going to the door, Marian called to the women in the kitchen. "The traitor is Sir Guy of Guisbourne, not Lady Alix. He fled through the tunnel. Go call for help and send them after me."

Returning to the edge, she eased herself into the tunnel, looking quickly to the darkness ahead. There was nothing visible save for the corpses, and rubble where the wall of stone and mortar built by the Sheriff had been torn down by the King. Marian sheathed her silver knife and hefted the swords lying there, testing them. Both those men were massive, and their swords felt unwieldy. One guard also had a long knife. Its heft felt good in her hand. Crouching low in the tunnel, Marian moved to the pile of stone and mortar. She extended the torch, peering through, then frowned. The flame of the torch was dangerous in the narrow confines. It offered more hindrance than help, for Guisbourne would see her coming and lie in wait. Better to dare the darkness and see his torch ahead of her. She set her torch securely in the pile of stone, then moved through into the next section of tunnel, crawling into dimmer and dimmer territory, until the dark engulfed her. She paused for a moment as her eyes began to widen in the dark, seeking light that was not there. So she kept moving, slowly, one hand searching before her, the other gripping the knife.

The air surprised her with dryness and an odd earthy freshness. Marian could feel it rising to her from below and let that faint cool touch guide her down. There were many small passages, but a main course seemed to go before her. She kept on through the dark, walking and crawling as the tunnel permitted. She bumped into several rocks hanging down, then raised her left hand head height before her, brushing it along the wall of the passage as she went. One opening offered a crude ladder of lashed timbers. Keeping her hand in contact with the rock, she went on as fast as she could, trying for silence. *He must not know I'm close.*

Suddenly she could feel no rock wall to her left and had to stop. The cave had widened into a chamber. Marian had no notion how large it might be, but the scent of the air was more pungent, its flow more brisk. *Why didn't I wait for help? Why didn't I keep the torch?* She listened but heard nothing ahead and, worse, no help coming from behind. Perhaps they had gone round to the brewery and captured Guisbourne emerging. Perhaps he had already escaped.

Marian moved cautiously across the open space. She reached out before her with her left hand and moved forward into the darkness. *Am I seeing light? Is this a trick of the cave?* She kept on until her hand found nothingness beyond, and she pulled back. *A cliff? A hole?* Then she heard a small clinking beneath her. She looked down and saw a very faint light reflecting back through a passage. She could not tell how far down it was to the level where that passage ran, and she could make out nothing beyond that faintness. There was no way to see exactly what lay below, or what to land on, or anything. She stepped out and felt herself falling through the air; she landed hard on rock several feet below, losing balance then catching herself. She froze but heard nothing from the passage. Then another faint clink sounded ahead of her, metal on rock.

Marian got to her feet and moved quietly into the passage. She could almost stand and was able to go quickly through the passage as it wound down through the rock. Her eyes were well accommodated to the dark, and the torch ahead was giving her light. She slipped through the passage, bumping into nothing, seeing protruding rocks, not needing to proceed by feel alone. She hurried forward and heard muffled sounds coming from ahead, wary footfalls, not the silence of ambush. *I can go faster. I can see, and he does not know I am close.* Then she saw Guisbourne moving ahead and tightened her grip on the dead guard's knife. The balance felt right, but she wished it had more reach. Marian moved quickly, quietly to close the distance.

But Guisbourne heard something, stopped, and pulled his sword. Marian flattened against the wall, her blood chilling as he turned back and thrust the torch toward her. "Who is there?" he demanded. "Who wants this blade?" She watched as he waved the torch, trying to see into the darkness.

"The Lady Alix." She answered him. "That's the name Bogo gave the torturer. But I know better."

"Marian," he cried out, startled at her voice. He moved toward her pushing out the torch before him, then stopped. His voice hissed with fury. "Stop. Go back now, Marian. Do not think I will not kill you."

She had never doubted it, yet the anger in his voice moved her. He did not want her death. Nor she his. Not even now, though she would claim it if she must. Marian moved back, keeping darkness between them, observing from his small stumbles that she could see much better. "Did you kill Geoffrey Plantagenet?" she asked him. Silence was her answer. A silence of assent.

At last he spoke. "You are alone. I can hear none other, Marian. None."

She moved back again, then farther. He kept coming toward her, his blade glinting in the torchlight.

"No Sir Robin lurking there," Guy called out, his voice twisting oddly, so that her skin prickled at the sound. "Only the three of us, Marian. You, me, and—" He paused, clanging his blade against the stone wall. "We three alone."

The madness in his voice startled her, and she retreated farther. As she went, she saw a little side opening, a natural chamber off the passage. Guisbourne was still coming. She thought it a small place, maybe only large enough to die in. Stepping back into it instinctively, she went still and held the long knife ready.

Guisbourne clanged his sword again, and it rang out. "Where's your torch, Marian? Or do you only want the golden Robin's torch? Do you think you see better without it?" he called out with a strange laugh. "Have this," he said, and threw the torch up the passage.

She saw it fly past the little opening to her lair.

"Not too bright for you, is it, Marian?" he mocked, his voice closer.

The tip of his sword appeared, sliding forward, and then the rest of the shaft emerged into the torchlight. *His voice feigns madness, but he moves with caution.* Marian saw a foot land softly, then his hand holding the haft. Two more steps—

"Is there another, Marian?" He clanged his sword against the wall again, almost missing rock and swinging into her chamber. "Did you fetch your Amazon's sword before you hunted me?"

Another ploy. He must know she would not face him unarmed.

"Have you the knife I bought for you? Do you want to put its snake blade into my heart?"

She saw another foot land, then pause. *He's seen this place. I must be first.* Marian lunged out of her hole and stabbed Guisbourne through the ribs. As the knife went in, she knew it was a flawed strike, not fatal. Guisbourne cried out in pain and jerked his elbow back, knocking her to the rock floor just behind him. He grabbed his bleeding side, pulled out the knife, and tossed it down the tunnel. Turning swiftly, Guisbourne began a swing that would sever her head. Marian ducked low, dived for his feet. As the sword passed over her head, she pulled her silver knife from its sheath, grabbed his belt, pulled herself up, and stabbed him deep in the chest, the blade cutting close to the heart.

"Marian," Guy cried, and fell to the rocks. He lay looking up at her, the flickering torchlight playing across his face. His eyes gleamed, alive with their own flame, but the knowledge of death was in them.

She could not speak, but she would not turn away from that gaze.

"Take out the knife, Marian," he whispered. "Finish what you started."

She knelt beside him, looking to see there was no weapon within his grasp.

"Wise," he murmured. He took her hands and fitted them to the handle. "I would have killed you. If I could."

"I could have loved you," she answered, knowing it even as she now knew his greater darkness.

"But you did not."

Marian did not answer. Leaning forward, she kissed him, for what might have been. His hands tightened around hers, pressing them to the handle. She drew back, looking into his eyes. The taste of his blood lingered on her lips.

"If you had, you might still have learned to hate me." His voice was hoarse with pain.

Guy held her gaze, demanding this last intimacy, giving her his life, his death, his love, his vengeance. She took it, pulling the knife free. A pang of anguish twisted her heart. He gasped, and the scent of his blood was hot and metallic in the air. She waited as his strength poured out, never flinching from his gaze. Between one flicker of the torch and the next, there was an answering flame burning within his eyes, then none. Only a pale reflection on their surface. She could not bear their bright gold gone so empty and closed his eyelids.

24 King Richard sat in a great carved chair in the chamber, Queen Eleanor in one but slightly smaller, son and mother radiating imperial presence. With Marian at his side, Robin made the proper obeisance. Yesterday, on the octave of Easter, Richard had been recrowned in Winchester, the ancient site of power in England. A politic move given the unsettled times, thought Robin of Locksley, newly dubbed the Earl of Huntingdon. He thought it equally politic to attend, albeit he was already weary of all the pomp and pomposity surrounding the King. Though Richard had been generous in his gifts and amiable in his demeanor, Robin had not expected to be summoned to this private audience.

"Rise, my two good friends," the King said with a welcoming gesture. Another graceful movement of his hand offered them stools beside a small table, where a flagon of wine and goblets waited.

"Come, refresh yourselves," the Queen said, smiling. "Pour wine for us all, Lady Marian."

Robin watched as Marian filled a goblet first for the King and Queen, then poured garnet-red wine for the two of them. Gold goblets, Robin noted, thickly set with pearls and scintillating gems. Not all of England's wealth was melted down, but all still served the King. Robin lifted his goblet in a toast. "To a long and glorious reign, Sire. May England find her greatest King in you."

Together they raised their cups and drank. The wine was rich and sweet, and Robin set his aside after the first draft.

Lion Heart remained seated no longer. Flushed with victory and excitement, he stalked up and down the chamber.

Robin listened as he talked, outlining his plans for England, asking advice now and again, and promptly dismissing it. After the obligatory courtesies, the King ignored Marian, speaking only to him. Robin caught a silent, questioning glance from Marian to Eleanor. He saw also the Queen ignore it and fix her attention on her son. Whatever the gambit, it was the King's to play. Robin traded his own swift glance with Marian, who nodded infinitesimally. Speaking to the King, Robin made it clear both he and Marian wanted the hostages brought home from Austria as soon as possible and the coffers of England swiftly replenished. So did Richard—but only to empty them once again. Then, as Robin had feared, the King's talk shifted abruptly from the selling of offices and new taxes to his plan to continue the crusade.

Folly, Robin thought. Guarded, he watched Lion Heart prowl the room and expound his vision, drinking down his own intoxicating words till he was drunk on dreams of glory. *Utter folly.*

Spinning around, the King approached him, clasped him by the shoulders, and smiled. "Come with me, Robin. I have need of men such as you by my side. We will sail to France, and from there on to Jerusalem. Together we will reclaim God's kingdom on Earth." His eyes gleamed, alight with fervor. The King was certain his offer was irresistible.

"More need of me here, Sire, if you are leaving England again." Releasing Robin's shoulders, the King frowned at his answer. Before Richard could press him, for his exhilaration was quickly hardening to resolution, Robin added, "I made a vow on leaving Jerusalem—never to return."

Lion Heart frowned, angry to be thwarted. "You mock."

"No, Sire. You are a crusader at heart; that is evident. I can only pray that your quest will succeed. But England is my Holy Land, my Grail. It is only here that I feel God's presence in my heart."

Despite what he had just said, Robin feared the King would not relent and he would be commanded to follow his sovereign into the hell he had once escaped. Outlawry would be better. He could feel Marian taut as a bow beside him and wondered what she would do when she found her new-made Earl fled to Sherwood, weaving his castles of twigs and vines. How could he dishonor all she had worked to attain?

Robin held the King's challenging gaze, grateful their audience was private, with little risk to the lion's pride. Robin wondered what part Queen Eleanor had played in this. Her affection for Marian was nothing beside her vaulting ambition for her son, and she liked few of Richard's counselors. She wanted him at Richard's side. That wish had kept her from meeting Marian's eyes. But it was Lion Heart who had spoken and Lion Heart, generous as well as proud, who heard Robin speak his heart. For once he listened.

"As you say, Sir Robin—I will have need for trustworthy men to protect the kingdom I hold, as well as for valiant crusaders to join me in reclaiming God's land for Christendom." The King's lips curled with indulgent amusement. "Someone must keep my wayward little brother from roaming too far from his own castles while I am gone."

So Prince John was to be forgiven. Despite all that had happened, the King could not see his brother as anything more than a greedy child, misled by others. Robin felt a swell of bitterness he quickly subdued. What mattered was that he would be neither compelled into service he despised nor forced to flee it. Impulsively he knelt before the King and gave his honest gratitude. "Thank you, Sire. In this I promise I will serve you faithfully and wholeheartedly."

King Richard smiled at him. It was a smile of simple human warmth, yet more than his power of command, his extravagant courage, or even his zealous aspiration, it transfigured this man into a King. By some strange perverse alchemy, the man shone now like a golden idol. Though Robin had thought himself immune, for a fleeting second he

felt Lion Heart's glamour touch him. It was an act of will
to lower his eyes, to bow his head, to deny the summons to
follow where Richard would lead. When Robin lifted his
head, the compelling smile had faded. The King nodded
his dismissal, amiable but distant. Lion Heart was in search
of men to share his vision and had little time to spare for
those who followed their own. Robin bowed deeply, then
moved back to Marian's side. Together they escaped.

■■■■■■

From the steps of the little chapel Marian watched May
dawn with tender radiance. On the horizon, pastel hues
tinted the blurred softness of the clouds into the semblance
of blooming roses, pale yellow and mauve, coral and blushing pink. In the fields outside Edwinstowe, hawthorn and
apple trees were lush with pale blossom, as if the clouds
overhead had fallen earthward and been caught in their up-
lifted branches. The cool morning breeze carried the dewy
fragrance of honeysuckle. Brilliant marsh marigolds and violets crowded the ponds, and spring flowers gemmed the
meadowland with vivid color—pink clover mingled with
red campion, sprightly bluebells, and lavender lady's
smock. Pale primroses and lush purple anemones blossomed in profusion as cool-scented hyacinths began to open
their buds. Nature tossed forth her largess in golden bursts
of cowslip, crowfoot, and cuckoo buds, while tall stalks of
broom and bright-hearted daisies swayed over gleaming
clumps of dandelions, buttercups, and satin-petalled heartsease. The hedgerows swarmed with hungry fledglings, and
glossy peacock, orange-tip, and brimstone butterflies fluttered by. Marian laughed as two of the blithe creatures circled Robin's head in a tipsy dance. He tilted his head to
watch, and they flitted off across the churchyard.

Wearying of regal pageantry, they had chosen humble
Edwinstowe, nestled on the border of Sherwood. This
morning the little village was a bustle of activity, preparing
for the jubilant May Day rituals. Robin smiled at her. "All
England celebrates our wedding."

Together they went inside the chapel to tend to the myriad last-minute details that clamored for attention. Agatha arrived soon after and took to ordering the draping of the beribboned pastel garlands with zest. By midmorning other guests had begun to make their appearance.

"By Saint Hugh's swan!" Friar Tuck exclaimed, entering. "It's a beautiful day for a wedding, Lady Marian."

"No one has made Hugh a saint," Agatha chided him.

"A saint on earth—and ever after, you wait and see," Tuck said. He looked about him, eyes twinkling with joviality and greed, "Is there some ale to hand, and gingerbread mayhap?"

Moments later Will and Much came through the door, and Friar Tuck bobbed with delight at the reunion.

"Tell us, will the King be coming to the wedding?" Will asked, after embracing Robin. "Much is all in a tizzy."

"No, we are not to be honored by his presence."

Will grinned. "And after you rode all the way to Winchester Cathedral to see him recrowned King of England."

"In royal regalia and riding under a silken canopy." Robin nodded.

"But he was King already," Much said, confused.

Robin smiled wryly. "He wanted to make sure the English barons remembered it after he had doffed his bonnet to the Holy Roman Emperor."

Much only shook his head, looking crestfallen. "I hoped the King would come."

"Queen Eleanor has come specially to give us her blessing," Marian told him. "She arrived last night and must leave after the wedding, to follow the King."

"Will he soon be back? England needs a king," Will said.

"Not soon," Robin said. "It seems there is much he must settle elsewhere."

"The next thing you know he'll be forgiving Prince John," Will muttered.

"The succession is not assured," Marian said quietly, exchanging glances with a disdainful Robin and a crestfallen Will. She did not care where King Richard went so long as Queen Eleanor returned quickly. Then England would have a worthy ruler, and Prince John's power would be severely limited.

The motley assortment of wedding guests grew: Sir Ralph, taciturn as always but beaming, old Sir Walter from Nottingham, Cobb and his family. More of Robin's men ambled into the church. Then Alan and Claire entered, exchanging glad greetings with all. The lovers had married in Winchester, and Eleanor had made a place for them within her court, where Claire's chief duty and delight were to sing with Alan. After choosing a seat near the front for his wife, Alan went back to accompany the Queen and Marian's grandparents from the hall of the local baron to the church.

Robin and Marian went to change into the wedding garments Cobb's mother had sewn and reappeared in time to welcome the Queen. Robin wore azure damask pure as the May sky. Across his chest lay a gift from Queen Eleanor, a rich gold chain set with sapphires, emeralds, turquoises, and tourmalines. The lustrous fabric of Marian's white gown shimmered with a myriad opalescence; the sleeves and paneled skirt were finely pleated, the neck and hem embroidered with tiny pearls, glimmering moonstones, and aquamarines transparent as water. Her hair cascaded down her back, and fresh flowers crowned her brow, the cool sweetness of their mingled perfume floating about her everywhere she walked.

At last all the guests were assembled, and Robin nodded for the ceremony to begin. They had chosen the simplest, as was wise. The poor, meek priest seemed like to faint with pride and terror at the assembled company of royalty, nobles, and former outlaws. He stammered a great deal at first, then spoke in slow clumps. Marian noted him darting nervous glances over her shoulder. At the Queen, she thought at first, but from the movement of his lips and the briefly audible whisper behind her, she realized he was so frightened he was being prompted through the ceremony by Friar Tuck. She heard Robin draw a sharp breath and hoped he would not laugh aloud. She cast her eyes down demurely and tried to still her twitching lips.

Yet when the little priest pronounced them wed, her heart swelled like an opening bud and tears misted her vision. His smile a white blaze, his green eyes alight with joy, Robin gathered her in his arms and kissed her.

> So, Lords and Ladies, if you will—
> Seek joy as jolly Robin bade.
> Search out the woods beyond the hill.
> Love and laugh in the greenwood glade!

Fingers dancing sprightly on the lute strings, Alan a Dale finished the envoy of his new ballad. His audience applauded and showered him with apple blossoms as he bowed. It was his last song, for Queen Eleanor nibbled the last spicy fragment of her gingerbread, laid aside her goblet of wine, and beckoned him to her side. She had stayed long enough to honor the marriage, but now she gathered her entourage about her and bade Robin and Marian farewell. The wedding party watched the Queen depart on her journey to London. Still flurried, the timorous priest kept bowing until the caravan was out of sight, then hastened to gulp a long draft of ale.

Those who remained joined in the village merriment, dancing about the Maypole. Will Scarlett seemed quite smitten with the pretty May Queen, and she to favor him over all the other handsome swains courting her. And at midday there was feasting, with honeyed lamb, new greens, aged cheese, and a baker's wealth of warm loaves and tender-crusted pastries. The assembly toasted their happiness, then devoured all that was set before them with exuberant relish. When the meal was finished, Marian saw Robin give a sign to Will; then he took her hand beneath the table. They rose from the gathering, slipping away as quietly as they could. In their rooms they put their wedding finery aside and donned their hunting leathers. They met Will behind the church, where he held their horses saddled and waiting. Will smiled at her and gave Robin a farewell embrace. Then they mounted and departed the village.

■■■■■■

The road soon led them into the sheltering embrace of Sherwood. Above them new bronze-green leaves unfurled on the oaks. Birds darted in a flurry of nest-building activity, nut thrush and swallow, wren and chaffinch, whitethroat and blackbird. Wildlife darted in grove and clearing. Tall ferns rose amid the long grasses, their fronds tight-curled, and green lords and ladies swayed together. Blue madder and scarlet poppies sprouted everywhere. Robin rode in silent communion with her, sharing the vibrant peace of the forest. Coming at last to the King's hunting lodge, they rode down the trail to the clearing where the great oak stood, branches bright with new growth, and dismounted.

Standing beside the thick trunk, Robin let his hands stroke over the bark, his expression pensive and reverent. "I became Robin of Locksley once again when I took my men to the siege at Nottingham. And for saving his life, the King has made me Earl of Huntingdon. But for all that, I've not yet ceased to be Robin Hood."

"Can you cease to be him, ever?" Marian asked. "Would you wish to?"

He laid his face against the great oak, and his eyes closed, as if he listened to a slow heartbeat deep within its core. "When I was sick . . . dying . . . in the Holy Land, I dreamed of Sherwood as life. These woods were the home that I returned to, more than Locksley Hall. But then, when I was outlawed, the forest became both home and prison. All the while I lived here I wanted to have Locksley back—to reclaim the life, the land that the law had stolen from me, to salvage some part of my father's life. But now that I have it back, and more, I feel almost as if my home were being taken from me again." He turned to her, smiling slightly, mocking himself. "Almost . . . I can come and visit after all."

"I do not think you will ever be just a visitor in these

woods,'' she said quietly, looking into his eyes, the color of
shadowed leaves now, but she had seen every green of the
forest there. "You will always belong to them."

"Perhaps." His gaze became intent. "King Richard is
off in quest of new battles. Glory is a drug like poppy, and
nothing will make him turn aside the cup, even though the
dregs of it are death. If Lion Heart does not survive, John
will be King after all . . . and John might think I make a
better outlaw than an earl. We may find ourselves living
here once more."

"Then I shall be Marian of Sherwood," she answered.

Robin smiled again, teasing, his eyes catching light.
"And we shall pass into legend."

She laughed. "Alan a Dale will do his best to make it so,
whoever is King in England."

"I do not doubt it," he said. "Come. I have a surprise
for you."

Robin pulled himself up into the great oak, and Marian
followed him, climbing into the welcoming embrace of the
great branches. Looking up, she saw a wedding bower
awaiting, the high wooden platform draped with the same
beribboned garlands that had decorated the church. Arriving
close behind him, she found the floor, the sleeping furs,
strewn with apple blossoms in a fragrant pastel flood. A
cache of food wrapped in cloth was set to one side, along
with ale and wine to refresh them. But now Robin was all
the sustenance she needed, and the craving hollowed her
with its sweet ache. Meeting his eyes, she saw the same
tender hunger consuming him.

They stripped slowly, uncovering their bodies to each
other's gaze, offering longing and worship in overflowing
measure. As one they stepped forward into an embrace.
Within it hunger vanished. Each timeless moment became
its own fulfillment as they praised each other with skimming touches and tasted the first sweet fruits of pleasure on
each others lips. Marian felt the breeze cool, the waning sun
still warm on her skin, as if the forest offered its caresses
along with Robin's hands and lips. Cool and warm blended

again in the touch of his tongue. Its moist heat left a glistening path of sensation in its wake, so that she shivered with
each luscious stroke on her skin. Her hands, her mouth
journeyed across him in turn, taking in all his tastes and
textures. With a pang she felt the rough scar of the arrow
wound on his back, familiar now in the landscape of taut
muscle and smooth tawny skin.

Still embracing, they sank down onto the softness of
flower petals and furs. Unhurried in their shared delight,
they floated, adrift on the fluid caresses of warm, wet
tongues, the flowing undulation of their bodies moving in
languid rhythm. They coiled one around the other, licking
over breast and belly to the hot juncture of thighs. Her
tongue licked up his flushed, straining shaft to its tender
summit, taking the small drop there like a sip of wine. He
delved into her open wetness, drinking from the source.
Eagerness grew, like the gathering rush of a river sweeping
toward a falls.

Turning to face her, Robin drew her close, his hands
massaging along her back, his strong thighs parting her
own. She surrounded him, wrapping her arms about his
shoulders, her legs about his hips. Centering the tender head
of his sex to glide between her moist lips, he rubbed there
slowly, nudging the portal gently, then sliding up to tease
against the swollen bud. A shudder rippled through her, and
another, and another. Robin whispered her name, and she
answered with a low sob of need. He entered her, searching
with every stroke. Desire sang through her, its sweetness
sharpened to new intensity with each piercing thrust. They
moved to its music in a rhythmic weaving dance, slow, then
quick, slow, then quick again. Their soft panting mingled
with the rising whisper of the breeze, and the rapid beating
of their hearts sounded in harmony with the thrumming
heart of the forest. She felt its throbbing swell within her.

Robin cried out to her, the sound a long, low reverbera-
tion as he surged forward. She felt the pulse of his sex, one
with the throbbing pulse of the forest. She felt him spill
forth, bathing her with liquid warmth. A sweet pang of

response quivered deep within her. Then she was lost, drowning in the same torrent as wild streams of honey and fire flooded through her veins. She melted from within, dissolving, merging with Robin and the dappled sunlight and shadow of Sherwood.

Drowsy, sated with rapture, they lay side by side on their bed of crushed blossoms and fur. Her skin tingled as Robin's fingertips played over her body, a drifting flow of tenderness. Around them the golden daylight slowly faded, the softness of dusk blurring the colors of the forest. In that deepening blue mist the glow of their joy seemed the brightest light, a glimmering aura surrounding them. For a moment it seemed the forest held its breath, poised for a second as a portal opened between the land of mortals and the ancient land of Faerie. Within the enveloping silence was sound, the soft, ceaseless rustle of leaves on the evening breeze. It seemed to Marian that they spoke, murmuring in a strange secret language.

"Do you hear?" Robin murmured, voice soft with sleepy languor. His arms enfolded her, wrapping her in his magic.

"Yes," she answered, "I hear." And it seemed in another instant she would understand . . . share the secret . . . step through the portal.

"Wherever I am now, I hear their whisper always, beckoning."

"Yes," she answered again, as the infinitesimal tightening of his arms called her to follow.

Closing her eyes, she entered with him into that living dream.

Author's Note

The Thief's Mistress weaves historical fact with beloved elements of the Robin Hood legend, adding a few golden mythic threads of my own devising. What liberties I've taken are there to help spin the tale tightly. The novel is extensively researched, but the single most vivid book used was *Eleanor of Aquitaine and the Four Kings* by Amy Kelly. The poems are mine, based on *Lyric Forms from France* by Helen Louise Cohen, and other sources that gave examples of the songs of the troubadours.